A NOVEL

Toads' Museum of Freaks and Wonders

GOLDIE GOLDBLOOM

New Issues Poetry & Prose

Western Michigan University
Kalamazoo, Michigan 49008

First American Edition, 2010.

ISBN-10: (cloth) 1-930974-88-4
ISBN-13: (cloth) 978-1-930974-88-3

Library of Congress Cataloging-in-Publication Data:
Goldbloom, Goldie
Toads' Museum of Freaks and Wonders: A Novel/Goldie Goldbloom
Library of Congress Control Number: 2009929867

Cover Design: David Drummond
Production Manager: Paul Sizer
The Design Center, Gwen Frostic School of Art
College of Fine Arts
Western Michigan University

This book is the winner of the Association of Writers & Writing
Programs (AWP) Award for the Novel. AWP is a national, nonprofit
organization dedicated to serving American letters, writers, and programs
of writing.
Go to www.awpwriter.org for more information.

A NOVEL

Toads' Museum of Freaks and Wonders

GOLDIE GOLDBLOOM

NEW ISSUES

 WESTERN MICHIGAN UNIVERSITY

To my mother, who first told me about Joan and Anthony and the Italians.

In war, there are no unwounded soldiers.

—Jose Narosky

From 1941 until 1947, eighteen thousand Italian prisoners of war were sent to Australia, at the request of the British government. In April of 1943, a recommendation was made to utilize the Italian prisoners as manpower on farms throughout Australia. The Italian surrender that followed the downfall of Mussolini in Italy had created a novel circumstance: prisoners who theoretically were no longer enemies.

Due to both the difficulties of providing guards and their new position as friendlies, thousands of Italians were sent to work on isolated Australian farms, unguarded.

There are people alive today in Wyalkatchem who can tell you stories about when the Italians came to the wheatbelt, and about Toads taking two POWs down to the Moore River for a spot of fishing. They'll tell you that there isn't a road to the river, not even a track, that it's a rough ride the whole way and that Gin Toad was six months gone and it's a wonder her unwanted child wasn't jolted free to land like a bloody rag in the dust. They'll sip their tea and suck their ill-fitting teeth and fifty years later, they'll still be tut-tutting over the way those Toads carried on with the enemy. They may tell you that schoolchildren pelted the wagon bearing the Toads and the POWs with stones and tomatoes, and that women waiting at the siding for the train to Perth pointed at them. Gin Toad had to stop the prisoners from waving and tell them that those women thought the Italians had killed their sons over in Libya. Those women thought they were murderers.

And if it's your lucky day, those old fogeys from Wyalkatchem or Binjabbering or Goomalling will pull out their black and fraying scrapbooks and show you the articles they cut from the papers, way back in '44, about Gin and Toad, and the Italian man, Antonio.

I

I was hiding in the orchard, pretending to check for creepycrawlies rutting on the beginnings of the fruit when the Italian prisoners of war arrived, descending from the sergeant's green Chevy: one fella tiny, nervous, prancing sideways, shaking his glossy black mane, a racehorse of a man, sixteen if he was a day; the other bloke a walking pie safe, draped in a freakish magenta army uniform, complete with a pink blur in the buttonhole that I reckoned was an everlasting. Some prisoners. They looked more like two obscure French artists mincing along behind the curator of a museum of primitive art. The curator, my husband Toad, pointed to the house, and I imagined him saying, "And over here is the Toady masterpiece—The Farm House—painted in a mad rush in 1935 before the wife had her first child—notice the delightfully eccentric stone chimney, the listing veranda, the sun-burned children lurking under the mulberry." And the tame cockatoo, Boss Cockie, saw them coming and raised his crest in alarm and muttered under his breath. "Shut up," he said. "Go away. Bad bloody cockie."

I turned thirty the year the Italians came to our West Australian farm, and I was afraid of them, so afraid of those oversexed men we'd read about, rapists in tight little bodies with hot Latin eyes, men who were capable of anything. Of course, we didn't know much about them, just what we'd heard on the wireless or read in the paper and if Mr. Churchill had said donkeys were flying in Italy, I do think we'd have believed him. We women of the district, none of us wanted the Italians, but who were we to say? It was impossible to get help for ploughing and seeding and shearing, the young bloods gone to splatter themselves all over Europe, New Guinea, North Africa, and even the old retreads in the Volunteer Defence Corps were busy drilling on the football oval. They didn't know that their crushed paper bag faces were enough to repel any Japanese invasion. Men were rationed, like everything else, and so when the government offered prisoners of war as farm labour, the control centres were mobbed from the first day by farmers in search of workers.

Oh, I knew those dagoes were coming all right, and that's why I hid in the orchard, crouching there in Wellington boots, the hem of my dress bunched in one hand. Over sixty trees were in bloom, and I was busy brushing petals out of the valley of fabric between my knees, trying to breathe, because the scent of orange blossom was chokingly sweet. And the rabbits—the bloody rabbits —had ringbarked all the newly planted almond slips, their buds already wilting.

I didn't want to put those men in Joan's old room. I didn't want them in my house at all. But we couldn't keep them in the shearing shed like a mob of sheep, so I was forced to scrub her tiny room—really just a closed-in part of the veranda, a sleepout—and beeswax the jarrah boards, and spread the old hospital beds with sheets white and brittle as bones. And, as a final touch, a welcoming note that I didn't feel, I stuffed some golden wattle in a canning jar and put it on a box between their beds. I'd cleaned the whole house too, so that if the prisoners killed us while we were sleeping, the neighbours wouldn't have anything to talk about, and I'd sent my children, Mudsey and Alf, to pick up the wee droppings that their poddy lamb had left all over the veranda. And lamb chops were on my mind, with mint sauce, baby potatoes and —on the side—a fricassee of brains.

I had a fairly good idea why Toad wasn't taking the Italians over to the room, and even though I knew it was wrong, even though what he was planning to do to them was possibly a breach of the Geneva Convention, I waited, gurgling with delight in the lusty orchard, attacked by platoons of bees drunk on orange blossom wine. All my senses were walking with the men, waiting for the sound of those baby-eaters howling when they were shoved into the sheep dip. They'd bellyflop into the stinking, arsenic-laden waters and they'd wonder about the greasy black pellets floating past them like mines and they'd be picking some of the sheep shit from their eyebrows right when Toady pushed them under again with his crook.

You'll have to forgive me for my language. Gin Toad is no longer a lady.

Oh, those men would be unhappy to be deloused the way we out here in Wyalkatchem delouse our sheep. They might even complain to the authorities at the Control Centre, but it would be worth it, because it would make a good story. It's a story we will be telling for years.

Toady told me that when he saw Antonio Cesarini's cordovan wing tips, he gestured to the man to take off his shoes. This consideration didn't save the men from a plunge in the long concrete cesspool that thousands of sheep had just swum through to rid themselves of fleas, ticks, lice and other blood-sucking parasites, but it did save their shoes, and especially the wing tips, which were such a luxury item, an Italianate extravagance. Toady had stroked those shoes while the men drip-dried in the hot spring sunshine; the leather looked as if it had been tanned in blood, and gave off a heady aroma reminiscent of the one and only cigar he had ever smoked. The soles were tissue thin, unscuffed, impossibly new. Toady had just resoled his ancient boots for the third time, with slabs of ironbark.

He tried to remind himself that the Italians were fascist pigs, cowards, and prisoners as well, lowly slaves in the Australian hinter-land, but it felt more like jealousy speaking, so he kicked the shoes back to their oily owner, and satisfied himself by thinking he had bruised the bastard things with his boot.

2

Their watching scuttled me as I moved from woodstove to table, carrying hot plates of lamb chops and browned potatoes and pickled beet-root and a monstrous loaf of homemade bread that could have killed a horse. They rudely stared at my scarf, which still boasted that it had once held Dingo Flour, and why not? Flour bags are made of soft cotton, and the stamped dingo isn't bad looking if you don't mind him showing up on your towels and your shirts and your underwear. They ogled my white skin, so different from their own burnt flesh that their eyes hung out on stalks and they nudged each other and whispered and I dropped the beetroot on the linoleum and scooped it up again and served it, just to shock them about something else.

"Would you like some chops, Mister Cesarini?"

My voice was strangled; I sounded like a trollop from Sydney, the kind of woman who might be glad that two young Italian men were seated at her table, their hands caressing her willow pattern tea cups. The heat lifted a scent of sandalwood and lavender from their skin, and dear Mr. Toad curled his lip and flapped his nostrils at them. Could they be wearing perfume?

"How about you, Mister Toad? Chops?"

His busy eyes had noticed everything—the tenderest chop had gone to the dago with the nancy shoes. He turned his head and glared at a red button on my dress, slightly below my heart.

"I'll take two, Mum," he said to the button, and with that I lifted the last chop, *my* chop, and placed it on his plate. He raised his cup to me, his pinky cocked like a dog lifting its leg on a fence post, and asked for more tea.

"Did you hear about the bombing up Drysdale Mission way?" he said.

"What bombing?" I said, terrified all over again that we were about to be overrun by hordes of little oriental men with single hairs sprouting from their chins. I was glad I had put Mudsey and Alf to bed early. Enough that they played out in our own pathetic air-raid shelter and lobbed mallee roots on the corrugated tin to terrify one another. Enough that Alf had pointed his two little fingers at the Italians and mimed shooting them, and then, when the big man clutched his heart and fell on the ground, ran and hid in the laundry, sobbing.

The first time I laid eyes on Alf, not only did he have his father's grated red skin, but there was another strike against him; he had that funny little hose between his legs that is normally found on all male infants. It made me squirm to think he had been in my belly. But from the start, there was something wise and innocent about him that put a hook right through my heart.

"Why are people afraid of dying?" he asked as I was making the beds. "It sounds like a lot of fun."

And a different day, "Are the clouds really angels, Mum?"

And once, "Who's the man standing next to the sewing machine?" When I swung around to see if a bagman had crept up on me, there was no one there. "The man with the yellow shoes," he said, pointing. My father, my real father, had yellow shoes, but he'd been dead over thirty years when Alfie asked this question.

He ran wild in the bush, dug underground tunnels with

15

Mudsey that radiated out from our air-raid shelter, developed inch thick calluses on his baby feet from the burning ground. He came home without his shirt, his puny chest brown as a piece of polished mahogany. In secret, he'd grown a watermelon behind the tank stand, and the day that Mudsey burst in, shouting, "Come see the bloody great melon out the back!" he rose up wailing and scratched her face. "You bugger!" he shrieked. "That's for Mum!"

Mudsey tried to immunize him, she did. She warned him that we weren't perfect parents, that we were full of faults and peculiarities. She told him we couldn't be loved with everything he had, but he stared at her with his thumb in his mouth until she couldn't stand the expression in his eyes and had to turn away. Each morning, as I bent to feed wood to the stove, he'd grab me around the knees and kiss my calves. "You're a yummy Mummy," he'd say, "the yummiest Mummy in the whole world."

He'd bail Toad up and demand to be taken along on the horse, and Toad, smiling, would lean down and lift the little bloke up into the saddle.

When he has grown up and left us, Alf will remember Toad hugging him after he fell from the big horse, and how his father brushed the red dirt from his baby face, and he will remember the great blue-black hooves of the horse. And he will remember swimming with Toad in the water tank, and the long body of the drowned king snake they found floating there. And Smetana, *The Moldau*, played every day on the Bechstein, the sound of it bringing tears to his eyes even as he listens again years later. He will remember the smell of the oats cooked in milk and the bread rising yeasty above the black stove and the round pool of yellow light cast by the lamp on the table on a cold winter morning and the hiss of the rain on the tin roof of our lopsided house in the sand plains of Wyalkatchem. He, who was raised in that solitude, will yearn for the silence his whole life and find himself floating away from crowded trains and business meetings and talkative lovers, to dreams of lying at the bottom of the abandoned air-raid shelter, looking up at the cloudless sky, the only sound the ceaseless thud of his heart in his chest.

"Says here," said Toad, rattling the newspaper, "twenty-one Jap planes bombed the blazes out of Drysdale Mission, first thing in the morning. Says there's an air force base up there, on the King Edward River, just south of Broome. Killed a priest and a bunch of darkies. Sad about the priest but good riddance to our native friends, say I. Bomb hit 'em in the air raid shelter." A ditch in the sand. What a place to die. "Ammunition hut exploded and now the mission is only good for toothpicks."

I leaned over to look at the date on the newspaper. Twenty-seventh of September 1943. The paper was more than two weeks old.

"Looks like the Japs are heading our way, eh? First they bomb Darwin twelve, thirteen times. Then it's Broome and Exmouth. What's next, you reckon? Lancelin? Yanchep? Maybe they'd like us to give 'em Fremantle on a silver platter."

"I heard there were Japanese submarines in Fremantle harbour," I said, "just like in Sydney. We're lucky they didn't torpedo anything."

The Italians weren't eating. Their faces worked, lines appeared and disappeared in their chins, it seemed that something burrowed under their skin. The beautiful one, Gianpaolo—who we later called John because we couldn't get our Australian lips to loiter on his name in the sultry Italian way—slopped his tea on the tablecloth and wailed, "*Basta!*" which I mistook for "bastard" and was horrified over. I blushed for him.

They were pitiable in their gratitude for a home-cooked meal and the pathetic clink of china. Poor men. The army had swallowed all the niceties, transformed women from wives and mothers to whores and hostages, made hot canned spam a red-letter meal. At my table, they looked like rabbits, trembling, suspicious that an iron-toothed trap lay under the tablecloth, unable to enjoy their first meal with a family in years.

Mr. Toad, his desire for the Italians' untouched meat scrawled all over his chipped Toby jug of a face, called for the pudding, and out it came, jam roly-poly, steaming sponge, almost spoiled jam and freshets of custard, like so much pus on a suppurating wound. It must have struck the prisoners that way too, because they stared at the pudding with looks of imminent emesis and pushed back their chairs.

"Thank you, lady," said the one with the Frank Sinatra shoes, and the two men slipped from the room, and I was left staring at my white fingernails, and at dear Mr. Toad's hand creeping across the tablecloth in pursuit of the abandoned chops.

Two days after we were married, he'd brought me up to Wyalkatchem on the train from Perth, the carriage cold and unheated, me wrapped in a blanket and shivering. As the sun set, the sand plains outside the windows, treeless to the horizon, were lit with a brilliant red light.

"But where is the water?" I asked Toad, and without turning, he replied, "There is none."

Abandoned stations flashed past the windows, but at one, a man ran after the train, shouting, "Paper! Paper!" and Toad kneeled on the cracked leather seat, raised the window and threw out the newspaper he'd brought with him from Perth.

It was a sixteen-hour trip on the slow moving train. "How much longer?" I asked again, as we passed the Number Two Rabbit-Proof Fence.

"Bloody government railway," said Toad. "Mentioned in

the Bible, they are. 'Creeping things that crawleth.'"

"Aren't you hungry, Toady? How much longer do you think it will be until we get there?" I was imagining a trim limestone cottage under a lemon-scented gum, the foggy clang of cowbells in the distance. The train had emptied out and we were the last passengers remaining.

"Here," he said, shoving a tin of pickled sheep's tongues at me. "That'll hold you." Sheep's tongues. The corpse of a meal moth lay trapped under the key.

"No, thank you," I said, handing it back and stalking to the tiny lavatory in the corner of the carriage.

My face, so white, looked back at me from the tin mirror. Even pinching my cheeks didn't improve my appearance. Albinism is the name for what ailed me. The total absence of pigment in the skin. Ugly was what I thought. Not oyster, cream or eggshell, not ivory, platinum or argent, not pearl or even alabaster. I was bone white. Everywhere. I drew a wet brush through my hair and my white white hair became transparent, like fishing line. I shut my eyes. I couldn't believe that Toad had wanted to marry me.

Earlier, Toad had told me about the farming near Wyalkatchem. The first-class land was forested, he said, and if it was cleared it made for beautiful grazing. The second-class land was mostly mallee and box poison. And the third-class land was gravel plains dotted with low scrub, stunted mallee, tamma thickets and rock poison. No trees worth climbing.

"Ha!" I laughed. "You probably picked the third-class land because it's all short, like you." I'd only been thinking that. I hadn't meant to say it out loud. He snapped his fingers, just once, and after that, hadn't spoken until I'd asked about the water, several hours later, not out of interest but out of desperation.

More than thirty years before the stationmaster helped me down from the train, the first white settler had staked his claim on the land near Wyalkatchem. Billy Law Macfadden, old Mac, built a bit of a place out between Warramuggan Rock and Twattergnuyding back in 1903. He was an old man, over sixty, and he called his farm Lonelykatchem, because he was the only white man for a hundred miles. Three years later, Toad's father took up land there too. He was advised to select forested land, first-class land, but, thinking it would be a hell of a job to clear it all, took third-class land instead. There might have been other men in the district, but he never would have known. In all that wild desolation, there was only one very old man, Toad's father, and Toad.

A man without a horse had to walk the forty miles to Goomalling to fill out the paperwork for a land application, and he had to carry his own water the whole way, both directions, in a kerosene tin slung from a stick over his shoulder. And Toad's father had been a man without a horse. By the time I arrived, Wyalkatchem had grown to a population of sixty-eight adults and forty-three children, counting the ones in the cemetery.

On the wall of the railway refreshment room were nailed two notices. One was for Hanrahans' Pioneer Boarding House: "Comforts, Conveniences, Cleanliness, Tariff Reasonable. Own Cow. Mrs. Biddy Hanrahan, Proprietess." The other notice was for a Popular Girl competition. "You should enter," said Toad as he pushed open the door. I knew he wasn't talking about the competition. He'd bought me a dark red lipstick down in Perth and told me to put it on "all over."

"Gawd, Toady. Don't even think of taking her to stay at Old Ma Hanrahan's," said the refreshment woman. "It's not a proper place for a lady." She held out an unsquare black plush cushion embroidered with a parrot. On one side was a strip of burnt fringing, for fancy. "You'd be best stopping here overnight and then getting Mister Flannigan to whip you out to your place in his gig in the morning." Her hair was pulled into a tight bun and a fat cluster of velveteen violets trembled on her bosom. "Or you could try the police station." She paused and then stuck out her hand and patted my shoulder. "That's good luck! We heard you was coming, deary, but no one really believed a woman would marry our Toad." She stared for a moment at my flat stomach and sighed.

"It's *not* good luck to touch an albino. But maybe it's good luck to touch an idiot," I said, tapping her shoulder.

So Toad and I spent the night in the police tent with a hard, thin, collarless man chained to a log. "He was only drunk and disorderly," said the policeman apologetically, when he showed us to our quarters. "Nuffink to worry about." In the night, the wind shifted around to the south and cold rain blew between the flaps of the tent and woke up the prisoner. "Bloody hell," he said, when he caught sight of me. He bent and, groaning, lifted the log. I watched him make his unsteady way back to the pub.

Five miles west of town. The Cemetery Road. An impression of dirt and disorder, a whiff of meat, a low zuzzing of flies. My new home looked like a broken bee skep, or a pile of twigs for an auto de fe. The door was nothing more than a chaff bag hung from a plank. A kerosene tin stuck out of a domed heap of rocks, and it was only later that I understood it was a chimney. The logs that formed the walls had been driven upright into the ground and draped with greased hessian sacks. The floor was made from a scree of crushed ant nests. Behind the hut stood a wooden wheelbarrow that had been used as a latrine for many weeks. "Fertilizer," said Toad and he rolled it out to a scraped patch of earth where a few onions languished and dumped the maggoty load on the vegetables. The hot desert wind rose and threw a handful of quartz shards in my face. A kookaburra laughed. *Fiddle dee fee. Fiddle dee fee. The fly has married the bumblebee.*

The water that ran off our first bark roof and into a tank was wine red and tasted like goat meat, strong and dark. Water from the dam looked like creamy coffee and tasted of mud. I settled the sediment with a few flakes of oatmeal. When we finally got a metal tank, the water tasted as if it was filled with iron filings. During a drought, Toad dug up the roots of the red mallee, shattered them with the axe and collected the water that was stored in the fibers. He followed pigeons at dusk to the small pools of water they drank from. Emus and parrots and magpies were reliable signs that water was nearby. Dew could be collected by dragging a blanket across the ground until it was saturated. Gum leaves exuded moisture at night and come morning could be sucked dry.

I had thought, when we were first married, that closeness might be possible. I left presents for Toad, under his pillow or in his boot, but it turned out he hated presents. He hated surprises of any kind. To him, they felt like pressure to be jolly or civil at the very least, neither of which he was good at. I had thought we might read the classics out loud by lamplight and take long walks together and laugh at the same jokes, but he thought it was funny that he'd once eaten his father's cat, and I liked Elizabethan riddles. We didn't have a thing in common besides the basic need for companionship and a joint wish for protection from the eyes and comments of the people of Wyalkatchem.

In those days, I still had delusions of grandeur, imagined that one day Mr. Toad and I would be lord and lady of our manor and the sere Australian hills surrounding our farm would miraculously sprout soft green grass dotted with daffodils and bluebells and sheep that never got flyblown. The wind would carry sounds of menial labor being performed by someone else, the honking of white swans from the dam would replace the incessant clanging of the windmill, and the Bedford truck would once again have tires and petrol.

In my youth down in Perth, at my ritzy private school, I must have read that ladies sat in their solars and embroidered items of beauty and impracticality, and so, in my dreaming, I bent to the yellow light of the kerosene lantern and with my needle—plink, plink— tried to trace the shapes of the wildflowers that rise after the winter rains, despite not being able to see the needle. Toad, wearing his favourite puce green cardigan, read the paper, or gargled his after-dinner port to the tune of "Waltzing Matilda," or, sometimes, "The Wild Colonial Boy," and once in a while belched educational titbits like, "Says here Bunyip wheat is turning out to be bloody good wheat," and, "Them idiots down at the air school are useless. There's a trail of crashed Kittyhawks all the way to Darwin." I think he would have made these pronouncements even if I wasn't there because he'd never mastered the art of silent reading. I can hear him now: his voice, so like the croaking of a frog in a bucket, his deep sniffs punctuating each sentence.

"There's a report here (sniff), of a POW in the Victoria Plains district (sniff). He stands accused of (sniff) indecent assault on a farmer's wife."

"Poppycock."

"They say," he hesitates, "she's in the family way (sniff)."

An utter lie, of course. No newspaper would dare mention such a thing. It is his own eager conjecture and predates the evil rise of pornographic reporting by four decades. I can't blame the woman, for perhaps her own legal love is as full of charm as my own dear Toad.

But a woman on a farm, a practical woman with hands polished by lye, fingers utterly lacking fingerprints, I can't believe she would dare defy her circumstances in the arms of our enemy. Surely she knew the delight her neighbours would take in her destruction? The way she would fade to white and cease to exist for the entire district, missing in action, forever.

And right as I am thinking this, a moth kamikazes the fragile mantle of the lamp; the mantle instantly disintegrates and, with a whiff of burnt talc, the moth is incinerated and we sit there, alone in a darkness full of night noises and the eerie sound of grown men whispering in a language we are unable to understand.

If I had to guess what they are saying, I'd guess this:

The Race Horse: What a strange pair.

The Big Man: She's so thin. And she's so white.

The Race Horse: I never saw an albino before. Aren't they dangerous? And do you think she's wearing a scarf because she has lice?

The Big Man: What about her husband? Unappetizing. She's probably thin because he takes her food.

The Race Horse: So when do we kill them?

3

In the first three years after I came to Wyalkatchem, our joint efforts built the farm up to six draught horses, two sulky ponies, eight milking cows, forty hens, a three furrow plough, a thirteen foot disc drill and a Mitchell harvester with a five bag grain box. Toad built a slightly better house, and I plastered it myself with mud made of anthill.

Clearing each paddock took two years. Trees were ringbarked with an axe. Toad bored holes into the sapwood and I stuffed the holes with plugs of salt petre. Salmon gums, because of their shallow roots, could be pulled over by a horse, and made a most satisfying thump when they fell. When the trees had all died, they were burnt on a hot day in February or March. Everyone burnt the trees at the same time of year. All over the district hung choking clouds of smoke.

While waiting for the trees to die, Toad fenced the paddocks. The year before seeding a field, he ploughed it and kept it cultivated through the summer. Four and a half acres was a good day's work. At night, I ran my fingers over the cicatrixes, the line of raised scars across Toad's back. I played them, as I had once played my Bechstein. "What are these, Toad?" I asked, but he moved out from under my hand and told me to bugger off.

We carted water by hand from White Dam at Naramuging, three miles down the road, and when the rains came, from a grassy soak to the north of the house. Farming was slow. Chaff for the horses was made from hay cut by the binder and tied in sheaves. I learned to shock the sheaves into stooks and leave them to dry, and Toad dragged them to the haystack. Twenty-five sheaves made a stook. Five tons of hay per horse had to be grown and cut and carried. It was impossible for one man alone. I no longer massaged cream into my hands at night. I no longer wore my mother's jade ring.

Kangaroos and emus destroyed the new fences, dingoes ate my hens, rabbits ate the grass, box poison killed the sheep and hard work killed the horses. Stinking smut made the wheat kernels foul and we lost the entire crop to septorian rust, which shriveled the grain, not once, but many times. There were a dozen easy ways to die out there: kicked by a horse, shot by a gun, thrown from the sulky, drowned in the dam, bitten by a snake, fell asleep in the sun, caught in the chaff cutter, burst appendix, laryngitis, childbirth.

Shanky Lamprell died in the middle of dinner, hand on his heart, right after saying, "Hold on a moment," from an exploded blood vessel in his neck. Sidney Baster died because no one knew enough to get the caul off his face after he was born. Joan Toad died of diphtheria.

The winter before Joan was born, Toad took me out on a night when the moon was full, to hunt possums. He showed me the claw marks deep in the bark of a gum that shone silver in the eerie light. He showed me the soft tufts of fur caught on the lower branches. He climbed up the hollow tree and thrust a gidji stick down into the dark bole and pulled out three chattering possums, still in their nest.

He said he learned all his horse skills from his father and all his bush skills from an old Aboriginal man, Billy Dick, one of the Balardong people, or perhaps one of the Nyaginagi. He no longer remembered.

Toad hunted the sweet-tasting emus in their nesting season, winter and spring, crouching with his face covered by a fan of branches. He gave me the oil from their legs to rub on my belly so the child wouldn't leave silver tracks in my skin. When he discovered that I craved meat, he rode to the Cowcowing Lakes and hunted mallee fowl, black swans, ducks, grebe, stilt and teal. When moulting, the swans were easily caught. He made me a sweet tea by boiling banksia blossoms. He roasted the spiny echidnas that wandered into my vegetable garden in a ball of clay until they were as tender as lamb. That first child, he was afraid of all that could go wrong. I found him cooking bardi grubs one day though, and I told him to stop. "Enough," I said, "you will kill us all."

He wore a kangaroo skin over his head and shoulders when it rained and advised me to do the same. It rarely rained. He kept a collection of women's corsetry out in the shed but I didn't find that out for years. That was all right. I kept secrets from him too. He never spent a penny he didn't need to and the day my piano and my glory box and my mother's mirror and the little boudoir chair I'd had all my life arrived on the back of a wool cart, he wept from the sheer useless waste of it all. My stepfather had finally sent my things, ashamed at last of all he had stolen from me.

When Toad had asked the director at Graylands Hospital if he could marry me, the doctor had told him that I was involuntarily committed and said he would need to seek permission from my guardian. So Toad had boarded a bus for Dalkeith and walked to my home, a large limestone house on the cliffs above the Swan River. He'd seen the lush rose gardens, the shade houses full of rare orchids, and the intimidating man with the swagger stick who was my stepfather. That man had looked at Toad and laughed and laughed, then wiped the white foam from the corners of his mouth with his fingertips and said, "Oh yes. Marrying you will do *very* nicely. Far, far better than Graylands." And Toad nodded, delighted to have made such a good impression.

Walking the road to White Dam, a year and five months after I first arrived. A narrow red gash cut through the virgin bush, littered with quartz boulders, tangled with the vines and shattered husks of the previous year's pig melons. Magpies, cockatoos, crows, corellas, parrots, galahs, wrens scream and cry and swing through the air and mob in the few standing trees. I have just passed a rock with a veil of lichen over its face and a golden wattle bending from the weight of its blossom, when I hear another walker, coming from the opposite direction. It could be anyone. It could be no one. After all this time, it must be an aural mirage. There's someone out on the Cemetery Road besides Toad and me? "Hullo," says the stranger, wiping her hand on the front of her yellow cotton frock before offering it to me. "I'm Mavis Wall-eye." Cockatoos scream. Insects buzz and tick in the undergrowth. Great plain of cloudless blue sky. Slow roll of the vast red land.

"Gin Toad."

"I know. I heard about you when I was in town. Well worth the walk to see somethink like you."

The sky over Wyalkatchem is hotter and bluer than any other place, and the winds are stronger, the thermals rising tens of thousands of feet straight up, lifting the litter of the desert in its embrace: shards of quartz and shale and flakes of limestone, spinifex, the lost tails of geckoes, scraps of paperbark, the hot smell of the red dirt, the taste of the sky like salt from the sea, cracked pieces of pottery, parrot eyes, wedge-tailed eagles looking for prey, the broken hearts of men and women, the souls of the children who died in that great isolation, sadness, unwillingness, anger, strands of horse hair, nuts and bolts, chicken feathers, sand.

Toad would return from the fields slick with sweat and dust and chaff, and hesitating, his hands in the kerosene tin of water that stood by the back door, he'd look at me, at the towel in my hands, and raise his eyebrows, and that was his way of asking if I might be available that night. When I nodded, he would lift the water in his cupped hands and dash it on his face, rub it over his head, rake the wetness through his hair with his unsubtle fingers, and then, smiling, take the towel from my outstretched hand. For a man who rarely spoke, gestures became important, the removal of an ant from my shoulder an invitation to another, different kind of closeness.

He liked to approach from behind, in the dark, on a moonless night when no stray gleam of light could illuminate my hair. He liked the sheets to be cool, he liked my shoulders to smell of grass, he liked to taste the skin at the base of my neck. He was embarrassed by the sound of the springs, by kisses, by talk of any kind. He liked, afterwards, to take hold of my smallest finger and to fall asleep with it in his grip.

But each morning, it was as if we were strangers again; as if, in the dark, he had lain with my twin instead of me, and I, with some other, unfamiliar man. He never touched me in the daytime, in the light, that man who ran his hands so tenderly over the horses, who touched his nose to their velvet muzzles and murmured to them as he gazed into their eyes. He had it in him, a capacity for love. But he hid it from me. He hid many parts of himself from me and not just this. And I hid from him too. As if closeness was dangerous. We were, each of us, afraid of the other.

Toad was out checking the fence line when I felt the birth pains from my first child, my Joan. I was pressing tea towels, the steam that rose from the iron tasting of burnt linen. Boss Cockie, perched on the window ledge, was imitating the sound of the sad iron. "Aaah. Ssssh. Hssss." I waited for the pains to go away or become less, but instead, they grabbed me and began, inexorably, to pull me down below the surface of the earth. I could feel the broken pieces of ant nest that formed our floor gouging tracks into my skin. Terrified, I ran through the wheat field to get Toad's help. He knocked me down with a right hook to the jaw and then dragged me back the mile or so to the house with a hard, set look on his face. I woke up, jolting along on his back, and the screams I heard were my own.

"Shut up, Gin," he said, "or I'll have to hit you again."

He'd seen that look in my eyes, he said, of an animal wild with pain, which either needs to be left alone to die or shot in the head. And the kindest thing to do is the hardest.

When we got to the house, he hefted me onto the veranda and pressed down hard on the top of my stomach, so that a wail rose from deep within me and I gritted my teeth and bore down on the source of all the hurting. And I vowed I would never again allow Toad near me when I birthed a baby.

Afterwards, he brought me a blanket and a towel for the blood and he sat with the new child in his lap, staring at her whiteness, her face with its startling transparency.

"Whaddaya reckon we call her Joan?" he said and so we did.

The next morning, I rose and baked six pounds of bread before the sun had topped the hill, and Toad came in from milking to corned beef and cabbage and a hot cup of tea. I'm proud of that.

These are the things that I learned to do after coming to Wyalkatchem: I learned how to make yeast, to bake bread, to make a bread pan out of an old kerosene tin, how to clean a kerosene tin and flatten it and smooth the edges with a rasp, how to trim the wick on a kerosene lamp, to clean the chimney of a kerosene lamp with a piece of newspaper crumpled in a ball, how to remove creosote from my skin with yellow soap, how to make yellow soap from ash and lye and fat, how to make lye, how to render fat, how to cook on a wood stove, how to split wood with an axe, how to sharpen an axe, how to treat burns from a woodstove, how to treat burns from hot ashes, how to treat burns from lye, how to treat a man who has been burnt, how to treat a man, how a man likes to be treated, how to make a maternity dress, how to make a layette, how to push out a baby, how to cut an umbilical cord with the knife used for castrating the lambs, how to feed an infant, how to hang a blanket in the boughs of a gum tree and rock a baby to sleep, how to sit quietly at night with a child in my lap, how to feel for a fever, how to boil willow for its cooling sap, how to paint a throat with gentian violet and listen for the smallest breath, how to make a coffin, how to line it with pieces of cotton, how to dress a dead child, how to lower a coffin into the ground, how to put one foot in front of the other and keep on doing it every day.

4

I am not used to having rapists sleeping in my house. Every squawk of the bedsprings from Joan's room jerks me roughly awake. It sounds like the Italians are having a bad night too; the racehorse screams and thrashes and is woken by the older man, but I'm not even tempted to bring him a hot water bottle, or some milk.

My children have not been murdered. Alf and Mudsey are in the sleepout on the western side of the house, in a heap of legs and blankets, Alf sucking Mudsey's thumb, their collection of bush tat blue and silver in the moonlight: magpie eggs, gumnuts, sheep's knucklebones in a jar, the skeleton of a mouse laid out in a matchbox coffin.

They are, both of them, unused to strangers. They have rarely seen people other than Toad and myself, certainly never people who knelt down to speak to them, laid chocolates in their moist ochre hands, smiled. Never men of normal height. Mudsey's sunburnt face swiveled between my white face and the unfamiliar faces of the prisoners, their mysterious glittering black eyes. She held her own dark arm up against the arm of the youngest prisoner and frowned.

"What's wrong with you, Mum?" she asked. She doesn't remember Joan. She doesn't know that I dreamt her white and was stunned by the redness of her face and the blueness of her eyes when she was born, her strength and her tyranny. Her dark secrecy.

When I finally fall asleep, my dreams are full of whales leaping out of a frothy khaki sea, their huge baleen grins aimed at me, their masculine elements raucous and ready, while I cower on a ledge that shudders in the wind of their passing. They leap and miss, leap and miss, and the platform bucks beneath my feet. Bizarre to dream of whales in the middle of a drought.

I wake up to the sound of hammering, and it's the whales I think I hear, battering the weatherboard wall next to my bed, and I scream, and scream again when my soul jolts back into my body with a feeling akin to being rolled in a thorn bush, and this time I think—oh my God! It's the Italians. They are coming for me.

But no. They rose early and are building themselves a humpy, a home of their own out in the orchard, with leftover boards and flattened kerosene tins and hessian bags and in their rush to escape us, they have knocked over the jar of wattle and spilled water has beaded on the floor forming hundreds of convex mirrors, a woman's expressionless face trapped in each one.

They build two rooms, a bedroom and a lounge, with a veranda along one side. A chimney is built; there must be a fireplace where they will warm their toes after work and cook eggs and potatoes. They are skilled builders—the chimney goes up straight and the veranda doesn't sing, and though they only work on it in the early morning and after the evening meal, it is finished in a few weeks. The Italians never return to Joan's room, and it's thankful I am for that small mercy.

Dear Toad hasn't finished our own little shack. He built this third house specially to hide away from prying eyes; beginning with the long line of gum trees to the north that mask it from the road, down to the two sandy hills, bosomy and maternal, that rise behind the shearing shed to the east, and which cast long shadows in the morning.

Between the house and the many outbuildings there is a hardpacked dirt yard, and this is often littered with pieces of kerosene tin which have been used as shingles and which regularly blow down from the roof; or the dead rodents which the dairy cats bring as sin offerings, and which decompose spectacularly fast on hot days; or pieces of steel boning that Toad extracts from Edwardian corsetry to create bulletproof vests for the old codgers in the Volunteer Defence Force; or scrags of wilted cabbage that fall out of the slop bucket on the way to the chooks; or the droppings of a mob of sheep that have broken through the fence (again!) and emptied out every inch of their digestive tracts right under the kitchen window. The children play in the yard, I hang laundry there, and Toad disembowels machinery on the hard red dirt. Now, the Italians have built a house in one corner, between the flowering gum tree and the rabbit cages, facing the field where we keep the horses. Turns out the Racehorse likes the real thing, potters out and feeds the horses bits of sugar and handfuls of grass, practises saying, "Orses, good orses," over and over in English. The Big Man paints words above the door to their hut: *Tobruk Hotel. A. Cesarini manager.*

One night, several weeks after their arrival, I find the Big Man, Antonio, sleeping in a rattan chair on our veranda. He has been fencing all day, and then, when he returned, he took the axe from my hand and split enough logs to fill the huge woodbox next to the back door. I could have done it myself. I have always done it myself.

Sleeping, he doesn't look like an enemy soldier. His head has fallen forward onto his arms and his back is sweetly rounded. He looks like a child in innocent pink clothing, his long black hair lifting in the breeze. He shivers. I don't want him to sicken and die from my neglect, so I step up next to him, and softly say, "Mister

Cesarini," then a little louder, "Antonio."

I am ashamed to wake a working man, but the nights are cold this time of year, and as the district nurse says, "A chill can kill," a fact well proven in this household, so I move closer, almost touching him, but not quite. I am not that bold. I have never touched or been touched by hands other than Mr. Toad's, who heard me playing in the madhouse at Graylands. He wasn't a patient like me. Oh no, not him. Just visiting an aunt in his grey wool three piece from before the war and an Akubra hat, well used. There was a Steinway in the dining hall, a grand old Steinway, and I was belting out Smetana's *Moldau* in my aggravation and bitter disappointment at being cheated out of my freedom. At sixteen, I had won the 1923 Open Piano Championship at the West Australian Eisteddfod, with by far the best piano solo, but another girl from my school, a beautiful girl with bouncing auburn hair and rosy cheeks, had charmed the judge. She was a tremendous fibber, that girl. She was too old to be in the competition, so she lied about her age and Professor Schallotsky thought she would look better than an albino on the stage in Europe as he took her hand and kissed her. He sent her to Germany to study under Teichmüller at the Conservatoire. That was my prize! That was what I had worked for, and it was taken from me! But the worst of it was, when I wrote a letter of complaint to the Trinity College of Music in London, they sent a message to the Symphony where I had been playing for twenty-five pounds a week, my running away money, and I lost my job. So Eileen sailed for Europe, a concert tour and history, and I, the better pianist, had to stay behind. I fell into my bed and didn't move for weeks until my stepfather tired of my presence and had me committed. Involuntarily. The folks down at Graylands weren't keen on letting me get away. They kept me there for four years, serenading the lunatics with daily concerts that could be heard all the way over in maximum security. It was fame, of a certain kind.

That day in the madhouse, Mr. Toad, a sawn-off stranger, stood close behind me, raising every hair on my neck, and when I was so squirrelly that I hit a wrong note, he leaned forward and shouted—he had to shout, I was well and truly into the current of the piece—"Will you marry me?"

At the time, it felt like escape. I was twenty and I already thought no one would have me, that I was broken in a way that couldn't be fixed with baling wire or square cut nails or glue. I had thought piano would be an escape too, from the fancy house in Dalkeith, where no one had looked at me after my mother died and no one listened to my music or asked about my day. I was an evil omen, a pale and hunched ghost whose own mother wouldn't have warmed her with a kiss. I would have married a bandicoot.

I stared back at him and thought he didn't look like a man who'd want to have his hands all over me. He was wavery at the edges, trembling so hard and so fast he didn't have an outline. I hated being touched. Too many children had pulled my hair on the school bus; too many adults had grazed my arm and then stared at their fingers to see if my whiteness had come off on them, like baby powder; too many people had lined up outside my cell at the hospital and paid their pennies to touch the lucky ghost girl. And I didn't trust their reactions when I touched *them*; shudders, shrinking, shock. My hands were unwelcome. Even Toad jumped when I put my hand in his after the wedding. The Justice of the Peace laughed at us then, Little Toady with his bantam legs, me squinting and blinking as the flash bulb exploded. "Plenty of time for that later," Toad had said, peeling his hand away from mine and wiping it on his tartan plus-fours.

So I wasn't about to risk touching Antonio, there on the veranda, and he didn't wake to my soft calling of his name. I looked at him for a while in the moonlight, and then went and got a blanket from my bed and came back to cover him but you cannot just throw a heavy woollen blanket on a sleeping man. It will not do.

Standing behind Antonio, I opened the still warm blanket, and with my arms wide, I leaned forward. Waves of heat rose from his flannel shirt, mingled with his man scent of hard work and sandalwood, and this warmth brushed my face as I hesitated there, trembling, my arms around him but not quite touching his flesh. I was afraid Mr. Toad would step out to piss, or one of my children would tattle at breakfast, "Mummy was cuddling Antonio on the veranda." I could hear the breathing of every soul in the house, and my own seemed as loud to me as an untuned violin. On the other side of the house, the children squirmed deeper under their blankets, Alf slurped on his thumb; a snake slipped across the veranda and left two tiny turds as evidence. The tin roof of the Italian's hut flashed like a semaphore at the clouds scudding over the moon, smoky white clouds, fraying at the edges, with deep purple bellies. I hesitated there, stung with an emotion I could not name.

Of course, it was only a moment. I left the blanket and went back to sleep. But it seems to me, when I look back on that night, that it wasn't night at all. It was bright day.

5

A rabbit skin—once you have made a quick cut up and down the hind legs and another around the head—slips off like a glove, and can be stretched on a frame and tanned and sold for a shilling to the rabbit-oh. The beak of a parrot is only worth sixpence and they're as hard as hell to saw off. A fox's pelt brings four shillings.

And if I was lucky enough to trap a dingo, the scalp was worth a whole pound. The rabbit-oh paid the money into Mr. Toad's moist hand, even though I was the one who trapped the rabbits and skinned them and tanned their soft little hides, and Mr. Toad put the money inside his trousers and afterwards hid it somewhere.

6

I was gloving the rabbits the first time I heard the Italians sing, their voices coming fitful on the battering wind from down near the windmill where they'd gone to feed the calves. Mr. Toad's wet shirts were tangled around the clothesline, and the wind flipped up the feathers of the blue-black chickens foraging for bugs in the dust around my feet. The wind whistled under the front door, lifting the hall runner a couple of inches off the floor, where it rippled like a snake and hissed. They were singing Verdi, two glorious and unexpected tenors accompanied by the brass of the milk buckets and the cellos of the bawling calves.

"Stone the crows," said Mr. Toad, emerging from the privy with his vest buttoned to his fly and a partially eaten apple saved under his suspender strap. "Aren't you done with them bunnies yet?"

He dropped into the rattan chair where Antonio had slept, checked his pocket watch and began paring his toenails with a pair of tinsnips. I sprinkled the hides with anti-weevil powder, and threw the shiny maroon bodies into the dog run, one for each dog, but the stupid beasts fought anyway, growling and tearing at each other and trampling the meat.

"Get out of that!" shouted Mr. Toad, and he stood and flung the tinsnips at the ringleader. The blue heeler yelped when the snips hit the side of his muzzle, and tucked its tail between its legs and slunk to the back of the cage, dragging a rabbit by its head.

"Bloody dogs," he said, squatting to inspect my work.

The Italians were walking through the orchard, swinging the buckets and singing. Mr. Toad smiled when he saw me listening, his lip pulling all the way up to his eyeball on one side and not at all on the other, and he clapped his hat on his head.

"Got them ones special for you, Pet," he said, leaning over me and patting me. "Asked for blokes that could sing or play pianer or something."

No matter that we were both still shy, ten years after our marriage. I couldn't help myself. I smiled back at him for the kindest gift he had ever given me, and before dinner, I played Verdi's *Nabucco*, for him and for them, because suddenly hearing rich, harmonic song was heartbreaking when we could barely hear the ABC orchestra on the wireless at night over the fierce popping of the static; when the local church choir with its orgy of voices was considered a high spot, a pin-nacle of culture.

The voice of my rosewood Bechstein roared through the house, the windowpanes tinkled in their muntins, dust was jolted free from the ceiling boards and flashed through bars of light. The Italians stood still in the doorway, their hats in their hands. I think they were waiting for something, or it might just have been that they wanted their tucker, the rabbit stew bubbling aromatically on the back of the Metters, but on that day, the day I played for my first real audience, I chose to think they wanted to join me, so I began to sing in a soprano I hadn't used in ten years.

They came, Antonio and John, to stand next to me and their voices joined mine like the convergence of two mighty rivers with a dry season creek, and Mudsey and Alf crept in from the kitchen and stared at us with their thumbs in their mouths, and their light blue eyes rolled from the men to me, from the men to me, and only

Mr. Toad still sat in the kitchen with my fine linen napkin tucked into the sweat-stained neck of his work shirt and his knife and fork strangled in his hands.

O, mia patria si bella e perduta!
O, membranza si cara e fatal!

The police sergeant had been round while I was out setting my traps, and during dinner, Mr. Toad slapped down two work books issued by the government in which we were to keep a record of how many hours the men worked, what jobs they were given, how well these tasks were performed, and what we owed our prisoners. They were to be paid one pound every week, but the money was given to the government, not to Antonio and John.

Each book contained a photo of a soldier in his dress uniform, looking pleased with himself and probably gloating over the excellent food he'd be getting three times a day from the army. All of his per-sonal details were listed in English. What a revelation: Antonio was forty, had five children and was a shoemaker; John claimed to be twenty-two (he must have lied when he joined up; he never needed to shave), unmarried, a farm laborer who'd enlisted in the cavalry and brought his own horse with him. I pointed at their pictures, tried to say the names of their villages, held up five fingers to Antonio, and he smiled and pointed at Mudsey and Alf and held up two fingers.

There was a pause.

Mr. Toad looked at me. Mudsey and Alf sat still in their bentwood chairs. A fly landed on a bead dangling from the crocheted milk jug cover and stamped its tiny feet. Yes, I nodded. Two. Maud and Alfred.

After the bread and butter pudding, Mr. Toad hauled out an atlas and opened it to Italy and the prisoners showed us where they lived, although I couldn't tell one place from another because the writing was so small and the pastel colours bled together, and

Antonio translated for John, who still couldn't say more than yes and no and I don't know. They pointed to Bardia where the Australian soldiers had captured Antonio on January 5, 1941, a hellhole in Libya just down the road from Tobruk, where John had been captured, and they trailed their fingers across the water to India and then down to Australia, to the west coast, and they looked up at one another then, and looked away. Antonio tapped his finger once on Fremantle and closed the atlas with a bang.

We went into the lounge and sang some more Verdi and this time Mr. Toad joined in, humming along to "Va, Pensiero" because he didn't know the words. He *did* know the words to some of the songs from *Madama Butterfly*, you have to give him that; he'd hardly had an education at all except for ploughing and crutching and wigging and castrating, so it was good of him to try. The men pressed closer and closer to the piano, their breath made the candles waver and Toad jostled Antonio so he could be the one to stand behind me. And Antonio leaned over my shoulder and turned the page at exactly the right moment. I knew then that he could read music and I turned to smile at him and saw Toad blush with shame, or maybe he was already jealous. I stopped playing and looked between them with my mouth open. "Don't be silly Toad," I said with a little laugh. "You know lots of things that Antonio doesn't." But even as I said it, I knew it wasn't true. I turned back to the piano and played "It's a Long Way to Tipperary" and other songs that Toad knew, until the Italians, bored, drifted away.

The next day in the orchard I was culling fruit. There was a pile of aborted peaches around my gumboots. My fingers were green and sticky and the wasps were enraged and had already stung me on the lip. He must have made a noise, because I turned and saw him there, leaning against the trunk of my favourite tree, the one with a treble clef carved into a branch because it was such a *melodious* tree. He was watching me and there was concern on his face. I covered my swollen lip with my hand and wished that Toad was nearby, but he wasn't. He was out moving the sheep to fresh pasture.

"Don't be ashamed of him," he said, bending down to wipe the dust off his shoes with a handful of grass.

Antonio knew what I was thinking right from the start.

I *was* ashamed of Toad in front of these men, embarrassed of his ignorance, although he was just being himself. He had no pretence to him, no artifice. Even though he was talented with horses and farming and bushcraft, he lacked even the basics of an elementary education. I deeply felt our inequality. When he mispronounced words in private, I corrected him, insistently, and in public I spoke over him, drowning out his mistakes with my Dalkeith accent.

"I'm not ashamed," I said. "Toad's a hard-working man. The salt of the earth."

He frowned and stepped closer. "He shouldn't make you do this work."

"What? These peaches? He doesn't make me. They're my peaches. I planted this whole orchard, and I take care of it too."

I reached up to thin another runty peach and he swiftly touched the front of my dress.

"But you are pregnant," he said.

I backed away, shaking my head. My hands were trembling.

"You can be injured. He should not allow this."

I crossed my arms over my belly, the belly I thought he hadn't noticed. The belly *I* tried not to notice. Toad was always very careful not to overexcite the pregnant ewes. Not to put the dogs among them.

"Don't talk about this," I said. "Don't touch me. We don't do that kind of thing here."

"Sorry, Missus. I didn't mean no harm. Look here. I will help you with your orchard. Maybe we can plant some olives. You can for sure grow olives here."

Boss Cockie, perched high in a red gum, muttered, "Shut up, *shut up*." His wings glowed urinous where the sun shone through them.

"We don't need olives. They're useless."

"Good for oil. Good for eating. I'll get you some." He moved to another row of trees. I was going to tell him to be gentle with the infant fruits, but he began to sing, and I stood still instead and listened. He had a voice worth listening to and after a while I began to hum along with him, not loud enough that he could notice. Distantly, Toad whistled for the dogs.

I'd seen in Antonio's workbook that his birthday was in two days, September sixth; I'd noticed the date because it was my poor mother's birthday too. And I thought I'd barter a linen pillow sham for some sugar from Mrs. Walleye, the neighbour, to bake him a cake, because maybe, just maybe, if I was kind to him, some Italian woman over there in Europe would be kind to one of our Australian soldiers.

Before bed, I went round my traps, resetting them if they'd already been sprung, a gunnysack trailing behind me that rapidly filled with bodies. In the paddock where the windmill and the dam were, the rabbits had come out to drink in the cool of the evening, and there were so many of them that it seemed the dam had overflowed and water was lapping the fence posts in silver waves. No wind blew and yet this silent ocean of rabbits rippled and shivered, the moon glittering on their fur. They drank our water and ate the pasture we intended for our sheep; they tunnelled under the ground and made it soft as a sponge, full of bunkers that collapsed under our horses' hooves and broke their legs; they were food for dingoes and foxes, both of which had another favourite food: lambs. They were alien invaders who were taking the very bread out of our mouths.

Those rabbits used my traps to comb their pelts. They sent out platoons to ambush unsuspecting tomcats. When I tried to poison them with cyanide, they got drunk on the gas and sang bawdy songs under the house. Rabbit partisans left long skid marks in the cheese and grenades in the oat bin. Saboteurs must have written our name on the back of the dunny door down at the local sleazy rabbit pub— "For a good time, come to Toad's and ask for Gin"—because we were absolutely inundated, no matter how many I killed.

Thinking of Antonio's hand on my belly, I slammed the back of the axe down again and again on the necks of the rabbits. When I was done for the night, I left their bodies cooling in a sack hung from the salmon gum outside the shearing shed, hit the sack one more time with the axe and went in to bed.

Mr. Toad wasn't sleeping. His bed was in the sleepout on the veranda next to my room, as he disliked sleeping in a room with a mirror in it, "Like having a big eye staring at your mug all night," he'd said when he dragged his enamel cot outside. The mirror was mine, Louis XV carved giltwood from home, propped up on a chest of drawers Toad had made from packing cases. But just because the mirror was there, didn't mean he had to look at himself. I never did. I thought he was lying about the mirror. I thought it was the sight of my white hair, uncovered and snaking towards him in the moonlight, that had turned his stomach.

"Gin," he said, "I was having a bit of a yarn with the copper and he reckons these blokes is daft." He meant the Italians. "Over in Yerecoin, one of them was sawing a limb off a gum tree. Stupid git was sitting on the branch he was chopping off and when he finally cut through, down he fell." He sniffed and laughed and the words of the hand sheet from the Department of the Army ran across the billowing hessian wall in sparkling, inch-high letters: "The Italian prisoner of war is a curious mixture, in that he can be made to give of good work if certain points are observed: 1. He cannot be driven but he can be led. 2. Mentality is childlike; it is possible to gain his confidence by fairness and firmness. 3. Great care must be exercised from a disciplinary point of view for he can become sly and objectionable if badly handled."

"Does it make you feel better than them," I said, "to repeat such an unkind story?"

It was the first time I'd not laughed at one of his stories, the first time I'd seen them for what they were.

"Singing bloody opera doesn't make a bloke a man," he muttered.

In the darkness, the glowing red tip of Mr. Toad's cigarette grew larger and larger, until it fell off and was lost in the seagrass matting.

"Best make sure that doesn't catch fire," he said, pinching out the butt and flicking it under his bed. He chuckled again, all malice, no mirth, and turned over.

The next morning, I saddled the tamest cow and rode over to Wall-eyes', my best linen sham folded inside my handbag, humming a few bars of "Va, Pensiero" over and over again. Antonio was one of the few people I'd ever met who knew how to use his voice like a musician, louder, softer, faster, slower, the tiniest of hesitations exactly where they wreaked the most damage. Mavis Walleye met me at the door, her eyes an unholy F-major green, her frizzy orange hair stuck to her freckled face.

"The whole district's talking about you lot, Missus Toad," she says, staring at my bony shins in their Wellington boots. Lord have mercy. Look what the cat dragged in.

"Good morning, Mavis. Nice to see you too. I was wondering if you have a bit of sugar you might let me have."

Her hand jerks on the screen door, as if she'd like to slam it in my face.

"We won't have men like that on our place," she says, clutching the top of her blouse together, an invisible Italian prying at the button, trying to knead her doughy breasts. "Things happen." News of Harry Walleye's capture had come on the Japanese radio station that broadcast men's names in an endless, painful list. There were no men at all on her place.

"I've used all my coupons for this month and I'd really like to bake a cake. I can let you have this sham if you'll let me have a cup of sugar. It's Madeira work on Irish linen." I am the very pink of courtesy. She sniffs the embroidery and grabs it from my hand.

"Who are you making cakes for, Gin Toad?" she says, and even though I can't blush, my eyes change from violet to something closer to a pale bluey-red, and she leans forward and hisses in my face, "Don't go thinking any man would look at you twice. You're a horror," and I hunch my back and cross my arms over my belly and think, "My God! This pregnancy is *such* a mistake." But I also remember that Antonio has looked at me twice. More than twice.

I stare at Mavis until she goes to get the sugar, and when it comes it's full of tiny ants that are just movement and the sour smell of iodine but I'll take anything I can get. I ride with knees and elbows flapping along the line of trees erupting out of the living red earth until I get back to my kitchen and call Mudsey to pick the bloody ants out of the sugar so I can bake the stupid birthday cake. She comes reluctantly, moist and dirty, and works in silence. Her hands accusing.

The rest of the day, I feel like I am wearing a magpie, the uniform of the English convicts, one side mustard yellow printed with black arrows, and the other side black, printed with mustard yellow arrows, my brain and my bloated belly and my unmentionables and my arms and my legs and even my heart, divided, for all to see.

After he blows out the birthday candles, Antonio tries to take my hand to thank me and I jump backwards into Mr. Toad, hiding my hands under my arms and shaking my head and squinting to see if he's coming after me, but he is just standing, solemnly staring at me and he is shaking his head too.

"*Cavolo!*" he says, "I wanted only to thank you. Excuse me."

"What is *cavolo?*" asks Mr. Toad, and in answer, Antonio holds up a head of cabbage, and makes of it a puppet and it sings in Italian, "Your tiny hand is frozen. Let me warm it in my own," and only I know what he has said, because they are words from the opera, from Puccini, and Mr. Toad laughs like a child entertained at a Punch and Judy show, not really understanding, and I laugh because I am so afraid.

7

It seemed to me that Antonio was a bit like the rabbits, popping up everywhere, underfoot. I'd be out pegging the washing and he'd be stitching up a sheep's flank, torn open on the barbed wire. "G'day, Missus," he'd say, taking off his hat and waving it at me. If I was riding out to check the far dam, he'd be fencing the paddock, or repairing the sails on the windmill, or ripping open the rabbit warrens, or napping inside a dead cow's ribcage, his shirt draped over the bones to shade his face. "Hullo,'he'd say, sitting up, "*Come stai?*"

Once, Toad was with me, and he pursed his lips and snapped, "Pull yer head in, Gin." Was it because I had touched the red buttons on my dress or because I'd slowed down to answer?

Toad jammed his arm around my waist and pulled me roughly against him, but he wasn't looking at me. He glared at Antonio and he may as well have been a dingo, peeing on a stump to mark his territory. This is mine. Antonio lifted his hat and bowed slightly. Always a gentleman.

8

My attitude towards religion has always been on the radical side. Seems to me there's nothing more religious than standing in God's almighty cathedral, the bowl of the earth, just as the sun comes up, and mist lifts from the ground, and the gum leaves are pink and gold from the light streaming through them, and every drop of dew on every spider web is a diamond on a glittering crown. The songs of the kookaburra and the fairy wren and the wagtail sounding better by far than the hokey magic of the organ: I've always said that the coffin of a church isn't worth a brass razoo compared with a spring morning in the bush.

The government, however, decreed that the Italians were to be taken to special services each week, services separate from those of the local Catholics, and that meant Father Duffle's, a round trip of three hours with the horse and gig, with Mr. Toad waiting at the end, hold-ing up his pocket watch and asking me why we were ten minutes longer than last week. Sex, I told him. Four minutes each for the blokes and two for the horse. He looked at me then, oh yes he did. A corrugation of gimlet saplings lay across the track to hold the dirt, and the occasional mallee root or lump of quartz jutted through, snickering in evil anticipation, ready to tip over the cart and leave us stranded hours from the nearest house. It was all right in autumn, when the track was dry and the bush hummed with lazy ripeness, but it was hell when the winter rains turned the slippery dust to mud, and hell again in the summer when the thermometer rose above a hundred every day and flies clustered on the spots of moisture that formed under my arms and down my back and in the corners of my eyes, and the road was littered with the bodies of kangaroos and dingoes and parrots that had died of thirst.

It was one hour there and one hour back and the Italians made bets on the local horse races and sang folk songs and opera and occasionally, tunes they had heard on the radio, like "Jealousy" or "Sorrento", but I didn't sing because I could barely see where we were going and I held my head cocked and my eyes almost shut and every jolt felt ominous as the gig dipped between mallee gums and the blue-grey scrub, towing a plume of dust and a cloud of ecstatic blowflies.

Two months after the Italians had arrived, I was used to this journey, and I began to relax. To practice Italian phrases. To ask questions and be able to answer some too. Once, rocking through the bush, our hips sliding on the leather seat, bumping and jostling one another in the way children do in the playground, familiar but impersonal, Antonio asked me how I'd met Toad.

"He heard me playing the piano," I said, skimming the truth.

"He wants his own radio, playing music all the time," laughed Antonio, but this was so close to what I thought that my lip drooped and he saw my sadness and held the edge of the seat, to avoid jostling me.

"Ah," he said, and after another moment, "ah."

"You are a good mother," he said later, in an effort to comfort, but we both knew it wasn't true. Ever since Joan, I had only done the basics, read the bedtime stories in a fast, flat voice, dropped the food on the table so the gravy splashed the cloth, pinned shut the places with missing buttons. Even a stranger could see that. "Are you looking forward to the new one?"

"Maybe," I said. "I'm not sure. It depends."

"It depends on what?" he asked, but this I was unwilling to an-swer.

"How about you," I asked. "How did you meet your wife?"

The traces jingled, the bush chattered, Antonio tapped out a Luxor and lit it, inhaled deeply and twin streamers of yellow smoke unfurled from his nostrils.

"She is a pure woman, my wife," he said. "I saw her in town, passing the shop where I made shoes, bringing soup to her grandparents every day. She has a long . . . " he paused, ran his finger from the crown of his head down to his waist and looked at me.

"Plait?"

"Yes. And it moves like a cat's tail when she is walking and I found myself excited by this."

He glanced at me again, hiding his mouth behind his hand. Daring but a little embarrassed too. I peered at him from the corners of my eyes, seeing him as young, ardent, infatuated with a braid, and I couldn't help myself. I smiled.

A photograph slid from his pocket, the paper warm, furry, domesticated, and he stroked it before passing it to me.

"My family," he said, and they were all there: in a ring, holding hands, dancing, three girls in white dresses, barefoot, with large bows in their hair, and two little boys facing away from the camera, their shorts pulled high up their backs by the dark targets of fabric suspenders, and there was a woman, barely taller than the tallest girl, her head thrown back, her mouth open in song or laughter; all the faces were turned towards her and she held their hands as well as their hearts. She was happy. They were happy. There was no doubt.

I wanted to wear that white dress and laugh. I wanted to know the man who saw her like that. Something broke in me.

"Very nice," I said, handing back the photograph.

He told me he always knew he would have a lot of babies. Because when he was just a little boy, just before he went to work at the shoemaker's, his father and three other men, strangers, came to him in the night and took him from his bed. It was spring, the ground was wet, and the moon was full. His father carried him at first on his back, and in the father's hand, like a staff, was a long stalk of sorghum. The other men carried grain too. And they went together into the forest. Under the trees, the faces of the men were a soft grey-lilac and their moon shadows ran along beside them. Antonio's hand around his father's neck found a sprig in a buttonhole and he pulled it out to look at it and it was a *cimaruta*, rue and fennel and pennyroyal and rosmarino tied together with a twist of paper, and he was surprised, because rue is the witches' flower.

"Oh, surely you don't believe in witches, Antonio?" I asked him.

"We had a witch in our village and she grew this flower next to her gate, because it is yellow and the petals make a pentagram. She was a good witch and honourable and she told us boys to rub the wormwood on our faces to grow a beard and it worked."

"That's so silly. You would have grown a beard anyway."

But he looked away and didn't say anything further and I was sorry I had spoken. Toad never cared what I said. A butcherbird startled away from the cart, flipping its tail.

"Go on. What happened when your father took you out of bed that night?"

He told me he smelled artemisia in his father's hair and on his hands and his unshaven cheeks, a smell like lemon. And this was his *father*, a religious man, with the witch's symbol in his buttonhole and her perfume on his skin! It made his blood run cold. But he would have been cold anyway, he said, because as soon as they got into the forest, the men stopped and stripped off his clothes.

My hands were tight on the reins then. I didn't look at him. It was an exquisite moment of the imagination for he is a good-looking man. I felt as if Michelangelo's David had fallen from the sky and landed—plunk!—in my cart. The same smooth bulge of the deltoid muscle, the same firm plane of the cheek.

He told me each man held him by a limb and they rushed him through the forest, spread-eagled and freezing. He cried and twisted and begged his father to tell him what was happening, but Antonio's father only put his finger to his lips. After a while, they came to a clearing and there was a large stone in the middle of the moss, and on the stone stood a clam shell filled with water, and a twig, and a broken antler, and a curling feather from a grouse, and a silver disc, very smooth, that shone in the moonlight. This, his father took up and angled to reflect the light across his face. "Here," Antonio said, touching his forehead, "and here," touching his cheek, "and here," touching his lip. And his lip was very close to me, and moist.

The cart lurched just then and I ducked my head, dodging an unseen branch, and Antonio continued speaking, looking sideways at me. He said one of the other men opened a wolfskin bag he had carried with him, and took out an axe and this too shone in the moonlight, and when Antonio saw it, he cried out and his father put his hand over Antonio's mouth and there were tears in his eyes.

"Ha! I know he didn't kill you. You're still here," I said, one hand tight on the iron rail so I wouldn't slide towards him. I didn't like to hear about a man crying.

Antonio swivelled on the seat and bent his head to look at me, one strong slap of a look, and then continued, "They were all speaking, but I couldn't understand the words. Some of what they chanted sounded like Latin, but other words were very strange, though I admit I was very distracted by the axe, very worried, and they may only have been speaking our own simple dialect."

He said there had been, after all, nothing to worry about because the man with the axe used it to cleave a chestnut sapling, to split it almost the entire way to its roots, and then the man shoved in a branch to hold the halves apart and laid aside the axe. Antonio sat, propped up against the stone and shivering. His father flicked water from the shell on him with the feather and it was cold. Like silver, he said. The men gathered around him and carried him to the sapling and now he saw that someone had nailed a picture of the Madonna to the heartwood, as well as a coin showing a man's organs. Antonio didn't say man's organs, he said *salami*, such an image! Excuse my words, but that was the fact. He said he had the goose skin all over. They put ash on his head and passed him through the split tree, like thread through the eye of a needle, three times. "My eyes were truly wet then," he said, resting his head on his hand, and his voice was low. "*Dio boia*. The men touched my tears and licked their fingers and I was sure I was going to die."

After this, they laid him on the rock and waved the stalks of sorghum and sang while one of the men took a needle and thread and sewed the tree back together again, with the picture and the coin inside. And they began to talk again, normally, and they smiled, and patted each other on the back.

"How traumatic. You must have hated them."

"Not at all. On the way home, my father spoke softly to me, telling me this was *La Vecchia*, the working of the craft, and it was done to the boys in our area to make them fertile."

How I cringed from that word. *Fertile.* I blushed to think of him imagining Toad and I together, at night, under the sheets, and I knew that whatever he imagined, whatever he was used to, wouldn't be as it truly was for me. Dark. Anonymous. Silent. I thought between him and his wife it would be different.

Antonio's father said, "My father, your grandfather, took me out to this forest when I was your age, and I, too, was passed through a tree, and see! I have eleven children, all healthy." He stopped on the path and pointed to the trees. "See, my son, see how many of these trees have a knot in their trunks, close to the ground, in the place where the coin and the Virgin are sealed within, and they have become a part of the living tree." And it was true, Antonio said. Many of the trees bulged near the base, and he realised that all those men with large families in his village, all those men had been brought there as boys, terrified and crying, and when they left that place, their fathers had shown them their future, just as his father showed him his.

"I was not surprised when my wife had a child every year. Even though my father had already died and I no longer lived near the same forest and I had never known the words, I took my own two boys out to a forest before I left for the army and passed them through a sapling and sewed a picture of the Madonna inside the tree."

I clapped my hands and laughed. "What a load of tripe. You Italians are so superstitious. I can't believe you think babies come from trees."

He turned away from me, and cleaned a line of dirt from under a nail with his teeth and spat over the side of the cart.

"I have never even told my wife this," he said, and then I was truly silenced.

I am thinking of this conversation as the cart lurches up the gentle rise to Keogh's farm and the Italians brush at their clothes and face forward, looking for friends amongst the crowd of POWs standing outside the slab hut that serves as the home of priest.

It's as vivid as a photograph: I see the house rearing back from its dying grass, the spavined veranda a foot from the ground, the floorboards sweating dust and termites, the flyscreen door with its cottonreel handle and the line of men squatting against the walls, rolling cigarettes, their faces hidden under the brims of their low-crowned hats. When I swing down, the hats all tilt slightly, just enough to see my legs, not enough to see the little lump of my belly. True, their own burnt and gloveless women are little enough to look at. I lean against the gig and the horse pushes its nose deep into the feedbag we have brought with us, and lifts its tail and with a fresh odour of porridge and new mown grass, drops a hot pile of dung onto a bull ant nest.

Prisoners have come from many of the local farms—Kings and Brennans and Waters and Ekvelts—and the farmers who brought them cluster together in moleskins and collarless shirts and elastic-sided boots, comparing their Italians, and their crops, and their sheep, and their wives, and darting glances loaded with suspicion and deep dislike at me; I am not an ornament to this district, like a fine set of china or a bicycle would be. No. They think I am a jumped-up, Anglified, better-than-thou, private school snob from Dalkeith who doesn't even talk like a real Australian and, even worse than all that, I am the only woman who has driven Italians—unsupervised—through the bush, not just once, which might have been understandable, but week after week, and now I am wearing maternity sacks, and what are they supposed to think of that, and even though this driving has nothing to do with me and everything to do with Mr. Toad's obscene desire to rummage through my drawers unobserved in search for hidden pennies and shillings, these men of the district will never grant me forgiveness.

Their conversation drifts towards me like a bad smell.

"Rabbiter was out layin baits yesterday down my way. Bugger all useless. What are we paying the bloke for? Them bunnies can smell the phosphorus, I reckon. Not a one of 'em killed."

"Should put out baits for the dagoes. They'll eat anything."

The farmers groan and laugh and cuff Richie Waters lightly around the ears.

"Eat us out of house and home, more likely."

"I reckon they could be spies . . . men like that. They swore to Mussolini to kill us all."

How I missed it before, I don't know, but Richie is wearing an army uniform, one side of his felt hat pinned with a rising sun, a pair of decent boots on his feet. The poster on the corner of the Wylie pub has finally had its effect and he's signed up, like so many others, to protect King and country from the barbarian hordes.

"Joe Dago can barely wipe his bum when he's finished in the crapper. Don't worry about them lot."

"No. Think about it. These bloody POWs show up and then Broome gets bombed to splinters by the Japs. It's connected, is what I'm saying."

"Yeah, and they're responsible for the bunnies too, right, Jack? Brought the bloody things over on the boats with them, just to buggerise around with us Aussies."

They are nodding their heads and laughing in agreement with Dick Ekvelt, a man who stands a hand higher than any of them, with a dripping side of beef for a head and two loose, rolling, silver eyes, the man most likely to murder someone with his bare hands. He makes a sign when he looks in my direction, to ward off the devil.

I am apparently reading a library book, sitting in the shade underneath the gig, not too bothered by the flies making a meal of the horse manure inches from my gumboots, with the priest's dog curled up, panting, against my back and the furthest thing on my mind being the conversation of those men over there.

"But really, what's to stop them being spies or saboteurs or something?"

And I want to laugh at them, for their poor weak minds, for how could the Italians ever be spies? There is nowhere to go, no way to make reports; we are a week's journey from anywhere strategic, from Perth, from Geraldton. We have no telephones, no electricity, the generator-operated wireless can only be heard for two hours on a clear day when the wind is blowing from the south and no birds are flying and the worms in the orchard are chewing with their mouths closed. On one side of us stands the uninhabited coast, thousands of rocky miles patrolled by sharks, and on the other stands the vast, appalling desert of the great red centre, studded with the bones of animals and men that have strayed there and melted into the earth. The bush is judge, guard and prison here, to the Italians, and to us, too.

Old Father Duffle wobbles out, the Italians wander off in twos and threes and fours, smoking, stabbing away in their quick language, waving letters and photographs. John stands in the centre of a circle of men, all waving money. He's a bit of a gambler, is John. A man who will place a bet on whether or not it's going to rain this year. The farmers stand up, brushing flakes of tobacco off their thighs. The priest shakes their hands and toddles over to me. His cassock is held together by dirt and huge stitches in white thread. The front is wet with spilled wine; he has some kind of palsy, his hands jitter and he presses them into his sides and smiles apologetically.

"Hullo, Mrs. Toad. Recognised you by your dress. Haha."

He says this every week, and it's true. Toad has allowed me two dresses and they are both the same: grey with maroon buttons.

I reply as always, "And I recognised you by yours."

He thinks this is funny and laughs like a rusty gate swinging in a stiff breeze until he sees my eyes drop to the book in my hands.

"What's that you got there, deary?"

I turn the cover towards him and his eyes widen when he sees my Italian dictionary, ordered up from Boans, and he wipes his squiggle of a lip, and smiles again, all scalloped black gums and concrete-coloured teeth.

"Ah," he says, "collaboration. It's a fine art. Never mind. You're a good sort, Mrs. Toad. How's the ever-lovely Mr. Toad? Has he found anything new for his—ahem—collection?" He winks and lays his forefinger alongside his blooming nose and I squirm with embarrassment, for out in the shed, Toad has a vast collection of Victorian corsetry with a sideline in engravings of women's undergarments; he clips these from the newspaper and colours them in and hangs them from the ceiling on sewing thread. Toad's a joke in Wyalkatchem. I'm all that stands between him and forcible castration at the teeth of Dick Ekvelt. He could have been a jockey, with his tiny body and his slim hips, his tumbled face and his way with horses, but he chose to stay in this district. They know all about him, these men, and they think they know all about me too. They think he married me because I look like a boy and there's truth in that. They think I married him because he somehow got me pregnant and I was stuck with him. There's no truth to that. He didn't go near me for months after we were married. Too shy.

Father Duffle isn't a priest for so long without knowing the signs of human discomfort and so he changes the subject and asks instead, "How's it going with your men?"

And his raised eyebrow really means, *how is it going with John*, because John is young and he has already sashayed his fluid hips over to Walleyes', where out working in the fields there are five red-haired daughters whose father was captured when Singapore fell and hasn't been heard from since. The Walleyes heard his name on the horrible Japanese radio station that reads out lists of Australian prisoners and describes in detail what will be done to such men. I think John, who speaks so eloquently with his butterfly hands and the fringed pool of his eyes, must have blazed a trail amongst these girls, whose only concept of a man until now has been the sepia photograph of their father kept under their mother's pillow. No one tells him he has no need to be secretive about his flirtations; despite all her protestations, Mrs. Walleye would gladly give him all five girls, and throw herself in for free.

Dick Ekvelt joins us without greeting me—slut of the district—and he asks Father Duffle if it's true what he heard, that people like me, albinos, are born when their mother is struck by lightning. The other farmers are standing, looking in our direction and they are silent, waiting to hear what the priest will say.

"Well, I've heard that," says Father Duffle, "but I've also heard it's from too much sunshine. Maybe Mrs. Toad can enlighten us. Pardon the pun, my dear." He leans towards me and pats my shoulder. "In the interest of scientific investigation, do you think you could tell us how it happened? Your defect?" And I can tell that he's actually curious, whereas the other men are snorting and rolling their eyes like so many horses about to kill a mayfly with one strike of their hooves.

Antonio has been watching me and he takes John's arm and they come striding past the men and swing up into the gig and I am unlocked, I can turn away from the priest, fly out from under the hooves, and I snatch the feedbag from the horse's velvet nose and throw it under the seat.

"Don't listen to them, Missus," Antonio says. "You don't have to answer every question."

I stare at him for a moment. Someone has taken my side. At last. It makes me feel powerful. Invincible.

"No," I call down to the men surrounding the gig, "it wasn't lightning. My mother ate roast goanna lizard. She built a hot fire of acacia wood, threw on a goanna and then, after about ten minutes, when it was bloated and black, she dragged it from the fire, yanked out its guts and scraped off its skin. Then she bunged the goanna back on the fire again until grease was oozing out and the fire was leaping up, white hot, and then she ate it. That's how you do it, so make sure you remember to tell your wives when you get home. Roast goanna."

I snap the reins on the horse's back and out of the corner of my eye I take in the silence of the farmers and the flayed face of the priest and then the gig is out of the clearing and back amongst the trees and I am laughing because hadn't those men just barbecued a goanna at the church picnic and hadn't they all been eating it, them and their wives and their children, and I wonder how many of them will be down at the blackfellas' camp next day, looking for Ma Jackamarra to give them a poison for the children that slept in their wives' bellies.

9

You're incredibly stupid, Gin. Go on. Admit it. A man, a stranger, smiles at you and you're so desperate for a little softness in your life that you think he must like you. Love you even. A hot tingle runs down your arms, a schoolgirl thing you've never outgrown, you perk up, smooth your hair, wet your lips, and there you are, throwing yourself at him. Ghastly. The self-deceit is what I'm talking about. What are you trying to do?

10

On Monday, Toad comes back from town and tells us that on Saturday the Country Women's Association of Wyalkatchem will be hosting a talent night to raise money for our troops; he points out that all families are not only invited but expected to perform, and that there is a ten-shilling prize for the best act. Mr. Toad is jubilant; he is certain one of us will bring home the prize. I am not so certain. We are not, either of us, best beloved.

Mudsey and Alf dress in their Sunday whites and run in and out of the Italians' hut, shouting and shoving each other and pulling hair. Antonio gives Mudsey a ribbon, Alf gets a chocolate from John, and there's hell to pay, Mudsey clawing Alf's face in an effort to claim the sweet held over his head, the ribbon rejected and trampled underfoot.

"Come here, Mudsey," I call from the veranda. "Let me do your hair." She stands still until she sees Antonio watching. Her hair is as soft as rabbit fur. She pulls free and runs off again, the comb still tangled in her hair.

"Bet a shilling you win," cries John, holding up a coin.

Toad whistles for us and places a box next to the surrey and all the runty members of our family clamber up, Toad last of all and he slips a brown paper parcel under the seat.

"Me togs," he says and winks at me, and the children drum their heels on the wooden sides and the horse starts forward before we're ready and everyone except Toad tumbles backwards and waves their legs in the air and Toad says, "It's a *glorious* wheat field this year, the heads big as drumsticks," and he leans over and bites my calf, the silly mutt.

"Leave off, Toad," I say and I beat him off, wondering what Antonio will think. John waves from their veranda and promises to look after the livestock while we are out painting the town red.

Horses stand tethered to the barbed-wire fence around the schoolhouse, and children pelt each other with honky nuts and dodge the girls playing knucklebones around hand-smoothed circles of dirt, the sun drops below the horizon and magpies cwardle-oodle and in the hesitant light, kerosene lanterns glow and women appear in the doorways in aprons, beckoning.

After dinner, we are called alphabetically: Atwood, Brennan, Bruise, Cleverish, Drake-Brockman, and some acts are marvellous, like Richie Brennan in a Red Cross nurse's cape, winding an unending bandage—he gets a lot of laughs for that one; or three of the King women lined up, carding raw fleece and spinning the rovings and knitting the yarn as it comes twisting off the spindle, all at one time, so a miniature blanket square is produced from woe to go in under three minutes; and some are bad, poems with lines missing or out of key songs, but none is so bad as Mr. Toad, poor dear Mr. Toad, who dresses in the cloakroom and emerges just as Mavis Walleye begins to gut the piano with a smutty piece of burlesque music. He wears my old woollen swimsuit with the drooping modesty flap at the crotch, and he has stuffed God-alone-knows-what down the front to raise a tremendous bust and my sun hat is pulled down to his painted lips and he prances on borrowed heels and around his neck is Mudsey's forgotten ribbon. Men whistle and he thrusts his hips and paws his bust and pouts his awful lips, and the women around me are frigid with disapproval and my own heart rips rabidly through my lungs, and I think it can't get worse and right then I see movement behind the modesty flap, and soon the children kneeling in the front are pointing at his crotch excitedly, expecting a Jack-in-the-box or a Punch or a sugar possum to pop out at them, and then, even the whistling men hush and their eyes are the eyes of dogs watching a snake and their necks burn red, and still Mr. Toad grinds and kicks shaven legs in seamed nylons and Mavis martyrs the keys like a bordello madam and I feel that with each kick he nails me to the bench, crowns me with barbed wire, stabs me endlessly in the eyes with the bayonet of his exposure—until Ekvelt yells, "Get out of there, you dirty bugger," and throws a rabbit bone at his head.

The music stops, the piano shudders with relief, and Mavis turns to see what we all have already seen, and she says, "Cor! Look at the size of the pizzle on little Mr. Toad."

And Toad, poor Toady, who is only five feet tall, a little man in anyone's book except his own, blinks rapidly and his mouth pinches together in a baby's fist and he walks stiffly, if you'll pardon the pun, into the cloakroom and district legend.

"Those bastards," he says on the way home, "they've never given me a fair crack of the whip. It's always been little this and tiddling that and throw him back, he's too small to eat, ever since I was a nipper."

"Brawn doesn't equal brains," I say, patting his arm, stunned at the focus of his distress.

"Strewth," he says, punching the dashboard, "they done me out of me ten bob too," which is more than a bit of an exaggeration. If I'd had the chance to play, it might have been *our* ten shillings, but the mongrels announcing the contestants bayed out, "Walleye!" after Toady's debacle and gave me a total miss, suspecting, quite rightly, that if I was allowed to touch the piano at that moment, none of them would have been able to hear for a week.

"What on earth gave you the idea of dressing in my swimsuit?"

The horse's hooves sound like gloved hands clapping; Mr. Toad's shoulders slump and he exhales a long breath on a descending note.

"What was I supposed to do, Gin? I can't sing or box or play an instrument. I can't crack a forty-foot stockwhip or whistle with two fingers or recite a poem from memory. I can't even stand up in a bloody soldier's kit and represent my country because they don't have uniforms small enough for me. Hell! If I go into Perth in December, people are looking for me pointy ears and Santa's bloody reindeer. The mob around here think I'm an old woman, a homo. By God! I surprised *them* the day I brought you home."

Indeed he did. The locals were so surprised when they saw poofy old Toad with an albino woman that they suffered an incurable case of speechlessness, and I'm thinking, he too has finally dried up, but then he blurts, "They thought I was good, Gin, until Ekvelt wrecked it. The men were whistling. They were laughing. It's incredible! They liked me," and he says all this with a wondering delight that causes my skin to inch along my arms, but it is not in me to tell him that tonight was so painful he should be lying in pieces on the floor, shattered. It makes me like him better, at the same time as being more ashamed of him than I have ever been.

11

Ever since the swimsuit disaster, Mr. Toad had avoided visiting our neighbors and begun shouting at the wireless, criticizing the way the war was handled by them in the know. He was nicer to the Italians and had me make vermicelli for them. He stood and applauded John's acrobatics on the horses, instead of sending him off to do the more pressing menial labor. It was as if, in rejecting the farmers' notions about him, he was also rejecting their notions about other things too.

It was a few months after the Italians came to our farm, and

I wonder if it was not merely coincidence, that Mr. Toad broached the idea of having an amateur theatrical night on Christmas Eve, just the Italians and us. I had to make an effort to block out an unappetizing image of Toad several times a day, and now, when I began to think of that horrible night, I soothed myself by thinking, instead, of Antonio: dignified, clean, kind.

But everyone else liked Toad's idea about the talent show and daily, they snuck around, negotiating partners and costumes and arguing about the best ideas. Papier-mâché was made—for what purpose, I knew not—and theatrical beards from fleece and hats from newspaper and Mr. Toad seemed to spend an inordinate amount of time in the outhouse, the interior walls of which had been mysteriously swathed in hessian sacking. Antonio asked me one Sunday to sing a duet with him and I—complimented—opened my mother's glory box, looking for the Victorian dresses and suits I thought opera singers should wear.

A bloom of scent rose with the lid, orange blossom and talc and camphor and moldy kid gloves, and I buried my arms in the first thing I saw, my mother's wedding dress, a bustled cream brocade wrapped around a corset from Paris that I'd hidden from Toad. The silk was cool and caught slightly on my fingers; it was beaded with seed pearls and draped with lace and buttoned with mother-of-pearl carved to look like castles. Under the dress lay a cutaway suit and a velvet box of enamelled shirt studs. I thought the suit would look good on Antonio. It was made for a tall man. Mudsey sat on my bed, disgusted. She was very much a child of the bush. Toad's child.

"What's all that tarrididdle, Mummy?" she said. She looked at me with her appalled, unfriendly eyes. Her sundress was a feed sack, bleached and tied in the middle with a leather string.

"Never you mind," I said and hustled her into the kitchen. "Here's a lovely bit of bread with golden syrup. Now off you go.

See if you can keep that Alf out of trouble."

Back in my room, I took out other dresses, stiff purple silk and brown polished cotton and a fine blue and white striped gauze, and fans of ostrich feathers and ivory and shoes with embroidered kid toes and tortoiseshell combs that looked like crowns and silk stockings with my mother's initials stitched on the calf and letters from my father tied with a pink ribbon and a bisque doll from France that cried "Mama!" when I picked her up and at the very bottom, a photograph of me as a child that I hadn't even known was there. In it, I wore a bonnet made of looped ribbons and they were tinted blue and so were my eyes and in that daguerreotype my skin flushed pink in a way that it never, ever will, and I felt so sad for my mother, whose husband, my father, looked at me the day I was born, excused himself and walked straight to the tent where men were enlisting for the first world war and Gallipoli and the chance to die for sheer stupidity. He didn't return to march in the ANZAC day parade, with medals on his chest but missing an arm or a leg or a chunk of his face. His mates said he stood up on the landing boat and took off his helmet and threw it in the water, then was hit by a bullet and fell over the side to be eaten by an octopus that was the biggest bloody thing they had ever seen.

In November I ordered up the music from Boans and hid it away so no one would know what we were up to. I waited till Toad went out to the furthest paddocks before taking out my magnifying glass and the score and working out the phrases. Antonio heard me pecking out the first few measures and he came inside and caught me squinting at the music. I tried to ignore him being in the room but he had the most extraordinary scent—sandalwood, licorice, and something else that was cool and clean. He was breathing deeply and evenly, watching me without speaking. I pushed aside the magnifying glass and tried some chords, as if they had been written on the score, but they were all wrong.

"What's the matter?" he asked, lifting the music to look at it. He picked up the magnifying glass. "What are you playing? Can't you see the notes?"

He smelled so differently from Toad, fresh and tasty. He noticed entirely different things. His shoes glinted again in the dim light.

"I'll open the curtains," he said.

I covered my face. I wished more than anything else to be normal, to have pretty pink skin and golden hair and good eyesight. I wanted him to like me. I looked up and saw myself reflected in the liquid surface of his eyes. I shook my head. "I can't see well," I said. "People who are white, like this," I touched the back of my hand, "can't see details. The dotted notes. Moving things. Especially far away."

He looked at me with great seriousness. "But you are a musician. You play so well. It must be very hard for you to learn the music, but you hide it from everyone. You keep secrets, Missus Toad."

I couldn't breathe well. His hand lay next to mine on the sheet of music. His shoes glinted. I thought briefly of Toad standing behind me in the madhouse and a sound came out of my throat and then he said, "Never mind about that. I will call out the notes and you will play them. That will be of help, yes? Yes."

And so, for a while, he stood next to me in the hot, dim room calling out notes, semiquavers and rests, and every so often, he paused and I would look up and each time his dark, dark eyes rested on my face and I looked away.

"Just play," he said. "Forget that I am here. I am the music stand. Or the metronome," and he smiled and nodded his head from side to side.

"I can't forget that you are here," I said into my collar. "I can't practice with someone in the room. I'd really rather you didn't watch me."

He sang a few bars of the melody and paused and I looked up again, waiting.

"Can you see me?" he asked. Which I found I couldn't answer.

"Your eyes aren't red," he said gently. "They're blue."

At this, I closed the lid of the piano. "Please go. It's very kind of you, but I'm not used to being helped."

He moved away, smiling, humming the bits we had been working on. I leaned over and lifted the sheets of music to my nose. The pages smelled like him.

"I will write that bigger for you," he said from the doorway. He came and took the pages from my hands and as he did so, his hand brushed against my stomach.

"Hello baby," he said, and he smiled again. "Do you think he will look like you or like me?"

"Like Toad, you mean," I said, flustered.

"Well, a girl like you, or a boy like me?" he said, but I didn't want to talk about the baby with him. I would rather have pretended it didn't exist. Besides the pink skin and pretty hair, I wished I had the waist I saw on his wife and no sign of any other man's claim on me. No swelling belly. No wedding ring.

12

Day and night, Mr. Toad and Antonio and John raced to harvest the wheat before the really hot days of summer, hoping to bring the bags to the siding the day before Christmas, but every morning we rose to hot, dry northerlies, temperatures over a hundred; we feared a storm, lightning, a fire that could destroy a year's labor. Mr. Toad gargled the news that there had already been one hundred days over one hundred degrees in Marble Bar and a record high of one hundred and twenty-three in Mardie. We waited for a night of powerful storms followed by a morning of calm, a bubble before the wind picked up again and a rise in the temperature so rapid that your ears would pop and the hair on your arms scorch and the back of your neck would be bleeding from the sand blown out of the paddocks and then the lightning would strike, again and again, uncontrollable, and huge fireballs roll through the fields and barbecue the sheep and blacken the wheat and leave men behind, fetal on the ground, nothing more than ashes.

But it didn't happen that year and we got the wheat in and the men limped onto the veranda and washed their faces and hands slowly in the kerosene tin sink and wiped them on flour sacks and capsized into chairs, their eyelids drooping.

"Well, that's it then," said Mr. Toad. "A record yield, thanks to you men." He nodded at Antonio and John and they hesitated and then smiled. They'd worked hard because he had.

"Thanks, Boss. We pretty pleased to be done with that." The way the Italians pronounced "that" it might have been "death" or "debt." They sat in the two chairs furthest away from him because each night for a week he'd dropped into bed, too exhausted to bathe.

"Now we're all looking forward to a good feed and a bit of a lark, eh, Mudsey?" Mr. Toad said, and Mudsey squirmed with pleasure and flicked a flea off her leg. If I'd said the same thing, she would have snarled. "What are you little shavers doing for our talent show, then?" said Toad.

"Not telling," said Mudsey. "Would spoil the surprise. How

bout you, Dad? What's all that rubbish in the dunny?"

"Yeah," said Antonio, "what you up to in the outhouse, Boss? We all want to know."

"Bet you a shilling it is telephone," said John. As if it was possible. Or even desirable to have a telephone in the outhouse.

Toady tapped his nose and grinned, "Might have something to do with our little shindig, but you'll have to wait and see."

"What about you, Mum?" said Mudsey and she squashed two flies fornicating on a smear of golden syrup with her bare hand and picked out the wings. "Piano?" She knew every secret in this house. Her face was blank. She looked at no one.

Antonio glanced at me and then looked hard at his plate of bangers and mash, a smile twitching the corners of his mouth.

"Obvious choice, isn't it?" I said, but I was laughing and my voice was the unconvincing voice of a woman who has illicitly been practicing arias for hours whilst crashing through the bush behind a flatulent pony. Mudsey walked past me and pinched my arm. John ground his teeth in my direction. Nobody had taken his bet.

I could hardly wait for the talent show; I longed to wear my mother's dress, to pin up my hair with her tortoiseshell combs and spit on the dingo scarf, to sing with Antonio for my family. Hearing news from Italy was as if I heard news about distant relatives instead of lecherous aliens and at night I twisted the knob on the wireless, searching for clues as to what might be happening near Civitella Maritima and Sant'Anna, and I cut articles written about Italians out of the papers and laboriously translated them, even though it was strictly against the rules, and pasted them into a scrapbook, and, at odd moments, I smiled at Toady, thankful that he had insisted on bringing the prisoners to our farm.

13

Since 1942, the government had mandated that POWs should at all times wear Australian army uniforms left over from the Great War and dyed magenta, as a sign of their inferior status. These uniforms, being made of a hot and itchy wool, became instruments of torture in the summer. Ekvelt and Brennan and some of the other farmers insisted that their POWs wear the uniforms, but Mr. Toad respected the men and gave them shirts and trousers of his own in which to work—much too small, of course—and I got used to the sight of our Italians in the shorts and sleeveless shirts they had hacked from the clothing, clearing the brush, throwing bags of wheat around like footballs, standing in the orchard boiling spaghetti in the wash copper. The men used bricks to scrub at the hated uniforms and daily hung them in the sun to bleach, and we turned a blind eye because, by God, when they got together on Sundays in their pink suits, they looked like an imbecile flock of flamingos.

I was, at that time, knitting a vest for Mr. Toad, a lovely thing with cables down the front, that I planned to give him for Christmas, and when it was finished I planned to make a blanket for the new baby. It seemed wrong though, not to give something to the men, and so I began to knit a vest for Antonio. But when that one was done, I realized I had to make a third or Toad truly would be suspicious.

When making Toad's vest, I had measured the length against his suit jacket, which I found draped over the top rail of the sheep race, but Antonio's jacket had shrunk or he had gained weight, and it was no good for measurements, so I thought I would go into his hut and check the size of his winter shirt, and one day, when the Italians were out with Toady, cutting wheat, I armed myself with a tape measure and pushed open the door.

Neither Mr. Toad nor I had been inside the Italians' hut, although the children ran in and out, as often as not with chocolates or lollies or little toys in their hands, things we couldn't give them, things Australians didn't have because of the rationing. John, that airling, gave Alf and Mudsey tailor-made cigarettes and matches and flat paper packets that held tiny rubber balloons that the children filled with water and threw at unsuspecting racehorse goannas and which sent Mr. Toad into fits when he saw the blousy remains leaking on the ground.

I was very curious what little bits and pieces they still had from their families back in the Europe I thought I would never see. Stepping over the threshold, I was blinded by the contrast between the apocalyptic sun outside and the deep, cool interior.

Far off, a galah called and, faintly, came the sound of the harvester, chucketta-chucketta, or that may only have been the blood pounding in my ears, and soon the darkness faded before me to a foggy mauve and I could see again.

On one side of the room stood an enormous old club chair, propped up on a brick and covered in ratty brown velveteen, and on the other, a kitchen table and two chairs, and the walls were papered with the *Sunday Times*; the bombing of Darwin and the lists of the dead and the recruitment notices all pasted side by side; a greenish photograph of Hitler, upside down over the fireplace. I turned and went through to the other room, the bedroom, and above John's bed was a photograph of a woman I recognized as his mother and a postcard of a horse and another of a man without a shirt and a framed picture of a horrible dripping heart staked with a cross. Fastidious, they were, in everything: their clothes, their bodies, their rooms, everything washed and groomed every day and reeking of otherness. Antonio's shirt hung stiff on a nail, the sole decoration on his side of the room or so I thought, but as I turned to leave after measuring the shirt, I saw a collection of tiny shoes on the window ledge, lined up from largest to smallest, each one no bigger than an inch long, a grotto.

The first shoe was high heeled, the vamp made of crow feathers and lined with red rose petals, the heel a sliver of polished jarrah wood, the black feathers slick and greeny-blue in the light from the window, the hidden red fold of the insole exhaling the scent of musk rose. The shoe took my breath away. It was obviously made for his wife. Stroking the feathery toe, I felt that I stood between Antonio and her, as if, by my touch, I had drained some of the power and comfort from his creation. Contaminated it.

The next five shoes were made of snakeskin and bits of bark and gum seeds and snail shells and bougainvillea and pressed Queen of Sheba orchids and the giggly fronds of bracken and purpley-blue hydrangea petals and red and teal and aqua parrot feathers and bottlebrush and skeletonised leaves and all of them were children's shoes, flat-heeled and round toed and smaller, much smaller, than the shoe for his wife. Last of all on the window ledge was the shoe that should have been for him, made from the white tissue of the paperbark tree, almost transparent, and lined with swan's down, an Edwardian boot laced with a single strand of pure white hair. This shoe stood a little away from the other six, and I never thought for a minute that it was a shoe for Antonio. I knew it was for me.

That shoe detonated in my chest, a landmine laid for unsuspecting tourists. Mr. Toad's unfaithful woman from the newspaper ran past the window, silently screaming, her bones breaching through her skin, and a snow of feathers, downy white feathers, fluttered down and melted on the hard red dirt. I backed out of the room, my fingers picking and picking at the tags of dry skin on my lips, and tearing them off, bleeding myself, letting out what I had seen in painful red droplets. I tripped on a dog lying before the door and I pulled its ears and kicked its rump for its grovelling stupidity in being comfortable on that cursed veranda, and I hated myself for loving that tiny white shoe; for letting myself think thoughts that must be murdered before they are born.

14

A whiff of powder, the crash of a bowl shattering on the floor, the movement of a moth around a lamp—each small reminder enough to conjure an entire scene, a day, a week, a year, as fresh as if all that happened, happens now. As if, once again, I am thirty and it is December 1943, and I am about to sing for my family.

"Mundungus is limping," says Mr. Toad, without looking at me. I am sweating in the heat, and the tightly laced corset has pushed some color into my face. "I wonder how that useless carcass of a mutt hurt hisself this time."

"Toad."

"What?"

"Are you ready for the talent show?"

He snaps his suspenders and sniffs and frowns. "You never dress up like that for me. Look like one of them china dolls."

"Well," I say and I stroke the boned bodice of my mother's gown, thanking God for the corset and the rationing and Mr. Toad's fondness for chops. "What do you think?" I turn around in a swish of silk.

"Very white," he says, shuddering, and goes into my bedroom, his eyes averted, to trim his nose hairs with my embroidery scissors.

The child inside me flutters against the steel boning, fighting its shrunken world, rattling the bars of its cage, and I hum a phrase from *The Moldau*. The dress makes a soft noise when I move. *Shush*.

I light the Aladdin lamp and the candles in the brackets of my Bechstein and I am arranging the sheet music when Antonio comes in and I hear his deep intake of breath. I turn, thinking to compliment him on how he looks in the old-fashioned suit, but he is staring at me intently, his dark eyes reflecting this unfamiliar woman in white, a mirage drifting in the uncertain light, and he slips the tips of his fingers into the waistcoat pockets and takes a step towards me, and staggers a little.

"You are beautiful," he whispers, and he clears his throat. "Beautiful."

His eyes slide from my face, my albino face, to my hair, hip length, white as falling water, to the gown pooled around my feet in ripples, then back to my face, and I flinch and hold one hand to my cheek, to cover myself.

He doesn't look behind him, he isn't ashamed or afraid like I am. He said this thing as simply as if it were the truth, and I cringe like a kicked dog, not confident enough to laugh and say, "I bet you say that to all of the girls," or even, "Thank you," for that would be worse; it would show that I knew he meant it. Between the shoulders I feel a stinging pain. And I hear the voices of all the people who do not see me as Antonio sees me. My stepfather, breathing over me in the night, my white skin pornographic to him. My classmates chanting:

Ghost gum, snow gum, paperbark, white,
Little Gin Boyle is an ugly sight.

His face as he comes around the corner, his lips as he calls me beautiful, his trembling fingertips in his pockets and his luminous shoes. I have been called some terrible names in this life, but now I only hear his voice in the mouths of my tormenters, saying, "You are beautiful."

Forward he comes, slowly, and the flames on the candles sway and grow taller and throw deep shadows on the comb furrows through his hair and the carved lines of emotion on his face.

"Come," he says, "let us make all ready," and he begins to turn the chairs toward the piano and takes up my knitting from one of them and hands it to me. As the soft stuff passes into my hands, his fingers briefly touch mine and he looks at me, then stoops and draws one long strand of my hair from a nail on the piano bench and rolls the white hair around his finger and slides it into his pocket without once looking away.

Alf, my small boy, my baby, is hiding under the last chair.

"I was spying," he says, "I wanted to see what you are doing."

"But Alfie," I say, "you would have seen us anyway in ten minutes, if only you had waited."

"No," he says mournfully, "you sing different when you sing just with Tony," and I wonder how many times he has watched us.

"Mummy?" he says, tipping back his head to look at me, "I also want to be beautiful."

"You are beautiful," I say to Alf and I kneel carefully, the corset cutting deeply into my hips, and touch his little boy hand with its bitten nails and caterpillars of ochre dirt in the folds between the fingers. "Only beautiful."

"Is that true?" he turns to ask Antonio, who nods.

When Mr. Toad enters the room, his cockatoo's crest of hair glittering with brilliantine, Alf runs to him and grips his knee and announces, "I'm beautiful, like Mummy." Mr. Toad frowns in surprise and shakes his head at me and sniffs, like a dog with a tick in its ear. "No, no. You are a handsome lad, like me."

And that is how it ends. Alf doesn't complain or deny his father's words; he bounces on his chair and says, "I'm handsome. I'm the handsomest one in the family," and for some reason this brings tears to my eyes, which I brush away before they can be seen and commented on.

Mudsey and Alf are first to perform on our talent night. Wearing lumpy plaster masks, they make a play about soldiers, or perhaps it's a play about fairies, or traitors or dogs. At one point, Mudsey recites a bit of "Wynken, Blynken and Nod." We are not sure when their play ends, and sit, waiting for them to continue, till Mudsey turns and skewers us with her wicked eyeball and says, "Now you clap," and we do.

Mr. Toad is vigorously polishing the seat of his chair with his bum, *swish, swish, swish*, and it's obvious he wants to go next. He's kicked over the empties under his chair a dozen times with his nervous feet. After Mudsey and Alf make their exit, he leaps up, snapping his suspenders, checking the time, grinding his teeth.

"I've been tryin me hand," he says, "at painting. I done one side of the dunny for each of youse. Come on." He picks up the lantern and heads outside.

"See that?" he says, opening the door to the outhouse and putting the lantern on the floor, stepping back with his bottom lip drooping.

It's a wonder.

Using only the blue medicinal paint with which we mark the sheep's backs, he has turned the dunny into an art gallery. On each wall is a monochromatic landscape, an imagined Italy with two men walking the steep hills. One of the men leads a thin and springy horse, the other points to a tiny house at the end of the road, with a light burning in the window. A pale blue woman floats in the sky on a piano with wings. Portraits of three solemn children hang from the branches of a snow gum tree. They are fat and tidy, dressed in the clothing of Victorian royalty. Down low, near the door, gallops a miniature Mr. Toad, one foot on the back of each of a harnessed pair of caparisoned rabbits. There is no perspective in these paintings, very little shading, the brush he used might have been a doctored toothbrush, and the paint has dripped in many places, but still we stand and gawp at Mr. Toad. His paintings are more than pretty cartoons. Our deepest longings, our secret wishes for home and love and power and escape are illuminated here, in the light of the kerosene lantern, on the rough-hewn walls of an outhouse. All the time, I thought he was the simplest of men, a man who never looked beyond the dirt at his feet, not the kind of man who would be able to see the longing on someone else's face. I never would have guessed that he knew all about my secret longing to perform in the concert halls of Europe. It makes me wonder what else he knows about me that I think is hidden. The coarse ticking of his shirt feels suddenly very close. I can smell the brilliantine on him, there, in the roasted night. And I have to step back. Give myself room.

Mr. Toad is unnerved by our silence. This, after all, is the same man who was encouraged to prance in high heels by the cheering of a bunch of men who have trained a pig to drink a bottle of beer and who can belch the national anthem in three octaves.

"Do you like it?" he asks, popping open the cover of his pocket watch and ducking his head, ready for pain.

"Toad," I say, "it's beyond words. I didn't know you could paint, that's all."

"But is it good?" he asks, the pocket watch ticking in his hand like a bomb.

"Bravo!" shouts Antonio, and we all jump. "*Magnifico!*" He slaps Mr. Toad on the back, but Toad still looks at me.

"Yes, Toady. Really good."

John inches into the outhouse and his shadow stretches out on the ground, as long as a king snake. He touches the thin blue man cast up on a Tuscan hill with the thoroughbred, traces the horse's bowed neck, its flowing tail, while the lantern hisses softly on the floor. When he turns, his face is soft and he lays a hand on Mr. Toad's arm.

Our shadows are distorted by their collision with the strange yellow light of the kerosene lamp. Our eyes black. Mudsey's head pecks towards Toad and butts against his leg, Toad's smile hooks upwards in fractions of inches. He hesitates in this rictus of pleasure, then leans down and plucks the lantern from the floor. We clear a path and follow him into the house, hushed and reverent. But I am careful now, not to walk next to Antonio, not to look at him. The sounds of the night become insistent, the ecstasy of frogs and the skittering of bats and the sad voice of the mopoke owl, and even the crunch of our feet across the flayed grass, and the rustle of silk and the snappings of twigs. The darkness is all leering shadows and breathing blackness, thrown up by the lamp, and I wade through this rushing sea, awed and a little fearful of his paintings, because they've shown me that Toad is not as simple as he looks.

And at last it is my turn, our turn, to sing and, as I rise, the hem of my skirt catches on a splinter of wood and I hear the fabric tear, a small sound like teeth grinding, crrr, and I know this fine and perfect thing of my mother's is no longer pristine. I think: it is only a tiny rip, small damage, and Antonio is standing next to the piano, waiting, his hand draped on his cummerbund, one long cobbler's finger resting on the button of the morning coat. His chest rises, the fabric expands, his finger beats time on the button.

We are singing from *La Traviata*: I am Violetta, a kept woman; Antonio is my Alfredo, my obsessive lover. I announce our duet in a shaking voice which is drowned out by the polite patter of my family's applause, and I don't know why they applaud me. They should stone me.

Da molto e che mi amate?

I lift my blind face to Antonio and ask how long he has loved me. And Antonio's voice, soaring, dipping, welling like a wave from the depths of the sea, sings, "*Ah si da un anno.*"

For more than a year he has been in possession of that unspoken love, mysterious, unattainable, torment and delight, that is what he sings, but he has only been here, on our farm, for three months.

Mysterioso altero.

We could be two lovers in a gondola rocking on the hips of the water in a Venetian canal. He looks down at me, his lips quivering with the force of his voice, he bends towards me and I lean towards him.

I can hardly bear to open my mouth in reply. The words sing themselves. "*Solo amistade io v'offro.*" I can only offer you friendship. I don't know how to love, I can't feel so great an emotion.

Our voices wind together; he sings, "*Croce e delizia al cor,*" and I sing, "Forget me," and we sigh together, softly. *Mysterioso.*

If I were truly Violetta, I would hand Antonio a rose. Instead, I look up at him, squinting, tracing the deep lines on his face with my eyes, and for this unveiling at the end of the farce, my family applauds.

Toads snorts, "Romantic rubbish" as Antonio sits down. John kisses his fingers and raises his eyebrows in appreciation. Mudsey makes retching noises, her version of praise, and Alf sucks his thumb, his knowing eyes resting on me.

And what of me? What am I thinking?

I am thinking that Toad has noticed the time I spend with Antonio, the way the Italian helps me around the house, the man's polite BBC accent. Toad has made an attempt to appear cultured in my eyes. The painting was so unexpected, so much a part of my world and not his. And too, I think he must have been working on it at least some of the times when I was practising with Antonio. This should make me grateful that he desires my affection, but instead, I only imagine him creeping around the farm like his own hand across the tablecloth.

From across the room, John's lewd smile cracks like a whip, catching me on the cheek, the shame of it taking my breath away. There is something naked and calculating about his face, his smooth brown cheeks and hungry lips. He looks from me to Mr. Toad and back again, and his glance is ugly. He'd bet his last pennies on the conclusion. John thinks he knows everything that happens on this stage.

But Mr. Toad turns towards John, unaware, and toasts himself in the warmth of the prisoner's glare, revolving slowly like a sheep on a spit.

"Toad," I snap, "come sit down."

In the morning, we hand out our brown-papered parcels, wooden riding toys for the children, cream wool vests for the men, oranges and tailor-made cigarettes for Toad. Mudsey and Alf search in every corner for overlooked presents and cry out with pleasure when they find chocolates in their shoes and chewing gum in the woodbox. Antonio laughs and claps his hands, before taking out his camera and snapping a photo of Mudsey, bum up in the air, rooting out the chewing gum, and of Alf, his mouth smeared with chocolate. "Now you, Missus Gin," he says, but I laugh and say no. It's the children's day.

When everything is lying around our feet, a mulch of good intentions, and the children are galloping through the house on their wooden steeds, John carries in the first of six pots he has made for us, moulded in the shape of old corsetry if I am not mistaken and planted with tomatoes and capsicums which tremble lush and round and juicy on their vines, filling the room with the scent of green tomato dust and fresh concrete. Antonio hands me a fur tippet with a matching muff, beautiful white rabbit fur that he has caught, skinned, tanned and sewed himself, with the same invisible stitches that made the miniature boot. Instead of waiting for my thanks, he twists away and begins to tickle Alfie, burying his face in the giggling boy's belly.

Toad takes a slim package from his roller desk, and, shocked, I find it is a small brass telescope, something the optometrist has said will help me see detail, but which I had written off as too expensive. In my hand, pressed against my eye, the glass reveals fine hairs on the tomato vines and the wink of light in Antonio's eye, where a tiny twin of the six-paned window swims. I open my hands, my mouth. I can't think what has spurred Toad to this kindness, and I am horrified that it comes now, when I feel so distant from him. I want to yodel.

"You are all too good," I say, my voice wobbling. "Thank you."

"Give us a kiss then," says Toad, pointing at his rumpled cheek. "Saved up all year for that gizmo. Must be crazy."

Antonio sits up. Alf stops laughing and cranes his little neck. The silence draws Mudsey from the other room. She, too, wants to see this rarest of events: her mother kissing her father. She frowns and giggles. "Mushy!" she says to Alf, poking him with her elbow.

Standing as far from Toad as possible, I wipe my mouth and dart my head in his direction, pecking him on the cheek. At the last moment, Antonio looks away. John licks his lips.

"Ha!" laughs Toad, blushing, adjusting the contents of his underpants. "Good girl."

Oh, but I am not a good girl. The unborn child sucks on my guilt, pedaling its toes into my bladder. I feel the drag down there, the tug at my inner fibers.

Alongside the creamy wool of Antonio's vest, I knitted a strand of my white hair, and now, as I inspect the room with my telescope, I see him discover the hair, trace it with his finger, look up at me and then back at the vest, fold it gently and smooth it with his hands, press it to his chest and carry it out to his hut, singing, "*Povera donna, sola. Abbandonata in questo. Popoloso deserto . . .*" but his voice is soon buried by Toad's bawling rendition of "Good King Wenceslas" and the children's screaming laughter.

I had thought, because the strand was nearly invisible amongst the wool, Antonio would not see it, would not know my intention, and I would be safe. But instead, I am as transparent to him as a sheet drying in the sun.

After the lunch of roast and Yorkshire pudding, the sweat is pearling on our faces and Mr. Toad mops his swampy neck with my linen, John fans himself with a plate. Even the flies are exhausted, not bothering to butt their heads against the windows, only idly tasting the drops of gravy and stewed tomatoes on the tablecloth. The fruit on the counter a little rotten in the heat. Chairs are pushed back, buttons opened, the windmill is silent in the dead calm of Christmas Day 1943.

"It says," intones Mr. Toad, flicking open the *Sunday Times* and sniffing, "that the Italian caught messing around with Mrs. Ahern over in Yerecoin copped ninety days in the clink."

This titbit falls on the table like a tarantula. Antonio shrinks away and eyes the wreckage on his plate, but Toad watches me closely and I am not sure why. Is he preparing to shock me with some sordid details he only *wishes* were true? Or is he suspicious?

"And here's another one. Looks like you blokes are making a big hit with the locals: 'Dago Menace Again Threatens Wyalkatchem Shire. The dagoes in the wheatbelt have become so cheeky, so arrogant, so devoid of common British decency that women, when approaching, are obliged to detour around them to avoid rude remarks.

"'One dago has been sent to prison for a cowardly attack on a returned soldier. This son of Italy stabbed the Digger in the back with a pocketknife so viciously and so deeply that the blade broke off in the unfortunate man's back. As an additional punishment, this man may not apply to return to Australia after the war.'"

"Boss," says John, "why a hell we wanna return? You wanna go back in prison after you out?"

"Well. That was uncalled for," says Toad, a fly sucking his lip. Forty-three wishbones dangle on a string suspended between two tacks on the wall behind him. "Australia is a lovely spot. Much nicer than Italy."

"Not nicer. No," mutters John, glaring at me as if I was the one who said it, and Antonio kicks me under the table. I kick him back.

"Toad," I say, "you've never been there. Maybe it *is* nicer."

"Traitor," he says and refolds the newspaper. He slaps me over the head with the furled paper and repeats, "Traitor. Good thing women aren't in the army or we'd never have any decent wars."

Antonio lays his hand on the newspaper when it rests again on the table. "I'll put the paper in the dunny for you, yes?"

Toad tries to slide the *Sunday Times* from under Antonio's hand and then nods. "Yeah. Beaut."

He shoves himself up and hovers like a blowfly over the shemozzle of the table, his nose an iridescent blue from the port in the pudding. You could light his breath on fire with a single match.

"Still," he laughs, "what happened to that bloke would be a good thing to keep in mind. In case any of you mob are thinking about a bit of slap and tickle with the missus here." His elbow jogs the wishbones and they snicker. "Buckley's chance of that, right Gin?"

"I think I'd best wash up these dishes before the flies carry them off. Pass me your plates." There is a spot of custard on my boot that is sliding towards the floor.

Antonio stands and takes a tea towel from the hook. He looks back at Toad with contempt and there is a little leap in my chest.

"Did you hear the one in the classifieds?" Toad calls after him. "'Italian gun, perfect working condition, never fired, slight scratch on butt from being dropped.'"

"Not funny," says Antonio. "We fired."

"What's Slap and Tickle, Dad?" says Mudsey. "Is it a game? Can I play too?"

"Now look. Little pitchers have big ears. Change the subject, Toad," I say.

"Too right you can play," says Toad to Mudsey, and he gives her a smack on the bottom and a tickle in the armpit that has her howling. "Give yer Mum a hand with them dishes." Her voice dies in mid-howl.

"How you get to be called Toad?" asks John, and everyone freezes. I peek at Toad but he is smiling.

Mudsey snatches the tea towel from Antonio and scours the cups. Smacks them down, dry as ashes, on the counter.

"Go and sit down, Gin," says Antonio. "I'll wash. You've worked hard enough today."

Toad blinks and frowns at me as I come back to the table.

"Us Toads is from Cambridgeshire back in the olden days. That's in England, see, and there was a lot of Toads in that place. They called us the Cambridgeshire Toadsmen and we had power over horses."

"I cannot believe," says John. "My family work with the horses for many years. We are expert. The horse only respect a man who thinks like a horse."

"Yes," calls Antonio from the dishpan. "Sounds like a made-up story."

Toad gets up and goes to his room and returns, holding a small leather pouch on a string.

"This," he says, fondling the bag, "is the secret to me power over horses."

Despite himself, John leans forward. "What is it?" he says. Mudsey pushes forward to look, careful not to touch my arm.

"What's that Dad?" asks Alf. Antonio returns from the kitchen and puts a cup of tea in front of me.

"Inside this here bag, I've got the breastbone of a toad. This was a secret me old Dad told me. Here. Look." He upends the bag and out falls a tiny, yellow, forked bone.

"It is nothing," says John. "How does this give power?"

"It doesn't. It's just a bone," says Antonio.

"It's not the bone," says Toad, "but what you do with the bloody thing. Listen. First, you catch a toad and skin it. Then you hang the body on a whitethorn bush with the skin next to it, until the wind has dried everything out. Then you bury the carcass in an anthill until the bones are clean."

"Toad," I say, "this is a disgusting story. I don't want the children to hear it. I'm sure you're making it." Antonio nods. "You've never told me anything like this before."

"Shut yer gob, woman. This has got nothing to do with you.

John's interested in me family history, even if you and Tony aren't."

"History, my foot. It's a yarn, if ever I heard one."

"So where'd I get the bone from then? Tell me that, smarty britches. Yer pretty quiet now." He touches the wishbone reverently. "It took me a month when I was just a kid. When it's eaten down to a skeleton, you bring the bones to a stream and bung them in the water." Toad suddenly screams. And we all jump.

"Shock like that is bad for a pregnant woman," growls Antonio.

"Why did you scream?" I complain.

"The *bones* would scream," he says, "I'm just demonstrating the facts for youse, like. And this little bone would float away from the other ones, upstream it goes, and then the Toadsman has to act sharpish and grab the bone outta the water before it sinks."

"Oh God," I moan. "Witchcraft. Spare me. Your ancestors were witches or gypsies or something arcane. And you never told me." I take a sip of tea and smile my thanks to Antonio.

"Wouldn't make a shred of difference," Toad says. "Anyway, Toadsmen were honourable men, every toff wanted one working in his stables. Total power over horses."

I do wish he'd stop saying that; it's the part of the story that's hard to refute, because Toad can do anything with horses. When the whole district went over to tractors, before the petrol rationing, Toad kept his horses. They're silly for him. They kiss him in the morning when he goes out to feed them. John knows it too and stares at the little bone in Toad's palm and shakes his head, but reaches out anyway, to touch it.

"No!" says Toad, closing his fist. "That's not the whole story."

"I love this story," says John. "I wanna hear the whole

thing." They smile at each other. Toad's creased old neck turns a deep shade of carmine.

"You take the bone to a place where a horse is buried, and you have to sit there overnight, and the devil is supposed to come and torment you. I never saw the devil but I did see me old man." He laughs. "And then a Toadsman comes to you and gives you three tests to try and make you give up the bone. One by fire and one by earth and one in the water, and that's the worst one by far. Dead against nature. And if you do all three of them, well then. You get to keep the bone and have horses follow you around like yer made of oats."

"Show me!" demands John, but Toad slides the bone back into the pouch.

"This one's mine," he says. Something happens to John's face. I see Toad look at him, see John slowly lift his eyes from the table and notice Toad watching him. The air blue and electric between them. Crackling. Eyes travelling over faces and then back to the *snap* of that moment, eyes locked on eyes. And then they both look away, their hands busy with nothing. Their faces damp. "Where's *my* tea, Tony?" Toad asks, pushing back his chair. "One last thing. Before you all scarper . . . I reckon we deserve a bit of a holiday." And this is when I know for sure that something invisible had happened at the table. We've never taken a holiday, and as far as I know, Toad has a personal aversion to wasting time. "Whaddaya reckon about hopping over Moore River way and slipping the hook to some bream?"

15

Toad drives our cart amongst the leaning river gums and stops, the horses wilting, soapy with sweat, bowing their heads to lip at the burnt grass, and the men force their cramped legs over the sides and get down.

The bush is silent, staring. Moore River was not settled land then, where the sound of an axe striking a tree or a plough ripping the fragile skin of the earth had become a common thing. So the cockatoos and the wrens and the magpies and the kangaroos which had come to drink hid fearful in the bush, watching.

The children are got down from the cart, their hair all stuck to their faces and dark with moisture, and their cries as they are lifted send a spray of corellas into the colourless sky. They are set in the litter under the stringy barks while Antonio ties a rope from one tree to another and hangs a blanket over the line to shade them.

It is a lonely kind of a place. The mud banks riddled with the holes of the snakes that swim in the slow stream, and the trees drooping over the water trail their branches in its coolness and the tannin in their leaves make the water as black as coal. Small silvery bubbles float on the dark surface amongst the scum of peppermint leaves and shards of paperbark.

Louder now, as if to break the grip the place has on them, Toad calls out to Antonio, to take the gun and get some rabbits for grub, and to John, to get wood, because even though the land is dangerously dry, we must eat, and the fire, too, will take the edge off the solemn place.

"We're all bloody starving, Gin. Get the lead out."

An echo of his harsh cry comes back, mangled, from the far bank, surprising him. He takes his sudden fear out on the frying pan, throwing it at me, almost as a necessity, to cover this weakness. But it misses, the black and lumpy cast iron disc falling into the dirt.

I boil potatoes, drop a gum leaf into the tea in the billy, scuff a damper bread under the coals, beat the maggots off a bit of lamb and drop it in with the potatoes. Smoke from the fire coils up into the still air and tangles on the branches overhead. Squatting next to me, much too close, Antonio prods the sandy berm surrounding the fire with a twig.

"What's this for?" he asks, one beautiful hand hanging limp between his thighs.

"Keeps the wind from blowing sparks into the bush. One spark and this place goes up in flames. It's as dry as dust."

"Ah . . . bushfire," he says, easing the waistband of his trousers. Flies rise away from his disruptive hand, and then resettle on the moisture and salt.

"Gin," he says, very soft. It is only my name, but the hairs on the back of my neck stand up. I am sitting on my heels, smoke veiling my head and I look at him. He is wearing the vest without a shirt, against his bare skin, even in this inflammatory heat and he draws his finger in a line over his heart. The fire seems very hot, too hot for mutton, and he looks a question at me, not stopping just at eyes.

I fumble for words, lurch after something to say that will not be an admission, but my mouth twists with the effort, my eyes tear. It is the smoke. Of course it is. For I do dearly love my husband and all this is a mistake.

He holds something out in his hand, a bauble, a trinket, I think, but it is Mudsey's ribbon again, bright red, staining his palm.

"This will look good in your hair," he says and stretches his hand towards me, a husband doing for a wife, tying a ribbon in her hair, a casual endearment, a sign of possession, but I fall backwards, away from him, and my feet flick forwards, kicking the side of the berm, caving it in, and the fire hisses, angry to be buried alive.

A puff of wind blows smoke and ash into my face as I lie sprawled and inelegant, my feet kindling at the edge of the fire. Antonio folds his arms. Pressing the wool against his chest. From high in the red gum comes the falling tremolo of a corella.

"Little mouse," he smiles and gets up and rubs his hands on the seat of his pants and strides off to kick the bushes, confidant in a way that seems wrong for a prisoner, and his image shivers a little in the heat rising from the fire. The corella lifts from the tree, its snow white wings flashing yellow as it tilts.

John and Toad are nowhere to be seen. The children's accusatory legs point out from under the tent like kangaroo bones in the hand of a witch doctor. "Snap!" cries Mudsey. They are playing cards. The bright and revealing calls of birds hang heavy between the muddy banks of the river. The trees lean closer, drinking the air in great thirsty gulps, beating at the smoke with their leaves. The river slides past. Slowly eroding its borders.

Two men rise from the water, their bodies sleek and dripping and for a moment, the smoke opens and I see their pale hidden skin, wrinkles and softness and potholes and pits, before they step behind the cart to put on their clothes. They are laughing and punching each other, frolicsome. Toad has John in a headlock, a father's rough embrace, and John writhes, happy and angry at being so held by one so small and pungent.

Toad drops to the sand, a black leaf stuck to his chin, the shirt under his arms dark with sweat.

"Tucker!" he says, his belly spilling between the gaping buttons. He drums an enamel cup on his knee, "Thank God for the missus, eh?" he asks Antonio. "Best thing I ever did. Meals on the table, regular-like, clothes on me back, tupping rights . . ."

I drop sand into the plate of stew I am handing him. Sod. He'd be laughing on the other side of his face if I ever told anyone about his peculiarities. I may not know much, but I can guess from the snippets of jokes and the whispered conversations I've overheard down at the CWA hall, that in Toad, desire has taken a deviant form. For one, he points to the beasts in our paddocks as role models in certain matters. It's only natural, he says. But for all that, he wants intimacy little enough to be the faggoty old ram we had to slaughter for humping the wethers and neglecting his duties.

Perhaps, for a sheep farmer, a woman is not such an exotic flower, for the private parts of a sheep look remarkably like a woman's, but exposed, for all to see and lust after, and the novelty must wear thin for a man who spends his days confronted with thousands, from the tight purse of the youngest lamb, to the yawning sack of the matron. It is all meat. To be tupped and bred, willing or not, until the old ewe is for the knackers.

After eating, the children fall asleep, curled around my feet, face down, and on each, the trickle of night spit is iced with sand. Their stomaches groan and gurgle, they huff and murmur in their dreaming. "Mummy," mutters Alf and I lay my hand on his head.

One by one, we creep closer to the fire, mesmerised by the trajectory of the sparks and the crying of the wood as it is consumed. We spear pieces of damper on green sticks, and the smell of burnt toast joins that of wood smoke. Part of the fire collapses into the embers and a shower of sparks rises into the endless night sky.

"Come on you mangy lot," Toad says, fidgeting in the silence. "Tell us something about yerselves. What kind of men are you?"

Perhaps it is impossible to sit in the dark with strangers and not talk about your lives. Perhaps men on long train rides, seated together, begin to speak out of a desire for the comfort of connection. The simple humanity of being born and dying and having things happen to us in the middle. No one will sit next to a man on a train who doesn't speak. He puts himself above the others, becomes inhuman, untouchable. And so it is with fires. We all must speak or be put from the circle.

So we take turns to tell our stories, oh yes, we tell them, and the fire rises into the night sky, too hot for closeness between us.

16

"I want Antonio to speak first," says Toad maliciously. He has not spoken at length to Antonio and does not know that he speaks English very well. He thinks Antonio will say no, no. You go first.

"Toad," I say, shaking my head, disappointed. But Antonio stands and says, "This is my story." His voice is lower, mellower, the voice of a storyteller, I think. He takes a breath, partly out of showmanship, and begins to speak.

"We were all in Bardia, in the north of Libya, pushed there by the British and Australian troops. Thirty thousand of Italians in this small, white town that once only held five hundred, without food or water. When the radio announced that the British let loose the Australian barbarians in the desert, we believed everything. A rumour went round that the Australians had bullet-proof clothing."

Toad interrupts, "Yeah. Bloody tin cans like Ned Kelly."

Antonio stares at him across the fire, expressionless, until Toad looks away and kicks at a twig in the sand near his feet.

"One man whispered that they take no prisoners, and after that, we all sat shivering, smoking our last cigarettes and not saying nothing. The wind had ripped off part of the roof of our shelter, and the constant banging of the loose iron sheets sounded like an air raid, and each time it went bang we'd all jump and then pretend nothing happened."

"Typical," says Toad. "Any of youse lot hear about Italian tanks? One gear for forwards and four for reverse."

"Shut up, Toad," I say. "Let the man tell his story. You're the one who wanted him to go first." I turn back towards Antonio and he looks like a man in a Caravaggio painting. Lit. Intense. Toad looks at him too and scowls, irritated that Antonio has my attention. Embers drift darkly past his face and he swats at them. John lies down in the sand, not following the story, bored.

"Our clothes and our food and our pride were left out in the desert along with the heavy guns and trucks, to be buried by sand. Men ran away throughout the night to hide in the caves. I should explain: The town of Bardia is built on cliffs above a beautiful little bay of clear water and these cliffs are full of caves. Afterwards, the Australians said that one cave had a thousand Italian soldiers, who were captured by eight unarmed men and a donkey. I wouldn't know nothing about that." He hesitates, touches the vest I made him and presses his lips together.

"The Australians somehow got across our anti-tank trench and then, within minutes, bombs were going off, two or three a minute and you couldn't hear nothing. The bombs would go off, right, left, right, left, never letting up and everything was covered in white-grey dust from the buildings what got hit. The air was full of it, and there were letters and photographs blowing everywhere in the black smoke, mothers and daughters and pinups and children hitting you in the face and every place was blocked with broken stone walls or fires and I started to think I should a gone to the caves. None of us were real soldiers. Most of our blokes were peasants and already knew how to fire the guns. My big worry at that moment was starving to death though, not being killed by shrapnel, and right after that, I was afraid of being captured and what that means."

"Well," says Toad, "Yer well and truly captured matey. I

reckon you know what it means now."

"For goodness sake, Toad. Leave him alone," I say.

John sits up and says "A woman must listen to her husband. Not the other way." So he's on Toad's side after all. Damn him.

"Thanks for that," says Toad after a moment. He hesitates, then hitches himself a little closer to John. They both stare into the fire.

"You are right, boss," says Antonio. "I *do* know what it means to be captured. But I think you do not. Australian POWs will come home to happy families, but for us Italian POWs, our families will be ashamed of us. For us, it is better to die than to be captured."

"That's dreadful," I say, but there is a lurch inside me. A man who has nothing but shame to return to, might not wish to return to his family at all.

"Being captured is not as dreadful as starving to death," Antonio says, gathering us back into his story with his eyes. They linger on my face for just a beat longer than the others. "While I was scrabbling around in Bardia, I found this ten pound tin of *estratto di pomodoro*, tomato paste, and since I'd lost the queer little can opener we were issued, I no way could get it open, and me hungry as the Madonna! Tomato paste seemed the most delicious thing in the world right then and I chucked it at the stone walls, stomped on it, kicked it and of course it don't open. So finally, I threw a grenade at it, just one of the little money box kind of grenades. This was in the thick of things, the town being strafed from the harbour, and there I am, detonating a can of tomato paste. And then, *buonanotte* to the musicians! There's bits of the tin sticking out of the walls, there's tomato paste dripping from the roof tiles, there's a seagull caught in the blast, skidding around in the muck. And of course I couldn't eat nothing. It made me so angry I could have touched hell with my finger."

"You can eat a seagull," says John. "I eat seagull lot a times and it's good."

I know Antonio would never have eaten a seagull and I smile a little to let him know I know. He laughs, telling this story against himself, but I think of him with a grenade in his hand and it scares me. He sees that too and begins to talk about something else.

"Then, I came across a little hospital. I thought I might be able to hide out there for a while. Most of one wall had caved in and the roof hung down in that place. You could shake the stone wall with your hand. *Porca miseria*! On the wall, there were chalked cartoons of British soldiers complaining that they should have got a discount on the Venus de Milo since her arms are missing, and jokes about Churchill and patriotic poetry about Il Duce. I searched for food but everything was full of rubbish and broken glass. I thought of the cavalry horses loose in the streets and the foam that builds up under their harnesses and I thought, if one went by, I would run out and lick the sweat off its body. I was that thirsty. Finally, I opened a door and I saw a steel table standing in the centre of the room and there was a big hole in the ceiling and through it, I could see the ash in the sky and the smoke and the mustardy edge of the sun.

"A breadstick of a man lay on the operating table, metal tools still holding the skin over his guts open, making a horrible smile with hard, black lips, and tiny black flies rose up when I came near. A rusty knife was under the table. The man looked to be about sixteen, an Italian boy, without even a bit of hair on his face, and taped to his chest is a picture of his mother, spotted from the rain."

Antonio looked at me then and he put his hand on his chest where the picture would have been taped, right over his heart, and Toad turned and looked at me too. I think Toad knew then. There is a moment when he turns away when I think he might say something, but he coughs into his shoulder and spits and wipes his lips and Antonio picks up the story again.

"I covered his face with my shirt and left that place, still looking for water. I was leaning down into a latrine, licking the wall, when an Australian soldier kicked me in the backside and shoved his gun between my shoulders. I asked him for water but he just pointed down the road, and so I walked in that direction. There were about twenty other Italians lined up with their legs out in front of them, and an Australian soldier squatting there too, a big man in his amphibious boots and his helmet and his white teeth. He grinned at us and pointed at things he wanted—belt buckles, epaulets, sashes, buttons, whatever we had—and he called over several men and measured his feet against their boots until he found a pair in the right size. Grinning, he gestured for the Italian to take off the boots, and then he put them on his own feet, but he didn't trade. He kept the old amphibians too and left the other man barefoot."

John kicks one of Toad's ancient, crumbling boots and they scuffle, "*Amphibians!*" laughs John, but Toad is in no mood for laughing. He hits John hard in the shoulder and tells him to stop. "Peace," says John, his hands in the air. Now, in the darkling glow from the fire, their bodies seem to have fused, they are sitting so close together. Toad sits very still and does not speak.

"After a while, we heard more men coming, and we stood up and marched out in Indian lines to the road and I saw that there were many men without coats or caps or boots, and the Australians had been drinking our wine and were drunk and feisty, catcalling and baiting us as we walked, four across, on either side of the Victory Road. A big sheet of dust ballooned up behind us, pink in the evening light, bloody.

"There were very few guards, and even as we walked, men ran to us to surrender, waving white handkerchiefs or towels or shirts, calling "*Ci rendiamo.*" In the bad light, our faces were only lit by the diesel oil drums burning in the sand, and the Australians were wearing our hats and our cloaks and our jackets, and it was impossible to tell enemy from friend. Italians surrendered to Italians, trucks went by carrying British soldiers, who called greetings to us. They thought we were Australians. And if we had wanted to, we could have walked off the road and into the desert or hidden in one of the truck carcasses blocking our way, but very few did. When a British lorry stopped next to us, we ran at it, begging for food, water, cigarettes, and when the driver threw out a few biscuits, we fell to our knees, tore at each other, shouting and hitting, lapping at the crumbs.

"After pulling along for a while, we were put behind barbed wire fences, a supply dump turned into a camp, and we sat in deathful quiet in the cold of the desert night. I asked our guard, a man who used his razor to pick his teeth, if we might build a fire. "Suit yerself," he said, and in the dark, we felt around for things that might burn, pages from a letter, a broken rifle butt, dung, and we got a fire going and soon there were fires all over the camp with men sitting around them, touching their lips where the skin was peeling.

"In the distance, we heard the roar of engines, many planes coming our way, and the men sat up straighter, nudged their neighbours, pinched their cigarettes out between their fingers, tore open the paper and scattered the ash. We knew the voice of our own planes. The sound grew louder until it was a scream and the sand under our legs jiggled, dancing against our skin, and then they roared directly overhead, the Savoias at last, and we rose with a cheer, waving, crying, but then we heard the creak of the bomb bay doors opening and the sound of destruction as it rushed through the air towards us.

"In the light from the burning men, I saw other soldiers,

wounded, and their blood was black on their faces and hands and they groaned. Under my feet were soft things, things that rolled when I stepped on them and things that squelched. Things that snapped. And the men were crying for help but I couldn't help them."

He is silent for a while and stares up at the stars. Toad throws sand at him and says to finish the bloody story. Antonio doesn't speak right away and when he does, his voice is slower than ever, halting.

"After all we'd been through, to be bombed by our own men. Italians. Of the three thousand men in the camp that night, only nine hundred and twelve boarded the ship for Bombay. I think it was the despair that killed them," he says. "I'm almost certain."

Hidden in the darkness, I dare to touch his hand for a moment. "That's so sad, Antonio."

"I dunno if I believe it," says Toad. "Even the Italians can't be such bloody idiots as to bomb their own men." I hear the click and pop of his pocket watch being opened. He sniffs.

Perhaps that is why Antonio has learned English so well. Why he has volunteered to work on an Australian farm instead of staying with the other Italians in the POW camp. A man like him would resent his country over something like that. Might be inclined to seek a life elsewhere. Antonio sits down and tosses a few bark chips into the fire. "Your turn," he says to Toad.

17

"Yeah. My turn," says Toad, rising. "And no one better bloody well interrupt me. Well, I've never yet seen a dead bloke with the tongs sticking up out of his guts, and it looks like the government blokes are giving me a miss on being a soldier, so I don't have much in the way of yarns. But I reckon I've lived through a fair bit too, so I'll tell you one of the stories what happened with me and me Dad.

"Me old man was a Digger in the Great War and used to go down to Perth every year for the ANZAC Day parade in his medals and whatnot. Unlike them other blokes but, he didn't only wear his uniform for the parade. No mate. He had me Mum keeping it in good nick and he polished all them brass buttons every Saturday night over bits of newsprint and by God, he looked like a hero, and he wore that uniform every day that I knew him, and when we were just nippers, me and me brothers had to salute him and call him Sir and he'd have us marching around the fowl yard, left, left, left-right-left. He was a cranky old man, alright.

"Doesn't sound so bad," says Antonio. "My children do that too, in the youth groups."

"Yeah. But remember. This was me dad and not some bloody boy scout leader . . . When we got a bit older, we'd scarper out into the bush when we heard him coming, and that really made him see red. He'd whack us around if he could catch us and after a bit of this, me two older brothers who were supposed to help on the farm ran off together and we never heard from them again. Well, they couldn't read and that, so they might have wanted to contact us, but there wasn't any way. Mum took on over that, crying and carrying on, saying it was Dad's fault because he was too hard on them and he'd tell her to put a cork in it and belt her one and then she skidaddled too and it was just Dad and me.

"Me Dad never had a good impression of me. Reckoned Mum nursed me too long or something and the first thing he did after Mum left was cut off all me hair and tan the hide of me backside, like I'd done the running. 'Just so's you know where your bread's coming from,' he said. Which didn't make sense if you think about it. Listen, if you mob reckon you've had it hard, you've got no bloody idea. Aw. Bring out the violins for the poor little dagoes. Their Mum's are going to smack their little bums for them when they get home. You'd be dog biscuits if you'd been through what I have. You'd be soggy sawdust. I don't reckon dynamiting a tin of tomato paste makes you a hero."

"That wasn't the main point of Antonio's story," I say, and at that, Toad snorts.

"Well then, Missus Educated, tell us what was the main point?"

"Not the hardness of the life. I don't know. The despair, maybe. The sadness of it."

"Well, my life was sadder than his, then. Not that I'm whining. Me and me Dad worked bloody hard in them days, clearing trees and burning out the stumps, shifting the sheep ourselves, and in between times, eating and sewing and that, but Dad got tired of me, got himself a tomcat one day in town and he called the bloody thing Sergeant Bollocks. He spent every spare minute he had training that cat, like he'd tried to train me brothers and me."

"I don't think cats can be trained. Maybe it was a little dog. Or a fox," says Antonio.

"No. Will yer just listen? It was a trained cat. Bloody fantastic, it was! The old man'd whistle and Sergeant Bollocks would come streaking through the bush and line up in front of him, quivering like a sheila. Me Dad would shout 'Atten-shun!' and the bloody cat'd stand up on its hind legs. It knew a hell a lot of commands, all of them from the army, and it wouldn't even eat until me Dad said the word. By God, he loved that cat. Carried it inside his coat on cold days, bloody dug the holes for its shit and wiped its bum with his hankie so it wouldn't get worms.

"One day, I was about ten at the time, we were out on a block we'd been clearing, bashing at the bark left on the stumps with the flats of our axes, and up comes this swaggy, man with a face like a broken cheese grater, and he says, says he, 'Can I join yer for a bit of tucker?' Me Dad and I, we just look at him, cause he was one of the first blokes we'd seen in a year. And this fellah, he sits himself down like king of the road and builds an abo fire, and hangs a black pot over it, which he fills with water.

"'What've you got for the soup?' says he, and me Dad just shrugs and goes back to his work. He never would give up a bit of grub to a stranger. The swaggy gets up and looks into the tin we've got with flour in and picks out a weevil and eats it. 'They're good for you,' he says, 'Almost as good as meat.' He offers me one, and then pulls a trap out of his swag and steps off into the bush again. We knew he'd be back any tick of the clock because he'd left his pot and his billy, and sure enough, after a bit, he came back and turfed some chunks of fresh meat in the boiling water, and followed that up with a couple of handfuls of leaves. Then, all persnickety, he pulled a wee tin of salt out of his hatband and pinched out a bit, and dropped that in the pot too, and Dad gave me a kick in the pants and told me to get over there and make a damper bread, which I did.

"It was a bloody good stew, and when we was wiping the grease off our chins, Dad says to the swaggy, he says, 'Mate, thanks for the tucker, and now I've got something to show you,' and he whistles for Sergeant Bollocks. He whistles and he whistles and the cat doesn't come, and after a while, Dad says, 'I've got this beaut trained cat. He's bloody priceless. He'll be here in a tick. Just wait till you see him.' And after another bit, Dad's still whistlin' like a bloody tea kettle, and the swaggy gets up and says, 'I've got to go shake some bushes,' and I notice that he's taken his billy and his pot and nicked one of our axes while he was at it, and that stew never *did* taste like rabbit."

"That's a good one," we laugh. I laugh too, even though I know Toad only said it to prove he's at least Antonio's equal.

"I'm surprised you can't taste the difference between a cat and a rabbit," says Antonio.

"I was just a kid."

"Still," says Antonio.

"Isn't that whole story just some old joke?" I ask.

"No," says Toad, sullen now. "It happened to me." He pokes at the fire with a twig.

"Now you," he says, turning to John. Lit from below, there is an expression I have never seen on Toad's face. He's eager to hear John speak.

John taps Antonio on the arm and they stand together.

18

"John's Story," John says and winks at Toad. "That much I can say by myself. I will tell my story in Italiano and Antonio will translate it to English and perhaps you will know something of my life before I came here." He looks at Toad when he says this, and puts his feet apart, to stand more comfortably.

"My life was just as difficult as your life," Antonio repeats after John, sentence by sentence. "But not for the same reasons. My father was a horseman," he says in smooth, high voice. "One of the *butteri*, the noble cow herders of Maremma."

"Is that so?" interrupts Toad. "Yer from a family of horsemen, just like me. Fancy that. No wonder you're so keen on getting hold of me lucky charm." In the darkness, I can just make out the morbid pouch in his hand.

"Yes, that is true," says John, his eyes on the arcane thing. "I remember riding in front of my father's saddle and he telling of our tradition, of kindness to the cows and love for the horse, the gentle bit we use and the small spurs, the quiet between us, and the smell of the sea and the marshes and the rosemary crushed beneath the horse's hooves all around me. My legs were tickled by the curly goat hair on my father's chaps. The silver cattle walked before us, their long horns waving like a forest of dead branches above their backs, dust from our passing settling gently over the olive trees."

"Now we know all yer secrets," says Toad. They each want what the other has. We have all seen John leap onto the back of a cantering horse without using a saddle or bridle. We have all seen the horses rubbing against Toad like house cats, purring deep in their chests.

"Not all," says John softly in English before he continues, and Antonio laughs.

"My mother, oh my mother, made me a little suede waistcoat with eight buttons like my father's and I wore a low felt hat like him too, but only he carried the real mark of the *butteri*, the *uncino*, a long stick of chestnut wood with a hook on the end, which he used for dividing the beasts, opening gates and picking up my little hat when it fell. I never dreamed that this would not be my life."

Something passes over his face and he begins to sit down as if he has already said all he means to say, but Antonio says a few quiet words to him in Italian, and he pulls his lip and wipes his eyes and stands to speak again.

"We lived in a stone house with a roof of cotta tiles, together with other *butteri*, on the property of the lord whose animals we tended, my mother, my father, my grandmother, my brothers, our animals and I, and before I knew how old I was, we were joined by a sister, and that was the end of our peace, because as soon as she could talk, she began to beg to join us with the horses. And we loved her, and pushed her from under the horses' feet and took her little hand with its bunch of weeds from their mouths, and we plaited bracelets for her from the long hairs of the horses' tails."

Again he stops and kneels in the sand, and this time, Toad puts his hand on John's shoulder and asks him quietly if he will say a little more, that it's really very interesting, and no wonder he's so good with the horses. John nods. His hand shields his face from the heat of the fire. His voice, now, is muffled.

"The land of the Maremma is very low and wet, having many birds and many mosquitoes, black clouds of them like the flies here, and at dusk they rise from the marshes like the velvet cloaks of the lords, rippling. The coat of arms for our lord had four letters on it—two Ms and two Ss, which stand for *Miseria, Malaria, Sudore e Sangue:* Misery, Malaria, Sweat and Blood, because the mosquitoes carry the malaria, and to make a living in the Maremma, you must give sweat and blood, and the last, the misery, that is the story I *will* tell you. Yes. I will tell you a story.

"My sister walked down from the hills at dusk every day with my mother, singing. As I came with the men, we too would sing and our voices would join together as we came on the horses. The mosquitoes bit the horses, because the animals are warm and full of blood, and they left the men on their backs alone. But they bit my mother and they bit my sister and because she was small and weak, she became ill with the malaria. She was only a child of three and even strong men can be killed by what comes from the spit of the mosquito. My mother and father were poor people, honest peasants, without fault, but they could not bring doctors, medicine. She became weaker and weaker until my little sister lay by the door and didn't cry.

"At that time, after the end of the war, the first war, my grandfather was still over there in Germany, and he was killed. A boy came on a little jingling bicycle, and he had a telegram for us, and he had to walk up the hill to our house, and the whole way, how that yellow telegram burned in his hand. It lit the whole valley. It was bigger than the sun. And my grandmother knew what it was, what was coming, and she hid in the cellar with the pumpkins so she wouldn't have to touch that slip of paper.

"The messenger also gave my mother a ticket to pick up a box at the train station, and on this ticket, amongst the German writing, we could see grandfather's name and so, we thought he had sent us a present before he died. And what bad luck, to arrive on the same day as the telegram. But we forgot about the ticket in our mourning for grandfather, and my mother took the ticket and pushed it into the frame of the kitchen window. Only after many weeks did my little sister call out from her place and say, 'What is that, there, in the window?' And my father saw it was the ticket and went to the station to get the parcel.

"We were all very curious what the parcel might be and took turns guessing while my father was away. But none of guessed what it really was, an enormous tin of German stock powder for beef soup. We stood around it and smelled the strange German smell of it and scratched at the strange German words on the paper label and were grateful to grandfather for thinking of us, even far away, even at war. Our lives were very hard then, very hard. Just as difficult as your life," he nods at Toad, "and your life," he nods at Antonio.

"The soup mix became very important to us, because whenever we were sick, my mother would make us a hot drink from the powder, and of course, she gave a cup to my sister every day and my sister got stronger and stronger.

"We had almost finished the tin when we had a visit from the local priest and he had a cold, so my mother made him a cup of the beef tea. But instead of praising her, the old man lowered his head and smelled deeply of the tea and frowned and asked her what she had used to make the drink.

"Mother brought the tin to him and opened it and he put his finger into the powder and stirred it a little and his face went white.

"'My God!' he cried, 'Did you not get the letter?'

"Which we had not.

"It turned out that the army had cremated grandfather because of the large number of casualties and the risk of disease, and lacking something better, shipped his ashes home in an empty tin of soup mix. He was not the only man brought home like that, and letters had been sent out, explaining the situation.

"We could have been upset, but we weren't. We thought that Grandfather made a delicious soup and that he would have been very pleased to help out in any way he could."

There is silence when he finishes. "Well that beats me," says Toad. "We only ate the cat."

"Stories show a little of what we are," I say.

"What a man is capable of," agrees Antonio.

"I ate the cat's balls. He ate his Granddad's balls," Toad says, pointing at John, but glaring at Antonio. "I bet if you went last, you would have ended up eating yer own balls."

"Don't be revolting, Toad. We're not crowning someone King of Hades here," I say. "They're just stories."

"That's right," says Antonio. "Just stories. Your turn, Gin."

19

I stand and tilt my head. "I suppose I should be glad it isn't ladies first. I honestly don't know what I should tell you since nothing remarkable has ever happened to me. Oh, do be quiet. Sit down Toad. I'll say *something*. How about a dream I once had? Would you like to hear that?" Their eyes are on me, glittering in the light from the fire, like the eyes of animals.

"I was standing in a close space, a kind of cupboard or perhaps a little jail, and small hands were reaching in towards me. Many children's hands. It was dark, see, but I could feel their hands, the tiny fingers, and I could hear the rush of their breathing. Smell it even. They'd been eating mints. More and more hands reached in, pulling at me, tugging at my dress, and then, just as it was getting unbearable, I discovered I had my number seven cleaver."

There is an absolute and profound silence. I don't know where the words came from. Even the fire is appalled.

"*Jesus*," says Toad, "Remind me never to ask *her* to tell a story again."

The air above the fire is so hot. My face is burning, burning. I am ashamed to look at Antonio, but he asks me "What did you do?" His voice from a far off place. My heart as loud as the rattle of a kettle drum.

"I cut their fingers off. I did. But they didn't bleed. New fingers grew and squirmed between the bars and came at me again, smelling of mint and lollies, smelling of baby soap and talcum powder and freshly sawn wood and I chopped and chopped at them with that bloody great cleaver until no more grew." I hesitate. "That's all. I don't want to say any more."

Antonio sighs and asks, "Did you really dream that or did you make it up?" He always knows. His eyes are soft upon me.

"Yeah. That's a weird one alright," says Toad, "I dunno what it means but."

"Neither do I," I say, "And the really funny thing is, I found a fingernail under the cleaver the next morning when I got out of bed." Antonio smiles. My face is truly burning now. *Bed*. What fool am I that everything on my mind falls out of my mouth?

"Ah, go on. Yer revolting," says Toad. "Don't listen to her." He hauls up both of my hands and shows them to the Italians. "She's got all her fingers. See?"

"Leave her alone," says Antonio. "No one said the stories had to be true."

"That's right," says John. "But mine was true. About the horses." He raises his eyebrows at Toad. *Snap*. A shower of sparks lift from the fire.

"I wanted you to tell a real story," Toad grumps to me. "You never talk about yerself."

"You know all my stories, Toad. You know there's nothing to say." Without embarrassing myself. And I see Toad pondering who I'd be ashamed to reveal my life to.

"In front of him?" he snorts and jerks his thumb at Antonio, and the Italian winces. "Yer embarrassed of yerself in front of a bloody *prisoner*?" An ember leaps out of the fire and amongst us. The word is terrible in the silence.

"Come off your high horse why don't ya? Antonio, mate," Toad says, grabbing the Italian's arm and digging his fingers deep into the muscle, "She doesn't want yer to know what she's really like, under-neath all the la-dee-da. Eatin yer granddad is nothing compared to what she's done."

"Don't exaggerate, Toad," I say, but it's too late. Antonio looks back and forth between us.

"What has she done?" he asks finally.

"Her?" says Toad. "She was in the madhouse and they had her in a straitjacket."

"I know," says Antonio. "And you married her anyway. She told me."

20

Mist rose around us that night as we slept and when I wake, it hangs from the trees like muslin and flaps wetly against my face, hiding the Italians and the children and even Toad is watery, as near as he is and bundled in a sheet. I stare at him, his shoulder blades jutting like breasts beneath his singlet, a trail of dark hairs idling down between the cleavage, and cannot shake off the guilt I had, over my ridiculous story. Everyone else had at least tried to say something about themselves. My story and Toad's final comment must make me seem like the most unreliable of people, a liar or an idiot, and I fret that Antonio will not wish to talk with me now. He will not trust me now.

And I am shaken by the dream that I've just woken from, a real dream and not one made up to win some bizarre kind of competition: of lying with Antonio in a tent made from translucent linen that is sucked in and blown out with our movements, in and out, soundlessly. But in that dream we are found out and shamed. I wake, trembling, and look for Toad, remembering the look in his eyes, of anger and rejection. And on the damp morning air rides the odour of soggy ash from last night's fire and the stench of the river, and there comes in me a horror for my dishonesty and for all the deceptions that creep into a life, all the moments when I have sought to twist the way things are and will remain, and the weakness in me that still hopes for change.

I sit up from the dell of tarry sand in which I had lain, and shove at the hair trickling out from my scarf and in the sound of the magpies calling to each other and the scolding of the wrens and the blurring sound of wings, snippets of dishonesty run at me, and poke with fingers, and do hurt as they can.

And so comes my stepfather, eeking the door of my room, breathing fumes over my bed in the bitter darkness, and he, not willing to touch my damned flesh with his own skin, drawing down the sheets with his swagger stick and light as air, lifting my gown to see what lies beneath, white and young and smooth in the moonlight, the night wind sweeping the fine hairs with icy fingers. Breathing as torture. I am asleep. So I tell myself. And I tell myself that for many years until I am gone from that place.

There is no denying now; the fog washes my face with white-grey seed, a wet stream both disgusting and cleansing, and I cringe from the stolen pennies cartwheeling toward me, the dingo scarf weaving through the slurry, grainy sugar full of ants, the telescope orbiting around the score from *La Traviata*, the white hair wriggling in the creamy wool of the vest, the indifferent face that I present to be pawed at when all I want is to open my mouth and bite at something, the lowered eyes with which I so often tricked Toad into thinking I was modest rather than secretive.

My children come and stand and point at me and it is minutes until I realise they are not figments, but real, flesh and blood, hungry and wet.

"What's wrong, Mummy? What is it?" says Mudsey, crushing snails with her toe, green foam of killed snail dripping from her unburnt skin.

"Why should something be wrong?" I ask, pushing her grasping hands away. "Nothing is wrong." Good women love their husbands, their children. It is love that has me haggard. Nothing more. "You need a hankie. The snot is all over your cheek." And it is. Yellow-grey scales of dried mucous streak her face and strings of pus join her eyelids. I spit on my finger, scrub and scrape at the crust until it is all lodged under the white of my nail.

"I'm hungry," she whines, twisting away from the clawing.

"Tell your father," say I, picturing fish impaled on hooks

and drowning in the sodden air, gills brown with exploded life.

And she goes and falls on Toad, and he sits up with a roar, tearing down the mist, batting at it until it eddies around him, whirlpooling under his chin. He hauls up his girl child and takes her down to the water, to teach her fishing and the love of a father, and soon they are back with concussed bream stiffening in their hands. He wipes the slime from his hands with a clutch of grass and flings the mucky stuff under the horse's feet. And that is breakfast.

"The Return of the Great White Hunter," he smirks, the filleting knife flickering in his hand and scales raining around him, glittering, dead. At intervals, the heads, with astonished mouths, fly into the bush and there is rustling after they land. Inspection.

"We caught fishes, Mum," says Mudsey.

"Fish"

"Dad says if we sing to 'em, they'll come and jump on our hooks."

"Really."

"He said not to sing out loud. Just in your head, like. Singing, 'Come, all ye faithful, par-rum-pum-pum-pum, a new fried fish will come . . .'"

I snort and gurgle, a drain of laughter. "Toad! You never taught her that!"

"Of course I did, Petsy. No better way to snag a fish." But there's a smile on his face and a Mudsey shining in each eye and I think that another woman might be able to love him fully. But I am appalled by Toad. That other woman wouldn't stand, hunched over, noticing the line of mold growing on the tongue of Toad's boot.

"Dad says what you have in your head is even more important than what you do."

"Well. I hope not," I say, and I mean this most truly, her

words raising that bitter dream in its misty tatters and my eyes flick to Antonio, who is returning from the bush, pulling up his suspenders, and Mudsey sees him too. Sees me seeing him.

"Tony!" she yells, "Dad and me caught fishes!" Like they have unearthed a twenty-two carat diamond instead of hauling a few carbuncled monstrosities out of a muddy stream. He is Italian, our Antonio, with all that that implies, and he cavorts around her, swimming like a fish, miming being caught, fighting the hook, and my daughter's eyes mirror the morning sun and she dribbles a little stream of spit in her laughter and catches it back with her top teeth, sucking wetly. Toad, I can see, is irritated to have his daughter's love taken from him. "That's enough of that tarrididdle now. Let's be having the fish, woman," he snaps. And then, "Yer droolin, Mudsey."

The fish tastes of rot and damp socks and tar. John holds his first bite in his cheek and spits it between the bushes after accidentally tipping the contents of his plate in the fire. "I'm going for a walk," he says. "Maybe I get frog legs for lunch." Larruping like a bullfrog, Toad pats the leather pouch that hangs around his neck. He winks at John. Mudsey and Alf elbow each other and giggle at Toad. They bog into their food, little wolves, unaware that fish should not taste of decay, and Toad praises his prowess as a provider and picks his teeth with a fine bone removed from the skeleton of his meal.

Antonio doesn't eat. He has a sheet of paperbark in his hand and a stick of charcoal from the fire. At first he writes a few words in a scrolling script, but then he says, "I can make shoes."

"Yeah. We know that already. Gee. Yer a funny bloke to bring that up now. Jealous about me fish?" says Toad, scraping burnt crust from his damper.

"For you. For your missus. And kids. I can make bewdy shoes. Last forever."

Toad eyes him, sees he's serious and smiles.

"Excellent idea," he says, his eyeballs devouring those Italianate tassels of the very first day; he is imagining the prestige a pair of fancy shoes will confer on him. "How do you do 'em?"

"Eh?" says Antonio.

"Make the shoes. How do you make 'em?"

"First," says Antonio, and my head jerks up. I struggle to get my eyes focused on him; there's something in his voice, some anticipation of pleasure that I can't connect to the construction of a shoe. "I mark the shape of your foot and cut a pattern in wood."

He pulls Toad's womanish foot in its boot with three soles towards him and gestures at the laces, hauls at the wooden heel, wrenches the old leather cages off in a fug of damp wool and footrot and peels away the fungal sock, flipping it downwind with the barest wrinkle of his nose.

"Now," he says, charcoal in hand, "we scribe," and he presses the mildewed foot to the paperbark and traces it, once with Toad sitting and once with Toad standing, and then it's the other foot and then he's looking at me and Toad pushes me towards Antonio. "Go on," he urges. "Don't be a twit," his hand on my back pushing in the exact center of the place where something quivering and electric has awoken.

"Don't," I say, a word that takes hours to say, but Toad pushes me forward, trembling under his hand. How could he? His face is cold and still, watching my reaction. "Nothing to be afraid of," he says, and to Antonio, "Her feet are perfectly ordinary. I can't think why she's carrying on."

I am sat on a log and Toad hunkers behind, peering around me to see all the doings and muttering approval. What's not to approve? Free shoes for the family at only a tiny hidden cost. He can't see my face, which is just as well, but he must be able to feel the sudden fierce heat rolling off my skin.

Antonio lifts my foot to his thigh and steadies it there, sliding the rubber boot off and laying it aside in the ashy dust, one cupped hand gliding from heel to waiting toes. He presses each toe gently through my thick lisle stockings, which are not coming off, no, never, and makes as if to draw my foot yet closer, grasps my calf to arrange things to his liking, pulls my foot higher still upon his thigh, and Toad, hateful Toad, announces it all with enchanted cries of, "That's it! Bewdy. Don't let her wiggle now. I'll hold her still for you." As if my first husband is stationed above the headboard on my second wedding night.

My foot, oh traitorous foot, is stretched upon the furred bed of paperbark and stroked with his stick of charcoal, pausing in the softest places, retracing every curve, and I feel his breath warm my skin as he bends to his work, one hand deep under my skirt, gripping my calf. He slides his belt from its loops and uses it to measure my instep, my ankles. A subtle scent of saddle soap. The belt still warm. The shwick of the knife as it marks the leather. The head between my knees. The crown of damp, black curls, the touching white skull. The trembling of his thumb as it enters the cave beneath my sole and probes the height of my arch. His charcoal wells between my toes and lingers there before withdrawing. There is sweat on Antonio's face. There is sweat on mine. My feet are wet with sweat. It is a warm day. So very hot. The slim eucalyptus leaves point straight down, exuding moisture. On the tip of each leaf trembles a drop of liquid.

The bones within me grind as I stand and the child moves in a wave, boiling me over. Antonio presses his hand on my foot a moment to steady me, his pulse pushing against mine, and his palm leaving a damp spot on the tan knitted stocking, a flower.

Deflated, Toad leans back and blows out his breath. He hasn't seen anything at all.

Antonio does not look up at Toad or me, just traces and

traces until he is done and then brushes the dust and small flakes of bark from my feet, first with one hand and then with the other. Almost painful, this parting gesture, and yet the one which I can still feel in my bones at night: Antonio sliding my feet back into the rubber boots as if they are buttoned with diamonds. Not a drop falls from the leaves.

After lunch, John lies on the bank of the river, downstream, away from the grizzling of the children, with his shirt off and his legs in the water, his handkerchief knotted at its four corners and laid over his face to keep the flies off. We, too, lie down to rest. On the other bank, kangaroos pant on their sides and listlessly chew leaves. Small croaks and buzzing sounds, ticks and trills come from the river, and once, a heavy plop, as of a larger animal dropping down to swim. Birds wheel and nip insects from the flotsam, or snatch them from the very air. A light breeze raises goose bumps on the water.

I must have dozed because Toad is no longer beside me. Quietly, so as not to wake the children, I stand and look for him. Ordinarily, I would be glad of it, but just now I feel compelled to search for him; perhaps it is my morning's pleasure, or the guilt of it, that pushes me past the limits of our camp and down near where John is sleeping on the river bank, his legs basted by the waters of the Moore, And so I come silently upon Toad, his chin resting in the crook of a tree and his trousers around his ankles. He doesn't hear me. His eyes are on John's hairless chest, and he presses himself rhythmically against the smooth pink skin of the salmon gum, rubbing himself there as he has rubbed himself against me. He jerks and twitches, shudders, leans more deeply into the tree.

Just then, John screams. A long, inhuman howl. He threshes his legs in the water and covers his head with his arms. We have heard his night screams before, when he is visited by men killed alongside him in Africa, or when the desert is once again sewn with machine gun bullets and ribbons of men's flesh and the rhinestone glitter of incendiary bombs.

Toad kicks out of his trousers and slides down to the boy. He holds that dark head and kisses that brow and that wet cheek and those lips and strokes those trembling thighs and even with my bad eyes I can see what is happening, and I am jolted by a feeling of compassion for him, for what he risks in order to find love, before I am swamped with my own desperate sense of abandonment. It is something no wife should ever see, although I have engaged in much the same behavior with Toad myself. Perhaps not as tenderly. Never in daylight. And after all, I am a woman.

I turn and am sick on my own two shoes, and when I am able to look again, there is a white bone in John's hand and Toad tries to take it from him. They behave as I have seen the dogs do when the female is locked away in the bitch box, licking at each other, biting shoulders and ears, rolling together, humping. If they were dogs, I would flick them apart with a stockwhip, embarrassed. But they are men. They turn and turn again, hands sliding on wet bodies, everything revealed under the brilliant sun, the water sparkling from the motion of their feet.

An image of Antonio and me, together like this, flashes through my mind and I suck in my breath and a little sound comes from my mouth, but I push the image away because we have not done this thing, we *should not* do this thing. How has Toad infected me with this misplaced sense of loyalty when he has no such qualms? He takes love when he finds it and damn the rest of us.

The brute. I don't even know the names for some of the

emotions I am feeling. I'd like to take a stick to his surging flesh. My hand twitches, I can almost feel the smooth wood in my hand, the shock up my arm as the stick strikes his buttocks. But this cinaedus is my husband. His shaven legs, his desire for John, his collection of ancient corsetry, maybe I'm the cause of it. The very whiteness of me, a poison that has dropped into his eyes, day by day.

I step back behind the screening trees and call, "Toad? Toad!" as if searching for him, as if I *want* him, and I take up a stick and break it between my hands with a harsh crack, the shrapnel javelined into the rustling underbrush.

"Toad? Where are you?"

I make myself sick. I smell of rot. This is the worst of all my deceits.

"Toad. I must speak to you," and when he climbs the slippery slope and his glowing face appears before me, I point wordlessly to my belly.

"What's wrong?" he asks.

"Everything," I say. "We have to go back."

I don't say *home*. It was home when he chose me and took me there. It can't be home now, because of the unchoosing. It wasn't good, what Toad and I had, but at least we were in it together, yoked together like mismatched beasts pulling a plough. But his beautiful boy has come between us now and gnawed through Toad's traces. I can't pull this plough by myself. I resent seeing him frolic while I stand here, abandoned in the field, tied to a burden I never wanted.

Antonio tries to speak to me on the way back to Wyalkatchem.

"Is the baby all right?" he asks. "What's the matter? Can you sit up?" When I slap at John and tell him to get away from me, Antonio growls at Toad, "What's happened to her? Why won't she say? John! What did you do to her?"

"*Niente*," says John. "Nothing happened. I did nothing wrong."

He moves closer to Toad, away from my scything fingernails.

"By whose definition?"

Antonio is sweating. He leans forward again and again to ask what is wrong.

"Leave me alone. All of you. Just leave me alone."

"Maybe the baby is coming? Is that what's wrong? Toad! You must know what's wrong."

II

1

Mudsey is under the house. The day is hot. Yesterday, she and Alf ate a two-pound bag of sugar in the dim light beneath the floorboards. They licked their fingers and pushed them into the sugar and pulled them out, fat with white crystals. No one came to find them or to stop them. Flies crawled on their sticky hands and in the wet corners of their eyes.

"What's wrong with Mum?" said Alf.

"Sick," said Mudsey, sucking her finger.

There was a considering pause and both of them stuck their fingers in the bag again.

"I know."

"Bellyache, maybe," she said.

"She don't use the dunny no more. She wets the bed like a *baby.*"

"You wet the bed," said Mudsey, looking at him, nose wrinkled.

"Nuh-uh."

"Yeah. Strewth, you're the flippin' Niagara Falls. Anyway, Dad says she's crook and when she comes good again, then she'll look after us, I reckon."

"Don't need any old Mum. Tony's better than any smelly old Mum."

"Don't say that."

"Why?"

"I don't like Tony anymore."

"Why?"

"Stop with yer stupid whys. Just because. That's all. Yer supposed to love yer Mum better than any dago fella."

"Do you love Mum?"

"Whaddaya reckon?"

Alf stirred the dust with his toe. "Look here," he said, reaching into his pocket. "I got a big key. Let's play house. I'll be the Dad and you be the Mum."

He pulled out a heavy, forged key with a piece of red embroidery floss tied to the end. It was the key to the glory box.

"Where'd you get that?" asked Mudsey, already knowing, already snatching it from his hand. "Give it."

She slides the key from her bloomers and presses the pointy bit into her palm. Alf went in to their mother several times a day. Just looking. He might have touched her open eyes, to see if she blinked, or the back of her hand, or her hair finally free of the scarf. He has walked around the windowless room and looked at the things hidden there. The hair receiver, stuffed with springs of hair rolled on his mother's forefinger; the Bakelite nail buffer, so excellent as a train; the gold ring with its flat green stone that hangs from a spring under the bed, unable to be removed; the black key to the glory box.

His mother didn't move. He could touch the glassy surface of her eye with his burr of a finger and she wouldn't blink. He has straddled her chest and peered into those eyes and seen nothing. Only the faint lift of her ribcage told him she was alive. That, and the stink of the sheets.

He took the key.

And now, under the house, she, Mudsey, has it, and she is no silly baby who thinks the key itself is treasure. There's a world inside that box.

Her father is harvesting grapes or planting cauliflower and broccoli and Brussels sprouts, February jobs, Mum's jobs, so she crawls from under the house, her dress tucked up in her knickers and the key out before her like a divining rod.

"Mum," she says at the door to the bedroom, "can I come in? Are you awake? Gee, you look crook."

It's the first time she has gone to see the breathing corpse on the bed. She stands next to the glory box.

"Thanks for letting me have a look, Mum. It'll just be a peek. I'm looking now," she says, still not moving, her eyes on the motionless sheet over her mother's swollen belly. *Cripes. She's got the bloat already,* she thinks. And pictures sheep exploding in a rush of foul gases and liquefied flesh.

"I'm turning the key now," she says and when nothing moves, she slips the key into the lock and twists it with both hands. She props the lid open with a frilly umbrella she finds on top of all the booty.

In half an hour, she has emptied the chest, and discovered the doll at the bottom. She observes the doll with bile in her mouth. She has never had a doll. The closest thing has been a stick with two burls on one end and a charcoaled mouth that she wrapped in a ratty old flannel and sang to, and all the while this magnificent baby was stuck away in the glory box. Her gaze flips to her mother, that appalling old waxwork, and then she lifts the bisque and carved wood child and kisses its face. To her horror, the top of its head falls off. The woolly hair was only sewn to a paper skullcap and pinned to a cork pate. With this parukh off, she sees a ghastly ivory knob jutting from the back of the baby's neck and a gaping wound where the top of the skull should be. Inside, a red rubber ball bulges obscenely upwards past a lump of plaster behind the eyes. As she cradles the doll, a dead silverfish slides out of the head and lands on her arm.

Shuddering, she claps the wig back on and ties her handkerchief around the head, then scuffles through the litter of old clothes for something else to dress her darling in: a pretty frock, a nightgown, a shroud.

"Victoria?" she says, trying out names, "Prudence? Elizabeth? Annette?" Because this child needs a suitable name, fancy, like the red shoes with Bs stamped on the soles or the glass earrings, or the silky little bustle draped exuberantly over the pantalooned bottom. And with the hankie on her head, she could be a bride. This gives Mudsey an idea, and she hauls the white dress from the pile, the one her Mum wore when she sang the screechy song at holidays. After tossing back the other clothes, she bundles the dolly in the slippery white stuff and carries the parcel off to her lair. On the way, she snatches up the scissors hanging on a nail next to the sewing machine.

Under the house, she leans the doll against one of the tree stumps that hold up the floor, and tells her about the farm.

"We got sheep, lots, smelly buggers, and wheat and cows and about a hundred fowls and horses and dogs and cats to eat the mouses and by golly, we got a heck of a lot of bunnies. They're bloody invading us.

"This here's the farmhouse, my Dad built it and that, over there in the gully is the shearers' quarters and down there, that's Mum's orchard, we got oranges and lemons, say the bells of St. Clemens, and apricots and figs and grapes and almonds. Olives now too, 'cause of the Italians. Mum likes Antonio, doesn't she just. He's always messing around with her. They like to play down in the orchard. Gotta watch out for bees in that orchard but. They got stingers and they'll stick you quick as look at you, and there's double gees in the grass that go right through your boots, and snakes under the water tanks. You see one of them, you run like billy-oh and don't look back."

Soon enough, she is chattering about Alf and Antonio and John and then she dries up and simply lays the doll in her lap and hums to it. The baby has painted eyelashes, a little O of a mouth and staring glass eyes that don't close.

"You're hungry. Poor liddle girlie. Your Mum didn't feed you nothing this morning," she says. "No worries. I got googy eggs and toast for you, and then you'll have a wee spot of milk."

She lifts the steel shears and snips a pearl off the lace. These are real pearls, point de gaze lace. Two or three other pearls sewn on the same thread slither down and drop in the dust. Mudsey pops a pearl into the doll's mouth. "Get that into you," she says, and wipes the doll's lips with her dress, then leans over and cuts a ratty square from the bodice of the wedding gown.

"Here's your pretty hankie."

She lays the doll in the dust, and ants scurry over the painted face, but Mudsey is too busy to notice. She uses both hands to force the shears open and shut, cutting out odd shapes: a bib, a nappy, a sarong, a shawl. She slashes two armholes in the largest piece and turns back to the doll.

"Ahhh! Get off it, you buggers!" she cries, crushing the ants against the doll, using spit and unwashed finger to scrub at the bloody smears of burst ant.

More ants come, attracted by the smell of death, and she shivers, waves the doll at them and the doll's hand swings out and hits the floor support and the clean little hand comes off, its childish cupped fingers beseeching from the dust and litter of scraps.

Mudsey picks up the hand and tries to push it back onto the doll's elbow. She looks up the sleeve for clues, and then, in a rush, tears off the fragile old clothes, not fiddling with the molded glass buttons, the tiny pins and hooks and ribbons and tapes. Off it all comes, the silk shattering, the pleated petticoats dissolving in her hands.

Underneath the finery is a chunky child's body of kid leather with a scalloped band across the chest. She inspects the intact hand. It is attached to the elbow with screws. The feet and shins are carved from wood, the head turns, grating, in the plump bust with its pale painted nipples. The doll's glass eyes bulge. The wig slips from under the handkerchief until it, too, falls to the ground. The brown net socks, the pointed shoes with their pompoms, the double-breasted red jacket, the tags of feather, even the earrings, all are discarded, one by one, and pressed into the earth under the house by Mudsey's eager movements. "Don't look at me!" she says in a fake, high voice, covering the doll's breast with her hand. "Don't touch me."

She pulls the good arm through the slit in the square of lace, and frowns at the pieces of bisque swinging from the other leather elbow. When shoving the pieces together doesn't work, she lays the broken hand against the upper arm and ties them with strips of fabric.

"Poor dolly," she says, "broke your arm. Don't cry. Mum will kiss it all better." She bends to kiss the bandaged arm, jostles it and the hand falls off again. This time, when she lifts the hand, two fingers are missing.

"Bugger the stupid old thing," she says, and she scoops a cat piss hole and buries the broken thing. Ants riot, surrounding the disrupted earth.

Mudsey settles to feeding her baby. So many pearls are cut from the gown that finally she can't force any more past the O of the lips and she grows tired of the game and the still, staring child with its raw wounds, and she goes to dress up the cat in the discarded clothes.

The doll lies face down. A light wind lifts a piece of lace and flutters it against the ironbark stump. The scissors, jammed open, are full of sand. Ants scuttle in and out of the doll's mouth and in the night, a possum scratches at the soft kid buttocks, at the seams, and a little sawdust trickles out. Days later, Alf finds the doll and chips at the plaster behind the eye sockets. He jams a screwdriver right through one of the glass eyes.

Mudsey returns. She pours golden syrup into the doll's mouth from a gallon tin. Treacle gets on the ground and on Mudsey and leaks from the open skull. Despite bandaging the empty eye sockets, she can't look at her baby. The ants move freely through the doll's body. The kidskin shivers from their movement. Pieces of the lambswool wig line the nests of many creatures; a tiny red scorpion lives in a shoe. Mudsey takes scraps of fabric to wipe herself in the outhouse. It's very soft with the pearls cut off. At certain times of day, she can see the cloth at the bottom of the pit, sprinkled with poo and lime. At other times, she stares at the paintings her father made and tries to remember Joan, her sister, the third child in the tree, the child with white skin like her Mum's.

2

Outside, Offenbach is being played on the gramophone, poor Jewish Offenbach, rejected by the Nazis in favor of the pompous Wagner. His barcarolle rocks me from my weeklong sleep, and my first thought is that they need to change the needle. It'll ruin the record. The tin of needles with its musical dog weighs down my stack of music on top of the Bechstein.

Before I woke up and heard the Offenbach, I remember a road with a cart going down it; the trace chains were jingling and the stars were out. The cart smelled of horses and of foreign hair pomade. It rocked from side to side, and a mast slowly rose out of the wooden planking and then the mizzenmast speared up and the canvas flapped and filled, and the air no longer smelled of horse, but rather, of bilge and tar and rotting seaweed. The ship, for that is what it was, heeled over, but my feet seemed glued to the deck. I rode along, my body weaving through the fog, and it felt to me like a very long time indeed, with the spray in my face and the wind blowing hard. There was a little man tangled in the shrouds, hardly a man anymore. His skin was gone, his meat had rotted, he was just bones held together with pale green sinews. When the wind blew, his legs straightened but the sinews were so tight behind the knees that the legs sprang back to a diamond shape and I saw him frog kicking across the sky. After a while, I saw a little hut with a lovely, inviting black door. Just inside was a ladder going down into the darkness of the hold. From below deck, I heard Antonio call. "Gin!" he said, his voice a sustained note on a cello. I had my foot on the first rung when I heard the Offenbach. I took another step. But the needle on the gramophone in the orchard was old.

> *Beautiful night, oh night of love,*
> *smile on our heady feelings,*
> *night sweeter than day,*
> *o belle nuit d'amour!*

In a stronger moment I wouldn't enjoy this music. This sap for witchetty grub people, white wrigglers. My hand-cranked gramophone is out there in the orchard, under the swollen almonds, and a sea of voices rise, singing along with the record, one voice clawing and scratching and spitting, a soprano that has never belonged to a gramophone woman.

Time flies, they sing, *carries away our affection, never to return!*

Do they even know what the French words mean? Toad's voice ratchets through the others, squawking, "He holds the broom like a woman." Laughter, singing, the scratch of the forgotten needle which has reached the end of *Les Contes d'Hoffman*. An unfamiliar odor hangs in the air, the smell of meat and wine boiled together, savory but fermented too. I haul myself upright to hear a crowd of unknown men singing with a guitar and a mandolin, and there is the clink of glassware and a kind of static that might be dancing and a softer sound I can't place, like but unlike the ocean.

Someone has closed all the doors to my warren and it is humid with the scent of my own unwashed body. Silverfish float in front of my eyes and rain down through the fetid darkness. Even lifting my head has left me breathless, my legs rubbery. The spine is stiff and unhelpful. And what to make of this hard bowl on my abdomen, this revolting bulge? I swing my legs over the edge of the cliff, my bed, and touch the floor with a toe, and the unwanted belly flops onto my thighs with an audible slosh.

I'd like to join Antonio in the orchard. To stand under the Southern Cross and taste the meat and sing. I'd like to wear a sleeveless dress like the Duchess of Windsor, and dance to "In the Mood" with his hand on the small of my back. But I have woken with the words "war fling" on my lips and a cold moist hand around my heart. Why would Antonio choose me over his wife and children? And me? I will be left here with Toad.

Trying to stand, blackness rises with me and I fall. There is a strip of purple light under the door. I crawl towards it, across the seagrass matting, penitent, my knees raked by the coarse fibres. Outside, it is evening, the orchard crowded with men, Italian men, the shadow of their beards blue on their faces like bruises. They stand around a fire and my wash copper hangs above the flames, a greasy spume boiling from its lip, and beside the fire, undulating on a wooden spaghetti box, is a man, John, wearing my dress with the dingo scarf knotted under his chin and my old rubber boots, and he lisps, "Come and eat, boys," in Italian but with a broad Australian accent and all the Italians laugh and Toad, standing back under the lemon trees, laughs too. Guffaws. John's face is smeared with white clay and he's wearing my dark glasses even though it's nighttime, and as he tucks his hair under the scarf, *my* scarf, I pull myself up on the banister and cry out, "Oh, stop! For heaven's sake, stop!" and then there is silence. The fire pops. Sparks fly up and strike the cauldron. The men's eyes are hidden in the shadows of their hats.

"Mother," says Toad, "Pet." He looks at the fire, at John and back at me. "You're up."

Someone giggles. And I realize with a rush of horror that I am no longer dreaming, that I am pregnant and wearing the thinnest of white nightgowns and that this is wet all the way down the back. Someone has been brushing at my hair but it falls all over me, wild, and I am barefoot and unclean.

"John! Give me my scarf." I point to his head, but he is already coming, the boots and the spoiled scarf held out. I knock them from his hands and almost fall with the effort. He reaches to steady me, his grasping hands coming far too close, and the spittle is out of my mouth and on the ground at his feet before I can think, before I can hiss, "Keep your hands off me."

John scrapes his face with the edge of his hand, as if the spit has landed there, and looks at the wet place on the splintered boards, the shiny dome of yellow-streaked mucus.

"*Serpente*," he says.

"No," I say, "you are the snake."

He kneels and, making the sign of the cross, sings, "*Croce e delizia al cor*," one hand on his heart, the other at his groin. "Not me," he says,

"I am not the snake." And he makes the horns.

"I saw you. In the river."

"Oh yeah? Such a *sporcacciona*. I didn't know you like to look. *Bellesponde*, beautiful arse, huh?" He stands and squeezes his buttocks and his hip juts. I can smell his fertile stink.

"I saw you doing things with Toad, despicable things, when we were all sleeping. That's why I wanted to leave."

"Toad is the *woman*," he says quietly, angrily. He steps closer. "He forced me."

"You're the one in the dress."

From where I had stood, watching from the bank, it did not look as if force was involved. The sounds, the splashes, the grunts, the cries, the usual stuff of mutual lust. "And I'd say nothing more about the subject, if I was you, unless you want the locals feeding you through a chaff cutter."

He stews for a moment and then turns and trips over the scurrilous dog, Mundungus, which has had its nose up his crack for five minutes now, confused over which man he smelled.

"John!" yells Toad and he runs and kneels next to the POW, but John hits at him with fists, turns his head away and scrambles to his feet. Toad is left there, in the dust, the dog licking his face with breath that reeks of rabbit.

"Well, good-oh then," Toad says. "Bonza. Bewdy. Glad you all could make it here to our lovely little shindig." He pats his pockets, searching for his watch, and, upon finding it, pops the lid. With a merry tinkle, the crystal falls out on his hand in tiny pieces. "Shit," he says bitterly. And offers the shards to the dog.

Shaking from the wind through my nightgown, I raise my voice, to John, to all of them, "You're a ridiculous lot. Look at you. Don't think you are free just because some stupid farmer lets you have a party in his orchard, lets you get drunk."

I see them wince, the moustache, the smoker, *il baffo, il*

fumo, tulipano, tormento, carbone, pezzolino, and the swamp, *padule*, my darling Toad. I see my own *ciabattino*, the cobbler, my Antonio, put his hand to his face, but it's not him I'm angry with. I hope he knows that. But Toad begins to stand and, thinking of him and John, I sink the boot in. I can't hold back.

"Until now you've had jailers and barbed wire but we didn't need to waste money on that. You do the job yourselves! None of you have escaped from here. None of you have even tried. You're pathetic. Do you hear me? Pathetic. Australian men, *real* men, would have been gone long ago.

"Just look at your limp leaders. The first sixteen Caesars were men who loved men. And your writers! Virgil with his Alexander! What is it with you Italians? Toad wants nothing to do with you. Just leave him alone."

"Oy," says Toad, "I can speak for myself."

"Shut up, Toad." Boss Cockie stirs in a tree and mutters, "Shut up. Shut up."

"Do you know what they say in our newspapers? I bet you don't . . . Hitler, your hero, is the pederast. Our good Australian men aren't deviants at all. You'd do best to remember that. Lad's love isn't on the menu over here. There is no third sex. Not here in Australia."

By God, the wind is cold. I shiver and the wet gown slaps against my thighs.

A sigh drifts from the crowd of men standing under the fruit trees; the gramophone needle touches the end of its groove and, scratching softly, moves backwards, again and again.

An unknown man, *il tosse*, coughs, and says, "What's that, Missus? What did you say?" They stare at me, hunching over their masculinity as if to protect it from my words, driving their slick shoes through the scurf of grass. I can hear the rattling of the dead stalks. Antonio steps from beyond the fire.

"We'll be sent back soon," he says. "The Allies have already taken the south." He's speaking for all of the men, but I think he, alone, doesn't wish to leave. The dog sniffs his wingtips, drips obsequious saliva on the glossy leather.

"Italy will never be free. There will always be foreigners running around," I say.

"But our friend Fritz will be gone."

"Oh. And Il Duce too. He'll be hung. He's probably been hung already. The Yanks will never let a fascist or a communist be in power over there."

"We choose our own rulers," Antonio says.

"You'll be lucky if the Italian people get to choose a ruler *fifty* years from now . . . you're invaded."

"We are rescued."

"Pooh!"

"We will be free."

"You are so stupid, Antonio. Italy now has ten thousand foreign soldiers running around its streets, legally raping its virgins, requisitioning all its food and housing, plundering its treasures and there's no reason in the world the Allies would want to give that up. It's not like Italy is some abominable sinkhole in Africa without a single decent restaurant. That, they might give up, but not Italy."

"Hen's brain. You speak as if the Allies are Vandal hordes, claiming my country for themselves."

"Oh no," I say, the words bitter as newsprint in my mouth. "They are smarter than that. They will never say that they have *invaded* your country. They will say they have *liberated* it from the evil Nazis. They are not occupying your country. No. They are merely helping to stabilize it, boost the economy, lend a hand where it's needed, but you wait and see. In fifty years, they will still be there."

"You are just picking a fight," he says, shaking his head, not listening at all. "I think you are angry at *me*, but take your anger out on my country."

Is that what I am doing? Why *am* I picking a fight? I want to punish Antonio in advance for the way I am sure he will abandon me. I want gibbous moons of his flesh underneath my fingernails.

"You think you're going home, don't you? Back to the wife and kiddies. But we still need you here and the oceans are full of German U-boats. You'll be kept here, a slave, until all our men are home."

"Is that why you are angry? Because one day I will return to Italy?"

"Why should I care about such a thing? You mean nothing to me."

"Many thanks," he says, blowing me a kiss, "for your blessings." He waves his hand, fanning me away from him. "I do not believe what you say. I am not surprised Toad's bed is in the sleepout. Some women wake up like flowers but when you wake up, the moon is crooked. I thought we were friends." He turns his back on me and returns to his countrymen.

He blew me a kiss. Suddenly, that's all I can think of. He blew me a kiss.

"That's right," says Toad, stepping up onto the veranda. "She doesn't know anything. Petsy," he says, turning to me. "Why don't you go have a bit of a lie down."

I give him a hard look that cuts right through his brain of margarine but he doesn't feel a thing.

"Come on, love," he says, tugging at my arm while I swat him. "These blokes is just having a party. Don't be too rough on 'em. Here. Have a sip of this beaut wine. They made it right here with a bit of this and that in one of me milk cans. Call it grappa but it's not just grapes, you know. All sorts of fruits."

I sink my burning face into the proffered glass and my palate, my gums, my throat go numb from the alcohol. I'd like to take back all my hard words to Antonio. I'd gladly stretch my neck out between the two nails on the chopping block and cut off my head with a blunt axe.

Toad drags me inside and behind us, Ponchielli's *La Gioconda* picks up speed, drowning out the murmuring of the men and the susurration of their hands against their trousers as they wipe away their contamination.

Later, in bed, I can't fall asleep. The grappa turns over and over in my stomach, the baby hiccups, the weatherboard walls move in and out and the swaybacked ceiling twitches.

"Toad?" I call. "Are you afraid of anything?"

"Huh?" he calls back. "What's set you off now?"

"I asked if you're afraid of anything." I shiver from the finger of cold wind running down my back. It is quiet out in the orchard now, deserted.

In the silence of Toad's answer, I get a strong whiff of Mrs. Walleye's stuffed tripe and banana sauce and hear the dog's claws click across the veranda.

If I was Toad, I'd be deathly afraid one of my neighbours would find out I really did like men instead of women and it's not just a rumor unkindly foisted on me by high-spirited young hoons. I might be afraid of being drafted or of the field catching fire or my wife changing her name and taking the children to a different country or falling into a full silo and drowning in the shifting wheat.

"Well, yeah," he says. "I'm not too keen on rats."

But that's not what I want. I don't want to know about the things that make him squeak. I want to know which things make him howl and beg for mercy. So I say, "I am afraid to be seen with my clothes off," just to get him started. Oh yes. This fear of mine keeps me from Antonio, from any man except Toad.

"Think I'm stupid?" he replies. "I know that. Remember that time when I busted in on you when you was, I dunno, dancing or something, in the nuddy in the washhouse? You acted like I'd bloody skinned you, wailing like a banshee, and you wouldn't look at me for months."

I remember it well. I was bathing in the only room with a lock, the laundry, and as I dried myself in the quiet, clean-smelling space, I began to hum and swing my hips, and only then became aware of Toad peeking in at me through the cracked door. He'd lifted the latch with the point of a knife. I slammed the door and began to scream through it, crying and frantic, ashamed and angry and all he could say was, "I was just getting an eyeful of me wife." Now that I know what Toad is capable of, it seems rather innocent. Theoretically pleasing. Only unusual in that it doesn't seem to be the way his desires run.

"Still," I say, "I really am afraid of that. I don't know why but it gives me the willies to have people look at me." The faint hiss of dead leaves tumbling through the grass. The banging of loose iron on the roof.

"I was afraid of me old man," says Toad, as if he might say something more, but then he laughs and says, "Everyone's afraid of their old man."

He breaks wind and sighs with pleasure. "You told me you was afraid of your old man."

"He wasn't really my father," I say.

"You used to be afraid of them blokes, Tony and John. I can't believe the way you woke up and came out raring to go. Sure gave 'em what for tonight. The way you had them blokes kowtowing to you. It was bloody amazing."

"Don't talk like that about them. Poor Antonio. He didn't deserve it."

Toad sniffs. "No. About time he got his comeuppance. It won't hurt him any. He's been way too full of himself recently, marching around this place as if he owns it. Ha! What was that you called him? A pederast? Did you make it up?"

I see again Toad clasped together with John at the river, and now, I wonder why on earth John responded to Toad's advance. I see Toad's stunted torso and the curlicues of peeling skin on his shoulders, his smooth shaven legs. A man who is not a man. And I am willing to overlook such things if Toad, too, will overlook my whiteness, my damaged body. But what does John see in him that I have never been able to see?

"Do you sometimes feel . . . ?" I ask.

"What? Spit it out."

I'm not sure what it is exactly. Do Toad's feelings for John mirror mine for Antonio?

"Loved," I venture, and there is the unearthly yowl of a cat on heat from under the house. I can't think how to ask what it is that John likes best about him, how he knew that John would respond to his caresses and not gut him with the fishing knife. Does he smile at John as I have smiled at Antonio? Does being with a man bring him joy? Does it bring out the tender love he has for the horses?

"Bugger it," Toad says, "I'm going to fix that bloody cat if I can get my hands on it. I'll wring its bloody neck." He throws his filthy boot at the wall and John wakes up, out in his hut, screaming from the night horrors, and the dogs snap at the bars of their cage, barking, and the rooster stands up on his toes and stretches his neck and crows, and the cockatoo screams, "Shut up! Shut up!"

"God, I hate this place," he says, hawking up a big one and

spitting it on the floor right where I will step on it in the morning. Antonio has never spat in my presence. Not even once. "It's a madhouse."

"Do you ever, oh, I don't know what, think that people . . . like you?'

I feel him looking in my direction, wondering. The trip to Moore River has changed him. Now he has begun to suspect me of the very thing he is guilty of. The cat yowls again, throttled by its own desire.

"No," he says, "I don't."

3

The solemn line of cows crest the rise to the shed, their morning whiskers wet with dew, udders swollen, teats full. Inside, they jostle, kick at the puppies tumbling in the gutter. One cow releases a flood of urine as it walks down the center and the others step daintily through the liquid, shine their splayed hooves in it. The children sweep the puddle into the gutter with their bare feet. Mudsey takes down a milking stool, the legs of which are blunt and uneven from years of being filed on cement, and closes the stanchions on the cows' necks. They press forward to eat the small pile of grain heaped before them. Their long mauve tongues stretch out endlessly, wetly, prehensile. In the low slanting light of dawn, the great swathes of spider web bunched from the beams glow golden and luxurious. The fly tapes twisting over the cows' backs seem like black lingerie, the cows warm and fertile, the splash of manure in the gutter smelling of the summer grass. It is silent except for the rhythmic grinding of the grain between cows' teeth. There is a yelp as one pup muscles another into the slurry.

I tie the soggy tail up out of the way and insert my awkward belly under the cow. I am like her now, swollen and dripping, waiting for gentle hands to relieve me. I wipe the cow's teats and throw the paper into the gutter, draw off two waste shots of milk and settle to draining the hot udder. Now the singing of the milk into the bucket is joined by the rustle of hay being pitched in tangled nests from the loft. Alf drags handfuls from the mass and shoves them towards the nearest cows, which brace their hind legs, hunker down, push uselessly with their massive shoulders against the metal pen, stretch out their necks and their tongues curl around the spun hay, dragging it closer until they can bite down on the goodness, lift it and shake it, golden dust raining down through the light and they settle to chewing, muffled as dawn on a foggy morning, with the eyes of the bull on their rear ends.

Toad tilts the bucket on his boot, milks swiftly with Clydesdale fingers, his head pressed into the hip hollow of the cow. Foam rises on the milk, the bull bawls, hay is pitched into his rick. The girl child, the small boy, their father, and I, milk. Silence. A breeze slides through the open door and strokes the cheeks, stirs the webs and the matted brushes of the tails.

When we are done and the cans of milk stand cooling in water, I want to ask Toad if Antonio will be sent back to Italy soon, or if he will be kept here for his labor. I feel like grabbing the front of his shirt and begging, but Toad's face is closed and he pushes past me, unseeing, and goes to saddle the horse. I almost call his name but his back is stiff, his shirt streaked with lines of salt from all the days when I have lain in bed and not washed his clothes, and his sweat has dried and dried again, like the water that rises through our land and leaves salt on the ground, spoiling the landscape, killing the soil. Vast lakes of salt sparkle just north of here, the Cowcowing Lakes, the Great Salt Plain, a crust of glittering white over bottomless, stagnant mud. A place where no bird calls.

There are twenty-seven small bones in the human hand, including eight rounded bones, like pebbles, held together with a network of ligaments and muscles, which form the wrist. There are more nerve connections between the hand and the brain than between any other part of the body. Every gesture we make is capable of providing powerful insight into our inner life.

Antonio is boiling bits of yellow root in half a kerosene tin and when

I get closer, I see he is dyeing leather. The roots give off a red color, so the Aborigines have told him, when the ash of a certain eucalyptus is added, but I think they are pulling his leg.

"You are very cruel." He throws a piece of root into the soup, splashing my dress. "I'm not talking to you. Telling us we are slaves!"

"Don't, then, but if it makes you any happier, I wish I hadn't said anything. It came out all wrong. I'm sorry."

He looks up.

Toad's abandonment has made me reckless. If he allows himself to love, why shouldn't I?

"I didn't mean you when I said all that nonsense in the orchard. I wouldn't say that about you. You are a good man."

I am almost gagged by these words. My mouth is dry and I clear my throat.

"Is that so? You think I am a good man?"

"Yes. Very good. Very kind."

"Is that all? Good and kind and nothing else?" He stirs the dye again and his gaze slips to my belly. "How is the baby? Does he move well?"

Toad never asks these questions. They make me squirm, and Antonio, seeing my embarrassment, changes the subject.

"There is much too much washing for you to do alone today. It is not a job for . . . " he hesitates and looks around,

" . . . my beautiful Gin."

The ground twists beneath my feet, as if I am standing on the back of a snake.

"This is not beautiful," I say, my face turned away and my hand where the child's head might be. "I am not beautiful." I pluck at the colourless skin on my forearm.

But he leans over the kerosene tin and says, "More beautiful than anything, a fertile woman in white." I promise myself I will not look at him again and look instead at his long, clean fingers. I can feel, quite distinctly, the thrust of the pulse in my own fingers.

"You are like the Venus," he says, "like the Maria in the church, smooth white marble, perfect. There is nothing more beautiful. Who tells you that you are not beautiful?"

I hesitate. "Toad." Shamefaced. "Everybody."

"We stop loving ourselves if no one loves us, Gin." He takes my hand between both of his, and holds it, warm and gentle, until I pull away.

"I will help you with the washing," he says, and so he does, despite my half-hearted protests, spending hours with me in the hot laundry shed, lifting the dripping sheets and cranking the handle of the mangle. Mudsey makes a puppet show for Alf with the broken pegs, both of them sitting in a big wicker basket. The peg without legs is Toad. I am the peg caked in cockatoo shit. Antonio's peg seems unbroken.

We work in silence, but I am exquisitely aware of Antonio's presence. There is a weight in odd parts of me that is pleasant and the longer I stand next to him, the stronger the sensation gets. His elbow touches mine. My hip touches his. Our bodies draw closer and closer, flowers bending towards sunshine in invisible motion. Mudsey gets up and takes Alf by the hand. The pegs fall from her opened lap into a tumble on the floor. "Come away from here," she says. She takes Alf's head between the palms of her hands and turns it to face the wall. He has been staring at us. "Let's walk to Melbourne." She tugs the little boy up, out of the basket, and leads him away. But were Toad to walk in, he would have no reason for suspicion. Nothing has happened. We are not like him and John, who rut like bunnies out in the fields and aren't ashamed to appear at dinner half-naked, sweating and laughing, their arms around each other's shoulders, smelling of sex.

Late in the afternoon, Antonio returns from watering the sheep, to help me take down the washing from the lines and carry the baskets inside. He sings, "*Maria lavava, Guiseppe stendeva, il figlio piangeva dal freddo che aveva*," over and over as he slips the pegs into their bag.

"What does it mean?" I ask, but he says it's just a nursery rhyme. Comforting. Nothing more. We fold the sheets together in the slanting golden light. The sheets are still warm from the sun and smell of the lavender water we rinsed them with.

"It's much better like this, for the child," he says, laying his hand on the front of my dress, just below my breasts. It startles me, but I don't pull away this time.

Before we go inside for dinner, he bends and wipes my old Wellington boots clean with a rag. My hand comes to rest, for a moment, on his head as he stoops. The wind sighs in the trees.

4

That night, driving the cows across the road, the lantern swinging in my hand, I am surprised by the sound of gunshots. I think they are gunshots, but it turns out to be the backfiring of trucks, and when I am only halfway across, army vehicles without their headlights on roar past heading north and the cows scatter into the night, bawling. The last truck swerves to avoid hitting our best milker and, instead, hits the stone gatepost and slowly capsizes on its side. Men in khaki jump out to stare at the wreck. Matches rasp and flare, cigarettes glow, their orange ends growing brighter and dimmer, and smoke drifts my way. The men wrangle over the best way to right the truck and no one seems to notice me, despite the way I must appear, as a roadside ghost.

"Hullo?" I say. "May I help you? Perhaps my husband can bring the team?"

Several men turn around, their faces tense, childishly peeved at the interruption.

"Yeah. Go on. You do that, love," says the nearest man. "Bloody twit," I hear someone else complain. "Who takes mongrel cows for walkies at night?" And far back, behind the truck, a single voice, "Shit. What happened to her?" But shouting over everyone, a city boy's voice, familiar and yet horribly out of place on the Cemetery Road. The voice conjures up a set of stumpy, orange-furred fingers, houses for fingernails buffed daily with egg white and flannel. These fingers dip into my mind, and stir up memories of another time.

"Malcolm?" I ask the darkness. "Malcolm McGuire?"

"Who's that? Who useth my name in vain?"

So it *is* him. My old arch rival in the music competitions, him of the tweed jackets, orange and green, and the bow ties and the damp red lips and the skin so thin the blood could be seen beneath it, moving in ugly rushes.

"It's only me, Malcolm. Gin Boyle."

Giggling from the soldiers.

"If you're gin, ducky, where's whiskey? I'll take whiskey."

"It's an old friend. A lady," he threatens in his unmistakable throaty contralto. I wouldn't want to hear how these men imitate him behind his back. "Give us a minute."

He strides toward the lantern, a soldier now, and peers at my face. Dusts his boots on the back of his trousers.

"Gin Boyle! What are you doing here? I thought you were off teaching at Liszt."

Everything I struggle to forget runs at me, leering, and it is all I can do not to sit down and bite my hands. Yet Wyalkatchem has been working on me these ten years. I'm a different girl than the one who played piano in Perth, and I won't let him see me cry.

"Silly boy. I've married a farmer and I've got three beautiful children. I live here now."

It's dark. He can't see my house, Joan's grave on the hill, the bathmat knitted from old stockings hanging from a nail on the back veranda, dripping. I could tell him any lie and he'd have to believe me.

"But what about your music?"

He means, don't I care that I'm playing for philistines, local larrikins more likely to pelt me with dirty underpants than applaud.

"What about you? Do you play in the army?"

"The army is temporary. But marrying a farmer . . . " His voice trails off. "God! What's his name?"

"Toad."

I hear his snort of disbelief, a puff of cigarette smoke lurches from his nostrils.

"What a bloody name, Gin. Hope he makes up for it." But I will never again rise to Toad's defense. I picture him, froglike, mating on the banks of the Moore River, his arms around John, streaks of black mud on his flanks. *Antonio.* I hold his name inside my clenched hands, inside my mouth. It almost comes spilling out.

The men strain to lift the truck, cows wail from ditches I'll have to get them out of in the morning; Malcolm stands beside me, watching.

"Hope we didn't clip any of the cows." He must have been driving. Lucky he didn't go through the windscreen. Lucky a cow didn't go through the windscreen.

"No. I don't think you did."

"We'll compensate you if there's any damage to your property."

"That really won't be necessary, Malcolm."

There is another pause, longer than the first and then he says, "You know, I always thought you were the best pianist I'd ever heard. Better than the people they brought in for concerts even. That first time I heard you, playing in the University competition, I wanted to go outside and eat rat poison, because I knew I didn't stand a chance. It was like nothing else existed for you but the music. You were always the best. No one could touch you."

And the day comes back to me, a hot December day when I was fourteen and we were puttering on the grass around the reflecting pond, a gaggle of potential piano illuminati, waiting for our results. We had already walked across the endless, squealing jarrah floor, been pinned by the eyes of the examiners to that instrument of torture, the backless piano bench, breathed and breathed again to calm our nerves and played our competition pieces with as much grace as we could muster, even though our formal clothes cut viciously under the arms and threatened to split across the back. Waiting just outside the door, you could hear the person who played before you, all their errors of judgement, and that first time, Malcolm was standing in line behind me, sucking a mint for his chronic bad breath, pretending to read Biggles.

I won that competition and every other competition I entered. Listening, appalled, Malcolm swallowed the mint before it was small enough and choked and was beaten on the back until he vomited and his mother scrubbed his mouth with her hankie and made him play anyway. I'm thankful I didn't hear him play. It can't have been good. I got to see him afterwards, when he came out and ran up to the reflecting pool and dived in between the lotus flowers.

"That was hell," he said, when he climbed out holding a mossy cricket ball he had found on the bottom. "I'm never doing that again. Who wants a game of cricket?"

We were supposed to wait for the results, but he led us off to the river, the Pied Piper of Perth or the King of the Lemmings, drying the ball on his crotch. There, on the narrow sandy beach, we cracked at the ball with slabs of spaltered driftwood that fell apart in our hands. We took turns bowling, but I'd never played. The ball dribbled from my hand and lay on the sand like spit.

"No! No!" he yelled from his place in front of the wickets. "Not like that. Here," he said, running up to me. "I'll show you."

He seemed not to notice my albinism, the way I'd swung wildly at nothing, unable to see the ball coming, my shyness. He grabbed my hand and pulled it behind and to the side, modelled the motion of bowling, showed me when to open my fingers and release the ball, and then ran back to his place.

"Come on," he commanded, "bowl!" but again the ball fell senseless to the sand.

He came and stood next to me, wondering how best to help. It was a hot day, and he was sweating in his wet clothes and without thinking, he unbuttoned his formal shirt, stripped it off and threw it on the ground. His singlet steamed in the glare from the river, small clouds of pond and perspiration lifting off his back and as he rolled his arm, demonstrating, I turned and saw the dark, curly hair in his armpit. I was horrified. The whole afternoon curdled. I dropped the ball and ran back, with tears in my eyes, to the University, where I found out I had won.

Afterwards, I would see Malcolm at every competition and he'd wave, pantomime hitting a sixer with an invisible bat, and the judges would choose me. He must have known he'd lose to me again, even when he got really good, when he became my main rival. He had every reason to be unpleasant, but he was unfailingly nice. And even then, in the face of his kindness, I didn't know what to do with those odd feelings I had for him, mostly gratitude for his incomprehensible liking of me, but also a pathetic little crush, and so I ignored him and didn't wave back, the temptation killed by the memory of the unchildlike hairs nestled under his arm.

Now I say, "That's nice of you to say, Malcolm. I always thought you played jolly well."

"Rubbish," he says. "No need to lie. My mother pushed me into it. Well, you know what she was like. Hello. It looks like they've got the truck upright."

He strides off to inspect the damage, taking my lantern and leaving me in the dark, but returns in a moment.

"Axle's broken," he says, not looking my way.

"I suppose we could put your men up in the shearers' quarters and sort you out in the morning."

"No," comes a voice from the hill. "No. Don't." It lifts all the hairs on my arms. No one turns. No one else hears it.

"We really couldn't. It would be far too much bother." But he's interested. He wants to see where I live, who I've married, and he can't keep this out of his voice. And only then do I wonder how he might view the unholy entanglement of John and Toad, Antonio and I.

"It's no bother at all." I manage to say. "We never get visitors. We'd love to have you."

"Right-oh then. If you promise you won't knock yourself out for us." And he shouts, "Missus Toad here is going to let us kip in her shearers' digs and probably throw in a hot feed in the morning too. Let's give her a huzzah, boys!"

I'm off, stumping down the driveway before he has to remind them to cheer, before he has to explain that I wasn't in some dreadful accident, before he has to order them not to stare.

The whole household is woken by the soldiers whistling "Colonel Bogey" and Malcolm, at the top of his lungs, merrily singing, "Hitler has only got one ball, Goering has two but very small, Himmler has something sim'lar, but poor old Goebbels has no balls at all." Of course, he joins the whistlers when they march closer to the house, but the bawdy version hangs in the orchard, vibrating amongst the fruit, and the children will hear it there in days to come and repeat it to themselves, under the house.

Malcolm and his men don't know we have prisoners on our farm. They may not even be aware such a program of prisoner labor exists. A lamp moves in the Italians' hut, but there's no mistaking the sound of twenty pairs of boots marching in time for anything other than what it is, no mistaking the smell of the bullying aftershave dispensed by the army, and the Italians don't come out, don't even lift a corner of their newsprint curtain and peek. I'm glad. I want to get Malcolm off the farm without him ever seeing Antonio.

"I'll have to telephone through to my commanding officer," Malcolm tells me after his men are settled. "They'll want to know about the accident. We're supposed to be heading up north. The Japs are bombing up there."

"Yes. I know, but we don't have a telephone," I say with a crooked smile of apology, slapping the kettle onto the stove, poking up the fire with a few sticks of kindling.

"Well then," says he. "No worries. Nothing to be ashamed of. The Depression got its claws into everyone. Mum even had to sell the Bentley, would you believe. Where's the nearest place that has a phone?"

This time I stand up straight and stare at him and it could be my mouth hangs open in the rude way of gilded youth everywhere.

"The nearest phone?" I say. "There used to be one in the Wyalkatchem pub but it's been out of order for ages. But we can take the gig in to the siding in the morning and Mrs. Flannigan at the post office can fire off a telegram."

"Bloody hell, Gin! You may as well be living on the moon! Your bloke had better be worth it."

He says this smiling, thinking it's true, and I don't want to be here when Toad walks in to toast his toes on the open oven door and the smell of gently warmed fungus fills the house and Toad, relaxed and comfortable, pulls white pieces of diseased skin from between his toes and eats them.

No one from my life in Perth has ever been here, no one has wanted to come and I—prideful—have not wanted them to come. It's a sad state of affairs to be ashamed of my own home, my children running around in bleached flour sacks with wheat seeds germinating in the dirt underneath their fingernails, the nest of mice I've been feeding that live in the plush armchair, my husband's collection of Edwardian corsetry out in the machine shed, the beautiful Italian in the tin shed, and most of all, myself.

"Come on, Malcolm," I say, hustling him from the kitchen. "Let's bring the tea out to the shearers' quarters. There's more room over there." I carry the kettle and he brings a rattling tray of stacked cups. As we pass the Italians' hut, there is a flick of light and he asks, "Who lives in there?"

"The hired men," but when I see him frown, wondering where we found able-bodied men during war time, I add, "They're POWs. The government has a program that allows farmers to hire them, since it's dead hard to get any Australian laborers. They've all gone off to fight Jerry."

"You have Krauts in there?" he asks, stopping suddenly. A single cup rolls slowly off the tray and falls in the dirt, cracking in two.

"Italians. They don't let the Germans out to work because we're still at war with them. The Italians signed a treaty. We've been learning a bit of their language so we can speak to them. It's jolly good fun."

Malcolm puts the tray down carefully and slips the broken shards between the cups, then steps onto the hut's veranda and examines the door.

"You haven't locked them in," he says.

"They're men. Not animals. And anyway, where can they go?"

"That's not the point," he says, angry, his voice rising, and I see that he, too, has changed with the years. "It's the law. You're supposed to lock these devils in at night. They could murder you in your beds."

"Don't be silly," I say. "They're our friends."

A shudder goes through him. He touches the line of ribbons on his breast pocket.

"That kind of comment is completely out of line, Gin. Married women can't be friends with foreign men. It's utterly inappropriate." He pauses, steps down from the veranda and picks up the tray. "These men are trained to take advantage of women whenever they can. It's all they think about. Believe me: you'd never want to be alone for a minute with these animals." Passing me with his tray, he says, "Pull yourself together. It's only a cup that's broken."

5

Before first light, Toad rolls from his bed and dashes out to the dunny to empty his bowels before the line of jigging soldiers snakes around the house.

"John!" he bellows from his throne. "Get the gig ready. I've got to take these jokers into town."

When there's no response, he kicks the door viciously for a while to get the POWs' attention and then bawls again, "Rattle your dags, you mob! I've got business in town."

The Italians cross from their hut to the veranda, buttoning their shirts, unshaven, and stick their heads in the open kitchen window.

"Need help, Missus? Wood?" asks John. He leaves the top three buttons on his shirt undone and strokes his hairless chest.

"God, you're revolting. Go find yourself something to do," I say.

"You will need a lot of bread today." Antonio smiles, lips only. "We heard the men last night. Who are they?"

"They're soldiers. They had an accident. Overturned their vehicle. Listen, Antonio, can you come in the kitchen and give me a hand with the bread? I think John can manage all right with the horse." I want to get Antonio under cover.

"That is right," says John. "Antonio is too good with his hands."

He makes a lewd gesture at his crotch, clearly visible from where I stand, and I snap, "I do wish you'd stop that, John. It's dreadfully crude."

"I got you!" he laughs. He pretends to be an aviator and flies away, arms out, buzzing the rabbit cage, strafing Mundungus. A manic kookaburra gurgles in the gum, like some berserker run amok in the bush.

"You wanted me at last." Antonio feeds sticks into the firebox. "I thank God." He kneels quickly, crosses himself, blows a kiss heavenward.

"Oh do get up. You'll get me into all kinds of bother. There's twenty soldiers out in the shearers" quarters just itching for action. Let's make sure the only kind they get is with their teeth. Tea. Toast with their eggs. It's just the bread I want you for. The kneading."

"Yes," he says, smiling. "I feel it too. The needing."

He stands and leans on the bracket above the old Metters stove, watching me stir the milky porridge and fry the bacon, but his weight upsets the shelf, and the bowl holding the sponge for the bread slides off and shatters on the linoleum.

"*Cazzo*!" hisses Antonio, and I drop the spatula on the stove top, where it slowly turns black. "I am killed."

A triangle of green glass sticks out of his calf, and a line of blood runs into his sock. His beautiful shoes are covered in grey, yeasty foam.

That foam is the starter for our bread for the next three days, and until I can grow more yeast, we will have to eat unleavened damper. Antonio stoops to pull out the glass, and the trickle of blood swells, red waves crest and spill down his leg.

"Stop." I kneel and press my thumb hard against the cut. "Don't move." I am on my knees, staring at Antonio's shoes, the child in my belly kicking my thighs. My finger on his skin, his eyes on my back. I don't wish to be caught like this. I find it embarrassing to be this close to his legs and their dark fur, his skin hot under my hand.

"You did that on purpose," says Malcolm. He stands in the doorway, his hands on his hips, his feet wide apart. "Dago bludgers taking the food out of the mouths of decent Aussie blokes. Typical. It's sabotage. And you," he says, handing Antonio a rag to wrap around his leg, but meaning me, "are disgusting."

"It was an accident. Antonio was just leaning on the shelf; I've done the same thing myself. Toad never put it together right and it's wonky."

"And the invisible Mr. Toad doesn't mind having Joe Casanova here drooling all over his little lady?"

"Antonio was helping me, Malcolm. That's what he's here for. And he got hurt."

"Ah," he says, "That's how you became so *friendly*. Get back to your quarters," he barks, pointing at Antonio.

A tap at the window. No one is there.

Antonio holds out the broken crockery. "I sorry," he says. "It is mistake. I too stupid." His English has regressed. Even while he rolls over and shows his belly, no challenge in his louvered eyes, he doesn't leave me.

A bee hits the open window, then bumbles along the glass and finally weaves into the kitchen, towing a tiny cigarette paper banner, tied to its waist with a white hair.

"What the hell!" Malcolm stutters for the bee. Boss Cockie screams, "Shut up! Shut up! Bad bloody cockie." Antonio covers his mouth with his hand. Several more bees follow the first, a fleet of buzzing biplanes on wobbly flight paths, all trailed by fragile Tallyhos, marked "Heil Hitler!" and "Vive Il Duce!" and, incongruously, "Happy Birthday."

Malcolm snatches a bee from the air, his eyes ominous, and spits, "Heil Hitler!" He crushes the bee in his hand, yelps with surprise, scrapes the dead insect onto the floor and plucks another one. He's boiling. It's "Vive Il Duce!"

"This is what bloody well happens when you don't follow orders. Anarchy."

He slams the window shut. Antonio edges for the door, I edge for the cleaver, and into this bubbling porridge comes Toad. He ogles my hand on the cleaver, Antonio rattling the door handle, the minefield of apian kamikazes and the froth on Malcolm's lip. Dear Toady comes in with the hair on his belly bouncing, his face split with delight. He's such a child.

"Good morning all," he says, grabbing Malcolm's arm and swabbing the froth with a handkerchief stiff from misuse. "We'll have you right as rain. Don't get your knickers in a twist. Gin told me all about the way you pranged the government's rolling stock last night. Good one! I wish they'd let me have a go at driving one of them trucks but they reckon I'm too important where I am. Gin tells me you can raise Cain on the pianer. What about giving us a bit of a concert before brekkie?"

Cold air slides off Malcolm's epaulets and runs over Toad's hands, unfelt.

"No?" says Mr. Toad. "Ah well. Who can blame a chap? There's no competing with our Gin. She's a bottler! Antonio tells me she could have been the next Beet Haven." Antonio grins. "But she married me instead. Lucky girl. Well, enough of the jaw flapping. I'm pining for a bit of fried spam this morning . . . it's the go on a hot morning. How bout you, Mal'?"

"You're addressing an officer," says Malcolm, pulling away, swabbing his mouth with a white fist. "I'd appreciate a little respect."

"Yeah, well, mate . . . wouldn't we all. It's a bloody crime, what the world's coming to."

"Beethoven," I say. Limp.

Toad flops into his chair and unbuttons the top two buttons of his fly. Has a scratch.

"Spam!" he purrs, "excellence in a tin. Why are you hovering, Antonio? Go help John with the nag. Somehow, you're always in the kitchen when there's work to do." Turning back to Malcolm, Toad says, "I'd love you to come see me collection. It's first rate. You can take a gander before we head off."

"Erm," says Malcolm. "Are you a philatelist?"

"No. Not that kind of collection," I say, before Toad can answer. "He wants to show you the sheep. He's really built up the flock." I lift the cleaver slightly in Toad's direction.

But Toad just laughs and thumbs his nose at me. "Don't threaten me with the cleaver, woman. I'm the boss in me own home. I'll show your friend whatever I have a mind to, and right now I want to show him me unmentionables."

Malcolm blushes.

"Corsets," I rush in. "Toad collects women's stays. He has a rather impressive collection of them, actually. All colours. Arranged by size. He's made cunning little stands for them so you can turn the corsets round and see the laces down the back. He's an artist."

"You naughty man," says Malcolm drily. "But I'd rather not. Thank you anyway. Perhaps another time." He raises an eyebrow at me. "I believe, however, we need to discuss another matter."

The window is lifted slightly, another bee eases in and Mudsey and Alf bob up, their faces red with suppressed laughter. From the direction of the dunny comes the sound of men fighting, a dog's yelp, an almighty crash as the crapper is tipped over and mobbed by a herd of desperate characters. Malcolm glares at me. "Bedlam!" he says as the last bee zags past his head, and he stomps outside to try to regain control.

I almost collapse against the red hot stove in my relief.

"What a prawn," says Toad, tilting his chair back against the wall and propping his foot up on the table to inspect his flaking toes. "I can't see what you ever saw in him."

"I was *never* sweet on him," I say, and try to convince myself that it's true. At least, I was never sweet on this Malcolm.

"Like fun," he sniggers. "You've got his love letter stapled to your forehead, along with another one I could mention." He draws a capital A on the table and waggles his eyebrows at me. "Eh, Gin?"

"Here's your spam," I say, slapping the enamel plate down in front of him, not careful of his toes, desperately anxious to get him out of my kitchen. I'm juggling razor blades here.

He slings back the tinned dog and the bubble and squeak, drains the cup of hot tea and belches into his hand.

"Bloody Mudsey," he laughs, kicking aside the broken bees on his way out. "I taught her that. Old Alfie was laughing fit to bust. And did you cop the look on old Sergeant Malarkey's face when he seen them bees coming in the window?"

"Toad!" I call, running after him as he scrabbles up the side of the gig. "I can't find my scissors anywhere. Do you think? I hate to ask, but I really need them. Do you think you could buy me a pair in town against the egg money?"

"You've got to keep a better eye on your things, Pet. You're a terror for losing this and that. Where'd that Mal fella get off to?"

"Malcolm? I took him out the back and shot him. Where do you think? You heard the lavatory fall over."

"Well, go get him."

When I return with Malcolm I ask again. Beg. "The scissors?"

"We'll see," he says. "Whacko the diddly-oh!" and he waves the whip over the horse and she lunges forward, straining, the wheels grating against the small stones of the road, the harness rising, stiff, but the gig doesn't move.

"Bugger it," Toad yells, ashamed of his apparent lack of skill in front of my old flame, and he whips the horse hard. "Bloody hay burner! I'll feed you to the sharks, I will." He wants to make sure Malcolm knows it his not his fault. It is the animal.

The mare rears on her thick legs and plunges forward, and

there is the sound of rending metal, wrenched nails, splintering wood, and then, with a final squeal, the gig is away, towing half of our new fence, posts popping out of the ground like corks, along with a great boiling mass of barbed wire, the air explosive with the smell of hot summer dirt and creosote. The mare panics, her eyes rolling, foam dripping from her mouth. She sidles and rears again, twists back, and strikes at the wire.

Antonio and John are almost wetting themselves, they are laughing so hard. "We got you a good one that time, Toad! We got you a good one, huh!"

Toad tumbles down in front of the wheel to see what they have done to the gig. While he was making love to his spam, the Italians took off the far wheel, fed the axle through the fence, and then reattached the wheel on the other side. They are unfazed by the damage. They built the fence and they'll fix it too, cracking jokes and warbling their favourite operas. I don't mind. The fence is right outside my kitchen. I'll be able to hear Antonio all day and maybe that was his intention.

"Ha!" Toady laughs. "By crikey! That's a good one. I didn't see that one coming!" He cuffs John lightly around the ears, punches Antonio in the most casual possible way, in the privates. But he punches him hard and then looks straight at me, daring me to change the expression on my face, while Antonio groans. "Oops," Toad says, smiling. "Sorry about that." The pet cockatoo makes a sound like a clock being wound up.

Antonio untangles the wire and releases the horse while John calms her with a meat pie. She lips at his hair and neck, and blows streams of moist air down his shirtfront. John looks round at Toad and lifts his thumb. "Works good, boss," he says, patting a leather pouch which hangs around his neck. They smile at each other.

I know it is coming. I have felt it coming since the first post popped from the ground and tilted and fell behind the gig. The sweat boils on Malcolm's fiery skin. Clouds race over his head, sucking up his steam in a shimmying tornado. He stands up in the gig, enormous, and the mare, unnerved, flicks an ear back at him and stamps.

"You there. You men. I will be reporting you to the POW Control Centre for insubordination and reckless behavior. I am a witness here to the most appalling conduct by enemy prisoners and I will not stand idly by and ignore it." Antonio hooks his thumbs through his belt loops. John makes a noise with his mouth that makes Toad laugh. "In addition, I believe there is illegal fraternization going on here. I am horrified, in fact, at the extent of it." He mutters some dark oath, looking at Toad and John now. "I believe this will be of most definite interest to the Commander of the camp. It is my duty as an officer of the Royal Australian Armed Forces to report this breach and to recommend the immediate removal of such prisoners."

Antonio and John both burst out laughing. Toad snickers. But I am not amused. If the men are removed, and the reasons divulged, we will both be destroyed.

"Get the egg out of your bum, mate," says Toad, closing on the gig, a stick in his hand. Antonio and John rise slowly. "Tell you what," Toad says, and the mare sidles away from him, rolls her eyes at the stick, "Tell you what. You take yourself into town. We've got better things to do than lark around with dingoes." Just before Toad whips the horse brutally across the flank, Malcolm sees the stick, the danger, and he drops to the bench, grabbing for the reins. Some of the barbed wire is attached to the axle and, dragging behind, it keens in a piercing B flat and strikes a shower of sparks from the stony road. A rabbit darts in front of the wheels and there is a snap as its back breaks, a moment in which I look away, and when I look back again, the gig is skidding over the cattle grid, taking the turn to town on one wheel.

The little bunny has dragged itself to the side of the road. Its hind legs aren't moving. It lies on the warm rocks and its body swells to a horrible size, and collapses, swells again and collapses, and then falls still. Mundungus walks over to sniff the corpse. The dog noses the rabbit, breathes deeply of its death smell, the dog's face sharp and hungry. I turn away to go inside and bang at the Bechstein: Ravel's *Pavanne Pour Une Infante Défunte*. Requiem for a dead rabbit.

We are isolated, but we do not invite isolation; every stretch of road has its markers for the lost. And the roads themselves have local names, friendlier than the ones given them by government workers who have never seen a fly-blown sheep. There's the Pig Slurry Stretch and Metholated Mavis's Gully and Kickastickalong. Every farm has its kerosene tin wedged between two stumps, or its Coolgardie safe on top of a Model T, and the people here say swing left at the kero tin or turn in at the motor and everyone knows what they mean. Antonio has hung a green milking stool from a stringy-bark at our turn-off. Toad's stool. Toad's tool. Toadstool.

Mister Cleverish will tell Malcolm that Toads live out on Cemetery Road, but he won't be able to find any road signs; they've all been taken away to foil the Japs when they invade. The blacks out the back of the pub will point in several directions, at the sky even. Mrs. Flannigan will pull up her skirt and show off her varicosities, take out her teeth and wipe them on her wincey petticoat and shower him with spit. She will nod and agree with him when he says Virginia Toad is a filthy slut. The baker, a man who shot off his big toes on purpose in the Great War, will smile and shrug, his rheumy eyes on Malcolm's decorations. And down at the siding, Kenny MacKenzie, readying the day's shipment to

Perth, of eggs and milk and butter and letters, will pretend deafness when asked for directions and offer Malcolm a hot beer, a wooden chair on castors, a plat of the township, a tanned kangaroo testicle bag filled with the bones of a mouse that was killed by an overly energetically flipped pancake which he found behind his Waterford stove and a piece of the pancake which he has had shellacked for evidence, and, when all this fails, a penny to put on the rail before the train comes. Kenny will drag Malcolm outside by the hand and show him the tracks and just for a moment, Malcolm will be afraid, will think that maybe, just maybe, Kenny is planning on tying him to the rails and seeing him cut neatly in three by the train, but then he will look at Kenny's idiot face, at the cluster of flies lounging in the spit running from his lips, and he will laugh at himself. He will feel foolish to be afraid of a retarded man. But he will be wrong. Because one day, after the war has ended and refugees are camped down near the train station, in the Reffo Camp, Kenny will tie one of those Balks to the rails just before the train to Perth rolls through. The man's screams will alert Mrs. Flannigan, her post office conveniently being built on the railway side of the main street, and she will squat next to the man and tell him that lying on the cold ground gives you hemorrhoids. She will say that she is one to know, before she makes him promise not to lie on the ground anymore and then, and only then, will she untie him, just twenty-three seconds before he is due to be mincemeat. Wyalkatchem would have been famous had this event occurred, and there are those amongst us who feel she should have been stopped because who wants a bunch of foreigners dirtying up the town anyway and it would have been a good lesson to them. But no.

Instead, Malcolm returns from town with the news that Felice Marasco—an Italian POW—has gone and gotten himself killed by falling backwards into a scarifier, and as a result, the

Control Centre was in an uproar and Malcolm could get no one interested in his story about the sorry goings-on out at Toad's except the old biddy at the post office, who fed him lamingtons and eels.

He's still buried here, is our Felice, and I feel most kindly toward him for protecting Antonio and me with his death. Even after all the dead POWs were rounded up one last time and replanted in some sanitized, deodorized, sterilized cemetery where there's not well-fed worms all over the place after it rains, they somehow managed to overlook poor old Felice, or maybe they never could find him to begin with. That's the kind of grip Wyalkatchem gets on you, with the result that he's out there now, in Wyalkatchem Cemetery's Roman Catholic section, in grave number fourteen. I still put flowers on his grave.

6

Antonio and I search for my scissors without much hope while Malcolm is in town. Things that are lost here stay lost. I am sure that while I was sleeping away Toad's dalliance with John, my most useful tool has surrendered and been sent to the penal colony for wayward implements: shovels used to decapitate snakes, tinsnips used to trim nails, scissors that sit up and beg for clemency when they see seven-year-old girls coming with paper and glue.

"Mudsey!" I scream, "get in here now!" I'm oblivious to the stunned mullet stares of the soldiers, Antonio's hand on my arm, the criticism of the cockatoos. "Mudsey! Where are you?"

A fat branch snatched from the ground and slapped across the corrugated tin siding of the Italians' hut emits a bullroarer of a noise, an ancient hungry bunyip's bloodyell, which Malcolm hears on his way to town and mistakes for a canon exploding.

"Yes, Mum," says the sorry cat's breakfast, wombatting out from under the house.

"Where's my scissors?" I storm. "Whenever I need my tools, they're gone. I can't stand it. They're *my* tools. No one else can have them. I don't have to share. No one else can touch them. Do you understand? You better find them right now!"

"I dunno where they are," she says, oh that little liar. "It was Alf what took 'em, I think. Shall I get him for you?"

"You stay right here. Alf!"

I surprise myself with this anger, and the more I crush it, the more it oozes out in the oddest places. Like a banana in a baby's fist. The stuff has to go somewhere.

"Alf! Where are my scissors?"

He, too, crawls from under the house, the sabotaged scissors clutched in chubby fingers and I run at him, then stop short and scream with frustration and disgust, stamping my foot, biting off every fingernail, past the quick, and spitting out the parings.

"You rotten kids. Nothing is sacred in this house. Nothing. Look at this . . . " I yank the scissors from his hands, shake them in his face. "Destroyed! The two sides can't even come together. What use are they?" Louder and louder. I stab with the scissors. Look sky! Look trees! Look earth! Look house! Look hills! This is what I have to suffer. The blades of the scissors hiss through the air, agape. This separation. This loss. "Oh, what's the use?" I cry and throw the scissors at the tree, hoping they'll take off someone's ear.

The soldiers watch this freak show and what a beauty it is: pregnant, mad albino, throwing knives at dwarves in flour sacks. Nice. Couldn't get in for a quid, and here, it's laid on for free. They're sitting in the branches of our flowering gum, safely out of harm's way, and I, feeling ridiculous, make a dash for the dunny and bugger-it-all-to-hell, it's still lying on its side, useless as any kind of haven.

Without turning around, I stand at the edge of the pit and brush at the flies which rise from the shit to stamp on my face.

"It's customary to repair things you break," I say, almost politely.

"La!" says the man who thought I'd been dipped in acid. "In't she fancy?"

The monkeys, however, swing down and lift the outhouse back on its footing, daintily spread the bougainvillea back over the roof and open the door for me, hats in hand. Ladies first.

Inside, I stare at Toad's painting of Italy, of the tall Italian man walking the hills, and I weep. What else is there to do?

And when I am done and stand to cast my offering into the hole, the newly rearranged bougainvillea letting in more light, I see scraps of white winking seductively from the bowels of the earth, white lace, familiar, and something falls inside me. For loss doesn't end.

It's not the way my children think. That if your dog dies, your cat won't die too. The dog will die and the cat will die and the child will die, and the sand from the desert will cover their bones, deeper and deeper, until no one remembers they ever existed, and the sand will be blown by the easterly winds out to sea and the grains will sink beneath waves that can't imagine a place where there is no water. And the man from the desert will be carried away by a boat that will cut through those waves and he won't even look back to see what was left behind. That is loss. That is loss.

Mudsey is forced to dredge up the remains of my mother's wedding dress. She asks if I want the doll too and I shrug. I don't care. She brings the lace, the doll's shoe, a decapitated leaking body of white leather with a broken finger laid on top, like a little corpse worm.

There is enough unsavaged fabric left for two small dresses.

"Wash your hands, Maud," I say, "and take your brother inside with you."

"Mum," she says, quivering, her hands placed delicately, the bones showing, "why did you stop liking me when Joan died?" She twitches on one foot, afraid of the answer, desperate for the answer, and I don't give it to her. I lie.

"Silly sausage," I say, "I'm very angry with you now, but it's not because I don't like you. It's because you ruined your grandmother's dress and Joan has nothing to do with that. Of course, in general, I still like you."

It almost chokes me but that's what I say.

I've never noticed before but I see it now: her eyes fade a little, from blue to grey and her face comes to an invisible point, about five inches in front of her nose. She nods, once.

"Yes," she says. "That's right."

Mudsey worries me. She is the one who carries all our secrets and does her best to hide them from the world. She calls out for a glass of water when Toad and I argue in the night. "Please, Mum?" she says. On the days when I am pounding my piano, lost in *The Moldau*, she takes Alfie by the hand and walks him out to the main road and back, again and again. "We're walking to Melbourne," she says, "and when we get there, we'll meet the King." She was my second born and until I saw the dust of dark hair across her scalp, I hadn't known it was possible for me to bear a child that looked like Toad, not like me.

When Toad isn't around to help me, Mudsey tries to, and she's been hurt carrying wood or hauling water or feeding the beasts. They're not jobs for a seven year old.

She watches me with her unwavering blue eyes, and I catch her later, practicing my accent, my gestures, as if she wants to be me. God help her. And now that Antonio's here, I catch her watching the two of us, every smile we share a smack in her face, and I wonder how long it will be until she tells Toad. Or maybe she won't tell him. And that might be worse.

Sometimes I think she'll be all right once I send her down to boarding school in Perth. She'll find out how the better classes behave, the way most fathers keep the rain off with an umbrella, not a kangaroo skin, the trick of being friendly towards people that you can't bear. But sometimes I think she'll hate it, and she'll run away and thirty years later she'll be living on a remote station by herself, running an animal refuge, letting kangaroos hop around her kitchen and cockatoos nest in her drawers. She'll have grown disgusted of public opinion, her hair will hang in a long snarl down her back, her legs will go unshaven, her clothes will stay unwashed, she'll pick up the kangaroo droppings with her bare hands and leave them next to her dinner plate to use later, as fertiliser in the garden.

No. It's not just the wood and the water and the beasts that have hurt her. Toad and Antonio and I have hurt her too, a more lasting kind of hurt to her character that I'd do anything to erase.

Malcolm brings back an expensive pair of scissors, a present he says. I cut out two dresses for Antonio's little girls before dinner on the floor in the lounge room, while Malcolm plays the Prelude to *Lohengrin*. He'd asked me to play something for him, and I'd just launched into Beethoven's *Hammerklavier* sonata, when he strode over, pressed his hands down over my hands, and said, "You always were a dreadful showoff." I am too. I would only play that piece for another pianist. To intimidate him. But Malcolm wouldn't listen, so I suppose I got what I wanted. His acknowledgement that, after all, I hadn't gone to seed.

"I won't have your man at the table," Malcolm says, pausing in the middle of the Wagnerish rubbish he's playing. The ticking of the mantel clock and the thumps of possums fornicating in the roof fill the room. "I don't care how friendly you've been until now. That man is dangerous. Your bint, what's her name? Mud? What kind of name is that anyway? Just be done with it and call her Keiko-san or Brunhilde. Your Mud told me you took both of those men on holidays with you! And they run around in civvies and where they got them from is as plain as day. Next you'll be telling me you give that Antonio the family gun and have him patrolling the perimeter."

I look up from the floor, my mouth full of pins and calmly say, "I do give him the gun."

"It's a crying shame," he says, the lid of the piano slammed to emphasize. "You used to be a decent sort." Lips drawn up like a woman's purse, he snitches around my pattern pieces. "Don't set a place for me. I'll eat with my men."

"Malcolm?"

"What, Gin?"

"Did you ever get married?"

He stares at me for a moment, his hand on the glass doorknob, and a muscle in his cheek jumping.

"I don't know why you ever married that disgusting Toad. There were men who liked you in Perth, educated men, and you were brilliant at the piano. You just went and threw yourself away. Where's your self-respect?"

"No one liked me. You're wrong about that."

"What in God's name made you do it?"

"He's a kind man. Works hard. Never killed anyone. That's more than you can say for half the men in Australia."

"He's illiterate!"

It's too awful, having to defend Toad. I think many of the same criticisms to myself, but I can't let Malcolm think there is any rift between us, or he really *will* report us.

"Don't exaggerate. He wanted me. No one else wanted me. From where I'm standing, that's pretty good."

"I liked you."

"You never liked me Malcolm. You don't like me now. Look at you. Your face has gone a horrible color."

"I did like you."

"Rubbish. You're confusing pity with liking. They're not the same thing."

"You had a lovely smell, like apricots. That day, when we played cricket. I could smell your skin on my hands afterwards."

"You didn't answer me. Did you ever get married?"

"No," he says and then, "my Mum told me albinos are sterile. She said you'd never be a mother, and see. You're not." And he goes through and shuts the door.

7

Earlier, Antonio, seeing me carrying the ruined dress, came and helped me fold it, and he said, "I remember this dress," as our hands met and parted, met and parted in the folding. Small black beetles pattered down as we shook the lace between us, and they rushed for the shadows cast by our legs.

"You want to be with me, Gin," he said, and the side of his hand touched the side of my hand. "Admit it." He slowed his movements, the sensation of closeness, of contact, almost unbearable.

In the corner of my eye, I saw Mudsey trotting towards the

orchard with a bucket swinging from her hand.

I held a finger to my lips to hush him.

"I am pregnant, and you have a wife," I said. "Children. Don't do this to them."

"My wife is a saint. A holy woman. A Madonna. But she expects me to live and be a man. It is usual in Italy, for a man to have more than one woman. Francesca will not be sad. Life is good for her, I think. I brought the whole family to Sant'Anna, very high up in the mountains and there, no one will find them. Now," he said, "I will save you too."

"I don't need your saving," I said. "I don't need your help." Malcolm had said that Antonio was dangerous, and he was. I was afraid of what might happen.

"Come here, Gin." He tugged at the fabric we held between us, towing me to the orchard. I went with him, but my heart hammered in my chest. He could have asked me for anything. Almost anything.

"When will you let me take your photograph?"

I shook my head. No no no no.

"Why don't you take a picture of Mudsey and Alf?"

"I already have photographs of them. I want one of you." He took my chin in his hand. "Look up," he said, "what do you see?"

"I can't see well. You know that I can't." I closed my eyes, afraid of so many things; that he would insist on taking my photograph, and later, looking at it closely, decide that I was not beautiful, not his kind of woman; that Mudsey and Alf would come to hate me for my betrayal, the slow and steady distancing from them that began well before Antonio ever came to our farm; that Malcolm would return from town and notice Antonio and I standing close together in the orchard. I had this morbid fear that Malcolm would mention my infidelities to my stepfather, down in

Perth, and somehow that worthy gentleman would be able to reclaim me. I couldn't keep my hands from trembling. It was as if I was shaken by an earthquake.

Photographs of Albinos. The Wonderful Lucasie Family from Madagascar! They have pure white skin, silken white hair and pink eyes! Their pink eyes stay open while they sleep! Exhibited at P.T. Barnum's Museum of Freaks and Wonders for three years running! The young son, Joseph, how strange and marvellous, can play the violin like a normal child. See how he holds the instrument in his white hands?

The man behind the camera disgusted with his work, the place, the smell of the elephants leaking through the canvas. Squeeze together now. Lift your foot. Just so. He puts powder in the shovel. A flash! A pop! They cry out and cover their eyes and he takes a picture of that too. There's a book in this yet. *Monsters of the Gilded Age: The Photographs of Charles Eisenmann.* It'll sell a million.

Smile for the camera, Gin. Smile.

"Just look. What do you see?" Antonio asked again, softly, and I opened my eyes.

"The children are picking berries. Mudsey is lifting up the bucket so Alf can put the fruit inside."

"Why are they doing that?"

My eyebrows bunched together. I couldn't think what he meant, but I knew his questions were leading me somewhere.

"Maybe they are hungry?" I ventured, wanting to say the thing that would please him.

He exhaled and ran his hand through his hair. His breath smelled faintly of aniseed. "Come on, Gin. You're not stupid. You can do better than that. You are a musician. Think about harmony and melody. They are separate and different, but when they flow together, they are so much more than each by itself, full of harmonics and overtones, fluid."

I blinked and squinted, more than ever an ugly albino in gumboots. But I attempted an answer for the only one who had ever called me beautiful.

"Partners? They work together?"

"Yes," he said. "The fruit that Alf picks would be bruised without Mudsey there to hold up the bucket."

"So?"

He stepped closer to me, very close indeed, his breath stirring the fine hairs on my face, and he looked at me with an amused smile. Small lines pleated the skin at the corners of his eyes. The smell of wood smoke clung to him. "They are each watching the other, to be ready to help when needed. They move together." His hands undulated, so suggestive that I looked away. "In harmony. Even a three year old has it all figured out."

He pushed the folded material into my arms. "Go clean your dress. I know you are sad to see it like this. I will make spaghetti for the soldiers."

"Why do you like me?" I said, not wanting to let him leave. I held the dress against my heart, to fend off his answer. "Why are you so nice to me?" The silk was rough in my hands. Catching on my calloused fingers.

"*Gingilla*," he said, with such tenderness that I almost cried out, "it is not liking that I feel for you."

The skin of my face melted. The muscles of eyes and cheeks and lips softened. I could feel myself changing. Oh yes.

"I hate you," I said. "You only want to photograph me because you are going to leave. After the war, you'll forget me."

"No. You will always be with me."

I felt as if I would suffocate. The fabric fell from my hands.

I knew then that I could break free of this place. That I was going to live in Italy. I ran my damp fingers across his cheek, his lips, his other cheek and then brought them to my mouth, tasting his salt. The sweat from his skin.

"Thank you," I said.

He called Mudsey *Pappogalla*, parrot, because of her chattering. He called Alf Ficuccio, little fig, because of the way the child ran around without his pants on. He called Toad *Pancionino*, pot-bellied stove. He called me *Gingilla*, and he spoke the name with a laugh in his voice, but he would never ever say what it meant.

Only later, laying the fabric on the floor, do I know that I will use it to make dresses for his daughters. At first, I simply wish to punish Mudsey, to make her jealous, but then Antonio's words return, *so much more than each by itself*, and my skin burns. I want Antonio's wife to think well of me, to believe that I am not a woman who would steal her husband. When she gets the dresses, she will write to Antonio and tell him how good I am. She will say I am the very best kind of person, an angel who thinks of others before herself. She will not know that I sent the dresses only so she would say such things about me to Antonio. That the dresses are not really for her children. They are for me.

The new scissors slice through the lace, and all my anxiety about Toad's and Malcolm's suspicions is lost in the rhythm of laying and smoothing and pinning and cutting—a soporific for distraught women—the blowfly butting its head against the window a grace note to a single chord played again and again, smooth and pin and cut. The rhythm is hypnotic. I am imagining myself as a boat, rising up and down in the swells of the warm blue sea off the coast of Italy, until, like a torpedo fired at close range into the hull of a tiny felucca, Malcolm bangs in with his demands and begins to butcher Wagner on my Bechstein.

"I won't have your man at the table," he says.

8

The soldiers bash their tin cups on the table in time with some ditty they are singing. A man squats outside the door to the shearers' quarters, rolling a cigarette. The tobacco won't lie straight in the paper. He rolls it and rolls it again, and each time, he glances up at me before starting again. Some tobacco falls on the ground and the man pinches it up and replaces it in the mashed cigarette paper. He tries rolling it up again. There is a set of rusty sewing needles in the band of his hat and one of them is threaded.

"Looks to me like yer dago has absconded with the eats. Don't reckon there'll be tucker fer me and the boys. Like that, see."

He licks the edge of the cigarette paper and smoothes it over. Twists the ends and fumbles for a match. Inertia appears to be his best friend.

"How'd you get like that?" he asks companionably.

Antonio brings out spaghetti sauce and homemade noodles and flat bread oozing garlic butter and sliced tomatoes with coarse salt melting in their juice and cucumbers and cold tea with chunks of lemon floating in it and the men groan from the smell alone, and spit in appreciation and loosen their belts. Toad glances at me in surprise. The food has always been my job.

"Aren't you the lucky one?" says Toad. "What did ya have to give old Tony to get him to make the grub or do I not want to know?"

I ignore him and hand out the plates. John and Antonio stand ready with ladles, while Toad pours the tea. Malcolm's face burns a deep and ugly red, seeing me standing next to Antonio.

"What the hell's this, then?" he asks, shoving his plate away.

His men stand up to see. Whatever it is, it smells good and they are hungry. But it's not chops and potatoes. It's not sausages. It looks like runny stew on worms.

"Carn! What's the hold-up?" It's the man with the cigarette, coming in from outside and knocking on Antonio's broad back as if it is a door. The man has a fine white line painted down the exact centre of the back of each trouser leg. Inked on his hip pocket are the letters D.U.N.E.

He takes a steaming plate of spaghetti and holds it out to be filled with sauce. He picks up a chunk of flat bread and slams it on top of the plate and licks his fingers.

"Bloody fantastic," he says. "If you'll excuse me French, Missus."

"I'm not eating it," says Malcolm, and he takes his plate and dumps it out on the floorboards. "He could poison the lot of us."

"Don't taste poisoned."

"You can't tell till after you cark it. You're supposed to feed it to the dog first. Or get the cook to eat it or something. Bring that Italian here."

So Malcolm stands over Antonio, watching him eat spaghetti, and Antonio's manners are beautiful. He doesn't make a sound. He doesn't spill a drop. He wipes his lips with the edge of the napkin, looks up at Malcolm and smiles.

"You must be disappointed that I didn't die."

"Let's eat. He didn't die," says D.U.N.E.

"Not yet," says Malcolm, his cheek twitching. "It could be suicide. Harikari."

But the men don't listen to him anymore and they mob the Italians, coming back for seconds and thirds, scraping the corners of the pot with their spoons. Antonio drops the ladle and bends to pick it up. Under the table, he touches my ankle. He has long fingernails, for a man. I stamp on his hand.

"Don't," I mouth, when he stands. "Please."

"Your ankle is much finer than Francesca's," he whispers. "She is still a peasant."

I am perversely pleased by this and walk around smiling until Toad slaps my arm and snarks, "Wipe the idiot grin off yer face, Gin. You've got half the men in the place looking at you and Captain Mal is ready to take an axe to Antonio." Oh. And he is one to talk, slapping John on the bum every few minutes, throwing his arm around his shoulders, his real emotion hidden under the blanket of Aussie mateship.

"If you were a prisoner over there, in Italy, wouldn't you try to knock off a few of their blokes? Well? Wouldn't you?" Malcolm hasn't taken any more of the food, and is still trying to cause a riot.

"Nah," replies the man with D.U.N.E. on his pants. "Reckon I'd be too busy just trying to stay alive."

After dinner, Toad and I find Malcolm sitting in a chair on the veranda with his boots on the railing.

"You should keep a better eye on your wife, Mister Toad," he says. "With you out in the paddocks, there's no end of mischief she could get up to."

Toad looks puzzled, but then he grins. "You don't know my Gin."

"Perhaps less well than I thought. But you have these men here, starved for company of a certain kind. And these Italians. They have a reputation, if you understand me."

"Oh, I understand you, right enough," says Toad. "But they

won't get nothing on with Gin. She's sharp as a tack and twice as cold."

"But, you see, I *am* worried, Mister Toad. I saw your wife in the kitchen this morning with her hands on the big Italian's leg. Panting, she was. What do you say to that?"

"He was bleeding," I say. "He cut his leg with a piece of glass." Toad's face is very still. He slowly closes his eyes and opens them. He slips his hand into his pocket to touch the gold watch case.

"You wouldn't have recognised Gin when I first saw her in the hospital," he says.

"You were in the hospital?" Malcolm asks and I nod numbly. Toad is going to ruin me.

"In the nuthouse, actually," says Toad. "They'd shaved off her hair and it was just coming back, short like, and they had her done up in men's pajamas and from the back you would have thought she was a boy."

Malcolm's face moves as if he has tasted something rotten. "Toad. I don't think Malcolm wants to hear this story."

"No, no. It's very interesting. I think he wants me to go on. Am I right, Captain Maguire?"

"I'm not sure what your point is."

"You see, Gin. He wants to hear the rest. I was in the hospital and I heard her playing from far off and I tracked her down and there she was, and every time she leaned forward, the striped flannel over her bum went tight and it was a beautiful thing to see, and I went over to her and asked her to marry me."

"By God, man. That's no way to speak of your wife," says Malcolm, abruptly sitting up and scraping back his chair. He's still operating under the erroneous assumption that Toad considers me his true partner.

"That's enough now, Toad."

"She kept on playing with her right hand and she twisted around on the little velvet thing with tassels she was sitting on and with her left hand she lifted up the front of her pajama shirt and tattooed across her belly in bright red letters were the words "DON'T TOUCH" and there was still a bit of dried blood in the foot of the H. She'd done it herself with a nail." Toad glares at me when he says this, and all his fear and dislike are in his eyes when he covers my cold hand with his own. "Didn't you, Petsy?"

There is an awful silence.

Then Toad says, "Most blokes don't want to see something like that right when they're plunging a woman. I think I'm safe in saying I'm the only man who'd want her the way she is." He's quite right. Antonio would never want me if he knew what he was getting. Damaged goods.

"A charming fiction," says Malcolm, very deliberately, not looking at me. It was not *Requiem for a Dead Rabbit* that I played this morning. It was *Requiem for a Dead Princess*. "With a husband as delightful as you, it's no wonder the Italian seems attractive."

The night when my stepfather lifted my nightgown and saw the red letters tattooed across my skin, I heard his intake of breath, the tap of his swagger stick on his polished boot. What he was looking for was gone. He didn't even wait until morning. He left the room and I heard a claxon wailing down the street and medics came into my room and took me away. I couldn't stop screaming. It was only when he sent me away that I understood my own longing, my desperate need for family and what that really meant: someone who would open the door for me when I came home and smile and hold me and ask how my day was and make me toast soldiers and soft eggs. Someone who would sing songs about five little ducks and three blind mice and later, someone who would giggle with me

176

at night, washing dishes in a sink made from an old tin, under a kerosene lamp hung from a nail in the window frame. And the black night would press against the glass and our two faces would be reflected there. Together.

In Graylands hospital, the idea of home became the metronome of my days; I could hear the blood in my eardrums beating *home home home home*. Every piece of music I played was played in common time. At night, I dreamt of the home I would make, if only I could get away from Graylands. If only I could leave the madhouse. I imagined the man who would stand under the lamp with me, both of our hands wet. The way I would arrange the furniture. The pillowcases I would make. The songs I would sing as I stood on the veranda waiting for him to come home. In the arts and crafts room, I made houses from empty shoe boxes, furniture out of folded cardboard, curtains from handkerchiefs. I made a toy man from clay and painted his face, but it cracked. I made a toy woman from papier-mâché and painted her white and used a red pen to write across her smooth white torso *I am yours*. One of the crazy people stole my little woman and I rampaged around the room, trying to find her, smashing the lopsided ashtrays and the pinchpots and the flaking masks until orderlies came and put me in a room by myself with soft white walls and urine stains on the soft white floors. A woman came by every morning and on the second day she shoved a rolled-up magazine through the slot in the door. I tore pictures of strangers out of the magazine and arranged them in pairs on the floor; they were my family. I gave them names and told them their histories, the stories of their lives. My great-grandfather was an especially kind and gallant man and I was convinced he would come to rescue me soon. My fantasy mother and father were dressed in evening clothes and held up martinis. There was a single lightbulb in the room that burned day and night. I tore out a picture of a girl and scratched at her with my nails until all her color was gone. I held the picture up to the bulb and the smell of smoke brought the orderlies and they took my magazine and the pictures of my family and put me in a jacket that bound my arms. But oh! My fingers played inside the canvas, every piece of music I ever knew, and I sang dirges for the family I had created while their pictures burned in the incinerator. I was not dignified but at least I was passionate.

The orderlies listened to me sing, but that was not the worst. The watching was. My stepfather had told me stories about albinos in circuses, in the lane of freak shows that led up to the big top. He'd told me the way those people had chosen to survive. I had heard about families of albinos, imported from foreign countries, who let their hair grow and permed it and charged a penny each time they were touched. I had heard about girls who had red dye injected into their irises, that made them go blind, because the people who came to the circus expected the albinos to have red eyes and spat on the blue-eyed children and called them fakes. I knew all this and dreaded the men watching me from the slot.

I taught myself not to sleep. At the click of the slot opening, I would turn and put my head between my knees and show them the back of the canvas jacket. When they pushed in the dish with my dinner, I lay on the floor with my face in the food and ate like a dog. Those lies we told around the campfire at Moore River, about what we ate when we were desperate, are nothing. In the hospital, I gnawed on my toes until they bled. I ate the buttons tufting the walls and the floor. I dented the tin plate with my teeth. I chewed holes in the shoulders of the jacket. I ate my own shit. I called for my fantasy family with the names I had invented but nobody came. One day, a man came in and cut off my hair because it was so filthy. I bit his fingers and ground my teeth on the soft places between the joints and then I bit the scissors too. The scissors cut my lips. I licked and licked and licked at the wet place for hours, thinking it was a remnant of something good to drink, a little salty like tomato juice, instead of my own blood. I ate the hair that was left on the floor. I snapped at the moths that lived in the stuffing of the walls, swallowing them in midair. I couldn't see them. I only felt their movement against my cheeks and turned and caught them between my teeth. Those moths caught in my throat. They made me cough. But I couldn't stop.

I don't think they would have let me out of that room, except for a visit from the Superintendent. They wanted to impress him. The doctors bribed me with a piano and a box of old photos, abandoned by the dead. I was easily bought. It's been ten years but moths still make me hungry.

It was into that desperation that Toad stepped with his, "Will you marry me?" He had his own desperation just then, an urgent need not to be a bachelor with funny pastimes in a rough district, but it was still unfair of me to say yes. To promise him something he would never get.

Still, that night, when Toad rolls into his bed, out on the sleepout, I sit up in my own bed and hiss at him, "How could you do that to me? Malcolm's my *friend*. I haven't seen him in years, and you whip him outside to look at your corset collection and then go and tell him every sordid thing about me. Have you no shame? I tell you, Toad, I won't forgive you."

"Oho," he says, not bothering to lower his bassooning voice. "What's all that about you and Antonio then? Nice. The bloody Captain of the Guards makes a dash into town—*my* town! —to make his report: "General, Sir, the bloody Italians are making a fool of old Mr. Toad. Tony Dago's doing Gin Toad in the kitchen while the cuckold's out lugging water to the filthy sheep.'"

Perhaps his voice is loud so that he cannot hear his own guilt shouting in his head.

We glare at each other across the dark room.

"Mummy?" calls Mudsey from her room. "I'm thirsty. Can I have a cup of water?"

"Shut up!" cries the cockatoo.

Malcolm is gone in the morning, all his men and he leaving on the early train to Perth, their truck left behind to be cannibalized for cogs and sprockets and rubber and canvas and rope and cigarette butts, and forgotten about until after the war when a government navvy will walk up the drive and halloo the Toads, unaware that he is the first person to walk up the road in many years, unaware of the devastation that is our place here in Wyalkatchem.

"Cooee!" he'll shout. "Anyone home? I'm here about the army truck." And Toad will slip out and draw the bolt on the dog run and sic the hungry blue heelers on the man.

9

With Malcolm gone, I sit at my treadle machine, feeding lace under the needle. I save one scrap, a skerrick of the bodice where Antonio's hand rested or maybe I imagined that, and I hide the fabric in my underwear drawer, touching it often, every day, lifting it, smelling it, balling it in my fist, printing the pattern on my skin.

The sewing machine is bolted to a table, and the table shakes. It has rubbed a groove in the soft wood of the window ledge behind it. There is a slight taste of machine oil in the air and at night, when my head rests on my hands, I smell the sewing machine, the fabric, the thread, Antonio.

He watches me sew from beyond the window, pausing as he repairs the fence to stare at the curtains sucked outside by the wind, at my white hands stark against the painted black of the machine body, the gold ring glinting on my finger. He wolf whistles, blows a kiss when the farm is quiet. If he thinks no one is looking, he slides grappa to me over the sill and brings his homemade triangular guitar to serenade me with arias from my favourite operas: Rossini's *La Cenerentola*, Verdi's wonderful *Falstaff*, and Smetana's *Bartered Bride*, strangely translated into Italian and lodged in my imagination as *Battered Bride*. Antonio is reckless. He snatches my hands, nudges me with his elbow, tugs the ends of my hair as I pass, walks back and forth between his work and the kitchen all day. Rubs at his nose as if he wishes to erase it.

Mudsey stops going to the Italians' hut. Then Alf. My children look between Antonio and me. They know something is wrong but can't say what it is. They frown and mutter in the secret language of siblings, and pantomime being sent off to boarding school. Being caned by the nuns. John wanders off to find Toad, ignoring my calls for his help. Even the dog steals meat from the kitchen and watches the rabbits that increasingly find their way into the vegetable garden, unconcerned.

Antonio brings me a cube of white soap he has received in the mail from Francesca, and lays it on the windowsill, cutting it cleanly in half with a knife. "Here," he says. "I want you to have this." He presses the soap into my hand and closes my fingers over it. The soap smells the way I think Italy will smell when I go there, a good clean scent of herbs and flowers, nearly indescribable, and I put it away with my scrap of fabric until Antonio says, "I would like you to use the soap. I want you to smell like that." Only then do I use it, carefully, on the days when he is repairing the fences in the home paddocks, but I save a tiny sliver in my drawer, to perfume my other relics.

"Everything smells good again, now that your stinking Captain has gone," he says, leaning in across the windowsill as I sit sewing. He breathes deeply. "Mmm. You smell good enough to eat."

"Oh yes. A single scoop of vanilla pregnancy with a bulging belly-button cherry on the top. Delicious."

"Yes, delicious," he says, licking his lips, but this makes me blush and I snap, "Malcolm doesn't smell bad. He's a gentleman. I think you are jealous of him."

"If I *am* jealous, I am only jealous of the way he stared at you."

"Silly boy. I saw you staring at his uniform. You probably wish you could wear your pretty uniform again and be a soldier."

"I do not wish to be a soldier. I do not wish to leave."

"Don't you want to go back to Italy?"

"Yes," he says slowly, "but not right now."

"What's that stink?" asks Toad later, sniffing at my neck. "What've you spilled on yerself?"

"It's just soap. For ladies," I say, my head bent low over the dresses I am sewing for alien children.

I have to strain forward with the metallic pout of the sewing machine thrust into my hard belly in order to drive the fabric under the needle. I've run the needle into my finger before. It makes a black hole in the fingernail, and I'm careful this time. I don't want to be marked.

The child inside me doesn't like the whirr of the machine. As soon as I begin to rock my feet on the treadle, the child squirms, I feel it turn away, its hands move to cover its ears and occasionally I hear a faint growl of complaint, the kind a dog makes if you poke it with a stick when it is sleeping. Down the exact center of the pregnancy are the thirty-three bumps of the child's spine. I can count them, sitting at the sewing machine, I can see them when I sit with knees drawn up in the tin tub out in the laundry, the slip of soap in my hand, pouring cold water over my head, my breasts, counting those bones in a line down to my white map of Tasmania. I can hear Antonio outside the door, breathing, looking through the crack and I let him look. Let him look. There's nothing to see but an old tin bathtub on the cold stone floor.

When I lie down and close my eyes, I still see the needle rising and falling, its single oriental eye pierced with cotton thread that runs out behind in an endless chain. I see miles of whiteness, a neverending white road, and far off, in the distance, five children walking with a woman in white. She looks like me at first, but then I see she has no hair, and her skin flutters behind her in streamers. It is a skull I see, a skeleton in a sheer white dress of skin, walking with those children, and as she turns and looks at me, the teeth drop slowly from her jaw and her bones fall in upon themselves, and the children fall down upon the white white road, their mouths open, and they are sewn into the earth by the leering eye of the needle rising up and down.

I finish the dresses. By God, in spite of my eyes, I finish them. They are very fine, French-seamed, lined with silk, the buttons cut from another dress in the chest, and the ribbons stripped from yet another. They are the best things I have ever made and Toad stops to admire them on his way to deworming the horses. I am sure he wants one for his collection of exotics.

"Reckon you're having twins, Petsy?" he says greedily, mauling my belly. It's nothing like Antonio's caress.

I have stopped answering Toad's questions about these two dresses and though it puzzles him, he's not upset. He doesn't need speech in a wife. He is more upset by his recent tiff with John, the way his beautiful boy has begun to hide in his hut instead of staying to chat with us around the fire. Toad rails about modern youth every night from his bed in the sleepout, but his look is that of a bassett hound, hungover, lusting.

"When will we be seeing the new heifer?" he asks, the day I finish, and the sadirons are heating on the stove. "When will you drop it, do you reckon?"

"Go to hell, Toad," I say and push him away before he can touch the smaller dress with one of his great horned fingers.

"Lover's spat," he says to Antonio, who has stopped to look on his way to weed the radishes. "The cow loves the bull, right, Pet?"

"Do you know," I say, "I once read there is a certain tribe somewhere, and when a lady is giving birth, they give her a rope to pull on and she can pull it as hard as she wants but she can't make a sound. And each time she pulls the rope, up above her, in the rafters of her house, there is a bloodcurdling scream, because the rope is tied to the scrotum of the man who made her pregnant."

Toad's face reddens. "You shouldn't say those kind of things in front of Antonio, Gin. It's bloody not done."

"Tell me something, Toad," I say. My voice is very quiet. "If we lived in that tribe, would it be you up in the rafters, or bloody Pedro, the bull?"

"That's enough of that," he says. "Antonio, go get a glass of that grappa you blokes made, maybe it'll do her good. She's half off her chop with the bub coming." He butts me in the breast with his dwarf's head, knocking me off balance and then hauls me to my bedroom, like some Neanderthal dragging his woman to the cave.

"You'll tell me," he whines, "won't you? When you're going to pop out the kid? If you tell me, I could whip you in to the district nurse. You'll tell me when it's coming on? You won't go animal on me?"

He's only worried about his livestock, his breeding program, so I give him my very best milker's moo, and, disgusted, he hands me the glass of homemade alcohol, and, lying on my bed, in the dark, I drink it.

The grappa enters, fires, burns, cleans, devours, exorcises. Toad's skin becomes golden and smooth after one glass. Swims there, sleek, in his element. After two glasses, Toad melts through the door. After three, Joan walks down the driveway, crosses the gully and bends to smell the Swan River daisies by the gate. She's older than I've ever seen her, coming back from boarding school, swinging her straw uniform hat in semicircles from its elastic, ribbons floating in the wake.

Straightening, she calls out, "Mum! I'm back!" She whistles up Mundungus, opens the door and looks inside the house, throwing a handful of sparkling gold dust to the chickens and calling again, "Mum?" I see clearly with these grappa glasses. Her uniform is grouted with mud and tiny spears of grass, spring grass, greenly haze the serge, not aiming for the sun, but simply sprouting. She smells of good damp earth, the smell of seeds soaked on a bed of cotton wool in an old cracked dish. She smells of the acacia wood Toad used to make her coffin.

"Mum?" she calls, as she wanders the yard, touching things, looking for me. She walks right through the Italians' hut; it's simply not there. She kneels to lick Mundungus and shake his paw. "Where's Mum?" she asks him, but he whines and rolls over. She touches the washing on the line, the door of the buggy shed, the knobby eyes on the flowering gum tree, the window propped open in front of the sewing machine. Her eyes widen. "Italy?" she says.

Touching the wood of that window, a glut of water runs down over her and her body ripples, wavers, separates into streams and rises, waving like seaweed in a clear blue sea, before blowing away, curling and twisting, until there is nothing left of her. A chicken pecks the ground where she stood. Cackles.

I was so happy when she was born, white like me, all my own child in every way. There was none of Toad in her. She ate meticulously, and kept herself clean and sang to the sound of my piano. She would have liked Antonio, but when she was alive, she kept me tied to Toad. Because of her, I thought more children would be born who would side with me, look like me. I imagined the families of albinos who populated the circuses, and I thought what a comfort it must have been for them, not being alone. Even in the face of paying strangers stroking their hair, they could have laughed at each other, pretended to be cats, held themselves aloof. I wanted that closeness. That degree of understanding. I still want that.

When Joan died, I let her be buried in her flannel nightgown. I let her hair be untied. I put a gingersnap biscuit in her hand and a glass of fresh milk by her side. I covered her with her blanket and I tucked her in. I kissed her eyes and sang her Brahms' *Lullaby*. I looked away from Toad's dry eyes and wouldn't let him nail down the lid. I wouldn't let him shovel in dirt. I climbed down inside the hole he had dug and told her stories I wanted her to know. I lay down next to her when the stars came out and told her their names, and the fantastic stories the Greeks made about them. When I was tired, so tired that orange lights exploded behind my eyelids and the ground swam, I closed my eyes and told her it was all right to go to sleep.

10

Antonio's address in Italy is in his workbook, on the letters he receives from home and on the postcards he sends his family every week. I've peeked at them before, Italian dictionary in hand, curious to see the words he writes to his wife; sweetheart, darling, love. I taste those words in my mouth, their tang, the roundness of them like ripe plums. Juicy. I want to say them to Antonio.

It's the work of a moment, to copy his address onto the parcel. Wrapped in tissue and brown paper, the dresses could be anything, a present from a stepmother to her children, even a package from one friend to another. It takes me over a week to find Toad's cash. I have to look when he is out in the fields with the men, discing and harrowing before the winter rains. Funny that I'd never looked before. He has been hiding the money, rolled up, inside a cracked old enema bag that is hung on the back of the door to the laundry. He knew I'd never touch the foul thing. Ha! But I find it and peel off five pound notes and blink when Toad asks if I think the Italians have come into cash recently.

"No," I say, "but old Walleye must have. She's been putting on the Ritz." His face is a picture as he imagines Mavis Walleye groping around in his enema bag in the dead of night, a torch squeezed between her shaking thighs.

I offer to take the eggs and milk in to Kenny Mackenzie, Toad wanting to make an urgent visit to Mavis about a horse he's heard she's selling, strange that I should mention it, and he accepts gratefully, with complete disregard for my swollen state, a state no decent woman would bounce around town in, but I lay no claim to decency and Toad has no concept of propriety.

This little oversight of his, however, will not go unremarked by the good burghers of Wyalkatchem, who are, after all, fully capable of observing that I am about to blow. There's speculation on the street and Bill Farr is taking bets, five to one it's the Italian's spawn, ten to one the Toad's. They think that's amusing. I see cash change hands as I walk into the post office; heads nod in my direction, a boy in woollen knickers steps in my path, staring openly. Maybe it's the dress I'm wearing, a little number I ran up from the leftover grey sacking Toad brought back from Perth on a bolt. It's a cousin to my usual grey dress, the one I stuffed in the firebox after John's flesh touched it, except this one has an enormous drop front that would perfectly expose my belly if all the red buttons were undone, just as the panel on a man's broadfall trousers is made to expose his cumbersome apparatus of fecundity. The door that drops open to reveal the bun in the oven. Apparently, this is not all the go in modern maternity wear, or perhaps it is the advanced state of things that alarms Mrs. Flannigan, or maybe she's just forgotten there's an albino within a hundred miles of Wyalkatchem.

"Ooh, dear," she says when she sees me. "Ooh dear. Can't be having that. Not right at all."

"What's not right, Mrs. Flannigan?" But the old chook is clacking her teeth and wobbling her wattles, brushing vigorously at her shawl of dandruff with liver-spotted hands.

"You can't come in here like that, deary. It's not proper. It's not English."

Since it's manners she's after, I say, "How are you going, this morning?" The parcel shivering in my hands.

"I wouldn't be dead for quids," she says promptly.

"Look," I say, pushing the parcel across the glossy wooden counter, "I've got to send this to Italy. How much do you think it will cost?"

"Italy? A man came in here the other day and said something about Italy. He said something about you too. Strange,

188

that. And Italy's ve-rry far. It'll be ve-rry dear."

That man would have been Malcolm, I think, and I hold my breath, willing the old bag not to remember what he said until after I have driven out of town.

Weighing the package, she glances at me, winces, and rechecks the address against a schedule of prices hanging on a cord behind the counter.

"We're not allowed to send things for those POWs," she says. "They're only allowed a postcard or an air letter. No parcels."

"It's not from them."

The post office smells dark, like oiled wood and the ink used on the rubber cancelling stamps. And a whiff of animal too.

"Then this is from you? Why would a lady like you be sending something to Italy?" She sucks her teeth, waiting for an answer. It makes her hiss, wetly, like a snake with a lisp.

"How much?" I ask again, holding out the pound notes, and turning sideways to look at the faces in the doorway. Bug-eyed, they are. The peep show open for business.

Her voice is raised and the pencilled eyebrows. "So. You're sending this here parcel to Italy, a country with which we are at war, as a *personal* parcel. I see. First, second or third-class mail?"

I don't know, so I smile a dreadfully fake smile and ask her to tell me what I can afford. She taps the carousel of rubber stamps and it turns, mewling, before she lifts one out and stamps my parcel and places it on the counter where every person walking in is sure to see it. *Francesca Cesarini, Sant'Anna, Toscana, Italia,* from Gin Toad, Wyalkatchem.

Before I'm even out the door, the peek-show yobbos boil in, goggling and snarking, passing the parcel from hand to hand.

"The old boiler's bloody sending it to the dagoes."

"Whaddaya reckon it is?"

"Buggered if I know."

"That'd be right. Zero brain power there. Don't pick yer nose or yer head will flamin cave in."

"Look at who's got tickets on theirselves! Weren't you the bloke who bloody failed the IQ test for the army?"

"Ah, turn it up!"

Outside, the same small boy in woollen knickers is standing next to the gig and he throws a honky nut at me. "Dad says you're a Haw," he mumbles and it takes me a moment to realize he has called me a whore.

"That's not very nice," I say, squatting, looking into his smudged face. "That's an unkind thing to say. Why do you think he said it?"

"Dad says the dagoes got you up the duff. He says you was askin for it. He says," he pauses to screw his finger into his ear and examine the clot of wax he extracts. "He says you're a Haw."

Still squatting, I reach out and poke him in the chest before he can shiver away.

"Then why'd you come anywhere near me? If I'm such a bad lady?"

I can feel the badness expanding in me, the desire to do hurt, pushing and pushing and pushing.

"Easy," he says. "Next time ask me a hard one. That bloke over there." He points to the veranda of the pub, where a line of eleven old buffers lean: hard, wiry men, farmers, men missing toes or eyes, all deeply interested in the proceedings. "That's me Dad. He dared me. Said he'd give me thruppence if I come up to you."

"Are you scared of me then?" I ask, wondering at the isolation of this town, at the way the fear of otherness has soaked into the child.

"Nope," he says. "I'm not scared of nuffink." But his eyes flick back and forth between his father and me and his hands, with their long grey nails, pick at his suspender buttons. If there was a loud noise, he'd be off like a shot.

"So," calls one of the men, perhaps his dad. "Is it Joe Dago's whelp?"

Mrs. Flannigan has come to stand on the road outside the post office. "Heard that off a soldier yonks ago, you jokers. Here's somethink better than a poke in the proverbial eye with a burnt stick, proof positive is what I reckon. She's sending fancy goods to the wogs," she calls. "Me customers was helping out, like, and they dropped her pretty liddle parcel, and it split open and that, and what do you know? It's got party togs in it. Party togs! And what's it for, is what we've got to be asking ourselves, when none of us has got clobber like that."

"I paid you five pounds," I say, turning on her. "I expect those clothes to get to Italy without being pawed about by a mongrel lot of bush larrikins. That's what the government pays you for. And as far as why I'm sending them, that's none of your business and never will be either."

Mrs. Flannigan clutches her bakelite beads and wobbles on her varicosities. The wooden clackers tumble about in her mouth, a statement of defence knocking them askew. It's the thought of the government that's upsetting. There's more than one irregularity in her books. I march past her, back into the post office, expecting the dainty dresses to be in pieces, hoping to tear strips off the men with my strong teeth. The men stare at the frocks, great chisel-headed hands gripped behind their backs, and they prop and shamble for the door, hairy and shrunken, when I push through them. They are too dumb to have touched the lace, too embarrassed of their own cobbled clothes and oddly dyed socks to destroy something precious and fine, obviously made for children. Even enemy children. For the bush folk have a religious fear of children.

This small part of me will be in Italy soon, in the very house where Antonio has lain with his wife. Antonio has his magic tree for power over fertility, Toad and John have their magic bones for power over horses, and now I too have a magic totem, a parcel that I hope will have the power to change my life. I climb into the gig and throw down the filthy pig's trotters someone has left on the seat, and gather the soaped reins, feeling the horse bite down hard on the bit, as anxious as I am to leave.

I want to go home and sit in my bathtub and pour bucket after bucket of sulphurous water over my head. I want to wash away this affliction. This place.

Jouncing past the scalloped fences and the sheep's skulls nailed to stretcher posts and the long lines of trees planted by the first settlers, I remind myself that God made the land and men made the cities but the devil made small country towns.

The following Friday, Antonio stands in the doorway to my bedroom while I polish the floor.

"John tells me that you sent a parcel to my wife. He heard it in town."

I keep my face turned from him. I don't reply.

"Why did you make those dresses for my little girls? Why didn't you make them for Mudsey?"

"I thought your girls would like them."

He strokes his hand up and down the wooden frame of the door. "Gin," he says and I turn. I like to hear him say my name like that, low and soothing. "Why does one person make a present for another?"

Does he mean the dresses? Or the vest I knitted for him?

"Caring." I mumble, embarrassed, my head bent over the beeswax I am spreading on the floor.

"But you don't know my girls." He steps inside the door. My eyes go to the window out in Toad's room. Mister Toad has begun returning to the house at odd times throughout the day. And where are the children? From down on the floor, at this distance, I can only see a square of brilliant blue sky.

"I know *of* them."

"Through me."

"Yes. Through you." I look up at him. I can't help myself. He is wearing the vest I made for him.

"So. The caring is really for me."

"If you say so." My face burns and I paw at the heat in my cheeks. The big mantel clock ticks once, and once more.

"Do you?" he says, kneeling next to me.

"What?"

"Care for me?"

"I suppose. If you put it that way." I have turned my head away again. He must not see my eyes.

"Is there another word you would use? Instead of caring?"

"I can't think of another," I say.

He pauses and looks at me while I turn the ring on my finger around and around.

"We use other words for such feelings in Italian," he says at last. He stands with a sigh and moves deeper into my room to touch the dragon key in the glory box. "What have you got in here, then?"

"Some things from home."

"Valuable?"

"Only to me."

"Could you sell them?"

"No."

"Turn around, Gin. I want to see your face. Won't you tell me one thing that's hidden in there?"

I rise awkwardly from the floor and hesitate before saying, "A bridal veil."

"Is it yours?' he asks, but I don't answer. My hands smell of turpentine and beeswax and now I wipe and wipe them on my dress, ashamed.

"Did you cover your face with it when you married Toad? Could he see your eyes?"

"I think you should go now. What if Toad comes back?"

"Did you wear it?" His voice so low I can barely hear him.

"No."

"Would you put it on for me now?" He takes my hand and draws me to the glory box. "I want to see it on you." He turns the key and begins to open the lid and I do not stop him. I would like to wear a simple white dress with my hair in a braid down my back and carry soup in a yellow pottery bowl to his parents with Antonio by my side, a long loaf of bread under his arm. Just then, Toad clatters across the squealing boards of the veranda, calling, "Gin? Where are you?"

Antonio closes the chest and slides silently out of the room.

"I'm here. Cleaning," I call back, my mouth dry and uncooperative.

When Toad appears at the door, Antonio is beside him, his eyebrows lifted, a smile twitching the corners of his mouth.

"Antonio says he needs to remeasure yer feet, Gin. He says you wiggled. He was just coming along to ask you." Toad stares at the greasy smears on the front of my dress until I cover them with my folded arms.

"What about you Toad? What's the matter? Why are you here now?"

He pinches my arm and when I yelp, leans in to sniff the stains.

"Had me a bad promotion," he says. Toad has been adjusting his speech for me. He is trying to learn fancy words from our dictionary, and has Mudsey read them out loud to him when he is holed up in the outhouse. "Perdition! Pergotory!"

"*Premonition*," I say, shoving his head away. "Well, you can see that everything's all right, so you don't have to worry."

"I should send you back. I don't trust you an inch," Toad says to Antonio. His voice entirely without passion. As if it's something he's *supposed* to say.

"But why, Toad?"

"Oh, don't be daft with me, girly. Think I don't have eyes in my head? I should have sent old Tony Stallion here away months ago. But what can I do? He's such a bloody help to you, and you with the bub coming . . . " His confused, ugly face collapses. "At least we'll all get a pair of shoes out of it. Do you have a moment right now to let Tony measure you up?"

Toad might be a lot of things but he's not a fool. He knows what's going on. Maybe he even expects it out of some lost sense of his own manliness.

When I nod, he goes into the kitchen to open a can of spam to eat on his way back to the paddock, and Antonio waltzes into my bedroom again. He stands near the window in Toad's room and watches my husband leave.

"Well, that was easy," he says, snorting. "You were worried for nothing."

"Not true. He knows everything."

"Then he is even worse than I thought."

He turns and comes to stand in front of me. "Sit down, Gin," he says, and I sit on the edge of the bed and ease off my boots.

"Show me your hair."

I pull my plait over my shoulder. "No. Not like that. I want to see your hair the way you wore it when we sang. After Christmas. Open it up." Like a present.

My trembling hands untie the piece of binder twine knotted

in my hair and the braid is unwound. Waves of fine white hair fall over my face, my shoulders, my back, my hands.

"Yes," he says. "Yes."

Toad has forced me to this. His love for John has pushed me all the way to this place. That is how I, a farm woman, practical and unvarnished, came to be sitting in the dark with another man, trembling and exposed.

"Don't look at me," say I, covering my face.

"Put your hands down," he says and I do.

A smile leaps in his eyes, as if he is secretly laughing at me. As if he knows that more than anything, I want to feel his skin against mine.

I will not reject him this time.

"Do you really need to measure my feet?"

He pulls the little boudoir chair in its frilly pink tutu close to me and sits down, his hands loose in his lap. We sit knee to knee, foot to foot. He doesn't answer me. His black eyes trace the contours of my face. Silence and darkness fill the room. A single bedspring squeaks. My stomach gurgles. I am flushed and confused by his gaze. It is hard to sit still.

Perhaps it is hard for him too, to hold back from desire. From lust. After a long, long time, he lifts my hair in his open hands and washes his face in the river of it. I feel my lips open to let some part of me that I have kept inside escape. Abruptly, he stands, bows to me and leaves the room.

That night, Toad is hiding behind my door when I go in to bed. He jerks me against him and crushes his face into my breast. "You're mine," he says, tugging at my hands. "Tell that randy bastard that you're mine."

He butts me like a ram will butt a ewe, and turns me around. He presses his protuberances against the back of my thighs. His arms are like the steel bands around a wooden cask.

"I'm pregnant," I cry. "You'll hurt the baby."

He pushes against me harder, and I close my eyes. I imagine it is Antonio's arms that pin my body, his hands that tear at my clothing, and I draw Toad's hands closer.

"Ach!" he says, sniffing my shoulder and pushing me away. "You even smell like him."

"I got a letter," Antonio says the next day, as if nothing has happened between us. We are planting cauliflowers and cabbage and beetroot and radish. "From my wife. She is a good writer." Adulterers always praise their wives to their mistresses. It makes them feel as if they are not really betraying anyone. I am obscenely huge, not fit to be anyone's lover. But once the child is born . . . Antonio prepares me for that time, and I am ready.

"What does she have to say? Only good news I hope." From translating the news articles into Italian, I can tell that Francesca often makes mistakes in spelling and has very poor handwriting as well.

"She says that in the spring there is much mud and the shoes weigh many tons more than usual." He leans over and lays his hand on my belly. "I saw him kick just now."

"Don't do that. What if Toad sees?" I twist away from him and drop three seeds into a shallow hole I have made with my thumb. "So strange that here it's autumn and there it's spring."

"True. We are in the wolf's arse over here."

It must be a literal translation of some Italian expression. I can't decide if it means something good or bad, so I smile and shake my head at the same time, and bend over the ripe-smelling earth. The child kicks and kicks and tries to turn, but there is no longer room. I stare at the letter in his hand and the sweat stands on my face when I think of the way he looked at me in my room.

"She says everyone is excited about the action in the south."

"The Allied advance?"

"Yes. Although she says everything is as usual where she is. She says a plane crashed on the mountain and they saw the pilot jump out. His parachute didn't have time to open all the way. She says they have sold the silk. The man's neck was broken. And he was naked by the time the priest arrived." He places a certain emphasis on the word *naked* that makes my face fill with blood but he doesn't look my way. He is busy sowing seeds. Is this emphasis my imagination? Or is there the shadow of a smile on his lips?

"Was he English?"

"Does it matter?"

"No. Not really."

11

These are the bush remedies for the things that can hurt you: kerosene on cuts and urine on burns, salt on bites, sugar on stings and boiled gum leaves for the worst kind of colds, emu oil for rash and a poker that's sizzling on festering wounds, a good scream, a good cry, a hot cup of tea, a pat on the back, a kind word, a Bex powder, a live pigeon split open and laid on the breast is a cure-all for jaundice, so they say, anyway. For weakness a cup of the juice from raw steak and for warts, stick your finger in the lime of the dunny. For the coughs that can kill you, dip a feather in tar and drop it in water to drink in the night. For snake bite, depending on which snake it is, the best of all cures is to shut up and pray. For love, hold a sprig of the everlasting flower, and for a broken heart, a cup of ammonia in the bath and a glass of something stronger than wine to forget. And for childbirth, they say to lie on the Bible. That'll do it, they say, she won't feel the pain. And if the pain makes her shout out and cry anyway, then hit the good wife on the head with a bottle, and at least you won't have to listen no more.

1 2

Three days later, there is slime between my legs and while I don't feel any cramps, I know that they'll be along to join the party any time now. John is sent to milk the cows, Antonio goes to shoot their calves, and cut the meat up for dogs. The children are off searching for eggs in the furthest paddocks. I wash my hair in castile soap and rainwater, brush dry in the sun. Long strands of hair roll and twist across the yard, pushed by wind. The clouds of the first autumn storm are huddling on the horizon, bruised and sagging before their first blow. Mundungus pauses, sniffs the chair leg, keeps going. The rabbits press so heavily against the chicken wire that their fur pokes through, in hexagons. I haven't worn my scarf in weeks, not since John and the party, and instead of wearing the dire thing, I plait my hair. I like the jolt this gives Toad every time he sees me and thinks the fairies have switched his wife for a succubus. A changeling. He stops calling me Petsy, and calls me, instead, Virginia. We avoid each other. Antonio watches my back. Smiles.

Antonio is squirting overripe tomatoes onto hankies, saving the seed for next year's fruit, when he hears me scream, a "No!" that seems to him to rip through the air like a circular saw, spraying pain like powder. He throws the stained hankies on the top of the rabbit cages and runs straight into Toad, who grips him by the arms and howls, "Bloody hell! She's done it again! Bloody locked herself in the laundry."

"Not in bed?" Antonio told me he was sure the deep cry he heard was that last cry a child tears from a woman's throat before breaking out of the womb. The dogs pace inside the run, whining, staring at the laundry shed with hackles raised and fretful eyes.

"She doesn't want me near her when she drops the kid," grovels Toad, filling with the smoke of pity. "God!" He collapses in the dirt. "She could do a perish on me."

"Stupid," says Antonio. "Open the door."

Toad looks at his hands, the scars from blades and hooves and wires that are in them. He doesn't move. Antonio is the one who lifts the lock with a knife and stands next to me where I crouch, shivering.

"Gin. Let me help you."

There is his shirt around me, hot from the sun and his hurry. An old shirt of Toad's, really, but warm on the back and the shoulders, and he lifts my plait from where it lies inside the shirt and lets it fall again, on the outside, and smooths the hair with his hand.

"I will take the boy now," he says, but waits. For some sign. Blood drips from beneath the dress, and makes a ruby puddle, ringed with little splatters. The baby, I suspect, isn't breathing. It is purple. Fermented. Not an albino. I nod.

The afterbirth is laid on the baby's chest like a hot, blood-filled pancake, and the limp child twitches from the heat. Snorts. There is movement of a reptilian kind. Antonio runs a straw into the baby's clogged nostril. To make him sneeze. He lifts the child and folds it against his chest, burying it in the thick black pelt. When the child's paw opens and catches fur between its fingers, a pained pleasure ploughs Antonio's face, and he lays his hand on the small wet head.

"Virginia!" Toad's face is white and wavering. His eyes jerk away from the glowing pool on the floor. "What is it?"

"A monkey," I say, sitting down in the blood. There are apes like me, with red backsides, beacons, telegraphing their willingness to mate.

"A boy," says Antonio, rubbing the birth grease into the child's skin. "Ten toes. Ten fingers. The tools."

Toad hands over the towel he is carrying, to cover the child and disguise it, but not before the raw boy releases a trickle of urine down Antonio's chest, claiming the man as his territory. There is some of the black tar that a child will excrete caught in the wet hairs.

"You must put Gin in her bed with the baby for milking," says Antonio, offering the child.

"Come on," says Toad, tugging my arm. "Get up." And then, bitterly, "You've done it again. You'd make a blowfly sick." Just as I begin to rise, the plait swings over my shoulder and touches his hand and he drops me, shudders, and rubs at his hand while I fall again to the blood on the stone floor.

"Take your boy," says Antonio, offering the child to Toad, but Toad backs away, shaking his head. "I am stronger than you. If you say yes, I will take this woman, your wife, to bed."

Toad's face is full of volcanoes. The two of them are equally strong, but it would be hard for him, as short as he is, to lift me other than over his shoulder, lumped, a hundredweight of wheat. He knows this is what Antonio meant, and worse. He knows Antonio is right.

I close my eyes for the eruption. My hands are pressed to my eyelids until there are orange and yellow and red fireworks and I laugh; at first, a weak bubble of spit popping between my lips, followed by laughter like vomit, spewing out frogs and lizards and snails and newts, and my own Toad, the mantoad, falls against the sagging wooden door, appalled and insulted.

He snags the baby which, even in his arms, clutches Antonio's hair between its fingers, and he says, "Take her. I don't want her." He whips the laundry door open, and slams out with the howling child.

I rub my hand against my cheek, the hand smelling of ferns after the bushfires have gotten them, remembering Toad's mud-streaked hand curved stroking around a brown thigh.

Then, as the wind bangs the door, I get my legs under me, the legs that I have never liked. Red ribbons unfurling down their whiteness, they ease me up to stand, ready to carry me where I wish to go. Only I do not wish to go anywhere.

There is hessian sacking draped on my back now, as well as the shirt, Antonio protecting and warming me with this old bag on my shoulders. I am defenceless against him. The part in my hair is thread-bare, revealing too much flesh, and the big man puts his hand behind me, getting ready to carry me. His hand smells of metal, of the gun he used to kill the calves. It is too much. It is the ultimate nakedness. "No!" I cry. "Don't touch me!"

"What is crawling on you, Gin?" Antonio says, his face as prim as an earwig. His lips very distinct. Some secret thought moves through his eyes and he removes his hand. "I will bring the wheelbarrow."

I am left in the laundry with the blood turning black on the floor and the yellow lye soap and the lines full of wooden pegs, so weak I couldn't knock the skin off a rice pudding. But there are bones in me, solid things pushing upward, bound about with all that dreadful whiteness. The little noise at the door is the squeak of the front wheel coming through, needing grease, Antonio holding the grey handles aloft to make it go.

"Now," he says. The barrow bows to me, and I feel a surge of gratitude towards my Italian, for sparing me, for not touching me.

On the floor, there are tins of ashes, and a bucket of fat, slippery from my heat, speckled with the droppings of mice. I remember when I first lost my footing, when I was no longer Gin Toad, the night I lay the blanket on the man's shoulders to keep the cold from him, and the clouds roiling with distress, and my husband all twisted by the winds of this place, so twisted he couldn't even lie straight in bed. And in the remembering I sit and am covered with bits of rags and shame from all that I have allowed to happen.

Antonio leans forward, but he lifts only a sapling with the bark scraped off, stripped and wilting, and here is his mouth opening, and inside, it looks like the bottom of a cockatoo's cage, white excreta in oddly shaped mounds. The tongue lifts and falls, and I close my eyes again, the wheelbarrow unsteady on its one wheel, threatening to tip.

The dogs have stopped barking. The trees are staring. Under the grey sky, everything seems brilliant and lunatic, the eyes of speechless things belligerent and disapproving, the wire on the cages burning. A cold wind rises from the ground and there are papers and leaves in it. The child screams from the house. Loathing itself.

The wheelbarrow cannot be made to go up onto the veranda. There are hands proffered, his hands, for grasping, and when ignored, he feeds his hands to his pockets.

The child cries on.

Standing brings a rush of blood and the man blanches from the flow, red and shining, but he holds himself steady, while I take tentative steps, unaided, towards the dark doorway.

"Should I come?" he asks, the Italian, on the inbreath.

"Don't you dare," say I, but soft in the voice because of the way the floor is tilting.

So he puts me between the sheets with shaking hands; they know their business, for they are practiced in the art of bedding a woman.

"I will send Gianpaolo for Walleye. A woman is better for this job. The wound . . . " Leaning down, the felt of his beard pulling his face into shadows, eyes glittering like jet, he says, "Poor Gin," with sympathy that slices.

I bat away his busy hands. "Who brushed my hair? When I was sick after the fishing. Who brushed it? Because it was brushed but not plaited."

"Aah," he says, turning away. "It was me. While Toad and John cut salt from the lake, I made dinner, and then came and brushed your hair."

"It wasn't you. It was Mudsey."

"Only me. It is very beautiful to brush the hair of a sleeping woman."

But this makes my flesh crawl.

"No. I am quite sure that Toad came."

He takes something from his pocket and bends from the waist to lay it in my hands. A crushed spray of flowers from the lemon-scented gum. A single strand of light unwinds from the doorway and, passing through that light, his skin shines gold. His pursed lips full and dark.

"Perhaps I did not see them come."

"Of course they came. They are my family."

"Many calves were born," he offers, by way of excuse, but the cows are no reason for anything at all, and their calves have been shot so there will be meat for the dogs.

"What will you call the boy? Is Alf named for Toad? Alfred?" For he has never heard Toad's name.

"I will never name a child for Toad."

"But, to give a son the name of his father . . . "

"One person soiled with that abominable name is more than enough. Agrippas Toad. It's not a name to share."

Antonio laughs; he hears the name as many others have: a grip arse toad.

"No. No. Not a good name at all."

"His name is Anthony," I say, and the district nurse fills in the birth certificate "Anthony Toad" when she comes, trying not to blink or shake the pen or look over at that other Anthony, the one from Italy, standing where no man not married to the mother should stand, in the darkest corner of the bedroom, his hands clasped over his groin. And the news goes round the bloodhouse when she pops in for a shandy in the ladies' lounge after work, that Gin Toad named her child after the father.

13

The rabbiter left late that night. He had a brutal headache. He'd spent the day riding the property with his poison cart, along the edges of the endless fences and around the dam, laying down baits for the rabbits. The pink and grey galahs fell in waves behind him, eating the baits. They were all dead before dark. Stupid birds.

Dehydrated from being in the sun too long, he ate the spicy stuff the Italians gave him and got drunk on their wine. They fought a little, Antonio and him, scuffling in the arid area between the laundry and the chook shed, just for the sport of it, though he took a couple to the ears and one to the jaw that made him regret the whole idea.

Afterwards, I saw them drinking more wine, out on the grass under the lemon trees, and the dog leaned on the rabbiter and licked his hand, and the man grew sentimental for the days before the Depression when he'd owned his own farm and his own dog and his own wife. The Italians lay out there on the grass too, and Antonio, his eyes the color of cauterized wood, told the rabbiter about how he had made shoes in a little shop in Lucca, before the war. He brought out the wooden blocks he was carving into lasts, and he made the rabbiter feel them. Antonio spoke of how the fascists came to the shop where he worked because they thought the owner was anti-fascist and they'd made the old cobbler cut his stock of leather into narrow strips and hammer nails through the ends, and then they'd made him run between two cheering lines of fascist dignitaries who each held one of the strips, whipping him with his own leather. They'd forced the old man's father and his mother and his wife to run and to be whipped, and when they were finished, they raped the owner's wife, and then they raped his mother, and she was in her eighties, and then, while Antonio hid trembling under the counter, they hung a sign outside saying that anyone who shopped in that place would receive the same treatment. After that, Antonio took his family and ran away to the hills above Lucca, to Sant'Anna, where he repaired the shoes of refugees who arrived from the towns in their city shoes, high heeled and tasselled and unsuited to the steep mountain paths.

The story went on and on, and the men drank the wine, and John praised the fascists and Mussolini and said that at least the trains ran on time, or something like that, and Antonio put his hand over John's mouth and nodded at the window where I stood listening. After a while, the rabbiter stretched out on the ground and went to sleep with his head pushed against the belly of the dog.

Antonio stood up, still saying something about the communists in Italy and their little red scarves, and he came into the house where the baby, the other Anthony, was crying, and he put the wooden box the baby was lying in across his knees and rocked it. When he'd done that for a long time, the child stopped crying and looked at him, with drops caught in its eyelashes, and quite strangely, a glaze came across his own eyes, and I knew that he felt how inadequate he was, as a father, across the sea, rocking someone else's child. Then he lifted the child and handed him to me, saying, "He's not an excuse anymore, my Gingilla," and the clocks in the house all stopped in mid-tick and the water that dripped in the laundry room trembled and did not fall and the beat of blood in my ears was silenced and then he went out again and woke the rabbiter to drink more of the grappa.

We are walking, Toad and I, along the edge of the dam, its edges chapped from lack of rain, another dry year though we should expect it, living as we are, in a desert. Toad is pulling at his eyebrow, the frazzled one that almost obscures his left eye.

"How could you, Virginia? They almost shat theirselves laughin at me last time I brung 'em the eggs. Bloody *Anthony*! You couldn't come up with something less . . . blatant? What about Edward? Didn't we speak about naming a boy Edward?"

"Oh, come on. You know the Italians haven't even been here nine months and so do all the sickleheads in town, if they'd just put their brains in gear. And so what if I called the kid Anthony? He's the patron saint of lost things, and it's a lovely name besides."

"The Patron Saint of Lost Things! Well, that'd be bloody right. Lost money. Lost scissors. Lost respect. What have you lost now?"

"God, Toad. What haven't I lost? Look, the name's beside the point."

"It's not, you know. The kid's going to have to live with that forever. It's like a brand." He'd like to knock my head on the ground like those fish at Moore River; his arm is jerking. "Bugger it, Gin, you could have asked. You could've said, 'Listen, darling, what do think of the name Anthony for our little poochy?' but you just bunged it on the kid and to hell with me. That mob in town all think yer having it off with Antonio, and maybe you are. I'd be the last one to know. You bloody never tell me anything."

"Well. What about you? Do you think I am? *Having it off* with him, as you so charmingly say, in that God awful blue-collar way of yours."

"I wouldn't put it past you."

"You don't have to believe me, but I'm not."

"Not yet." He rubs his hand across the bridge of his nose. "God! I spent me last farthing on a bloody telescope for you and you use it to make eyes at an oily foreigner. The wife's turned into a slut of epic proportions."

Mundungus is disturbed by our voices; he growls softly in the back of his throat, almost a whine, looking from Toad to me. Toad pushes the dog's muzzle away. It's too close. Stepping on him. I can smell Antonio's aftershave on its fur.

"Oh, and you're so innocent of that yourself." The dog, Mundungus, trots to the edge of the dam and noses something there. "The pot calls the kettle black."

"What do you mean by that?"

"You know exactly what I mean."

"Come on. Spit it out, you bitch."

The dog is gone, over the lip.

"You. And John."

"What about it?" Innocent.

"When we went fishing."

And now there is his silence, blooming, as he realizes what this means, his head a big cauliflower wedged between his shoulders, red dust caught in all the crevices, mouldering. Toad's always been a humble little man, laughably mediocre. But there's nothing wrong with mediocrity if it's honest.

"Ah," he sighs. "It's not what you think."

"No? I don't see how it can be anything else. For God's sake! You were both naked. Taking turns. My eyes are bad, Toad, but they're not *that* bad."

The dry heat of the summer is gone now, though the air still crackles. He twists in his shrinking clothing, the seams pricking, and tells himself that he is still a man. I see his struggle, the effort to find words in his own defence. But there is nothing.

Quietly then, burning in the last rays of the sun, Toad says, "I think I'll head back. You might want to look over the rabbits." And he calls for the dog. It's an excuse not to have to continue further with me, which would be, quite simply, intolerable. So he licks his dry lips and fingers the useless watch in his pocket.

A black rabbit lies in the shade cast by the windmill. Before he leaves, Toad says, "You can count how many rabbits you have by the black ones. For every black rabbit, there are ten thousand normal ones." He points with his finger, and his hand twitches in time with his pulse.

"I don't want to know how many rabbits we have. They're revolting."

And I'd shoot it, that black one, if I had the gun here, because we are trained from the time we are small to hate the things that are different from us.

"No," says Toad, "They're not revolting. They're just bunnies and it's an interesting thing to know, I reckon."

The rabbit, I see now, is dead, the eyes gone from the sockets, a mat of fur in the shape of a rabbit. Toad nudges the head with the tip of his boot. It is very rotten. The boot. And the head.

So Toad leaves—walking back along the track past his shoddy monuments to manhood: the dam, the cows, the orchard, the house—scuffing at rocks, looking for something else to kick. Even the dog has abandoned him. Under his arms bloom two white rings of salt left from his sweating.

We had depended on one another. Nothing more. He had bred the sheep, found the water, lifted the things too heavy to bear. I had prepared food for him, strips of wrinkled bacon, the folded grey nodules of sweetbreads. I had made his clothes, his children, his bed. It wasn't happiness. It wasn't love. But it had been tolerable, so long as there was nothing else.

I had stopped thinking about things that I wanted many years before, perhaps at the very moment when I heard the other girl's name called as the winner of the Eisteddfod. Instead, I only thought of what had to be done. Today. Tomorrow. The next day.

I had not wished for love. I had not had the strength to wish for anything except the smallest, most possible things: a chop, a cup of sugar, a pair of scissors.

And the poison that the rabbiter had laid was out there in the dank grass, by the side of the road, in the weeds, under the fences, any place where the water might attract the pests. It lay there in tidy one inch pellets, a mixture of phosphorus pressed together with bran and pollard, and in the moonlight the rabbits came closer and closer, their whiskers trembling, for they smelled the bran and knew it was something good to eat, but in the end, they smelled also the cold metal of the machine that excreted the bait and the clamour of the phosphorus and even the unwashed hands of the man who fed the poison through the machine, and so they turned and left and not one bait was taken by the rabbits and the baits still lay out there, when Toad and I took our walk and Mundungus followed us and swallowed one and died with purple gums and his teeth through his tongue.

So now I have this fourth child, another stake anchoring me to this place. This then is my crime: I would like to steal away from these responsibilities. Poor Anthony. It's not his fault he's not albino. It's not his fault he was born after Antonio had claimed the shell of my heart. Empty skin hangs from the baby's arms, not fattened with a mother's love. His cry for me is no child's cry. He can feel me slipping away. Oh little child! Sometimes I hold you late at night and that mother instinct rises strong in me and I press you against my breast and breathe in your baby smell of milk and bleach and talcum powder. But when the sun rises in the sky, you open your mouth like a bird. Feed me, hold me, rock me, you demand. Be my mother, not his lover. Wipe my bottom, clean my nose. If you look at him that way, I will vomit on your shoulder, leave yellow stains upon your lap.

And yet, there are moments when he lies quite still and his fragile hand wanders over to my red buttons and he grasps one and pulls at it and his face changes from grey to rose, and his cheeks fill from his blooming smile, and in those moments, I am his.

Later that day, just before true dark, Sergeant Cleverish rides out to the farm to speak to Antonio and John, and to Toad, as their boss.

"Complaints are coming in to town a bit too often about you lot. Now, you understand, I don't believe a word of it! But if anyone files a complaint down in Perth, I'll have to start believing and then I'll be out here like a shot and you Italians will be cooling yer heels in the clink for three months."

"What are you implying?" asks Antonio, but John punches him in the arm and grins and says in Italian, "Don't be a dick. You *know* what he means."

"Shut up!" cries the cockatoo. "Pig's arse! Shut up! Shut up!"

"By God," says Cleverish, "I could take that bird in on

charges of public obscenity."

While he is here, old plod has a taste of the grappa out on the veranda. I shift a dirty nappy off a rattan chair so he can sit down, but he stares at the damp spot and folds his arms. He leans against the wall where the rabbit traps hang, and the dingo traps, and he strikes a match on the sole of his shoe, and lights a tailor-made.

"So the kid's not a whitey," he says, offering the packet to Toad. Antonio and John stare at his outstretched hand.

"Right," says Toad.

"And not dago neither, by the looks. Reckon I've won me bet, then."

Toad shrugs.

"The people in town speak a load of rubbish a lot of the time."

I would have said *all the time*.

"What will you do if you lose these dagoes, Toad? You need them up here. What will you do if they're taken away?"

"Don't take them . . . " I start to say, but Toad sniffs, pops his pocket watch in warning, just once, and I wish, suddenly, that the odor of baby shit was not so pervasive, that I hadn't wiped the railing with the mustard-stained nappy, anxious to look respectable in front of the constabulary. And just at that moment, Mudsey and Alf begin to play a duet of chopsticks on the piano, horribly out of synch, a tinkly, jarring clash of sound, entertainment for their baby brother. Who begins to scream, full throttle, startled out of his dreams.

"You lot would just love to see us fail," Toad says. "You'd crow, you'd bloody lay eggs. Is that what you want? To see us fail?"

Antonio and John smirk.

"Jesus," says the sergeant, feeling guilty, the buttons across his shirt straining. "Toad, no one wants that. It's my job to tell you the law and that's what I'm doing. You just have to keep your end up." He pauses, remembering the debacle at the town talent show, and finishes in a rush, "People talk. There's been some discussion round town about possibly blacklisting you lot. Because of. You know."

The music faster and faster, louder and louder, wildly dissonant, and the cries of the baby rise with this crescendo. The glass in the windows tinkles. The floorboards vibrate under our feet like an earth tremor.

"No," shouts Toad, to be heard above the fracas, "I don't."

"Can't you shut those kids of yours up?" pleads Cleverish, but I stare at him with eyes of stone.

Before he leaves, the sergeant says, "By the way, there's a dead dog floating in your dam. You'd best fish it out before it poisons the water."

"God," says Toad, when he's gone. "The stupid geezer's worried about what's going on in town when there's mutiny right here under his nose. Yer lucky I didn't turn you in, Virginia."

"She's done nothing wrong," says Antonio.

"Depends what you call wrong," says Toad. "And nobody asked you for your opinion, you nong. Yer part of the bloody problem. Why don't you go get Agrippas, wife? The kid's bawling again. And shut those bloody kids up. I'm about ready to turn yer piano into firewood."

"His name is Anthony, not Agrippas." We're fencing with sabres, deadly sharp on both edges. Any minute someone will bleed.

"Like I said, that Agrippas never shuts up. If you were any kind of mother, you'd be able to get him to stop."

"If you were any kind of a father you wouldn't be mucking around with a bunch of antiquated women's underclothes every night, instead of helping me with him. You wouldn't like men *in that way*. You're not normal."

"Look who's calling me abnormal!"

Antonio and John had been following this disagreement with their heads as though they were at Wimbledon. *Smack! Shlack!* Out! Now, John is edging away.

"And you lot," snarls Toad, noticing them at last, "what are you lookin at? Get out to yer humpy."

The policeman, Sergeant Cleverish from the big family of Cleverishes who live in town and buy and sell pigs, will return again. He'll come in April and in June, reminding us of our responsibilities and letting us know that an optometrist is coming to town in July. Each time, he will carry away a couple of bottles of grappa in his saddlebag.

It's the grappa that's keeping the dingoes from our door, not whatever it is that we do to fit in, to be accepted, and in June, to test my belief in this theory, I bring a cup of tea to Antonio in full view of the sergeant and loudly say, "See you later, love," and blow the Italian a kiss.

Nobody says a word.

The sergeant presses one nostril closed and ejects a frothy stream of mucus from his nose, a bushman's blow, which he pinches off between his fingertips and shakes into the hydrangeas. Toad seems to shrink, his broad back sinking lower inside his shirt.

He leans against John and John lays an arm on him.

Antonio raises his hand to shield his eyes from the biting sun, and he almost closes his eyes, looking at something very, very small, far away, on the horizon.

14

From inside the dunny, Toad mispronounces words from the dictionary. He's still in the Ps.

"Pucelle," he bellows so loudly that even the corellas startle and launch themselves screaming from the trees. "A prostitute, a courtesan, a mistress. Purgatory: a place of spiritual cleansing in which souls suffer for a time to expiate venal sins. Can you hear me Virginia? Are you aware of the meaning of *venal*? Putrid: morally corrupt; aesthetically abominable; contemptible."

15

Antonio's making the paper pattern for my shoes now. He learned the work during a three-year apprenticeship in Lucca at a shoemaker's, he says. Hides came fresh from the slaughterhouse, dripping, and they'd soak them in limewater, the big oak barrels standing in a corner of the cellar, and every day he'd go down and haul out the hides and stir up the lime. His hands full of the shedding hair, wet and clumping. After four or five days, he and the other apprentice, he can't remember the boy's name anymore, scraped the skins smooth with long, blunt knives. They liked to joust with these blades, liked to pretend they were Athos and Porthos, shout "*En garde!*" and pin each other to the moist walls and growl about debts unpaid and ransoms and jealous love and morbid duty. They were ten.

The hides were transferred to other barrels, he tells me as he cuts out the patterns for my new shoes. The skins were pickled in salt water for a few more days, and the boys hid cucumbers in the brine to eat at lunch because the old shoemaker was long on pasta and short on vegetables. Later, the dyer came, a thin man with lines on his clothes from leaning over the vats that made him look like a twelve inch ruler, and with bark and flowers and earth he produced yellows and reds and browns and blacks and once in a while, a special order, a pale pale blue from the little flowers that dotted the hills in spring. Glancing up from his work, Antonio says, "Pale blue would be good for you. Match your eyes."

"Go on," I say. "I want to hear everything about when you were little. I want to know everything about you."

"Everything?" he says, looking up at me again.

He tells me they took the best leather from either side of the spine near the rump for the parts that showed, but the soles came from the cow's hips, and the belly leather was used for laces and patches and anything that didn't need strength, and the neck could be cut and stacked and used for heels. On shelves, upstairs, Antonio's boss kept every last he'd ever carved and there were hundreds of them, tied together, with the name of the person they'd been made for inked on the toes and the marks of the old man's fingers were on the wood were he had touched it. I momentarily lose track of what he is saying, thinking only of Antonio's fingers leaving marks where he touches me.

The yard with its litter of weeds, fading away, and the way I am dressed and the stench of the dye as it boils in the tin and the cries of the children as they torture the cat. Only his eyes and the way that they look at me are real. Those hands and their warmth on my skin.

Antonio is still talking. Still teaching me the things I will have to know. "And hanging overhead were the patterns, the brown paper pieces pinned together, shapes for brogans and court shoes, for sandals and booties, vamps and insoles and quarters in every size, and the *tramontana*, the afternoon breeze, would set the papers rustling like old aunts whispering in the attic, whispering about the war, whispering about the fascists.

"No, no!" the old man would shake his finger at them, "quiet now, ladies. We have to work."

I love his stories about Italy, about his life before he was brought to Australia. "Tell me another one," I say. "You should write a book and then everyone will want to travel to Italy."

"You want to go to Italy?" he asks, arching his back over his hands to ease the muscles. He rotates each shoulder. His hips undulate.

"I'd go with you," I murmur.

"But what about Anthony? What about Mudsey and Alf?"

This question hangs in the air between us. I don't even look in the direction of the children, where they are burying themselves under leaf litter and dust.

"Toad could watch them."

Antonio sings while he works on the shoes, opera mostly and sometimes love songs from the radio, picking up soft pieces of leather and examining them, rejecting, taking up others. If I am not standing next to him, he stops often and straightens and looks towards the kitchen. He calls me by the name he has for me, *Gingilla*, and I wave.

16

After dinner, when Toad can't get the radio to work, we read out loud, sometimes a chapter from a book sent up from Perth, but most often letters that have arrived. The baby is passed from lap to lap until he falls asleep, sucking his fist, and then I rise to tuck him in his box. Toad almost always chooses news of shamed women from the papers. Antonio translates the letters his wife has written and he and I try to read between the lines, guessing the identity of the aunt who came to visit (he has no such aunt), or the bird which nests in the eaves (maybe there really *is* a bird?).

"Shut up you two. You're as thick as thieves over there." Toad shakes the paper at us and sniffs. "Get me a new cuppa tea, Virginia. This one's cold." He talks about the secret weapon Hitler plans to use against England.

"They say it is not poison gas, but something truly terrible," I say.

"Ten to one, it's a bomb that can blow up a whole platoon in one shot," says John, and Toad nods.

Another night, Antonio reads a letter from Italy. "'I have sent Anna and Giobatta up the hill to hide blankets and pots and food. Today I buried all our important papers in case the German retreat comes through here.'"

"What does Anna look like?" I ask later, as we dry the dishes.

"You will see her yourself,"answers Antonio, "in Italy." He nudges me in the ribs. "Eh, Gin?"

And one night, in a small voice, he reads, "'I go to pray every day for peace. Most of the village is there and we sit with our hands folded. I have felt you sitting next to me. I have smelled your cologne. The feeling was so strong that I had to turn my head, but you were not there. I have carved your name under the bench I sit on in the church and I touch it with my fingers as I pray. Perhaps I cannot recognize you anymore. You will not recognise me when you come home. I am almost skin and bones. When I think how you used to hide my chocolates before the war to keep me trim!

Ha! Now I know the real secret to staying slim.'"

Toad stomps off to bed after this letter is read, and Antonio shrugs and moves over into the vacated chair. I wish Antonio had not read that letter, although I, too, like the smell of his cologne.

"*You* never have to work on staying slim with Toad around," he says to me. "Even right after a baby, you are like a blade of grass." He forms a tiny circle with his hands. "A waist from the seventeenth century."

John snorts, and makes a circle with his thumb and forefinger that he jerks suggestively in his lap. "The boss can hear you. You should watch out for youself. One day he is going to put the knife in you guts, like this." He twists his hand in an ugly motion and a chill passes through me. "Just because he is small, don't mean he is not dangerous. Like red-back spider. Like scorpion."

In April, Sergeant Cleverish brings Antonio a little envelope, much colored around the edges, and after Antonio reads it, he goes out in the paddock and lies on the ground and cries. The cows encircle him with their heads lowered. They come closer and closer. When he makes a loud sound, they startle and the calves run to hide behind their mothers.

When the sun goes down, I put Antonio's dinner on a plate and walk out and balance it on a fence post. "I've brought you something to eat," I call. "Please get up. Please come inside." He doesn't move. About a hundred feet away, the letter has been impaled on a barb in the wire and the paper is very white in the fading light, fluttering in the breeze. I lift the letter from the fence and bring it back to the house and paste the torn edges together again. I translate it with my Italian dictionary, and I touch the crayoned lips on the page and for a moment I think that I have become a monster, and I do not like myself.

Dear Papa,

Is it fun in Australia? I hope so. Me and Mama pray for you every day. I took the children to the woods today and we saw a man there, hiding in the bushes and he was afraid of us. Isn't that funny?

I have drawn six smiles on here. They are from all of us. We kissed them. If you put your lips on them, you will get our kisses. They have all our love inside them.

Peppe goes to every man in town and asks, "Are you my Papa?' He has forgotten you. It is time for you to come home. I have not forgotten you. Neither has Mama.

Come home soon,

Love,
Your darlingest girl,
Anna

His house might be pink or turquoise or blue. It might have a bed made of feathers in the attic and goats down below. It might stand in a dimple of woods with cherry trees blooming around it in spring. It might have a well in the courtyard with water so cold on a hot day you'd shout out to touch it. He'd keep a watermelon down in the well, cooling, and he'd lay the sweating pink slices on your skin at night and lick the juice from where it had run beneath your breasts.

17

Antonio tells me he has seen shoes made of cat hide. He has seen men come down from the mountains wearing squirrel skin on their feet, or guinea pig and once something he tells me that looked human to him. Like human skin. The people in those mountains are *rough*. Their shoes, he says, don't have a right or a left: they are made on straight lasts like shoes from a hundred years ago, by men who don't know anything about comfort. Hard men who make their tools out of pitchforks and peelers and sieves.

"But you don't live there?"

"No," he says. "You don't need to be afraid."

He sits Alf in the dirt at his side and gives him a piece of scrap leather and a little hammer. He has made rockers for the baby's drawer and he presses the rocker with his foot in time with the beating of his own hammer. There is a dreaming look on his face. When Alf looks up at him, he tweaks the little boy's chin and hands him a short piece of flax with a knot in the end. "Which story shall I tell you today?" he asks the boy.

"The one with the ogre and the four feathers."

And so they work.

The quarters are stitched together, his needle moving fast. It is the curved and lethal looking needle we use to sew up gashes in the sides of the sheep. He lifts the vamp, dripping, from a bucket of water where it has been soaking, and dries it on his apron. Then, with short, stabbing stitches, he attaches it to the quarters. He stands and shakes the apron, and Alf stands too, and flaps the front of his little shirt. Now, he takes the last and tacks the insole to it at the heel and the toe and draws down the upper. Alf holds it in place while Antonio sews it tightly with flax. When he is satisfied, he looks up and smiles at me.

"It will be a good shoe, Gin."

"Oh, because you made it, I suppose, Mister Shoemaker-to-Kings-and-Queens?" I am charmed and not only because he is so kind to my boy; not only because he has made the child a wooden hammer with which to pound.

"Just Queens," he says, and bows low over his extended leg, sweeping off an imaginary hat.

"Go on with you!" I laugh, and some hurtful impulse makes me ask, "Did you make shoes for your wife and children, back home in Italy?"

Antonio's smile fades. He stands up straight and plays with a button which is coming loose on his shirt. "I think, in English, there is an expression, 'The shoemaker's children go barefoot.' It is the truth. I never made shoes for my wife or for my children. That they could wear." His eyes move towards his hut, where the tiny shoes are lined up on the window ledge, and he wipes his flushed face.

"Like me," I say. "I have not taught Toad or Mudsey or Alf music. I could, I suppose. Perhaps," I say, hesitating, afraid, "perhaps, one day, I can teach your children to play."

He frowns again, and the button comes off in his hand. He stares at it. "I don't know, Gin. Do you want to come to Italy? To see where I live? It's not like here. The people do not even have food to eat." There are odd flats in his voice, and he turns the button over and over. "Would you *really* want to come? After the war?"

"Oh, I don't have to," I say, watching his hands. "I would only come if you wanted me to. Teaching your children was just a silly idea I had. I thought you might like it but I've never taught anybody; music is so personal. I don't think I'd like to be in a bad mood, and have to hear someone *else's* bad mood music on top of everything else. Selfish of me, but there it is. Every emotion I feel comes out in my music."

"Really?" he asks, raising an eyebrow. "So I can hear what you feel if I listen to you play? What you are feeling right now?"

In the rabbit cage, the bunnies jostle for position. The big grey male clumsily mounts the little white female and begins to thrust and shudder.

"Come," I say, and I take his hand, and pull him away from the rabbits, towards the house. "Listen."

Inside, the room is dark, so I light the candles on the piano and he laughs softly and says, "Such pretty candles. Like a funeral."

Before I push up the lid, we hear the soft sound of Alf's little hammer, rhythmic, a metronome of sorts, or a drum, and louder, the sound of the baby beginning to cry in his drawer, the little meddler, and he, too, cries with precision, a rising crescendo in a syncopated rhythm with the percussion. I play something in a minor key, accompanied by Shoemaker and Bawls, novice musicians, something that will tell Antonio everything he wants to know, if only he knows how to listen, until Mrs. Walleye bangs on the window frame and yells, "By God, Gin Toad! You're the worst mother that ever was! Can't you hear your own kid howling?"

She doesn't see Antonio, leaning against the piano, with the end of my plait twisted around his fourth finger like a ring, or Mudsey, lying under the piano on a sheepskin rug, the soles of her feet pressed against the lacquered wood. Mavis Walleye ducks her head under the frame and now I can see the small whiskers in the crevices around her mouth and her two-tone forehead, tan below the hat line and white above.

"What do you want?" I ask. She would not ride over to our farm without a very definite purpose. She would not contaminate herself.

She twists her head and looks around the room and, her eyes

getting used to the darkness, notices Antonio, who has dropped my plait and stepped away from the piano. Her hand snatches at her blouse, at the cameo pinned under the collar. "Might we speak *privately*?" she says. Her voice lingers meaningfully on the word and her eyes dart several times towards Antonio.

I wave her in. She thinks I mean through the window, and after a pause, hoicks her dress up on her thigh and throws her leg over the windowsill. At the top of her stocking is a fat and glistening blue vein.

"The door," I say coldly, "is around the corner."

I seat her on the couch and offer her a cup of tea in the best china. Antonio brings in the hiccuping baby and lays it in my lap. It tugs at my breast with its hard little beak. The house smells of laundry soap and vinegar, and is faintly urinous from the nappies drying on the veranda. It is May fourteenth 1944, the beginning of winter.

Mavis rubs at the mark her lipstick has left on the edge of the cup. It is taking her a long time to get to the point. While she blathers about the price of wool and the best way to remove lice from the legs of chickens, my finger rests on the second octave C and occasionally taps it. She jumps each time. Quivers like a blancmange. The cup is let fall and a wavelet of tea drowns the biscuit in the saucer. She stares at the dissolving biscuit with revulsion.

"Oh, Missus Toad," she says. "It's me eldest. Kathleen. I think she's had a little indiscretion with your Italian man, nothing permanent, mind."

And I feel there is something wrong with me. The air in the room becomes black and bitter. It is certainly not John she speaks of. He has no interest in the fair sex.

"The Italian . . . " I say, but cannot say more.

"She's ever such a good girl, really. Never had a speck of

bother from her."

"Mrs. Walleye," I begin.

"They didn't do nothing out of the ordinary. Very pure. Just the normal frolicking of young folk."

"Who?" I manage, and hear dimly the beating of the hammer outside.

"I've just said. My Kathleen and your John."

"John!" I say and press several piano keys at once.

She nods and one spring of her hair falls from under her hat and bounces against her pencilled eyebrow.

"I think it must be him. I haven't seen him with her, mind, but he's the nearest one of those Italians. As a mother I must do as I feel is right, and I honestly feel that this romance must be nipped in the bud. Between us, don't you agree?" Here, she bobs her head vigorously, like a chicken about to bring up something stuck in its craw, and several more sausages of hair tumble down and jostle against one another. "It seems," she says, bobbing and stretching her neck, "that my Kathleen is in a little spot of . . . " She pauses and clears her throat. "*Trouble.*" There is a dreadful emphasis on this word, and she says it much louder than she intended and blushes furiously and swipes at the joggling hair.

"I know you never wanted none of your kids, Gin, except maybe that first one, the ghosty one like you. So I was wondering, you know, if maybe you had come up against one of them doctors . . . "

"We had Doctor Bott out when the children were ill," I say. "Didn't help and cost a packet." I play C sharp.

She turns the tea cup around and around, and her hand is shaking and the biscuit is nothing but mush.

"I do wish you'd stop that."

"What?" she says.

"What fiddling. Those cups are rather delicate."

"Sorry," she says, but two minutes later, she's doing it again and I am forced to lean over and push the cup and saucer into the middle of the table.

"No, no," she says, staring at the cup. "I didn't mean that at all. The other sort of doctor. The *other* . . . "But now she sees on my face and in my eyes that I know what she means and am deliberately not answering her, and she brushes at her hair again and lifts the tea cup. Now I cannot help myself; I turn to the piano and begin to play. Discordant clangs and bangs. Poor old Mavis looks as if the chords are hitting her in the chest. "Mrs. Toad," she says, rising, but I drown her out, and she sits again and waits till the end of the piece.

"My!" she says, "that was dreadfully loud. I've never heard anything like it. What was that piece called?'

"That was Eric Satie," I say, and I can't hide the note of triumph in my voice. "A Frenchman. And the piece is called *Dried Up Embryos*."

She stands then, and bangs the cup down. The handle snaps off in her fingers and she drops it with a clink in the saucer.

After she leaves, I play the Gymnopédies and the child sleeps in its rag-lined box, lulled by the dreamy music, and Mudsey, who heard everything, stands beside me and watches my hands.

I think it was then, while I was playing, that Antonio dipped his bare feet into some herbicide he found in the shed and stamped a giant heart into our newly planted lawn with his killer feet. In a couple of days, there is a shrivelled, yellowing heart-shape in the deep green grass, which Antonio joyfully points out to me.

"Am I supposed to thank you for that?" I ask, but his eyes glitter and he says it is a present. From the heart. I only hope that Toad, being shorter, cannot make out the shape of this gift.

That night, after tossing and turning for hours it seems, I get up and go out to examine the grass again. In the moonlight, the dead heart is even more obvious. There is a prickling sensation in my neck. I root around under the house for the milk can of grappa and dip out several handfuls to settle myself. When everything seems sparkly and brilliant and the pet rabbits are grinning in their cage, I take the pitchfork and start uprooting the grass. This, I discover, is exhausting work, and I go back for another handful of the grappa, and as I tilt my head back to drink, I remember, a little uncertainly, that grappa is alcohol and alcohol is flammable, and so I set a back fire and burn the grass, instead of digging it up. This is an example of the kind of thinking that drunk people do when they decide to leap across rivers at night with towels pinned to their shoulders, or climb the Sydney Harbour Bridge with a rose in their teeth.

I believe I was dancing, an undulating belly dance, involving drunken hip motions and imaginary tassels, sprinkling the grass with grappa, and I have a distinct memory of lurching inside looking for matches and hitting my head on one of Toad's corsets, so I most likely was in the shed and that would explain why there weren't any matches in the drawer. But I must have found matches because I remember trying to shake some out of the box and seeing that a fair few matches are already lying on the ground, and when I look down, I see a piece of buttered toast stuck to my calf, and I am not at all sure where that came from. I strike a match against the box and that is when I see Joan standing in front of me and she puts up her little hand and says, "Don't," and I feel cold all over when she says that; but the match lights, and with a tremendous phwoomp, an explosion really, the grass goes up, the flames weirdly burning in the fumes from the grappa, about a foot off the ground and blue.

Parts of my nightgown are burning too, and even in the state I am in, I can see that this isn't good, and there is quite a bit of pain in my leg, sharpish, and my legs fold with a squeak, and this sitting is the only good thing, because some part of me smothers the flames on my nightgown and I don't burn up.

The grass turns black and when the fire can't find anything else to eat, it slinks back, makes a few desultory and rather pitiful leaps and then goes out. Ribbons of grey smoke lift when the wind blows, but that's all.

"What was that all about?" says Antonio, running and very red, tussled from sleep, the mark of his hand imprinted on his cheek. "You might have been burnt. Where's Toad?"

"I was burnt," I correct him, and lift my nightgown to show him the red patch on my shin, but I'm still confused and instead of showing him the burnt leg, I show him the leg with the toast stuck to it. He peels off the bread and eats it slowly and licks his fingers afterwards.

"I couldn't let Toad see that thing you did with the weed killer. And what about Mudsey and Alf? They've got eyes in their heads, you know! That was dangerous."

"Why?" he asks, sitting next to me. "I only wrote you a love letter. Why are you embarrassed?"

But it's not embarrassment I am feeling. It is fear.

"Antonio. Listen. If we are caught, you will be sent away. I couldn't stand it. You have to be careful."

"Toad will not be angry. A man is flattered when another man desires his wife." He draws his finger slowly down the back of my hand.

"What are you saying? He already is angry. How would you like it if an Australian soldier was lusting after your wife, over there in Sant'Anna?" The blood pounds in my ears from watching him eat the toast, from the movement of his skin across mine.

"It's not the same. Toad wants John more than you." He touches my eyebrow. "Ash," he says.

"Not true. He wants *both* of us."

His hand hesitates on my face. A pause. A silence.

"When you talk about your wife, all you ever talk about is protection. And safety. And yet you are so reckless when it comes to me. To *my* safety. And you didn't answer me. Would you like it if another man went around touching your wife's eyebrows?'

"Over here," he says and he looks out across the moonlit paddock with its blanket of motionless rabbits, "I cannot protect my wife. And she worries about every small thing. After a baby, she is not like you.

She is so anxious; she will not let me near her for many months. You seem . . ." He does not say what I seem like. His fingers are warm in the cool night air. "I had a letter last week . . ." He fishes in his pajamas, and then, blushing, realizes he is wearing not a shirt but nightclothes.

He tells me about the letter, and I try to appear interested, even though I would rather not hear her words, unless they are about me, praising me. Francesca, it turns out, is taking classes with someone local in the art of self-defense. She has learned to break any grip, to avoid being shot, diversionary tactics and the fine art of strangling a man. She is afraid, he says, of being raped by the Germans (whom she calls Uncle Fritz) or the terrifying black Americans (Uncle Sambo) or the owner of the place where she is staying, a man without teeth or hair. She looks under the bed, he says, before lying down.

And she resents that Antonio has food here and clothing when they have none, and that he forgot to tell her not to send packages, and that he didn't praise her for her mouldy cake and lumpy socks.

She doesn't understand, he says. He had wanted to spare her pain. He had wanted her to think he was still living under the same circumstances as her, even though they were separated by oceans and continents. That they were still connected. He had wanted her to think that he was still at war and a hero, instead of what he is: a prisoner standing on the black grass in his pyjamas, shivering.

He wonders who is giving her such lessons. It cannot be a woman.

"I would not want a man to lie with my wife while I am away," he says finally. "But this is not true of Toad. He is not a caring person."

"Why is it wrong for your wife to have a friend, but it's all right for you to sit here with me in the dark?"

"Am I just a friend?" he asks, sliding the palm of his hand back and forth over the back of my own hand. His hand is moist. Frictionless. "Is that all?"

My skin is luminous in the moonlight. He moves his hand to my thigh.

"No. Stop. This is not what one friend does for another." I still his hand and push it away. "Please don't do that unless you mean something by it."

He turns his body towards mine, cups my face between his hands. His eyes each hold an image of a moonlit woman moving closer, closer.

"I mean everything by it," he says.

On the way to milk the cows in the morning, I stop to inspect the grass. But it is hideous in the daylight, completely different than I remember. Where had we sat? Where had he leaned his warm body against mine? All is cold ash. I stare at the destruction, the pitchfork with its prongs uplifted, and wonder if the ash will give us away. If, even now, there is a flattened place, an imprint formed when we sat there together, a single shadowy shape as if something has been spilled.

18

Uno, due, tre,
La Virginia fa il caffe.
Fa il caffe di cioccolata!
La Virginia i' enamorata.

John sings his little rhyme as he walks down to hitch up the horses. As he mixes molasses and pollard. As he combs his hair in the sunlight. The words are simple. I am grateful Toad has never tried to learn Italian.

One, two, three,
Virginia is making coffee.
Coffee with chocolate!
The virgin is in love.

19

Toad tells me, early in June, that Laubman and Pank, the optometrists, will be coming to Wyalkatchem together with other travelling doctors and snake oil sellers. I plan to go in to town again, something I have not done since the debacle at the post office, and have my eyes tested. The district nurse can take a look at the infant and determine if I am starving him; there may be fabrics to purchase, or foods we normally can't get; and in the evening, they will be showing a film, *The Wizard of Oz*. Despite the expense, we will all go in to town, even the Italians.

I mention my idea to Toad over breakfast and he scowls at

me. "Yer just giving the town more to talk about. As if they don't already have enough."

"But Toad, maybe there'll be news about the invasion."

And at this, both Italians lift their heads and smile. Antonio has avoided drawing Toad's attention, but just yesterday, when we heard the news at lunchtime of the fall of Rome to the Allies, he shoved his chair back and leaped to his feet and clapped his hands and shouted. "That's it!" he said. "The war is over." It's not surprising the Italians want to hear about the Allied march into Rome, the collapse of Nazi rule throughout Italy and maybe even an uncensored hint about what has become of their families.

"Don't bust a blood vessel," muttered Toad, but he patted John on the arm.

In my bedroom, I stare at the baby sucking his lip in his box and at his sunburnt skin and wonder briefly if I could leave him behind, but then I chastise myself. What kind of a mother am I? The voice in my mind sounds remarkably like Mavis Walleye, who has gone to Perth with her eldest, "to enroll the dear pet in Teachers Training School."

"What is so amusing?" asks Antonio, walking in with a clean nightgown and bonnet. Without waiting for an answer, he begins to dress the boy. He chatters to him in Italian, threading the thin arms with their loose skin through the flannel sleeves, squeezing the flaccid cheeks until the baby smiles.

"I haven't been to the cinema in many years," he says. "What is it about, this *Wizard of Oz*?"

I explain the film is based on a book about a girl and a tin man and a dog and a scarecrow and a cowardly lion and several witches.

"Aha!" he says. "So you also believe in witches."

When he passes the baby to me, a pleasant smell rises from the child's skin, of Velvet soap and sun-warmed cloth. Antonio's arm is pressed against mine and he looks directly into my eyes. The baby turns to my breast and makes a wet spot on my dress with its mouth, sucking on the cloth. "Sometimes I wish," says Antonio, looking at the place and still pressing with his arm, "that I was a baby." Everything he thinks is in his eyes. It is very still in the room. He has just shaved and beads of water are caught in his hair and in his eyelashes.

"Don't start that," I say, almost unable to get the words out. I turn away, hitting him with my elbow, but gently. "Toad is just outside."

"You should feed him before we leave," he says, and so I sit down and open one button on my dress. I expect Antonio to leave, or at least look away, but he doesn't. He raises his eyebrows. "Go on," he says, touching his own buttons. When I hesitate, he says, "You want me to love you as a man loves a woman, and yet you will not show me your breasts?"

This frank talk, the word *breasts*, makes my face sting.

"Go on," he says.

I open another button but it's not enough to feed the child. The infant turns his face to me, pursing his lips and kicking his legs in frustration.

"More," Antonio says, and I slide another button through its hole.

Despite the miserable pretence of sleeping when my stepfather crept in to look at me, I had wanted him to touch me. I knew that now. I had burned for his touch. For *any* touch. His lifting my nightgown with his swagger stick instead of warm and human fingers had, more than anything else, been the cause of me crouching in the bathroom, raking a ten-penny nail through my flesh and gouging at the wound with the point of a sprung pen nib dipped in red ink. "Don't touch," I had tattooed, never dreaming there'd come a time when I would regret the presence of these words on my skin.

I pull my blouse open a little, but hold the fabric bunched over the old red tattoo.

"Take it off," his voice echoing from every corner of the room.

"No," I say. "I can't." I don't want Antonio to know I am damaged. I don't want him to know about this other Gin who would allow a strange man stroke her thighs, who would lie awake waiting, night after night, for a human touch. Even from someone strictly forbidden.

"At least feed the child," he says and he watches as the child puts its mouth to my skin and he swallows when the child swallows.

After a while, he says, "Open your blouse more. You are smothering the baby."

Very slowly then, I undo the last buttons and let the blouse fall open. He looks and his eyes trace the ugly scar and his face fills with pity.

"So it's true," he says. He looks and looks until I am ready to scream. Now he knows what I am, truly. There is nothing left to hide.

"Touch me," I say.

"Yes," he says, taking the drowsy baby and putting him in his drawer, outside the room. He returns to me, closing the door.

III

1

Rumbling into town, John and Toad ride together on the front bench. I sit in the shade of the seat, out of the sun, and Antonio has the baby draped across his knees.

Mudsey and Alf are going feral in the tray. There is something of the carnival atmosphere on the main street: the CWA building has hung out a large pair of cardboard spectacles; deckchairs are being carried out to the side of the town hall; lines of horses with ribbons in their manes twitch at the hitching posts; malingerers in colourful cast-offs slouch against the wall Bill Farr has made of empty beer bottles. It's just gone noon and children are already eating long striped sugar lollies and setting small fires.

A semicircle of citizens gather on the road outside the butcher's shop, their eyes on the radio old Mr Cleverish has attached above his door, waiting for the ABC's lunchtime news broadcast. Toad pulls the cart up alongside them. Antonio hands John the baby, gets down and holds out his hand for me. I shake my head, a tiny shake. I look down at my lap and then up at him again and a smile stretches slowly across my face. I touch my top button. He retrieves the child, pats him on the back to quiet his mewling, and then John springs lightly down, blows on the horse's nose and rakes back his own hair. The Italians stand next to Mabel Bruise, though she crosses her arms and twists away from them. Today I don't care. Today everything seems possible and pleasant; even my least favourite neighbour seems less like a sausage casing stuffed with slugs. And maybe today we will hear what has happened in Italy. There were rumors that the Allies would land in the Maremma, and since this is John's home, he is laying bets that the Americans have never abandoned this plan. The Maremma is so safe, he says. Quiet. Unpopulated. The perfect place for an invasion. "Except that they will be miles and miles from anywhere with only crazy cowboys like you to show them the way to Rome," replies Antonio. Now, he says, if they were to land at Viareggio, they would be on the road to Pisa and to Florence. And your family, snipes John. And so they go on at one another.

They are interrupted by the crackling and buzzing of the radio. All eyes turn upward, to the little deity perched on a shelf above the door. Mr. Cleverish stands on a stepladder and adjusts the volume on the Bakelite box; his red and cheery wife twiddles with the aerial. We hear part of the BBC chimes and then the grave voice of John Snagge saying, "D-Day has come. Thousands of Allied troops have begun landing on the beaches of Normandy in Northern France at the start of a major offensive against the Germans. Thousands of paratroops and glider-borne troops have also been dropped behind enemy lines and the Allies are said to have penetrated several miles inland."

"Kill the bloody Huns!" screams a woman in the crowd, and she struggles to get closer to the radio, but is pushed back with elbows. "Where's Normandy?" asks someone else. "How the hell should I know?" says a third. "Shut up!" hisses Mrs. Flannigan. "You can't hear hardly nothing with all the yapping."

"The Prime Minister, Winston Churchill, has told MPs that Operation Neptune—the code name for the Normandy landings— is proceeding in a thoroughly satisfactory manner. Upwards of four thousand ships and several thousand smaller craft crossed the channel to the northern coast of France.

"The Allied Naval Commander, Admiral Bertram Ramsay, said the landings had taken the Germans completely by surprise. There were no enemy reconnaissance planes out and the opposition of coastal batteries was much less than expected. He said, 'We have got all the first wave of men through the defended beach zone and set for the land battle . . .'"

Antonio and John wait until the very end, but there is no news of Italy. It is all the beaches of Normandy and an entirely different invasion. The Italians turn, their eyes downcast.

"They have forgotten us," Antonio says. "What will become of my family?"

"I'm so sorry, Antonio," I say, taking his hand. "I'm sure the Allies will liberate them as soon as they can. And if not, well, you'll still be safe here with us." With me.

"Shit, don't touch the bloody dago on the main drag! Do you want to get us all killed?"

"For God's sake, Toad. I'm just being kind."

"There's no such thing as being *kind* to another man. It's called something else."

But the argument is moot. At my words, Antonio gives me an odd look and pulls his hand away from mine. He pushes the baby between Mudsey and Alf on his wadded up jacket and squats at the edge of the road, rolling a cigarette. John still stands, turned away from the radio. A woman enters the butcher shop and the bells jingle merrily.

"I want a drink," John says in a ragged voice, and he takes a step and stops again. He puts out his hand as if to grasp something and a woman pushes past him, hissing, "Rude man."

"Old bag," he replies.

"Come on John," I say. Even now I have no sympathy for him but I offer him a thermos of tea and an egg sandwich and he takes them and puts them up to his mouth.

Later, in the CWA hall, the optometrist shines a bright light in my eyes and says, "You're close to blind in strong sun, aren't you, Mrs. Toad? And I can tell you haven't been wearing those dark glasses I gave you last time I was here." He pauses, taps his front tooth with his pen and then says, "Do the locals give you much gip about being an albino?"

He is genuinely concerned, but I can't bring myself to answer. What could he understand about a place like this?

"My sister," he says, by way of explanation. "I got into this field because I thought I might be able to do her some good. Fix her eyes. Silly," he laughs. "I know it now. She's got it worse than you. Lots of problems with involuntary eye movements. Nystagmus. Rather unattractive in a woman. Can't find a nice man to settle down with. Well. You know. She's been pretty unhappy over the years."

"I'm sorry," I say. "I don't understand. What does your sister have to do with me?"

"She's a . . . an albino. Just like you," he says, blushing to the roots of his sparse grey hair. Lots of problems with involuntary lip movements. Rather unattractive in a man. "I thought, you know, you're both the same."

"I honestly don't know what you mean," I say, snatching the dark glasses from him and ramming them into my purse. "I'm not the same as anyone else, any more than you are."

He was probably about to suggest that his sister and I exchange letters, pen pals sending each other words of support and comfort for our miserable, unloved condition. Maybe he's even thinking of a late-life cohabitation, very modest and discreet, a dignified rumpy-pumpy between consenting women. Just *friends*. But I *am* loved. And by a man. It's rather sad, after all, to see how he blushes and fumbles with his casebook and sprays his receipts on the floor. Bending, he murmurs, "I was just trying to be nice. I didn't mean anything by it. I didn't intend to hurt your feelings."

The poor boy. In his innocence, he thinks he can hurt my feelings today. An axe murderer couldn't ruin my mood today. But my years in Wyalkatchem have made me cynical. Too caustic. A bar of soap with too much lye in the mix. Instead of washing out the unwanted words from his mouth, I have burnt him, and his tongue touches the corners of his lips before he speaks, probing the damage.

"Don't worry," I say now, contrite. "You didn't hurt me." More than can be said for him; his stricken face with its narrow chin and drooping moustache tremble from my unkindness. He reminds me of a dog we had when Joan was a baby that put its eyes up and wobbled its chin if the meat was late, and left me feeling guilty.

And so I feel now. Bah!

He starts, and I realize that I have actually said this aloud and now I am truly forced to mollify him, to apologize to this twig.

"Tell your sister," I say, lifting my hand in a gesture of peace, "That there are people in the world who find albinos very beautiful."

The doctor sucks one end of his moustache; perhaps this accounts for its limpness. He looks at me and looks away. He is blushing again. How beastly to communicate ones every emotion like a signal lamp; he is obviously not one of those people who find albinism attractive.

Before I leave, I say again, "Tell your sister what I said. Tell her that you met an albino woman who is loved."

He opens the door for me and there, leaning against the warm bricks, is my Antonio. The optometrist sees Antonio turn to greet me and hears my own sharp intake of breath and all is revealed. The blinking little man scuttles away from me, almost letting the door close on my hand, the brute.

Mudsey stands with her clammy paw trapped in John's hand and she pulls against his grip, trying to get away. She flicks her finger at his leg. Stamps on the toe of his brilliant shoe. "I'm not yours," she says. "Where's me Dad?" Antonio passes me the baby. Alfie sits in the dust. He has caught a gecko and the tail has come off, and he is trying to push it back on again. The gecko is no longer moving.

"Where's Toad?" I ask, and Antonio jerks his head towards the hotel. Men are drinking on the veranda, but I can't see Toad.

"Let's go," I say, striding past the Italians, glaring at Mudsey. She imagines I am going to send her down to boarding school. She imagines I am a malevolent angel fully capable of casting her forth from her rubbish-strewn Eden. "We don't have to wait for him. We'll have our picnic on the football field."

Next to the weatherboard schoolhouse, there is an enclosed patch of rusty grass where the children and the railway workers play sports. Long ago, someone hammered stakes into the ground at either end and, every so often, the teacher goes out with a bag of flour and marks the edges of the field. She sends the children to trample the cotta-colored ant nests. The ants bite the children and they run away screaming and swatting at their legs, and the nests appear again, almost overnight, big enough to conceal half-grown heifers.

Last year, before the Italians came, there was a new teacher who was terrified of the ants. Each lunchtime, she went out and soaked the nests with kerosene and set them on fire. She smashed ants that made their way inside the building with rolled up maps, and ordered new charts when those grew tattered. She had a morbid fear of the ants, and her students, kids who grew up on farms and had been nibbling on ants since infancy, laughed at her and decided to give her something to remember them by.

They secretly brought ashes from home and filled the fireplace in the schoolroom with the grey powder. They puffed handfuls up the chimney flue. They dug up an entire ant nest and one famous boy stood on the tin roof and carefully dropped the nest down the chimney during mathematics.

The red ants, disturbed in their domesticity, swarmed out, vengeful. They marched through the ashes. They poured over the brickwork. They climbed up the walls. Thousands and thousands of ants. A little girl in the first row pointed her finger and screamed, "Ghost ants!" The teacher approached, cane in hand. Then another child, further back, screamed, "They're everywhere!" and someone in the back solemnly said, "It's the ghosts of all those ants Miss has killed. They've come back to get her."

And by that time, *grey* ants were raining from the ceiling and drizzling down the windows; they were thick on the desks, and the smallest children had been bitten and were crying. These were not the ants that everyone knew lived in the paddock and which were red.

The teacher trembled, closed her eyes, put both hands on a desk and hung her head. Ants from the desk swarmed up her arms and inside her dress, grey ants, *ghost* ants, and when they bit her, she opened her eyes and screamed and screamed, and felt them swarming under her stays and she tore at her hair and her clothes and ran from the room, ran for the horse trough behind the schoolhouse and washed herself in the green water, and scrubbed herself with her broken fingernails and her hair was down in dripping dags and one cork-soled shoe floated in the water. She didn't notice that the ants in the water were red, not grey, and that a scum of ash floated there. She walked to the hotel, water leaking from her dress and leaving twin tracks of wetness in the dust. She packed her bags and stood shivering, still in the sodden dress, still with a little pond scum in her hair, at the railway siding until the evening train arrived and carried her off to civilization.

The farmers in Wyalkatchem are proud of their children for being able to scare off a licensed teacher. It shows guts and planning, qualities much appreciated in a farming community. They're not ones to tolerate those who are different in any way, those who show weakness.

I struggle to tell this story to Antonio in my best Italian while we find a place to spread our blanket. He smiles at my little mistakes, but I am sure he knows I will be an asset to him in Italy and not an embarrassment. John interrupts to ask in English where Toad has gone.

There's a stunted York gum leaning over the fence on the north side of the paddock, dripping honky nuts, and all the horses are clustered in its shade. The field is dry and cracked since we haven't yet had the winter rains. The sky is almost white. Other farmers have driven into town, and had the same idea as us, of having a picnic beside the school. They, too, have come for the doctoring, or the dancing, or the entertainment, or, most likely of all, the company. Some of them have illegally brought their Italians and now the football field is dotted with blonde heads and black heads on blankets, bent over and gnawing on old hens' legs.

Mabel Bruise, in a shrill voice that carries and turns every head, calls across to me, "Gin Toad, where *is* your husband? Don't say he was too . . ." she pauses and smiles a mean smile, "*short . . .*" she pauses again and giggles, ". . . of breath to join you." She laughs in a high, snorting whinny and the horses flick their ears at her. Even though she is so grotesque, there are now mutterings of disapproval at seeing me seated on a blanket with not one but two of those randy Italians and no protector in sight, and backs are turned and children's eyes are covered and stories are told of bad women they have read about in the press.

Shielding his gesture with his body, Antonio slides his fingers under mine and squeezes my hand.

"Take me away from here, Antonio. Please. Take me back to Italy with you."

"Gin," he says, dropping my hand, "I am a prisoner."

So we eat our meat and our cake and choke it down with swigs of lukewarm tea, but it's not the picture I imagined when I packed the food this morning. The shine is gone.

After lunch, Italian men gather at the stone horse trough to wash their hands and faces. Australians who have said that the Italians are a dirty race suddenly find the ants fascinating so they will not be witness to this refutation of their beliefs. They dry their greasy hands on the front of their trousers and speak together about the germs that swarm in watering troughs.

One of the Italians has bought a ball and they kick this around and their white teeth flash in the sun and they jut their chins and finally call out a challenge. Standing, the Australians flex their knees and pull their cabled jumpers over their heads and spit on their hands. Their women hurry to fold away the blankets and bring the children to the fence. The Italians make a few experimental kicks and discover that when the ball hits an ant nest, the ball flies up sharply, at an unpredictable angle. They discuss this and other matters in Italian and choose a team; Antonio is included but not John, and I wonder why, since John moves like a dugite on fire, but then I see the Australians lined up, and they are all huge men with fists swinging by their sides like kerosene drums.

"Give 'em hell, boys!"

"Carn the Aussies!"

"Bust a gut!"

"Stick it to them wops!"

It seems likely this will not, after all, be a friendly post-picnic game, but rather, our own reenactment of World War Two, the African Campaign played on a minefield of anthills.

A red-tailed hawk tilts overhead, eying something in the grass. Its shadow passes over my hand. The Italians strip off their shirts and the women standing next to the fence gasp at all that naked flesh. Old Missus Flannigan touches her lip with her gnarled finger, slides her fingernail along the wrinkled rim of her mouth. She nods her head and her eyes smile, but it doesn't reach her lips. She's much too cautious. Her eyes dart, again and again, to my Italian, to the flesh that is all mine now, and each time, she looks away and puts her hand to her breast and fingers her bra strap through the serge of her dress. She catches the eye of another woman, likewise engaged, and they smirk and blink at each other in embarrassment at their shared fascination. Antonio looks good. Even from here, I can see the turtle shell of his stomach and I remember tracing those deep lines with my fingers.

To be perfectly honest, I would rather sit and talk quietly about Italy with Antonio than watch him in a game of football. I would rather hold his hand on the blanket and listen to him hum a few bars from the *Moonlight Sonata*, or Chopin's *Nocturnes*. Even listen to the creak of the fabric over his chest as he breathes. The motion of his hands as he slices an orange into quarters and licks the juice from his fingers. This is what I want. I have never cared for sports. It seems far too similar to gladiators and tawdry circuses but in this, I hold the minority view. Here in Wyalkatchem, the people have their football and cricket teams, hockey and lacrosse, lawn bowls and even golf, though there's not a shred of difference between the putting green and the rough, and balls are regularly eaten by passing dingoes. I have no idea how any of these games are played, what constitutes a win, or what equipment they require. I usually can't see the ball, and it looks as if fast moving dabs of colour are crashing into other fast moving dabs.

I jump when a man on the field blows a whistle. Several men simultaneously trip over an anthill and themselves. Antonio butts the ball with his head, Dick Ekvelt marks it and tucks it under his arm and there are screams of "Foul!" and scrambling men on other scrambling men, and a dog dashes in and bites the ball. It's complicated. I know there must be rules but what they are, I can't tell, and in the confusion, I find my eyes following Antonio through the melee. Admiring the way he slices through the crowd of men, glowing in the bright winter sunshine, an impossibly deep and delicious shade of Italian chocolate.

"Mummy," pleads Mudsey, blocking my view again and again with her thin, child's body. "Stop staring at him." She knows disaster when she sees it.

I push her aside but she steps in front of me and tugs at my hand. "Please."

"Whatever are you talking about?" I ask, my eyes never leaving Antonio. "Here's thruppence. Go and get yourself a fizzy drink."

The Australians curse the weather, the ant nests and the way lunch is roiling in their pendulous bellies.

Next to the town hall, where the deckchairs are, a band warms up and their squawks drift across the field; the band leader's voice flares, "And a one and a two . . ." and the band begins to play "The Star of the County Down," well below tempo, but there is a real musician playing the fiddle and now we can all hear a young man singing the ancient words to that song. It's almost a hymn, and very moving, it is, and the men halt their game and turn and listen.

When the singer comes to the last verse, I can feel Antonio looking at me; that side of my face burns while the man sings:

No pipe I'll smoke, no horse I'll yoke, though with rust
   my plough turns brown,
Till a smiling bride by my own fireside sits the star of
   the County Down.

The coarse men in the field join in with the chorus, throwing their heads back and roaring. There is a moment at the end, as the bagpipes exhale, when I am sure that every man, woman and child in Wyalkatchem can see what exists between Antonio and me, and I am not ashamed. I feel like doing a little shimmy in front of them all, a victory dance. The red-tailed hawk drops into the scrub and hops and then flies up again, with a snake twisting in its talons, but somehow the snake is able to flex its body and strike at the hawk, and the bird staggers in flight and begins to fall.

It's the way he stands. The way he combs his hair. The glow of his skin under the hot sun. He is the kind of man that holds cigarettes between his thumb and his first two fingers and blows out the smoke in a long, unending stream. He is the kind of soldier I had been afraid of when I crouched in the orchard. The kind of man that women look at twice before sucking in their tummies and pushing out their busts.

I am not the only woman who looks at him during the game. He has that effect. But I am the only one who fills his eyes. I am the only one who knows the way he has of making his woman happy before seeking happiness himself. I am the only one who has the chance of a different life because of him.

Don't leave me here.

The game begins again, softened a little by the old love song. Antonio, however, is still looking at me, almost as if he is waiting for something. He waits and waits and his team mates hit him on the chest as they run past or try to grab him by the hand. Women turn to see what he is looking at. Toad, returning from the pub or wherever he has been, follows Antonio's gaze and sees me lift my hand and wave and smile a bottomless smile of joy.

Toad sees Antonio salute me then, out in front of all Wyalkatchem, and bow and lope off down the poxed field; and he sees Mudsey catch my hand, which still wobbles in the air, and bite my fingers; and he even sees Alf, holding a glass of lemonade and frowning. He sees it all and understands what it means and he takes out his watch and opens the case and stops the hands. He looks at the broken crystal for a moment and then closes the case and returns it to his pocket.

The Italians are very easy in their ways, hugging and kissing as if it were the most natural thing in the world for two grown men to touch each other. They sing out compliments and make gestures with their hands and I am sure they must be winning for they never stop smiling. I recognize some men from the orchard, one with a habit of grasping his chin and tugging at it, who kicks the ball backwards with his heel, and another who coughs as he runs and shouts, "Bonzai!" after every collision.

The whistle is blown and the men come out of the field, sweating and joking, and the Italians all swat Antonio on the back. The Australians offer him cigarettes and bottles of beer. Basil Herring, the pig farmer, raises his thick red arms and shakes his fists playfully at Antonio and says, "You set the very devil of a pace for us old codgers."

"I'll have to try harder then," he says.

The Australians laugh ruefully. They didn't see what happened after the break. One by one, their women claim them and drag them away, whispering and darting glances filled with loathing at me.

Antonio walks over to me, grinning. "Let's sit down for a minute, Gin," he says. "I'm not what I used to be." He is breathing heavily and his back is bent. He looks around, but the grass is brown and crisp and ants walk through it in long, straggling lines. Instead, he leans against a fence post and takes a piece of damp cheese from his pocket and sniffs it, before throwing it on the ground. There is no sign of Toad now. He might have gone back to the pub, or off somewhere with John.

We hear voices from nearby: "It's not proper. Toad must know what's going on. How does he leave his children with them?" says one. "And her! She's speaking in wog now. I heard her. They could be talking about Toad and he wouldn't even know."

"Appalling," says another. "In broad daylight! Don't even have the decency to hide themselves from honest people's eyes."

"Can hardly blame her though. The Italian's a real man," says Mrs. Flannigan. "Did you get a good look at the bum on him? Juicy! And compared to that ugly Toad! He can put his shoes under my bed any day."

"Shut up there. That's not talk for a woman."

"She's giving him something. Look! She's putting it right in his hand!"

"It's only a sweet"

"They used to hang women for less."

The umpire blows the whistle again, and Antonio, who heard everything, turns and puts his face close to mine. His eyes and his lips are smiling. "Maybe I'll have to give you up for Mrs. Flannigan, eh?" he says, before following the others to the field. I suddenly see Toad on the other side of the field, hunched and glowering, an evil omen from a Grimm story.

The sunburned Australians drip sweat; it runs down their faces and saturates the backs of their shirts, and the rasp of their breathing can be heard in the silence between the shouts of the men and the thuds of the ball. They have given up chasing the younger Italians and now huddle around the goal. One man, a bachelor, wears a singlet with a hole in the hem, and he lifts up the front to wipe his face. His belly has dimples. Another man reaches up to scratch the crop of melanoma on his bald scalp. His fingers return again and again to worry the purplish lesions. The

Australians are irritated with themselves, and in consequence, the harder they try, the more often they trip on the uneven ground and drop the ball and knock into their neighbors. They are becoming exhausted.

The Italians, seeing this, move faster and faster, almost dancing, spinning on their toes and opening their mouths in joyous shouts that show their small, white teeth. I know Antonio is tired though, and above all the other sounds, I can hear his breathing, and the creak of his shoe when he turns and the wet sound his hands make when he leans on his knees for a moment.

A cloud passes overhead looking like the map of England and the teams pause to look at it and to point and to offer comments about other interesting clouds they have seen, clouds like biplanes and cockerels and guillotines. They wonder if it portends rain.

"Why did they stop?" asks Mudsey, sitting up from where she has been lying, rolled up in the blanket. Alf is floating ants in his lemonade. "What are they saying?" She doesn't understand that these are not children, but mostly old men, or middle-aged ones, who were rejected by the army. Who can no longer run for an hour without feeling poorly in their bones. She wants the Australians to win.

"They have called it a draw," says Antonio, trotting up to us. He bends and kisses the baby noisily on the head while looking sideways at me.

"What? No winner?" says John, joining us. "I bet a ten that we would win."

"Can there be a winner in war?" Antonio asks. "All are losers."

He picks up his shirt and fans himself with it. Only then does he notice that the band is still playing.

"Why did you stay?" he asks me. "You should have gone to

hear the music."

"I wouldn't have missed your game for the world."

"Is that so?" he says and he hums to himself as he buttons his shirt.

When Toad crosses the field, I tell him the game has been cancelled on account of age and he looks at me strangely.

"I think we should go home," he says, "you're making a spectacle of yourself." But the children cry and beg and pull at his clothing, and the Italians are surly, and I say he can walk home by himself but we are all staying for the dancing and the film. He jerks his head and glares at the people standing near us, but they won't look at him. They are avoiding him entirely.

"What a life," he says with feeling, and touches the pocket watch through the cloth of his trousers. He looks again at me, and there is a struggle on his face, some kind of pathetic pleading, but I cannot understand what it is that he desires. "I bought you some material," he says. "Grey. It looks that good on you. Ladylike." He coughs a meek and embarrassed cough. The very *weed* of a cough. And drifting from him, from his armpits and back and the palms of his hands, there is the smell of fear, as if a pot of burnt lentils oozed acridly from his pores. "And if your heart's set on it, well then, we'll go to the flickers."

With most of the football crowd, we carry the tired children toward the town hall, where the band is playing and Baker's Open Air Theatre has been set up. Corrugated sheets of iron fence the picture garden and there is even a ticket booth of sorts: Kenny from the station sits on a crate with a fan of tickets in his hand. Inside, there is no roof and no garden. Some wag has stuck a hot pink whirligig in the sand near the front, and it looks, if you squint, a bit like a fluorescent sunflower. They are using the side of the yellow-painted town hall as the screen. The actors will all look jaundiced. Sergeant Cleverish helps Paddy Baker with the cinematographic plant and then takes a seat. He nods to Antonio and John and several other POWs sitting nearby. Even though cinema going for POWs is, no doubt, banned by the government, we all understand that tonight will be educational and therefore not covered under the law. This whole day stands outside the law. It seems the people of Wyalkatchem finally feel some kindness towards the Italians.

"Look," says Alf, pointing. There is a box chained high in a gimlet tree outside the fence, and an Aboriginal man climbing up towards it. "What's he doing, Mum?"

A small bird, indistinguishable in the brothy light from any other small bird, swoops between Toad and I. "Saving himself two shillings and sixpence," says Toad, wrinkling and unwrinkling his eyebrows in appreciation. He'd have us all swinging from the branches if he could.

Poor Alfie is exhausted. His head bobs and his eyelids flutter. His thumb creeps towards his mouth. But he wills himself awake and his little eyes fly open, startled. He doesn't want to miss a thing.

I tuck the baby under my deckchair on a flannelette blanket, but Antonio reaches down and lifts the scrappy thing onto his lap. He strokes its bald head and puts his finger into its fist. He turns and kisses his little namesake's cheek. "Remember how my daughter put her kisses in the letter?" he whispers. "I put my kisses in your baby."

I hesitate, my face very hot, but no one has heard a thing. Then I bend and kiss my child in the tenderest spot, the fontanelle, where Antonio just pressed his own lips. The child's eyes open for the briefest of moments to reflect Antonio's pleased face. "*Our* baby." I whisper the lie as if it's the truth.

The projectionist struggles with the Essex bio box, attempting to bolt it to a wooden box in the fading light but mostly pinching his own fingers. He yelps and fusses. He cries, "Damn it all to hell!" and kicks the box and throws down the wrench in disgust.

Toad says, "Watch out. I'm going to give that bloke a hand. Otherwise we'll be here all night." He pushes past the line of knees, picks up the wrench, and within minutes has aligned everything and tightened the bolts. He starts the generator with one tug and the projectionist, an old man with huge, blindingly white false teeth and eyes like a bassett hound's, shakes hands with Toad. They mutter together, and the man opens a canister of film and unspools a foot or so, dangling it in front of Toad's eyes. Toad shouts and turns and runs to us, and calls John excitedly, "John! John! Wait till you see! The flickers are made of photographs all joined together. Come on. I asked the man if me mate might have a look-see." He pulls John up by the arm and drags him to the projectionist.

Toad lays a yard of film in John's hands and says, "Hold it up against the sky, like." He lays his hand on John's shoulder, and several people turn and begin to giggle before John shrugs out of his embrace and drops the film. "Get off me, you poof," he says loudly, and several more people turn around. Toad's delighted smile crumples. He abruptly walks to his chair, yanks Alf into his lap and presses his face into his son's back. John reaches out to touch him, to apologize, but Toad shivers away, muttering, "Get off me, you poof."

The band is warming up again, since it's not quite dark, not dark enough for the film anyway, and the crowd is restless, ready for a spot of dancing. "Anyone have a birthday tonight?" calls the bandleader, but no one does. "What about an anniversary then?" A man one row in front of us raises his hand. I have never seen him before.

"How many years have you been married?" asks the

bandleader.

"Sixty-seven," whispers the old man, shrinking from the attention.

"Sixty-seven!" exclaims the bandleader. "Well, Sir, you've got something to teach us all then. You and your wife, that's it, bring the old girl up here and we'll play something for you."

"Oh no," says the old man. "I couldn't." But his wife stands and takes him by the hand, and helps him out of the deckchair. She gives him his cane and holds his hand and they shuffle to the front. No one is talking anymore. Our eyes are all on the broad old woman with the plain face and the shabby flowered frock, and the old man, with his thick arm around his wife. The old woman pats him on the cheek and he lowers his head towards her.

The band plays softly behind them, and two men in the audience stand to sing when they hear which song it is, and Antonio stands too, and then John, and then another man. Antonio's voice in the cool night air sends me straight back to my bedroom, to the moment after he put the child outside the door.

I'm in the mood for love, simply because you're near me . . . The old man and his wife hold each other and sway; the old man's head rests on his wife's shoulder. When the song finishes, the man leans down and kisses his wife tenderly on the lips to the whistles and cheers of the audience. She touches his cheek again and smiles and draws her thumbs through the wetness under his eyes.

"Wait," says the bandleader, coming after them as they start for their seats. He raises his hand as if he will take the old man by the arm and stop him, but then his hand falls to his side. "Wait," he says again, more softly. The old man and his wife hesitate.

"Yes?" says the old man.

"We want you to tell us the secret of staying together for so long." He means, but does not say, the secret of a happy marriage.

The old woman peers out at the audience and she says, as if

it is very simple, "I never argue with him. He is always right." And the man pulls her hand up to his heart.

"We are the same as two peas in a pod," he says.

It is utterly silent as the old couple go slowly back to their seats. Antonio slides the picture of his wife from his pocket to his lap. He doesn't look at the photograph, but he touches it and sighs.

I put my hand over the photograph. "That could be us," I say, "one day."

"Yes," he mumbles, crossing his arms over his chest. "God, it's cold."

Softly, I sing for him as he once sang for me, "Your tiny hand is frozen. Let me warm it in my own," and I twine my fingers between his, but he shakes his head and pulls away.

"Don't," he says and looks across at Toad, who still has his face hidden in Alfie's back.

"Imagine! To be married for sixty-seven years. Do you know those people, Toady?"

"Don't talk to me," Toad growls.

The band begins to play another song and several couples move forward to dance. "I'm not going," says Toad. "Don't bother asking." Is he talking to me? Or to John?

"Are you going to dance, Mum?" asks Mudsey, tugging at my dress. Her nails are bitten to the quick. She has seen me slip off my boots and roll down my stockings. My bare feet are tapping in time to the music.

This, then, is the dance.

She strikes a match and holds it to his cigarette. He takes the match from her and drops it on the ground. He draws her cupped hand to his mouth and blows gently into her palm. A gleam of light falls on her neck. "Dance with me," he says. She stands and strokes the dress smooth over her thighs. He takes her hand and they walk to the front of the picture garden. She breathes the clean smell of soap and his sweat from the game. They move away from the other dancers, away from the musicians. He speaks to her in his low, slow voice, in his beautiful language. When he moves, she moves. What he feels, she feels. Four legs. One heart.

Her braided hair begins to fall as they turn, and he takes a wisp and holds it in his hand, inhaling the scent of her. Her throat as white as marble, the nakedness of ear and neck and wrist. She leans against his chest to hear his heart beat, *da dum, da dum*. He lays his cheek against hers and thinks of the heat of stone in sunlight, the smooth, chiselled texture of her skin. He wants to taste the lids of her downcast eyes, the softness of them delicious. They do not speak about the danger of this dance, about the people standing in the aisles, watching and jealous, or merely outraged. He makes a low groan of pleasure, just to be holding her so. The whitest places between her fingers. The gleam of her teeth within her lips. The pale blue dimple at the base of her neck. Their clothes full of the scent of their love.

Was this imagined? Dreams born of wishing? How could the town have allowed it? Where was Toad? Was he sleeping? Maybe there was no dance, no breath caught in the palm of her hand. Just the white hot desire of it.

"Where are the sandwiches?" Mudsey asks, just as old Paddy Baker gets the film rolling and announces loudly, "First off, mateys, we've got a newsreel, and then the main flick, the almighty Wizard. Keep the noise down or you'll be booted out and no refunds. No spit balls, no squirt guns and no hats allowed." There is a rustle as hats are removed and placed on the ground under the chairs. "If you need to use the facilities, on no account walk in front of the projector. Beer and nuts available when I change the reel. This film brought to you courtesy of the Wyalkatchem

Returned Soldiers' League, the Country Women's Association and the Junior Footballers. Now sit down and shut yer gobs."

The newsreel is a short black and white film entitled *San Pietro*, showing fighting in an Italian town, but for some reason, the projectionist can't get the sound to work. It is unlike any newsreel I have ever seen. The people are much closer. They appear to be *actually* dying. The camera lingers on a woman who lies in a gutter, still holding a bunch of flowers. A black line of something comes out of her mouth. Her leg is bent at an awkward angle, making it appear as if she is in the middle of one last happy skip. The camera shows buildings, mostly the remains of stone houses, being hit by large projectiles that flash through the screen, and a hand reaches up to wipe dust and distemper from the lens. The cameraman must have been standing right next to the building when it was hit. The signs in the little shops are in Italian. A bicycle lies abandoned on its side. A barefooted boy runs down the middle of the street, looking back over his shoulder, and when he sees the bicycle, he lifts it and tries to ride away. He is no more than six. A puff of dust rises near the bicycle and the child veers off to one side and crashes into a building. He could be Charlie Chaplin. The band raggedly begins to play something comic. Perhaps it is meant to be funny, but no one is laughing.

"Switch it off," calls one man, "the women shouldn't be seeing this."

"It's only actors," says the Paddy Baker, the showman.

"No," says the old man in front of us. "It's real. That body there is missing a leg."

Antonio, sitting next to me, leans forward in his chair. His hands grip the wooden rail under his knees. His breath comes and goes, his face shines with sweat, and a muscle jumps in his cheek.

A cold wind blows from the east, smelling of sheep piss. There's not a single mosquito out tonight. The film goes on and on.

John has closed his eyes and covered his ears, even though there isn't any sound. I can hear Antonio's voice. He murmurs, "God help them. God help them. God help them." Even though the bricks of the town hall are visible underneath the film, the images are no less real. No less terrible. Thank God, Mudsey and Alf are asleep.

Antonio raises shaking hands and spreads them in front of his face, blocking his view of the screen, but the ticking of the projector, the flashing lights up there against the bricks, the groans of the audience pull him back again and again. He looks around the edges of his hands, and his eyebrows draw together and he hunches his shoulders, as if in pain. American soldiers launch mortars against the town and cheer as buildings collapse. The film cuts from the sprawled, dismembered Italians to the laughing, gum-chewing Americans.

"You don't have to watch," I say, putting my hand on his arm, but he shivers me off and leans a little further forward. He is almost off his seat, breathing down the neck of the man in front. A woman runs across the screen. Her hair is plaited and she carries a small child on her hip. She staggers and drops the child and keeps on running. The camera focuses on the child. It is just a little boy wrapped in a cardigan and he lies on the road, wailing. Antonio sits very still. He has forgotten to breathe. An old woman in black walks down a mountain of rubble, balancing a coffin on her head. Three women sit in the sun, children in their laps; one of the children holds a scapular in its hand and sucks at it. When the film finally stutters to a close, Antonio leaps to his feet and says he needs to take a walk.

"Don't be too long," I call, "or you'll miss the Wizard."

"Shut up, Gin," he says. "I don't care."

John pushes past me. "How would you like it if that was Australia?" he says. He says he will go to see what has happened to Antonio. There are a lot of Italians leaving.

Paddy Baker gives the thumbs-up sign. "Breathe a little easier now that those greaseballs have left. Works like a charm every time. Puts the wind right up them."

There is discussion in the deckchairs while the projectionist threads the new reel, about what we have just seen.

"Can't really blame the Huns for killing those dagoes. Not exactly the staunchest supporters."

"Hopeless. The lot of them. See they are on the losing side and bloody change sides. Spineless wonders."

"You're a mob of fatheads. That was *us* bombing the Eyeties, not the Krauts."

And a woman calls out, very softly, "There's Italians here with us tonight. Have some pity."

And Toad says, "For God's sake, Gin. Don't stick your oar in or we'll have a riot."

But she calls out again saying, "It's people like us that you are talking about. Men with wives and children and mothers."

And Mrs. King says, "Poor men."

And someone else says, "I told you to turn it off. Now the women have all gone soggy."

The projectionist says he'll be ready in a tick and the chat subsides. People are pulling blankets over themselves now, or taking out cardigans. The wind is getting stronger and the tin walls rattle and the Aborigine swings on the crate and the leaves of the gum tree hiss. The Italians return and slump in their deckchairs. Antonio comes in last of all, shivering. No one is talking. The moon rises, a sharpened sickle in a field of magician's velvet. Anyone could be cut and they'd never feel it. What the trick is going to be is anyone's guess.

2

In the beginning of the film, the farmers laugh at all those men fussing over so few animals. "With fools like that, no wonder the Japs caught the Yanks sleeping at Pearl Harbor," yells the projectionist, which sets the tone of audience participation.

"How did Dorothy's hair get so long so fast?" asks the old lady, half rising to point it out.

"And short again," adds her husband. "Remember when our Sheila cut her own hair?" They put their heads together and laugh like a family of mice.

"I paid good money to see a *color* film," shouts a man near the front.

"That's right!"

"First the sound, now the color. What's next?"

"Keep your hair on," says the projectionist, placidly smoking a cigarette. "It's coming."

And when Dorothy steps out into Oz in full color, there is a gasp and several women stand up to see better. "Oh! Look at that! Did you ever see such a thing?" they say, and the people behind them yell, "Sit down! Sit down! You're blocking the view!" The projectionist stops the film and shines his torch on the offenders and says if there's any more trouble, out they go, and after that, everyone is quiet and meek as lambs and they only sing along under their breath.

I nudge Antonio when Dorothy meets the scarecrow. "Love at first sight." His hand is ice cold from the wind and he pushes me away. I look around for the baby and see the top of its head inside his jacket. "You're as cold as a frog," I tell Antonio and shove my hands up the sleeves of my cardigan. It's not often that I will risk a touch.

Alf is shivering so I move Mudsey, who moans in her sleep

when I touch her, into his deckchair to keep him warm. Antonio leans over me and whispers to John in Italian, "Francesca would love those shoes." He means the red ones. "I'm going to make her a pair just like that."

"What did he say?" asks Toad suspiciously. He yanks my arm and glares across at Antonio. "Here. Switch with me," he says and tries to slither into my deckchair.

"Leave off," I say, shoving him back. "I'm comfortable where I am."

"Be quiet up there" complains a man from behind us.

"That bloke there in front is too tall," whines Toad. "I can't see anything." He tries to haul me out of my chair again.

"I can't move away from Antonio. He's got the baby in his coat." If the baby cries, I'm right here. "You think you can nurse him?" There are titters from behind. "I'm not switching." In the middle of Toad's tussling, my ankle bumps against Antonio's.

"That hurt," he says. His voice cold as wet cloth. Up on the screen, they've reached the Emerald City.

"Bugger it," says Toad, subsiding into the sagging belly of his deckchair. He lets go of my hand. He pulls Alf's thumb out of his baby mouth with a wet pop. He thinks he can win battles the way he has always won battles. He thinks that just by marrying him, I will always be his devoted serf, making him cups of tea, letting him service his livestock, but my gratitude has faded. I am not fighting with him exactly. Just withdrawing, and one day he'll wake up and discover that the trenches on the other side of no-man's-land are empty.

Now, I look up to see the Wicked Witch of the West skywriting "Surrender" with her flaming broom.

I am ready to abandon everything I have here. The flimsy house with its dogs and its cows and its rabbits. The dirty brown children and the clean white grave on the hill. My husband with his cracked terracotta face. It's not surrender. It's a strategic retreat.

I push my foot against Antonio's. He shakes his head and moves his foot away.

"What's the matter?" I ask, but he suddenly stands up and switches places with John. The great stretch of stars overhead looks like a highway and the icy wind from the heart of the continent is strong enough to blow us all head over heels, skidding across the sky; enough to blow the bark off the trees and leave them standing bare like naked yellow skeletons. Dorothy taps her shoes together and Antonio fondles his photograph and Toad pops his watch and I hold my handkerchief to Mudsey's bleeding gum. While she was eating the sandwich, a tooth came out, and she swallowed it and now she's afraid it will grow in her belly, like a tree. Silly poppet. It's not trees that grow down there.

"Switch seats with me John," I say, leaning across to Antonio, brushing his leg with my elbow. His skin twitches, a horse dislodging a fly. "The baby might wake up." John looks at Antonio's set jaw and back at me.

"No," he says.

"Poor Virginia," snarks Toad. "Lost the little lover boy, did you? Boo hoo." He shows all his sharp teeth, a baboon's threat, not a smile.

The film ends and the band mewls "God Save the King."

"Wasn't that wonderful?" the people of Wyalkatchem say to one other.

"How charming."

There are goodnights and a rising fizz of frogs. Toad lights the lamps on the sides of the wagon and then, remembering, extinguishes them again. There is a wail from the Aborigine in the tree.

"Blackout," says Toad, "and that one's afraid of the dark." He nods towards the tree. "They are, you know." We climb into the wagon in darkness, and the horse takes us back to the old torture chamber out on Cemetery Road.

3

"Dry and cold as a witch's tit," says Toad, two days later, staring at the sky. "Half the lambs will die before the bloody rains come. There's no feed in the paddocks." The cauliflowers we planted a month ago are the same size. Yesterday, we used some of the last water to wet down the crutching yards, so we won't suffocate in the dust raised by frantic livestock. We got up at four this morning to muster the sheep in the Bore Paddock, riding down there with steak sandwiches in our hands and the dogs running alongside. By seven, we had the sheep in a mob and were driving them through the gates to the yards near the shearing shed. The dogs run across the sheep's backs with their tongues out and a jolly smile on their lips. They know what's coming.

This morning we're marking and crutching the lambs, cutting off their balls and their tails and the wool on their faces and bottoms. Wearing long canvas aprons that hang almost to the ground, we chose our partners with an eye to who can do the dirtiest job. I hold each lamb against my chest and Toad does the cutting. When he lops off the tail, he throws it in a bucket at his feet. The dogs mill around, excited by the smell of blood, and Toad flips the dripping tails towards them. The ewes bleat for their lambs from the furthest yard.

Toad castrates with a knife though a lot of blokes around here use their teeth. It's easier to get a grip that way but Toad is squeamish. He can't see himself biting off balls with his own front teeth. I've seen men do it, yes I have, with their faces down in the greasy wool and blood on their chins. He looks up and says, "Lamb tail stew tonight, eh?"

When we sit down for smoko under a tree, Toad squats next to Antonio, wipes his bloody hands on his apron and rolls himself a cigarette. "Did 'ya hear the one about Graham Robertson?" he says, not waiting for an answer. "Dumb galoot was trimming his sheep's feet and managed to whack the end off his thumb with the cutters. By the time he bent down to pick up the thumb, his dog had already run over and eaten it. You gotta be careful with these knives," he says, flashing the razor sharp knife inches from Antonio's face. "You never know what might get cut off."

The sheep in the jetting run stare at us with yellow eyes. Their smell is unlike any other. It sticks to the hands. To the feet. To the hair. To the tongue. We spit and spit again, and our mouths still taste of sheep.

Antonio straightens in his place, takes off his apron and hangs it in the tree. "I'm done here," he says. "I'll go work on the shoes now, if you will let me."

"No," says Toad. "Get back here, Mister Cesarini."

"Too late," replies Antonio. He jerks my plait up and cuts off the tasselled end with a rough shwick of his bloody knife. "She's mine already." He throws the twist of hair into the bushes. "Mine." He winks at Toad and spits, rubs his hands on his pants as if he has touched something obscene and, striding past, kicks me in the back with the edge of his shoe.

Toad sees only my hair in the hand of his enemy. His eyes bulge. He leaps to his feet. "You better watch out, mate, or I'll come after you one night with me ball-cutters. Bloody stallion makes a nuisance of himself with the mares, that's what I do. You hear me, Tony?"

But Antonio, who seems less and less like a prisoner every day, calls for Alf and my child runs to him, carrying his little wooden hammer.

I am invaded by thoughts of Antonio. The simplest actions of my daily life a reminder. Kneading the dough, my hands squeeze his flesh; smiling at my children, the smile is only for him; pulling carrots from the grip of the earth, my hands slip on his flesh, all him; his invisible presence at my side day and night. Oh, love. That is what this insanity must be. This willing loss of all previous existence. The wind's fingers in my hair reminding me of Antonio, *mio caro*. An obsession. A form of madness. The woman in Graylands who walked in endless circles chanting a single word, her actions understandable at last. Antonio. Antonio. Antonio. I splash his name upon my face, water my lips with its sound, dive back into every memory of every stolen moment I have shared with him as if it is now. As if it can quench my thirst for him. His name written on a loop of tape within my mind, so that when I open my mouth I am afraid that instead of what should be said, "Yes dear, the toast is ready," I will say his name. Antonio. Antonio. Nothing left in there but Antonio.

Words dangle from the furniture now, small manila cards with holes punched in the top. Each hole with a red thread looped through it so it can be tied to convenient nouns. *Davanzale, forbici, seno*. Window sill, scissors, breast. The beautiful Italian tripping off my tongue as I go about my morning work. Knife and board and garlic. Hand and heart and soul. Each word I learn bringing me closer to my desire. And now, when he comes to eat, I have to force myself not to rush at him, wanting only to breathe him in.

4

In the beginning of August, he gets a letter from his wife dated June fourth 1944; it arrives with a Red Cross package containing condensed milk and coffee and cigarettes and soap and chocolates, and while Toad and I hold our hot cups of unsweetened tea between our hands, and mallee roots pop behind us in the Metters, Antonio sullenly reads parts of the letter aloud. "'Dear Antonio,'" he says, "'planes flying low all night, we can see flashes of light far down the coast and the ground shakes. The farmer says the people in the cities will have many stories to tell on winter evenings *a viglia*.' Like this," Antonio explains, "sitting up around the fire." He says that everyone knows the Allied troops are within six miles of Rome. The fall is coming soon—but what if the Allies can't cut off the German retreat? What can we expect then? What will their retaliation be like? On the radio, we heard Alexander telling everyone in Italy to help the Allies as much as they can. But we also heard the Germans saying they will punish us if we assist. What to do?

"Get the hell out of the way," Antonio answers himself in a bitter tone, a carnivore biting at words. "Maniacs chop down anything that grows and shoot the rest." He's still miffed about the newsreel, it seems. I can wait. He sips his creamy coffee.

The last time I went into town, the clerk at the shop took my coupons and tore them up and spat on them.

"Where are your coupons, Missus Toad?" she said, glaring at me over the wreckage of my ration book. "You can't buy nothing here without tickets." I haven't told Toad but he must notice that the pantry shelves are empty. I won't be looked at by that girl again.

"'At midnight, shots from a low-flying plane,'" Antonio

continues reading. "'There are fires in the forests.

"'On the fifth, we hear the Allied armies have entered Rome by Porta Maggiore, and are chasing the Germans up the road to Bracciano and Viterbo. Many friends arriving this morning by foot. The German Red Cross came huffing and puffing up the hill to see if he could hide here. Two bombs fell in the valley, near the bridge. Someone (who?) is trying to blow it up. Anna doesn't even look up when she hears a plane any more. She runs straight for cover.'"

"Do you want to hear more?" he asks. He addresses Toad. Lately, he never speaks to me. I am grateful for his caution in front of Toad, but it's too late for that. Toad has seen me put everlastings in Antonio's room. *Flowers for eternity.* I bring my Italian hot breakfast in bed, crumpets and hot strawberry jam and mushrooms fried in butter, but he must be ill, for he cannot eat it. What ails him, I do not know. He has everything he wants now.

"You deserve this whole bloody mess," says Toad. "You Italians. How many good Aussie blokes did you kill, huh? Five? Ten? Gin, did you forget Antonio is a murderer?"

"I didn't murder anyone." Antonio slaps down his letter.

"Kill then. How many blokes? Did you put a bullet in their brains like you did with the calves? Or did you shoot them in the guts, so they'd die slowly?"

"Stop it, Toad. Leave him alone."

"Did you get a medal for killing Australians? Did you? How many Hail Marys did the priests tell you to say so it wouldn't be a sin to kill? Huh? Got no answers now, do ya?"

Antonio rubs his eyelid. "I didn't shoot anyone."

"Like fun." Droplets of sour spit fly from Toad's lips as he shouts. "I just hope you know you'll never be forgiven."

"Stop it," says John now, patting Toad's arm. "The Australian soldiers killed too. That is war." Toad stares at John's hand as if it is a cockroach.

"Nobody remembers before they enlist that they are being paid to take the lives of other human beings," says Antonio. "Killing a man in defence of your country is still killing a man." He rubs his eyelid and begins to read from the letter again. Proclamation of Eisenhower, coast of France, rumours, Tiburtina, no water in all of Rome, German line of defence in hills above Civitavecchia and Subiaco. The news rushes past me for I am still imagining my Italian with a gun in his hands. That was Toad's intention.

"Listen to this," says Antonio. "This is amusing." He has a bitter look on his face and he looks my way for the first time all evening.

"Many people are arriving here every day. Two girls came who called themselves Red Cross helpers. They stayed behind the church until their real profession was revealed by a constant stream of male visitors."

Toad directs a glance full of significance towards the children lying on the floor, but they are already asleep, face down in the sheep-skins. Alfie's foot trembles. Mudsey's arm is crushed under his cheek. I lift this substitute love into my lap and kiss his cheeks. His small head butts against my ribs. His breath is warm against my hand. Antonio. Oh wicked obsession. Oh warm breath in my palm.

"Yes," Toad says, after a moment. "We have our own little *comfort woman* right here." He pinches me on the arm. "Though she seems particularly cheerless lately. Can't think what's gotten into her."

"Antonio," I say, ignoring this last. "I wrote to the people down in Perth who are in charge of POWs."

"Mmm," he says, leaning forward to add more and more condensed milk to his coffee. Antonio. Antonio. Antonio.

"They've sent me a letter. Apparently, if you want to live in Australia after the war, you have to go back to Italy and then someone here offers to sponsor you. Write and say that they'll look after you financially. I thought, you know, you've stopped talking about going back to Italy. I thought you might be thinking about staying here in Australia."

"So?" he says, dropping the wet spoon on the doily, "what's that got to do with me?"

"I've done it. I've written the letter saying I'll sponsor you."

"Pig's arse, you have," snorts Toad, rearing up out of his chair. "I'm not giving a penny of me hard-earned dosh to this bastard."

The dogs begin to bark their faces off and all the cockatoos scream in the tree and Boss Cockie shrills, "Shut up! Shut up!"

"You put her up to that, you mongrel. It's not enough to be dipping yer donger in what's mine, now you want my money too."

"I didn't ask her to do that," says Antonio, shaking his head. "I don't want to live in Australia. I want to go home."

"Liar!" shouts Toad. "Admit it for once, why dontcha? You'd kill me if you thought you could get away with it." He flings an ashtray at Antonio but it skates over the big man's shoulder and hits the windowpane, shattering it. Wind straight from Antarctica rushes in between us with a sound like hail on a tin roof.

Antonio stands and shoves Toad in the chest, and Toad falls against the table.

"I don't want your wife," says Antonio, his fists up and ready. "Even if you gave me a million pounds, I wouldn't take her."

He is very convincing. If I didn't know otherwise, I would think he was telling the truth.

Toad pants, "Get the hell out of my house."

"I could kill you now," Antonio says, "if I wanted to." He

presses his fist into the flesh under Toad's jaw. "Like that. I could take your head off."

Peace! Peace! I speak in my softest voice. "But if Antonio can't go back to Italy? Then he'd have to stay in Australia. Wouldn't he?" I ask. "We owe him something, after all this time, Toad. That's all I've done."

"Filthy mongrels!" cries the cockatoo.

"It's supposed to be quiet in the bloody country, for God's sake!" Toad screams, jerking away from Antonio's fist. "Shut up!"

There is silence and then Boss Cockie mutters, just beyond the window, "Shut up! Shut up!"

"No one cares what you say, bad bloody cockie," says Toad, attempting to stuff a rag into the shattered window. It's ruined now and unlikely ever to be repaired. The yellow spill of light from the lantern rises and falls with every blast of wind from outside.

"Cuppa tea?" I ask, trembling. "Antonio? I didn't mean to upset you." My joints crack from the cold. This fight is what I have been waiting for. But Antonio takes out the old photo of his wife. God. How I hate that picture! I would like to throw it in the fire.

"I won't know her when I see her," he whispers, warming his hands on the tattered paper.

"Milk?" I ask. I shove the sugar bowl with its hard lumps of congealed tea towards him. Doesn't he want something sweet? Toad sprawls across the table, picks out the lumps and puts them in a matchbox to eat later, out in the paddocks.

"Those were for Antonio."

"Haven't you got eyes, Virginia? He doesn't want them. He doesn't want *you*." He turns to John, who's pretending to be asleep with his back against the fire. "It's a bad go that Badoglio mucked around so long the Germans had a chance to fortify and hold on to Italy," says Toad, his hand stroking up and down, up and down on his neck. "I thought you blokes would be scurrying off home any tick of the clock. Not that I want you to go."

He is looking at John, but John stands up and puts on his coat and says, "It's a bastard." I am used to him now and know he really means *it's enough*. He doesn't want to talk about what just happened in this room. He doesn't want to go out to the air-raid shelter with Toad and make the walls shake and the bunnies run away. He doesn't want to talk about what's happening in Italy. He hasn't had a letter in four months. Every time a letter comes for Antonio, he tries to smile and be happy for his countryman, but the veneer is very thin. You can see the frightened youth on the other side.

And when a letter *does* come for him, it's not from Italy, but from Perth. It's a letter demanding his presence back in the Control Centre, where he will be sentenced to ninety days in solitary confinement. "What?" says Toad, tearing at the tuft of hair that sprouts from the top of his forehead. "Not *John*! Those idiots! I told them *Antonio*, not John. My God. They've totally muffed it."

"What do you mean, Toad?"

His eyes are slitted, the eyes of a fox in a trap, crafty. He's planning to sink his fangs into me. "I should have done it long ago."

We are still standing near the gate after seeing off the sergeant. Toad begins to break rusty curlicues off the old iron scrollwork. The mass of fine lines in his hands fill with dirty brown powder.

"What should you have done long ago?" I ask, although I can sense his answer filling my throat.

He paws at the latch and this too crumbles in his hand. Flakes drift down on his boots and become lodged in the laces.

"I've dobbed on you and him, Virginia. When we were in town that day, the day we went to the flickers, I went over to the

Control Centre and told them it's true. About you and the dago. Captain Murray said they'll be arresting Tony soon and he'll never be eligible to live in Australia."

"You bastard! How could you? It'll be all over the papers! You've ruined everything for us." He catches my flying hands with fingers that are gritty with rust. My face, I know, is disintegrating.

"But not for you and me. We still have a chance," he says. I remember his sad little gift of grey fabric. "I couldn't let it go on. I can't bear it. Not in me own home. It's not right. And bloody Tony would wipe the floor with me if I tried to fight him with me fists. It's the only way I could get rid of him, see." His hypocrisy is stunning. This is the man who still runs, hand in hand, to the air-raid shelter with his Italian lover. That is all right, but what I do isn't? His voice rises, "But those bloody no-hopers down at the Centre have got it all bollixed up. Probably on purpose," he spits. "They're probably laughing at me right now. Cleverish cacking himself the whole way back to town."

It's a dreadful thing he's done, but, knowing Toad, I'm guessing he messed up the reportage himself, somehow blurted out the exact opposite of what he wanted to say, somehow blurted his great love for John.

I won't be the topic of conversation at every dinner table for weeks to come, after all. Antonio won't be imprisoned and barred from Australia for life. We are not revealed. And maybe it wasn't Toad's letter at all, but a result of that other romance, the poor boy mistakenly implicated in Walleye's pregnancy, I'm willing to bet. The girl hasn't returned and the mother was yellow and shaking when I saw her passing the gate at a gallop.

"Can't stop," Mavis said, whipping up the horse. "I've got a train to catch." She waved her thin hand at me and something flew up from it, in an arc, and hit me squarely in the forehead. It was her wedding ring. "Keep it!" she called. "And tell that Toad to come and get this bloody nag from the station."

I hock her ring and mine too, down in Perth after the war, and stuff the money in my brassiere, a start towards the fare to Italy.

5

Cleverish is out again the next day too, tapping a newspaper against the side of his boot. It reminds me of my stepfather and the hackles rise on my neck.

"What now, Sergeant?" I keep the gate closed between us.

"I need to speak to you and Toad. Alone." His voice has a tone in it, implying doom, or destruction, or at the very least, discovery.

But it can't be that. He has no real evidence against Antonio and me. Touching Antonio's hand in the street was nothing. Smiling at him, speaking to him in Italian, giving him a sweet, all of it is nothing. Not enough to take my Italian away. Not enough to declare me a moral hazard and an unfit mother. But there is still a roaring cavity in the center of my chest and the wind tearing through me is as cold as ice.

When Toad comes to join us at the gate, Cleverish unrolls the newspaper and hands it over the fence. He pulls off the little tag I attached to the gate, *la porta*. Looks at it and frowns.

"Shit!" cries Toad, "Will you look at that! A thousand POWs escaped!" His head swivels. He's looking for *his* POWs and alarmingly, they're nowhere in sight.

It seems from the paper that on August fifth, there was a mass breakout from the Cowra camp. Just after two in the morning, there was a single blast from a bugle and then four large groups of Japanese prisoners stormed the perimeter fences and threw themselves over. They had emptied the straw from their mattresses and set their huts on fire, a stray bullet cut the power lines and then all the lights went out. I imagine machine gun fire, the high pitched screams of the Japanese and the moans of the men impaled on the barbed wire fences. Over 700 men escaped and 231 Japanese were killed. At the bottom of the article, I read "No Italians took part in the uprising. They remained indoors and experienced no casualties." And then I can breathe again. The Italians are not escaping.

"Some old biddy wouldn't give up two Japs that were hiding in her house," says Sergeant Cleverish. "She wanted to give them tea and scones first. Imagine that! What on earth was she thinking?"

Toad snorts, but I give him a killer stare. "She was thinking they were hungry. She was thinking they needed food." Toad is glaring right back at me. "She was thinking those men needed her." His eyes goggle.

"What?" sputters Cleverish, his face as motley as boiled beef. "What?! They're not human beings! They killed four of the guards!"

"And you wouldn't? Are you saying you wouldn't do that, if it meant escape?"

"It's different," he says, but at that, I can't listen anymore and I go to mash beetroot for the baby, and I take intense pleasure in crushing the flesh, watching it ooze between the blades of the mill, red and pulpy.

6

Mudsey finds the doll again, stashed at the bottom of the woodbox, wrapped in newspapers. She watches her mother and her father, but nobody checks on the wrecked thing. It just lies there and the newsprint is slowly transferred to its face, so that now, when she peeks, news of the war runs across the pink cheeks. The broken arm is gone.

Early in the morning, while her family are out planting veggies, she takes the doll and rearranges the kindling and escapes to the hill that rears up behind the shearing shed.

She sits on her sister's grave and unwraps the doll. It is completely unlovable. She puts it down in the sand next to the stone bird that is the grave's only marker, and begins to scratch away at the hill. She feels unlovable too.

Alf sees and leaves the garden where he has been burying thinned beets. He stops on the way to wet his hat, but ends up crouched next to her, digging with his little shovel.

"Are we digging to China?"

"No," she says. "We're going to give this dolly to Joan."

They dig for a while in companionable silence.

"Doesn't she have a doll?"

"Dead people don't have dolls. Here. Don't knock the sand back in."

She takes his hat and wrings it over the sand and pats down the wet place to make a crust. They work at the hole until their mother comes out of the house with lemonade and pikelets, and then they run down to eat.

"We're digging a hole to China," says Alf, forgetting.

"Oh, says their mother. "That's nice." She hasn't noticed

where they are digging. Her eyes are on the Italian man. "When will you get there?"

"Tomorrow," says Alf.

"In August," says Mudsey, simultaneously.

"Well, that'll be lovely for you. Bring me back one of those pointy hats when you get there." She hesitates. "Maybe you'd like to dig to Italy instead? Italy is really nice."

"We're *never* going to Italy," says Mudsey tightly, and Alf and she go back to dig.

Days pass and it doesn't rain and the hole gets deeper and deeper. Mudsey and Alf can stand in the hole now and not be seen from the house. Sand slides down the steep walls and covers their feet.

"Wet it! Wet it!" cries Mudsey fiercely and they pat down the loose sand with water and dig again. They carry out their diggings with Alf's seaside bucket. They lie on their backs in the bottom of the hole and stare at the sky. They forget that they wanted to give the doll to Joan. The doll is buried in the pile of sand they have dumped near the edge of the pit. Now, they only talk about digging to China.

"Show me Chinese eyes," says Alf, sitting up, and Mudsey does. "How can they see?" he asks. "Like Mum," she says, because their mother is blind in the sun but still manages to see everything. Almost everything.

One day, they are digging and Mudsey's fingernails scrape against something hard. She thinks it is a rock. She tries to get her fingers around it. "Get the shovel," she tells Alf, but when he throws down the toy shovel painted with pastel animals dressed in rompers, she yells, "Stupid! Not that one. The real one." It takes him a long time to drag the heavy shovel up the hill from the garden, and when he finally gets there, he sees Mudsey has gone. In anger, he slings the shovel into the hole and it hits the bottom, breaking something into splinters that fall into a hole beneath the hole. "Mudsey!" calls Alf, "I broke into China!" He runs to get her and finds her cooling off under the house. She, however, is sceptical. A sceptical six-year-old.

"Nuh-uh," she says. "Liar liar pants on fire and I smell smoke!" Together, they climb down into the pit and peer at the hole within a hole. "It's a Chinese house with a wooden roof," she says finally, pulling at the splinters. A large piece of the wood comes away. Underneath, just barely able to be seen, is a tiny, withered, yellow hand, its fingers curved around something dark.

"Why doesn't it move?" asks Alf, poking at it with a stick. "Don't Chinamen move?" But now Mudsey remembers that they were not really digging for China and she looks up, searching for the stone bird that marks he grave. She pulls Alf away from the hole within a hole, dragging at his shorts. "Come away from there Alfie," she says. "I'll give you a lolly." She kicks sand towards the hand with a sick feeling in her guts. "This is a stupid game. Only pissy babies play this game."

"No it's not," he shouts, and tries to jab the yellow hand again. She slaps him on his face, twice, and breaks the stick. She jerks his little arm and says, "I'll tell Mum on you if you don't get away from that."

After she gets him out of the pit, she climbs back down and retrieves the shovel. In the sun, she thinks she can smell the hand. She thinks she sees it expanding, like a prune in water. She thinks the fingers are reaching for her.

That night, she dreams of the hand and climbs into bed with her mother for the first time in years. She curls against the warm back and holds the tip of the plait. Her feet are ice cold. Her nightgown is wet. She tries not to close her eyes.

In the morning, her mother pushes her out of the bed and says she smells of wee, but then notices the look on her face and her trembling, and asks what's wrong, but she can't say. She falls asleep at breakfast and her mother doses her with cod liver oil. Alf says they broke into China and saw a Chinaman and their mother smiles.

She creeps into her mother's room night after night and lies under the bed with her eyes open. If she sleeps, she sees the wrinkled hand mushrooming over her head, pressing against her, suffocating her with its smell of old skin.

She watches Alf and doesn't let him go near the hill. She tells him to grow up. They can't dig to China. When he asks about the hand they saw, she tells him that it was a turkey foot she hid in the sand. To trick him. When he cries and says she's mean, she cries too and says she's sorry. Very sorry. So so sorry.

7

I am singing on the veranda. It is loud enough for Toad to hear. It is loud enough for Antonio. It is loud enough for all who wish to hear my song. The words move through me like a wind, a hurricane, blowing through my hair, brushing against the folds of the old grey dress, threatening to rip the buttons off like bloody spatters.

O mio babbino caro, mi piace e bello, bello . . .

Oh, my beloved father, I love him, he is so beautiful . . .

Mudsey and Alf stop what they are doing and come to look at me. They stand with their mouths open as tears roll down my face.

Vo'andare in Porta Rossa a comperar l'anello!

I want to go to buy the ring. I am ready. At last, I am ready.

8

A cold wind from the south blows steadily over the hill and clouds pile up on the horizon. Change is in the air. I know it. I feel it in my aching bones. I feel the change coming in the pressure behind my eyes. Even the ants and the beetles and the snakes know it and abandon their nests and mass on high ground.

The land opens its mouth, waiting for water. The trees are black against the sky, with strange white shadows along their limbs. An emu blunders out of the bush, looking for water, its huge beak open and its tongue protruding like a desiccated earthworm. A deep drumming comes from its throat. The wind touches the hand that has lain for so long in the dark and blows sand into the hole within a hole and the fingers close on the sand. Far off, beyond the furthest trees, there is a flash of light and a distant rumble.

A small man comes and stands on the veranda and he stretches out his hand. A tall man opens the door and joins him and they both light cigarettes, leaning on the railing.

But the rain does not come that day or the next. The storm passes by to the south of them and the land still lies on its back with its mouth open, desperate now for water.

The small man stands in the garden and kicks at the rows of dying plants. He wheels a forty-four gallon drum into the rows and pours a ladleful of water onto each seedling. He pulls up radishes and wipes them on his shirt and tastes one. He makes a face and spits it out on the ground. The big man points at the clouds, but the small man shakes his head. From the house comes the sound of a piano. The big man turns and frowns at the house and the small man looks at him. He walks over and tries to hit the big man, but trips on a clod and falls and the big man helps him to stand again.

The wind blows the smell of the dying sheep and cattle all around them. The drum of water is all there is left for the house, for the garden and for the dogs. The windmill is still pumping up a little water from underground for the livestock, but increasingly, it smells so strongly that the animals won't drink. Increasingly, it comes up rust red and full of sediment. Even the rabbits are leaving.

9

That is what it is like, the winter of a drought. We look up into the sky for salvation, but nothing comes. Clouds gather, but then the wind blows them past, pushes them further north or east. The land withers. Toad ploughs and seeds, without rain, but with a puny hoping, and the wind lifts the soil and the seeds in great billowing sheets that blot out the sun and hit the sides of buildings like gunshots.

A chain of salt ponds stretch across the south-east end of the Shire, and drain into the Mortlock River just north of Tammin, but it's a salt river and a dry one at that. There's no fresh water to be had for love or money.

That winter of 1944, we lost over half of our sheep and had to butcher all but one of the dairy cows. Rotting sheep lay by the fences, and the air was full of the stench of putrid meat and the zuzzing of blowflies. Everybody washed in the same pan of water, and then the clothes were washed in it and then the floors were washed with it, and then the cow shed was cleaned with it, and what was left was fed to the garden, by the teaspoon.

John was taken to jail and did not come back. Sergeant Cleverish came for him unannounced on a day when Toad was miles out repairing a well. That beautiful boy cried when he was told he had to leave. He said to tell Toad that he would miss him. He said to tell Toad that the bone really worked. I had not known that John believed the story about the toad's bone, much less that he had made one. And an image of Toad and John clasped together on the river bank in an amplectic embrace, the mating grip of an amphibian, rose up before me to block any proper goodbyes.

When Toad came in and I told him that John was gone, it seemed as if his eyes retreated within his head and his face shook. He nodded, once, and I pitied him then, oh yes I did, for wouldn't it have killed me if it had been Antonio who'd been taken away. Toad was, after all, a man who could feel love and show it too.

Toad wrote to John but never got a reply and eventually he returned to his former pleasures. Sergeant Cleverish donated his mother's purple striped corset with the lurid red flossing and for a while, Toad was busy building a stand that could adequately display this masterpiece of Victorian engineering. Perhaps I had something to do with the arrival of the corset, being tired of seeing Toad draped on odd bits of furniture. He was depressed for so many reasons; the loss of John as lover and extra pair of hands; the merciless drought; my obsession with the Italian. Perhaps I bribed Sergeant Cleverish to rummage through old Missus Cleverish's trunks in search of corsetry. I had not touched the grappa since the night I torched the lawn, but I still knew where it was kept.

Antonio, too, seemed deflated. I tried to entertain him, putting Chopin on the gramophone, playing the opera we had sung together, bribing Mudsey to take little notes to him, scribbles that she must not have delivered for he never answered them. I cut up apples for him and arranged them in the shape of a heart. Going to work in the orchard, I walked so close to him that the backs of our hands touched, but he didn't speak. "Remember that day?" I asked hurrying to catch up with him, "When we went to town?" I waited for him to turn and see my desire for him, but he stood, stoop-shouldered, staring at the aborted lemons on the ground. I wasn't sure if his misery stemmed from the loss of John as a friend and countryman and never ending source of salacious gossip, or from seeing that appalling newsreel, *San Pietro*. Or maybe it was because I was unskilled in flirtation. Maybe there was another step to this dance of which I was unaware. Either way, when I knocked on his door, he didn't answer and if I stepped into his hut, he retreated to the bedroom and shut the door between us. He no longer ate in my kitchen but took his meal out to the hut.

One day, I stood next to the woodpile with the axe in my hand, waiting for the chance to have a private word with him, but the sun went down and he never appeared. Funnel web spiders loaded with green poison leapt out from between the logs as I paced, alerted to my presence by the vibrations set off by my footsteps. They dangled at the ends of their silken bungee cords, swinging slowly. And then climbed back up to their lairs, unsatisfied.

I stood there in the deep dark until I heard Mudsey banging on the wall and calling me to knock down a tree snake from the ceiling over her bed. "Keep on banging like that and the bloody snake will fall right on top of you," I yelled back at her. The stack of wood by the back door got lower and lower until I was forced to chop my own wood again.

Since there was no rain, Antonio had plenty of time to work on the shoes. By the beginning of August, he'd already given Toad and Mudsey and Alf their new shoes, but the shoes he had begun for me were taken off the last and put aside. Now he worked on a pair of red slippers *a la* Judy Garland and he came to me with his hat in his hand to ask if I had any sequins or glittery things that he might have for the shoes. Privately, I would have preferred a pair of practical work boots, but who was I to look a gift horse in the mouth? I still had a tube of glass sequins at the bottom of the glory box and I handed it to him with a smile. I mouthed "I love you," but he looked away at the critical moment. "*Gracie*," he said when he was already halfway out the door. He left me standing there, yearning for the liquorice scent of his body, for the taste of his fingers.

1 0

On Monday, we all oversleep. The sky is so dark that the rooster doesn't crow, and without the line of bawling cows outside the shed, needing to be milked, Toad and I think it is still night and turn over and go back to sleep.

When I wake up, there is a strange smell in the air, electric and unpleasant, and I can't think what it might be. The house is very cold, icy drafts skittling across the floor and rubbing against exposed ankles, jumping up and rattling all the windows. Even after I light the little stove in the lounge room and throw some more wood in the Metters in the kitchen, I still have to pull on a thick jumper and a pair of woollen socks. My breath can be seen in front of me, smoky. It will get up to eighty degrees at lunchtime but it's probably not even forty now. Bitter winter.

Mudsey and Alf skid around on the jarrah floorboards in their socks and I warn them not to touch the isinglass in the stove door, or even to go near it. There is still half a glove stuck to the glass from last year. The clock in the kitchen has stopped and when I ask Toad what the time is, he shakes his head and shows me his pocket watch, which has been stopped at three forty-nine since the football match between the Australians and the Italians.

Nothing else is said between us that morning. Be careful of

the stove. What's the time? Even the children aren't talking. And every so often, Toad walks over to the wonky window with its shattered glass and looks out at the sky. We are all waiting for something.

Mudsey and I are hanging laundry on the line when she puts her hand on her hair and says, "A bird just poohed on me." We both look up to see what kind of bird it was and a large wet drop of something lands in my eye. Because of Mudsey, because of what she said about the bird, I cry "Oh!" and put my hand up to my eye, but many drops have already fallen, and my face is wet, and my dress is soaked through on the shoulders, and there is the shush of the rain hitting the dusty leaves and the smell of the wet earth and the rain and the taste of the sky on my tongue. God, how good it is to let the clean water roll over my face; cavort in my ears and down my neck. I put my hands in the air and there is no thought of taking shelter and the laundry droops on the line, all of the hems in the slurry, forgotten. Mudsey strips off her dress and twirls in the rain and the mud splashes on her calves and she opens her mouth and lets the rain fall in. Toad comes out of the house and puts his hand into the sheet of water cascading off the roof. He goes inside and comes out again, carrying a bar of soap. Even though the rain is as cold as ice, he steps into the waterfall with a shout and soaps himself, clothes and skin together, cavorting and twisting. Alf first cries, "What is it? What is it, Mummy?" He doesn't remember rain. But then he runs from puddle to puddle, jumping in every one. Antonio calls from the veranda of his hut, "Stupid Australia. First there is no rain. Then there is an ocean." A mouse is swept by in the current of a stream that cuts through the middle of the yard. Antonio watches it go past. I can't get him to come and stand in the downpour. I try to pull him off the veranda, but he is stronger than me, and he doesn't smile. "Leave me alone," he says. "I don't want to get wet." I leave my handprints on his shirt and laugh at him. "Stick in the mud," I say. "Wet chook." And that sets me off laughing again, because he's totally dry. "Come on," I urge, "Come out here with me."

"I'm not going anywhere with you," he says. "Stop it."

When Mudsey's lips turn blue and her skin is prickly with gooseflesh, I bring the children inside and stand them naked in front of the fire and hang fresh clothes for them there too, so when they are dressed, they are warm and rosy and smell of wood smoke and I kiss their heads.

"Come here, darlings," I say. "I'll play you a tune for the rain." Their cheeks blush from the attention. From the *darlings*. I play them Chopin's *Raindrop Prelude* in D-flat, which is a sad piece, even though I am so happy, convinced that Antonio will be taking me to Italy, that I will escape this place, and even escape the grim satisfaction of my children, but out in the rain, while I am playing, Sergeant Cleverish, a freshet of water pouring from the bash in his hat, hands Antonio a telegram from Italy. The envelope is so wet he can hardly tear it open. He stands in the rain, trying to shelter his head with his arm. The telegram is falling apart in his hands. He reads it and he reads it again and he says a word. No, he says. And then no again. No. No. He kneels in the mud. No. He beats off the hands of the man from town. No. He holds up the telegram and reads it again and looks up at the sky and his face is a river and very slowly, he lies down in the mud and the rain and curls up there, wet and dirty like something a cat coughs up, and saying no and no again.

Sergeant Cleverish knocks on the window before I am finished playing and pushes up the sash. "I won't come in," he says, "But your man has had some bad news." He says *your man* with some delicacy, a kindness I won't soon forget. "It's very bad, Gin."

"What is?" I ask, and he shrugs.

"The usual. The war."

"Has someone died, then? What's happened?"

"Not just one someone. The poor bugger's whole family has been killed."

"No! What was it? A bomb?"

He shakes his head. "The Germans."

"But they were safe. Antonio said they were safe. What happened?" My heart beats faster at this news and I keep barely keep myself from smiling. It's a dreadful thing to think, but I can't help it. Antonio is mine now.

Cleverish doesn't know who murdered them. He only saw the telegram; the news of 560 dead at Sant'Anna and amongst them, Antonio's family. He says it's not a mistake, the Germans are butchers; he's not at liberty to say but Sant'Anna is going to be the least of the atrocities.

"Not for Antonio," I say. I am wicked to the bone. Casualties. Strategic losses in war. And I wear the uniform of the conqueror.

No, not for him, Cleverish agrees. And asks me in the same breath if there's any of the grappa left.

Together, we go out to find the milk can with its load of mind rot, and discover, instead, Antonio curled up and blue from the cold, in the mud. My Antonio. We get him onto the veranda and rub him with chaff bags and Toad brings blankets from his bed and lays them over Antonio's shoulders as I once did.

"I'm so sorry, Antonio. I know how hard it is. I had a child that died," I say, seeing the Italian's ravaged face, not knowing what to say. It is not our way here, to lay out our emotions like spices in a marketplace. Tears are like salt. The tiniest pinch is enough. Antonio looks at his hands and the pieces of wet paper between his fingers.

"Her name was Joan. She was just like me. White. Like a

statue." That's what he said about me. But there's no flicker of recognition on his face. "She thought, just by wishing, she could make good things happen." I stop. I can't keep on talking. I have lost one. He has lost six. An empty space in the heart creates an empty space in the mouth.

"Why did she die?" he asks, very low. I almost can't hear him. The rain on the tin roof is deafening.

"She was eight," I say. "She never knew there was anything different about herself. She thought it was a gift, being born an albino. That it made her somehow special and protected." I remember Antonio winding my white hair around his finger. *Bella*, he called me. Beautiful. Something hot rises in my throat and behind my eyes. Antonio has shown me all the things that Toad could not. He is my god and my creator. I will not see him broken. I *cannot* see him broken. "The children got diphtheria. Some people had come up from Perth, to shoot ducks, and they brought it with them. At first the little ones were only feverish and coughing, but then they became very weak. It was hard for them to breathe."

"Why did she die?" he asks again, not lifting his head, and this time I know he doesn't mean Joan. His lip is bleeding. A drop falls onto his wrist and is rubbed across his eyes. And now I only want to speak about my own loss. Toad puts his hand on my arm, the greedy pup. He thinks I am vulnerable to his advances now. I knock his hand away. I don't want him. I want Antonio.

"The doctor said I have to watch the children, because with diphtheria a skin grows over the back of the throat and suffocates them. He showed me how to put two fingers down their throats and tear out the membrane. He wouldn't let me bring the children to the hospital because of contagion."

Antonio looks at me for a moment and his eyes fill with bitterness as he mashes the telegram in his hands.

"It can't be true," he says. "She said she was going to hide in the caves if anyone came. She's still alive. I'm sure of it. They're all up in the caves, hiding. *Dio boia.*" He begins muttering in Italian, the words not making any sense. Maybe he's praying.

"It must be a mistake," I agree, but Cleverish grips Antonio's shoulder and shakes it and says, "The telegram was sent by a man who got away, an eyewitness. Someone who knew where to find you. He saw what happened. He knew who your wife was." The words limp out of his mouth, apologetic, but Antonio flinches at the word *was*, and groans and lists to one side, his bones creaking, the timbers of his great limbs waterlogged and sinking.

"I fell asleep," I bobble on, a jolly boat in his wake. "I fell asleep. It wasn't my fault. I'd been awake for so many nights tearing out those bits of skin. I fell asleep. I didn't mean to." Words, words, words. I cannot look at the wreck of Antonio. The rafter drips, *plink plink*. There is a hole in the toe of my boot. A damp smell rises from Toad, of linseed oil and mouldy chaff. "It was Joan. All the others got better but Joan died."

"You did yer best," Toad say, patting me on the back with his horny hand. "Buck up."

"Shut up Toad," I say, "I'm not talking to you. And anyway! You slept through the night and didn't get up even once. What would you know? You never wanted Joan to live from the moment you laid eyes on her. From the moment you saw she was white, like me."

I turn slightly away from Antonio and can no longer see his face, the curve of his spine, and it is a relief. Such a relief.

"Ah God, woman. You've got me mixed up with yer old man. I *loved* Joan. I did. And you told me to go to sleep that night."

"Yeah. But you didn't have to. You could have stayed up

and kept me company."

"Would she have lived then? That's so unfair. She was crook, Gin. She was dying."

Antonio stares out at the rain, his face twisted, and tears run from his eyes without stopping. They fall from his chin and gather in the chalice of bone at the base of his neck.

And what would the sergeant think if I were to draw Antonio's head to my breast and comfort him? Lay my hand upon his cheek? What poison would the neighbours think I had swallowed?

"A lot of children in the district died," says the sergeant, glancing at Antonio and rubbing a hand over his own head. "You did a good job of nursing your kids, Missus Toad. The doc said so. Your kids had it bad. He didn't reckon any of them would live. You were bloody lucky to keep the two."

"You've never seen her grave," I say to Antonio. The conversation hard for me but destroying him. I would give him my mother's veil if I could. To cover the shame of a grown man crying. "I could show you Joan's grave." To spare him the shame of crying in front of the men. *Liar.* "It's the nicest place on the farm. Up on the hill. Gets all the breezes." As if there can be something good about the death of a child.

He doesn't answer. He makes no sound. His mouth moves as if he is chewing something that tastes bad.

"Come on, Antonio. Stand up. A walk will feel good." The dog would have put its wet muzzle into his hand and it would have been a comfort. "Will you walk with me?" I say, holding out my hand, my face averted to avoid pity.

He jerks to his feet but he won't let me take his arm. The second we step off the veranda, we are saturated. The bags on Antonio's shoulders must be heavy for he shakes them loose and drops them in the mud. Toad watches us go. His face is turbulent, sad old Punchinello.

The mud sucks at our feet and after a few steps, Antonio sits down and pries off his shoes and hurls them against the rabbit cages. I point towards the hill and pull at his arm, because he seems glued to the ground. He hunches over his bare feet and puts his muddy hands over his eyes. And howls. Like a dog. And when he lifts his eyes again, they are red and glittering. Inhuman.

How I am slain by a man with tears on his cheeks who allows the arrow of pain to pass through his heart and who allows himself to feel it. As I do not allow myself to feel the loss of Joan.

I tug at him until he rises and then we trudge up the slope, slowly, the rain slapping our faces. It is only when we stand on top of the hill, our hands and knees smeared with mud, and I am wondering why I ever thought this would be a consolation, that I see the gaping hole, the hole to China.

"Oh God! No!" I cry, thinking dingoes, but Antonio slides down into the pit and kneeling, wrenches back the wood. He stoops and touches something in the hole within a hole and his eyes fill again

"It's your fault," he says in Italian, and then louder, in English, "Your fault. It's because of you, because of what we did, that she is dead." Nonsense, of course. It is only the grief talking. And yet, a crack of shame runs through the porcelain of my face.

"That's superstition. She died because of the war."

He nods, and then stands up. "Gin. Come down here."

But there's nothing that could force me down into that hole. Not even Antonio. I remember lying down there with Joan, still fresh in her nightgown, with her white hands blooming like lilies. "No," I say. "No. I'd do anything for you, but I can't go down there."

Antonio scrambles up the disintegrating side of the pit and I back away. "Gin," he says, and he rushes forward and takes me in his arms, his cheeks wet and cold.

"I love you, Antonio. Please let me help you." My mouth against his chest, thinking he must, at last, see what I see. An opportunity. A chance for us. But he tugs me towards the grave. We struggle. I cannot go down there. I will not. It is as if he wills me to feel as he feels. Oh God! I cannot. I will not. No. The edge of the pit crumbles and we lose our footing and slide, together, sideways down into the muck. He makes a sound deep in his throat as our bodies come together in a heap. "Look," he says, and his face is white as he lifts the piece of wood. "Your little girl is still here." There is her hand, much withered and the biscuit clutched within it, petrified by the dry winds and the sand and the salt. "It's your fault," he says again. "*Tu porti iella*." He tells me I bring bad luck. The worst luck.

"I didn't mean to fall asleep," I whisper, and I am so tired and so cold now, I wrap my arms around my body, shivering, holding myself together. The longing unbearably strong in me to touch her hand. To stroke it. But instead, I cover the yellow thing with a piece of the shattered wood.

"I thought they would be safe," he says, and his voice breaks when he says *safe*.

"I thought I could save her too," I point to the wound in the hill. "But I couldn't. I could only try." I pat a handful of the cold earth over the wood and scrape sand from the sides of the hole, my fingers numb, moulding it over the place where Joan lies. The wet sand stings my hands. Sometimes, the children, Mudsey and Alf, find a shell in this sand, as if this land was once the bottom of a vast ocean. Sometimes they find bones, as if it is the graveyard of a continent.

"If I wasn't stuck here," he says, "I could have saved them." His looks up at the sky, at the rain vomiting down. "Your stupid country," he says, biting at the words. "You should have let me go.

We became Allies and still I am your prisoner! You should have let me go to fight the Germans in my own country instead of trapping me here. Cutting tails off lambs." He turns to look at me. "Barbarians," he spits. "You are all barbarians."

"Shut up! Shut up!" screams the cockatoo.

My hair snarls upon my face. I hear whimpering. It is him. It is me. It is us.

"We are not the ones who killed your family, Antonio. It was the Germans."

"You! You caused them to be killed with your evil eyes!" he cries. He, who said I have blue eyes. Not red.

"Superstition again," I whisper to the grave at my feet. "I wanted them to live." *Liar.* I cannot leave it alone. I must know at any cost. "But maybe, now that it's happened, it will be easier for us. After the war."

He rises with a roar and pelts me with sand and pieces of fractured wood, hits me with his big hands and cries, "You are a stone fortress, not a person. When you opened your gates, it was not to surrender to me, but to *capture* me. Do not call this love. You have no idea what love is."

I have no answer. It's true. I let him hit me until he is tired and then I pull myself out of the pit and walk back to the house without him. Toad is still waiting.

From the middle of September, in the damp, hidden places, rise the wildflowers of the wheatbelt: the blue fairy orchid, the flame grevillea, fields of pink everlastings, the yellow hakea and the sandpaper wattle, the praying virgin orchid and the strange bloom of the warty hammer orchid. The labellum of this flower is brown and speckled like the abdomen of the thynnid wasp. The orchid even smells like a female wasp. The male flies down and grasps the dummy female, intending to fly away and mate with it. But the orchid is firmly attached to the sandy soil from whence it sprang. And the thrusts of the male trigger a form of hammer in the orchid which slams shut, slapping pollen on the wasp's back and leaving him marked. For the orchid, this ensures survival. But for the wasp, it often means death.

I avoid Antonio's sadness as I avoid all problems. I do not write to the authorities, thinking he will come and speak to me. I don't want him to be taken to Graylands. Is that where they take even enemy soldiers? Perhaps there is another hospital for them. I want a chance to rekindle his desire and give him a chance to recover, and so I ignore his needs and focus on my own. I forget to shield him from the letters that dribble in with their condolences from elderly aunts in patched black dresses, and their descriptions of what, *exactly*, had befallen his family in those mountains in the north of Italy.

For two months, he sits in the big, lopsided velvet chair in his hut, and stares at the miniature shoes he had made for his family. He touches them and holds them to his lips until they fall apart, until all he has, lined up on his thigh, are tiny pieces of bark and feather and leaf. And then, those too begin to crumble. And finally, he has nothing and just stares at the place where they had once stood, at the window ledge and beyond it, at the arid land stretching to the desert.

Daily, I leave Anthony to cry in his box on Antonio's veranda, pushing him closer and closer to the door with the wash stick, until Antonio comes out and steps over the box on his way to somewhere else. He swats at Alf and tells the little boy to stop following him everywhere. To go and find Toad. And one day, when I leave Anthony on the Italian's veranda and go to make lunch, I find the infant on my return with Boss Cocky between his baby fists, strangled in his hands. Feathers on his lips.

Two months after he received the telegram and almost a year since he first came to the farm, Antonio revives. He stands at the window of the kitchen, his hat in his hand.

"The parrots are too many," he says, with his face turned east. The parrots, what we call twenty-eights because of the way they scream—*twenty-eight! twenty-eight!*—are a serious pest, and especially after the rains, swoop down in clouds and nip the buds off the fruit trees, eat the heads from the grain, peck out the eyes of the weaker lambs. It is late spring. Early morning. There is beard of green across the unshaven fields.

"I need the gun," he says, "And a box of bullets," he says, "To go shooting."

I am grateful that he is speaking to me again. Perhaps he is beginning to accept the loss of his family and look around to see what can still be salvaged. I lick my lips and smile at him and smooth my hair back behind my ears. The only thing unusual in his request is the demand for a *box* of bullets. Parrots are not so stupid that after a few of them have been shot, they continue to sit there as targets. A handful of bullets would be enough. But I only think that afterwards.

He asks, too, for some meat and some bread, and I, only too happy to please him, give him the best I have, the end of the corned beef, a lump of queen's pudding, the last of the pickles and four fat slices of toast. I tuck an everlasting flower between the slabs of bread for him to find later and smile over. I watch him, that spring morning, heading east with the parcel of food tied up in his spare shirt and hung from the sight of the gun. I wave to him, but he didn't wave back.

When he doesn't return by nightfall, I am not worried. I sing *Five Little Ducks Went Out One Day* to Mudsey and Alf when I put them to bed, and Toad, cautiously, suggests that maybe Antonio is tired of my company. He smiles his crooked smile and ducks his head out of a kind of modesty, a pudeur that is uniquely his. I would like to scratch his eyes out.

"I don't think so," I say, and that's when I see Toad is winding up his pocket watch and setting the hands.

The next morning, I look in Antonio's hut and see the hated pink uniform folded up on his bed. "He's gone!" I cry, running to Toad. "Escaped." I picture Antonio with the little pink flower in his hand. Waiting for me to join him. And I bite all trace of a smile from my lips. So this is how it is going to be.

Sergeant Cleverish comes with the dogs and the aboriginal tracker, a man named Ute, but it has been raining again and we've had the sheep through the yards and every time the dogs head east, Cleverish jerks their chains and says *come orf that, you blithering mongrels*. He is sure Antonio is heading for the coast or down to Perth. Probably walking along the railway lines so he doesn't get lost. The police aren't so concerned either. They think he'll show up in a week or two, tired and hungry, with blisters the size of jellyfish on his feet.

But we are interviewed, Toad and I, separately, and when it comes out that I've given an enemy combatant meat and bread and a gun and money (Toad tells them there is money missing. "Five pounds," he says, "From me enema bag."), they lose the friendly look of country policemen and begin smoking evil-smelling cigarettes and shouting, and Sergeant Cleverish, who I think understands my situation and maybe even has a little sympathy, tells all those men in front of Toad that I am the Italian's mistress and have given birth to his child.

"That's not true," says Toad crossly. "Anthony is all me own kid. Spitting image of his old man." And then they look at him with such pity that his ears burn red and threaten to fly off into the bush, even though what he said was the truest truth. "She was preggers when those Eye-ties got here. Bloody doctor. If he wasn't arsing around chasing floozies, he could tell yer that," he mutters, but no one listens to the words of a cuckold.

"Wasn't it you, Mister Toad," they say, "That made a report at the Wyalkatchem Control Centre back in June, to the effect that your wife and this Italian were involved in an adulterous liaison? Just so. It seems likely that the missus here has letters from her lover stashed somewhere round abouts," they say, turning away from Toad to hash out their own theories. "There might be something incriminating amongst her things."

Excuse us, they say, as they tear apart my glory box, their butcher's hands shredding the Victorian dresses, ripping apart the fragile umbrella, wiping their perspiring faces on the little scrap of fabric I've kept from my mother's wedding dress. Pardon the noise, they say, as they pry boards from the inside of the Italians' hut and poke bayonets into the plush club chair, as their boots scuffle the last little bits of leaf and fur and bark and blossom to dust.

"Did you ever see your Mum talking with the Italian?" one man asks Mudsey, squatting next to her as she rocks Anthony in a blanket tied to a tree.

"Nope," she says. "Wouldn't be proper." She stares the man down and he goes back to opening and closing drawers, thanking God that his own little girl looks like a little girl and not a hound from hell. Thanking God that he lives in the city.

They take away the wooden lasts Antonio carved, and the shoes he had begun for me, and his pink uniform, and my white rabbit fur tippet that I've never dared to wear, and they take photographs of the paintings in the dunny after laughing at them and inking rude comments below my portrait, and they wrap up the scrapbooks I made of newspaper articles, and they even take photographs of Anthony as he crawls after scorpions on the floor, and finally, they even take Alf's little hammer and leave him howling in the dust.

A stream of carts and jigs and men on horseback go by the driveway, craning their necks and the word goes round town that Gin Toad has helped a POW escape, and that the Toad let her. They can't say who is more to blame. The husband. Or the wife. But the townsfolk of Wyalkatchem, Western Australia, are eager to blame us both. "That wicked woman come in here and I give her what for!" says Mrs. Flannigan, thumping the counter of the post office. "I always knew her for what she was." *Slut of the district.*

The first time Toad takes the eggs into town after Antonio does his bunk, Kenny looks at the eggs and purses his lips and shakes his head so that his eyeballs rattle. "Not buying," he says. The hotel isn't buying either. The bakery doesn't need them. When the same thing happens on the second and third day, Toad takes the eight dozen eggs and throws them, one by one, at the Johnston buildings along Railway Terrace. People watch from inside with their windows closed, the lace curtains shuddering. When he gets home, he butchers all but six of the hens and drags them out to a paddock downwind of the house and burns them. Then he comes inside and hauls out my mirror and my chair and my glory box and burns them too. He wants to burn my piano, he tries to, but it is too heavy to move. And last of all, he hitches the horses to the big iron rake and ploughs all the hot ashes under six inches of dirt.

A month later, the policemen are back and asking us more questions. Did Antonio get letters from a priest in Perth. Or Melbourne? Who did he know? They haven't found a single piece of evidence besides my own admission that I gave him food and a gun. "So, when he headed west," they ask for the umpteenth time, "Where do you think he was going?"

I answer as best as I can, but my reputation is ruined by the suspicion of these men. I will always be known as that woman who diddled the Italian POW and helped him escape. All my life, I will be remembered as a traitor and not invited into the homes of my neighbours. All my life, the post office will hand me my mail, opened, smeared with jam or grease or turds; handwritten comments in the margins of the personal letters in red ink. I will be forced to drive to Goomalling to buy food and even there, people will eye me with suspicion, remembering something they heard back in 1944. If I buy a ticket to board the train in Wyalkatchem, the local train will roar past, not stopping. "Whoops," they'll say. "Sorry about that." Even Toad will be shunned, as if, finally, I have managed to rub off on him. I cannot forgive myself everything but I can be forgiven for not wishing to help the police.

And the last thing I warm my cold cold hands on, the thing I never give up to anyone, is that memory I have of Antonio walking up the hill towards the *east* with the morning sun making a flaming halo around his head and the fresh new grass all aglitter and his back as straight as a wand. No. I knew he wasn't going towards the coast or the railway tracks or the Italian delicatessens down in North Perth; he was walking towards the desert and the hot killing places out that way.

I search for a note or a letter telling me where to join him, but he only left behind his pink uniform, neatly folded on the bed, and the pair of red shoes he made. I find them when I go into his hut, the morning after he leaves. They are standing in the doorway as if they will walk away by themselves. I know they are his wife's. I don't even have to try them on to know he's made them for her. When I bend down to touch the sequins on the toes, I see that he has written something on the inside, in red ink. *There's no place like home.*

The parcel I sent to Italy comes back marked "address unknown" and I burn the little dresses and the shining red shoes in the kitchen stove one morning when even the birds aren't awake.

Epilogue

For months I read the newspapers carefully for the names of recaptured prisoners and for the notice that the Italian POWs were being returned to Italy, but on the day that they were rounded up from the district there was no warning at all. Men were pulled from the fields without even time to collect their meager belongings, pitiful souvenirs of time spent in the Land of Oz. Mudsey, in the schoolhouse down on Flint Street, saw them go by in Cleverish's green truck and she said there were children who jeered when they saw the Italians leaving. She watched the truck rolling south, and hoped that at last her life might return to what it once was.

Antonio's name never appeared in the papers and I allowed myself to think that he was still alive out there in the bush, or that maybe he had managed to get away to Italy. Toad complained when he saw me with my nose stuck in the newspaper. "Stop looking for the bastard, Gin. He got what he wanted. He was never planning on taking you with him." But Toad didn't know everything.

After the war, when money was a little easier to come by and the rationing had ended, I began to travel down to Perth to play with the orchestra again. It was Malcolm who got me the job. The regular pianist broke a finger in a fist fight with the oboist and Malcolm had filled in, all the while protesting that he knew this *real* pianist rotting up in Wyalkatchem, and then, when the director heard that the rotting pianist was *me*, I was suddenly wanted. Desirable. Such an offer they made me, for a few hours of doing what I would have been doing on a Sunday afternoon anyway! But after the war, people were silly, a little mad. They only wanted to be happy, to be entertained. They wanted to sing and dance and go to the concert hall and forget there ever was such a thing as a war.

I never told Toad. He assumed I was going shopping, or visiting Mudsey who I had sent down to boarding school. Mudsey! Huh! She barely spoke to me anymore. Her back had seemed permanently bent over the baby, rocking him in that grey army blanket tied to the gum tree. Permanently turned away from me. It was as if she was deaf. Her face all closed and secretive, her sunburnt cheeks accusing. She lined up gumnuts and mowed them down with twigs. *Ack ack ack*. And then torched them. When I told her I thought it would be for the best if she went to boarding school, she shoved me hard in the belly and ran to Toad. No. I wasn't visiting Mudsey.

It would have irked Toad to know that I had gone back to my old life in Perth, and even more so, that I kept the money I earned playing in the orchestra out of the enema bag. He thought, perhaps, that we were cautiously repairing what had been smashed during that incautious year.

God help me, I kept the money in a savings account in Perth under my single name, Gin Boyle, and one fine day in 1948 I had enough to buy a ticket on an ocean liner bringing other war brides to Italy. I brought Alfie down to Perth and bought him his uniform for boarding school.

"Why?" he asked. "Why can't I stay home? Where are you going?" His mouth opened and shut like a gate in the breeze. Squalling. The train came late that day and it was raining.

A month later, I departed with a ticket and a passport and a new black silk dress that came down low in the front. Toad, when I told him I was leaving, went out into the shed where he kept his corsets and cried. A dreadful noise like a nail being pulled from a board.

"Give it up, Gin. He's not there. He's dead," he said the next day, but I didn't believe him.

I said I might bump into Antonio in the streets of Lucca or Sant'Anna or Pietrasanta. He could just walk up to me and say, "Hello, Gin. I've been waiting for you." I was haunted by him. I saw his face everywhere. I followed strangers down the street, hoping they'd turn and be him. Once, I saw his reflection in the window of a teashop on Murray Street. He tilted his head to the side, winked and was gone.

"He'll be there," I said. "He promised me."

Toad snorted and retired to the dunny, to his dictionary. He was up to the Vs.

"Vagary: a departure from regular or usual norms of conduct or propriety. Vanquish: overcome or defeat an enemy by some means other than physical conflict."

In Italy, I took the slow train from Rome to Lucca and then traveled in a bus full of peasants to Pietrasanta and Barga and Stazzema, to Ponterosso and Seravezza and Viareggio; all the towns that were bombed by the Americans in the late summer and autumn of 1944. Too late to save Sant'Anna.

I spent almost the entire time in Italian post offices searching through phone directories for an A. Cesarini. In Massa I found him at last. Or I thought it was him, but it turned out to be his brother. This Cesarini met me at the door to his house, a small child humping his baggy woollen trousers.

"You must be Gin," he said in Italian and winked. His eyes were dark, like Antonio's. "Come in. My wife's not here at the moment." He bent to put the child outside the door and the ground under my feet tilted. There was a greedy look on the man's face and I caught him licking his lips and smoothing his moustache. I asked him if he'd seen Antonio and he said that after the massacre, they'd been told that Antonio, too, had died, down at the Control Centre in Northam. So that's the lie the Australians put about when they couldn't find him.

Who knew what lies Antonio had told his brother about me?

"Come in," the man said again. He had none of Antonio's subtlety and none of his beauty. There was a fat cauliflower wart under his bottom lip that had three stiff black hairs protruding from it and when he licked his lips, he licked the wart also.

"No thank you," I said. "I only wanted to know if you had seen him." I began to leave, but then turned back. "What does Gingilla mean?" I asked.

A slow and wicked smile spread across his face. "A plaything," he said. "A toy."

On the rattling old train from La Spezia to Viareggio, I sat near a group of teenagers who laughed and fell against one another as the train swayed. One young Romeo lifted a strand of hair from his Juliet's cheek and there, she touched his face, and prickles of envy and desire ran down my spine. Their easy affection, their frank love, was not something I experienced at their age, and now I am envious of their facility. Oh yes. Jealous. That was what I was. No plaything *she*, or so I thought. Why couldn't I so casually touch another person? What held me back, so tightly wound? Why was I in Italy, running from place to place, in search of a ghost? What had I left behind in my true home? What had I lost forever?

Now I knew why skin is meant to touch skin. I closed my eyes against the naked faces of infatuation, their blithe caressings. Oh, Antonio. For the remembrance of you, turning the sheet of my music, the shadow of the curve of your hand breaking like a wave across the page. Oh for your breath stirring the fine hairs at the base of my neck as you called out the notes. The train fled, shrieking across the coastal plain. The Romeos laughed. There was surely ash in my eyes that day, swept in by the sea breeze with the stench of the brine, the stench of the ash, the stench of that train so far away in Italy. My own heart beating too loudly. Too alive. And Antonio must surely be dead.

On the beach at Viareggio. Clouds as grey as whales. The ocean howling, waves rearing up, frothing at the mouth. The wind raking my hands. Howling. Antonio not here. Perhaps he was never here.

The beach was empty. The wet sand at the edge of the water mirroring the sky. Where was Mudsey? Where was Alf? I had spent all my time wondering about Antonio, and my own flesh and blood was lost to me. They would love this coast, rough as it is. Would it have been so hard, after all, to have brought them too? And my forlorn child, Anthony, was he crying now, and for me? Would he still reach for my red buttons when I returned?

The lacy train of the wave's wedding gown swept across my foot and I was gone from that wild, grey beach, gone from the Mediterranean, and washed back to that night when I too wore a wedding gown and Toad said that I did not dress that way for him. I ignored him then. I was to blame for what became of the Toads of Cemetery Road. I should have done for Toad what I did for Antonio, but my heart wasn't in it. From that first time when Toad wiped his hand on his plus-fours, my heart was not his.

And then, along the beach, just at the edge of the ocean where water and earth and sky were all one, right there, a man came walking with a long stick in his hand, and attached to the stick were dozens of balloons, and the man was white. White like me.

"Ciao," he said and he blinked in the strong wind and his white eyelashes fluttered against his pale blue eyes. He turned his head to look at me, sideways, the glance of people like us who cannot see but are not blind, and he smiled.

"A balloon?" he asked, and he untied a red one and laid the string in my hand. Oh Mudsey. Oh Alf. They have never played with a real balloon. Only the prophylactics of our enemy lovers.

A small child, not my child, ran down from the boardwalk, shrieking and pointing at the man, at me, at our whiteness, his words incomprehensible. Surely, not here, not in Antonio's country, no. His voice sharp as a stiletto. He thought I was the man's wife. He thought we were magical creatures risen from the sea. He touched my arm and gazed into my eyes. And ran back to his father who was standing, leaning against a lamppost, waiting.

Mudsey irons her navy serge uniform by laying it under the mattress of her boarding school bed. She thinks, not of me, but of revenge for her humiliation. Alf, so small and gentle, wets the bed and cries at night and sleeps upright in the closet, so the boys in the school cannot find him to torment. And Anthony crawls between the house and Hotel Tobruk, A. Cesarini Proprietor, his baby knees full of sheep shit and double gees, his nappy wet and dragging on the ground, and he cries, "Mummy! Mummy!" and

Toad appears from his corset shed and picks him up and chucks him under the chin and feeds him a lump of sugar congealed around a drop of tea and wonders where I am and if I am ever coming back and if he even wants me to.

The little birds ran from the waves, their silvery legs flashing. The sun struck the glass-green of the waves, shattering them into hundreds of brilliant spears of light. I closed my eyes against their stabbing. The wind roared.

Climbing the steep path up to Sant'Anna that first day, the great white stone head of the mountain with her broken nose and her cancerous lesions above me, I heard the sound of the water trickling down her face, falling through the bracken into the cisterns and the sound of the birds like thousands of tiny chimes and the men, singing at their work, arias from the opera that reminded me of Antonio walking back from feeding the calves. By August, the water would diminish to the merest trickle over a wide and thirsty lane of stones. Only later, after the hottest month, did clouds build up, swullocky over the pink houses, and send the wind to knock on the green shutters.

Now, sitting on a bench in the *piazza della chiesa*, the wind blowing plane leaves across the scorched earth. I know what befell Antonio's village of Sant'Anna.

A small boy showed me the tall stone house where Antonio's family lived, and I sleep there, though it lacks a roof and the windows hold no glass. Besides me, the boy is the only one who lives in the village now. I walk over this ground and see the lumps of congealed metal and the burnt terracotta tiles that lie in broken piles around the houses. I hold in my memory an image of a man with a sodden piece of paper in his hand, saying no as he kneels in the mud. The boy lives in the house near the church. He brings out his grandfather's hat, with its bullet hole. He tells me everything he saw, everything that happened that summer when Italy was invaded. He stares at me and crosses himself. Wondering if my hair has turned white from the pain of this knowledge. From *feeling*.

I have tried to hold Sant'Anna away from me as I held Toad and Antonio and my own children away from me. I have never wanted to feel anything, to lay *feeling* on my heart and let it sink its claws deeply into the bloody beating muscle at my core. Once, long ago, all this was just a story. A love story. About an Italian man and the albino woman who loved him. Now I see Antonio's wife and his children and his village and his existence. I *feel* their reality. Now the story is alive and true and terrible.

Sant'Anna lies below Stazzema, as if the town has crumbled down the mountain, houses dotted along the limestone road. They are named, these houses, l'Argentiera di sopra and di sotta, Vaccareccia, Bambini, Sennari, Franchi, La Case, il Pero, i Merli, i Coletti, Fabbiani, i Molini beyond them all, almost at the next village of La Culla. Some are clusters of buildings, generations living together in tiny villages of their own making, and the houses are made of marble, because the hills are made of marble and the heavy beams are chestnut wood because of the chestnut forests that cloak the sharp shoulders of the mountains, and even the road is only a scrape through the mountain's skin that reveals her white bones. On three sides, the mountain cups the village and on the fourth, is the steep drop down to the Ligurian Sea and on clear days, islands bob in that sea, playfully.

The mountain people are fearful of their mountain, and love her, and lift plants from her rocky soil and shake the roots to free them from pebbles caught there, but they catch the pebbles in their hands and lay them gently back again, on the mountain. They take the *vetrilla*, a little weed they use to polish glass, and the *pungitopo*, a type of holly, pulled up and down inside chimneys to rid them of creosote, and monk's pepper, growing in the deepest shade. There are olive groves and grape vines lower down, but higher, near Sant'Anna, the harvest is mainly chestnuts and mushrooms, and so the people make *polendina* and *castagnaccio* and chestnut ravioli and chestnut bread, and higher still, even the trees don't grow and there is only the clatter of the feral goats on the white marble tors, their droppings like so many piles of gleaming olives, and now and then the sound of boots and the clink of metal and the swearing of men.

There is a story about these mountains that the people do not tell newcomers, and they even hide it from themselves and only sometimes, when the men sit in the back room of the *osteria*, their faces full of grog blossoms, will the story spill out and the men nod and look at the ground and slap down the cards, angrily almost. It is an old tale, about a girl and the boy she loved, a young man who rejected her for another. But she would not be rejected and lay on the ground and said, "I will not move from this place until you say you love me," and he, laughing, ran away to another place and did not return and time has covered the girl and her sadness and yet you can see her still, her long, twisting white spine and the hunch of her shoulder and, most awesome of all, a sight that thrills tourists and horrifies the real mountain folk, her eye that cannot see, a perfect circle within the mountain that is blue with the sky in the daytime and black at night and no stars shine in it at all.

They say that one day she will arise and with a cry, shake off those who scurry up and down the white roads, and so they are careful. They speak politely to the mountain and lay the pebbles gently down upon her skin.

During the war, the war that had nothing to do with them

and their lives, there were many men running and hiding amongst the chestnut trees, some with red scarves, some with green, herring-gutted men from Germany and France and Spain and England who raped the women, and Gurkhas who raped the mules or the men or each other, running and hiding and talking and killing, and none of these men feared the mountain, but they would, eventually. And there were many women and children who came to the village to hide but also to live because below in the valley there was no food. Their clothes were held up with string and pinned with thorns and their shoes were wooden *zoccoli* and the wives wore the steel wedding rings Mussolini gave them instead of the gold. The people no longer commented on the thinness of arms and the weakness of legs. The roundness of the children's bellies was only a horrible illusion. Here, in Sant'Anna, they ate the wild goats, if they could catch them, and the olives and the chestnuts and the *funghi*, the excellent porcini mushrooms and the truffles, and the vegetables from the gardens that weren't destroyed by the comings and goings of men, and the squirrels and the wild carrots and the hedgehogs and the occasional dog or cat or child's pet guinea pig; and the people who really lived here, having lived here for centuries, from the time of the Etruscans, muffled their resentment and covered their dislike of other places, and let the strangers stay in the stalls of the animals that had died.

In the little school which stands on the edge of the olive terraces, Antonio's children listen to two news broadcasts a day and the sound of martial music makes them spring to their feet and stand at attention. The teacher asks, "*A chi la vittoria?*" and they respond with a shout and *il saluto romano*, "To us! Victory is ours!" On the door of the school is a poster in German and Italian. It is a list. Of crimes. Punishable by death. For some reason, the Germans think that Sant'Anna is the center of the Garibaldis.

Laughable. This village of old people and women and children. One of the crimes is the tearing down of posters. Another of the crimes is assisting the partisans.

"*Budella di Pio Nonaccio*," says one small boy, in imitation of his father, who comes and goes at night. "Who believes this shit anyway?" But he doesn't say anything else, because maybe his friend's father is a fascist, or maybe he's a communist or maybe he's a partisan or maybe he's a collaborator. No one knows anymore.

The same poster hangs on the door to the church and on the beech tree that guards the entrance to the town. The women who live in Il Pero, near the church, have painted little red flowers in all the white margins of the poster so it will be beautiful. As it was, struck through with nails, just below the circular stained glass window of St. Anna and just above the order demanding all the residents to leave the town and go to Sala Baganza in Parma, it was simply too grim. No one is leaving. They trust the partisans. They are sure that those men who stalk through the woods, ambushing Germans, setting off avalanches that block the roads and stealing guns off the back of trucks, those men will protect them. They trust the German commander down in Camaiore, who says this is a white zone, a safe place to live. They don't believe the village will be destroyed by righteous German retribution for the actions of the partisans. That's what they think, even the refugees from the cities, though they have seen German tanks crushing houses and gardens and children under their tracks, and they have seen partisans dangling in the market squares, upside down, bayoneted, naked, with the thin blue lines of their intestines hanging down to the ground, snapped at and fought over by dogs. The little old man outside the church told me they thought they were safe.

A rabbit runs out of the alpine forest early on Saturday morning.

Something has scared it, for it runs towards the church of Sant'Anna and then darts behind a stone wall. Fog lifts from the valley, rising up from the sea with a little breath of salt and drying seaweed, but the village is still shaded by the mountains, Monte Lieto and Monte Gabberi.

Today, perhaps, the partisans will come down from the crags, skipping down paths that their grandfathers' grandfathers named in their youth—scraped arse, the rump of the mule, the blonde rat, he-who-doesn't-make-it-doesn't-make-it, the vagina; their home paths, the almost invisible roads of their lives, and the phantoms of the dead white cattle will donk their phantom bells stepping out of their way, and the men will splash a while in the little stream Baccatoio which flows all the way down to Valdicastello, and they will stroke the breast of the mountain and some will come through the gate behind the house of the witch and some will walk in by the mule path and some will simply be standing outside the church when the people come for mass and no one will know how they got there, and they will be strong and brown and well-armed and they will speak the dialect of the district and many of them will be the fathers of the children and the husbands of the wives, and the Germans, those old clawscrunts, will pack up in shame and go home.

But on this morning, a hot Saturday in August of 1944, the partisans do not come down from the mountain. They stay hidden within the trees when the Germans arrive and block off the exits with old Viennese pastry chefs manning flamethrowers.

Wulf Kreipke will be humming Liszt's *Un Sospiro* for piano in D-flat major when he barbecues a six-year-old boy in suspendered shorts. The child will go down with his head thrown back and his arms wide and for a second, Wulf will see a flash of copper in the little hand, before it melts and fuses into the blackened flesh. He will dream about that flash of gold for years. No broken Italian father will come to get him in his shop in Vienna. No one even knows what he did. But every time a customer hands him a coin and the light is coming through the front window in just the right way, he will cringe.

Private Horst Kansteiner, formerly a student of Natural Sciences in Berlin, will remember nothing. Except sometimes an image of grey continents splitting and dividing over a weeping red sea, a rain of ash, a smell of roasting. He will remember carrying the great pack on his back and the weight of the nozzle in his hands, the rear trigger between his fingers, the front grip, the faint click and hiss of the ignition before a different sound, a sound he can't remember any more, and the way the colors drained from the sky, and he wakes, howling from the weight, tearing at the burden on his back, and his palms will feel the weight again, the weight, the awful weight.

The Sixteenth SS Panzergroup marched four abreast from Mulina di Stazzema, and from Capriglia Montornato, in the darkness before dawn. They had mules and traitors to guide them. They had salt. They had sausage and cheese and brandy, flamethrowers and machine guns and potato mashers, the stick grenades that can demolish a barn. The scent of the macchia mediterranea rising around them, the dense undergrowth of grey-leaved plants, aromatic. Far off, on the top of the mountain, a rooster crowed.

The early risers in Sant'Anna will die wearing ragged clothes but most will die in their undergarments. Whatever they wore to bed on a hot Friday night. A bra. A slip. Nothing.

They are raused from their homes, thinking the Germans simply want to speak to them. No panic. Let me get my pants. One little boy hops to the grassy square in front of the church, prodded in the back by a German gun, trying to get his other leg into his shorts. Most people there are barefoot, the children's hair unbrushed, their eyes gumbled, the testiculous old men abashed in their pissburnt drawers, the women in their petticoats turned away towards the church with their arms up over their breasts.

Don Innocenzo, their priest, averting his eyes from the machine guns set up under the plane trees, hurried to the captain, or whatever he was, to make peace, to intercede.

"Yes, yes, yes," he said, "of course we are supposed to have evacuated. Naturally. We want to please." He thought the Germans had come to assist in the unwanted move. "But, sir Captain," he said, looking up at eyes like the fog over water on a cold morning, "we are only old people, women. Children. Not even a mule between us and how should we move to a place we have never seen in all our lives?"

For a moment, the commander looked at the priest, at the white dust on the hem of his cassock, and the white dust on the priest's black shoes, and then he ordered, "Kill them all." And the soldiers who came with him, some of them all the way from Germany, who were trained to follow every command without thinking, hesitated, and in the hesitating, the commander pulled his own pistol from his pocket and shot the priest in the forehead and a star bloomed on the skin of the dying man, a four-pointed red star as the skin pulled back from the wound, and then the soldiers mowed down the old men in baggy underpants and the women in curlers and the children, even the babies, vicious partisans all, they will say when they are asked why they did it, vicious criminals, the Saturday filled with the rattle of the guns and the screams of the dying and the tinkling music of the hurdy gurdy that the Germans brought with them to keep it all civilized.

When the killing stopped, when there was silence, and the bodies lay on the grass, leaking, they dragged out the wooden benches from the church, dark wood carved in the sixteenth century, and piled them on the people who had loved the old carving, and other soldiers with flame throwers came and burned them all together with the wood to make sure that nothing remained there of the hundreds.

Then they burned the church.

Then they went, house to house, and looked for more things to kill. And the houses angered them, because they were made of stone and were empty and plates of cold food stood on the tables and the stone wouldn't burn. So their rage was all the more when they found things that cried and moved and tried to get away, and thus it was, that on the twelfth of August 1944, seven children found hiding near the large, stone bake oven where the entire community baked their bread, were thrown inside and the door closed on them and locked, even though the oven was hot and the fire was burning and the children were crying.

And thus it was that Antonio's children were found by the soldiers, hiding in the rafters, and pulled from that place, and their heads were crushed with rifle butts and all five of them, even the smallest, as light as a prayer book, were run through with stakes and hung from the walls, their toes not touching the ground and the blood on their faces running into their eyes, and then they were shot. And this in front of their mother, Francesca, Antonio's wife, unprotected, unsaved, begging them to stop, while a young man held her and laughed and then killed her with a shot to the back of the head. She was glad of it. The shot to the head. Her whole body opened and glowed, the sweet air of the mountains rushed into the cavity as she fell, and she saw Antonio's face, just for a moment before she died, thankful for the vision.

At midday, the Germans stopped for lunch and ate sausage and cheese in the warm glow from the houses. The man with the barrel organ continued to play and the commander gave out brandy and after they'd eaten, some of the men sang, and some of them were sick, quietly, in the bushes. And then they went down, after the survivors, to Valdicastello, and they caught quite a few who still couldn't speak for all they had seen was lodged in their throats and had burnt their lips and the Germans carried away these last few witnesses and left their bodies near a river, many miles away, tied by the neck to fencing posts. All shot. And some few were tied to the wreckage of a German motor lorry, to the headlights, to the door handles, to the radiator cap, a loop of wire around their necks, with the stinging flies moving in and out of the soft places, and a bullet in their skulls. And to explain it all, to make it clear and sensible, a note: *Thus shall be done to the partisans and all those who give them aid.*

And the men lying there were old. Grandfathers and great-grandfathers, with nails stained black from working the earth, who had never learned to read.

On my final day, the huge purple bees of the Appenines hum amongst the lavender. Down in the valleys, women bend over the unmade bed of the earth, their arms all circling down and shuddering, like the fleshy organ of a bull, impregnating the field. The roads striped with the light that falls between the shadows of the chestnuts. In the woods uphill from Sant'Anna, I find trees that bulge at the base, a legacy of the families that have lived here. I find a flat stone in a clearing and a broken antler lying upon an altar.

A red dog walks ahead of me through the village and stops when I stop, turning its head to look at me. Waiting. When I try to pat the dog, it moves away, climbing the stairs between the houses. Again, it stops and looks back at me. The moss that grouts the stones is black. It smells of smoke. A cold wind lifts the fur on the neck of the dog, stirs the waxy leaves of the trees.

The dog wants me to follow him. He slips into a narrow

corridor between two houses, turns the corner and disappears. The air in the passage is still. I lean my head against the rough stones. Such a cold place on such a warm day. And dark. Full of shadows. On the wall, at chest height, are a line of holes. And lower down, another line. The ground is covered in teeth of stone and shattered tiles and javelins of wood. The wind makes a sound as it plays over the holes. A soughing. A sighing. A cry.

"What are you saying?" I ask the wall.

But the holes make no reply.

Francesca and her children whisper and point at me, kneeling there in the razor-sharp garden of destruction and my fist salutes the line of holes, and then falls. Falls to the lower line and my hand opens and my fingers file at the splintered edges, gently. There are black droplets around the holes. The marble is cold. The tip of my finger fits exactly inside one of the cavities and there, deep inside, I can feel the colder metal case of a bullet, lodged in the stone. This is death. This is how death came for Antonio's children. The glittering children put their own fingers in the holes and laugh and push at one another and they blink when I look at them and move away, melting into the stone, fading in the beam of sunlight that passes between the buildings. I did not cause their death. Antonio was wrong.

Come, Gin. You have destroyed, but it was not Sant'Anna which you destroyed. It was not Antonio. His children were not your children. Your children are still alive. Come, Gin, take hold of what is truly yours, take it up in your hands and do not let it go this time. Do not let it go.

Amongst the broken tiles something dull and metallic winks. Calling me. Faintly, faintly, the song of the sea and the hiss of the waves on the sand from miles away.

In the corner of my eye, the flick of a hat ribbon floating in the air. The odor of burning olive wood on the wind. A whiff of cordite. The fluting voice of the bullet holes, lisping their own songs, childish songs learned at the knees of mothers who are gone now too.

There is a pain in my chest as I bend to take up the dull and ruined thing from between the schist. My eyes are full of ashes. My mouth is dry. I lay the incomplete circle in the palm of my hand, just below the shallow impression under the joint of my fourth finger. From a ring that is no longer there. That was sold and can no longer be reclaimed. And this circle too is a ring, an old metal ring, blackened by fire, burnt through and incomplete. It weighs much more than I expect. I think, when I touch it, that it will be something light. As light as a white dress and a face turned upwards and caught in that motion by a photographer who no longer lives. As light as a shoe made of feathers and leaves. As light as a child who is loved. Weightless. But instead, it is unbearable to hold. So very heavy that it falls from my hand, turning slowly, twisting end over end, through the cold air of that place, falling forever, that black metal ring.

Author's Note

The characters that appear in this novel are fictional, but Wyalkatchem, the West Australian wheatbelt and Sant'Anna are all actual places. The bombing of Darwin, the POW outbreak at Cowra and the massacre at Sant'Anna are historical events around which I have woven a fictional story. I am grateful to the National Australian Archives, the Battye Library of Western Australia and particularly, Il Museo Storico della Resistenza in Sant'Anna, Italy for providing the research materials and the objects and photographs which ignited my imagination. Thanks, too, to Tom Field and Anne Glaskin, for their wonderful early memories of living with Italian Prisoners of War. It is often their distinct voices which the reader can hear in the novel. Many blessings also go to Paul de Pierres, the historian of Wyalkatchem and a true gentleman, to Dinah Voisin of Peralta, Italy, and to Medea, surely the most unforgettable of all translators. Kelsey Thompson of NOAH (National Organisation for Albinism and Hypopigmentation) helped me understand the experience of those with albinism, down to the buttons.

My readers' generous and thoughtful suggestions helped mould the final shape of the novel: Andrea Barrett, Martin Cloutier, Emily Forland (a most charming agent, as well as a reader), Shterna Friedman, Aryeh Goldbloom, Irma Goldbloom, Tzipora Goldstein, the marvellous novelists of Fred Shafer's Novel Workshop, and the best Toad-sized writing group east of the wheatbelt, Gerald Burstyn and Matthue Roth. Thank you all. And to my eight children, each one as beloved as an only child: Special credit for your patience and your endearing fondness for macaroni and cheese.

Joanna Scott and the people at AWP saw the potential in my work, just as I was considering selling junk on eBay. I am grateful.

I am deeply indebted to both of my editors for their clarity and for their ability to help me birth the novel within the novel: to Georgia Richter at Fremantle Press in Australia, and especially, with love, to the incomparable Fred Shafer.

And most of all, I would like to bless my dearest friend, Bruce Aaron. Without his encouragement and his ongoing support this novel would still be languishing in the drawer. Many, many thanks.

ACKNOWLEDGEMENTS

Chapters 16-19 of Book I were excerpted and published in *StoryQuarterly* in August 2007.

The descriptions of Aboriginal culture, specifically with regard to the capture of possums and emus on page , was taken from the introduction of the book *Goomalling, a Backward Glance: A History of the District* by Barbara Sewell (Churchlands, WA, 1998).

Goldie Goldbloom's fiction has appeared or is forthcoming in *StoryQuarterly*, *Narrative* and *Prairie Schooner*, as well as in anthologies in Australia and the USA. She won the 2008 AWP Novel Award and the Jerusalem Post International Fiction Prize. Her stories have been translated into more than ten languages.

She lives in Chicago with her eight children.

AWP AWARD SERIES IN THE NOVEL